THE M████████CE

The car door opened.

A heavy work boot clomped onto the blacktop, followed by another. Worn jeans covered tree-trunk legs, a plaid flannel shirt stretched across a barrel chest and broad shoulders. Black belt, big silver buckle shaped into the head of a rearing horse. The left hand was free; the right held a wooden-handled ax. Head silver, edge sharp. The face—

Scott couldn't make out the figure's face. Whoever it was *had* a face, he was sure of that. But even though the parking lot was well lit and he was looking straight at the man, Scott saw…nothing. Not a blur, not a shadow. Nothing. While he felt sure his eyes *saw* the face, it was as if his mind refused to register its features.

The man without a face closed the car door with a solid *chunk!* He stood for a moment, gripping the ax with both hands, slowly turning it around and around.

Scott felt an icicle of fear stab into his spine. It was the Riverton Ax Murderer. The man had never been positively identified, let alone caught. During the course of the investigation, the prime suspect had committed suicide and the killings—after a final tally of eight—had stopped.

"This hasn't been a good night for you, has it, Scotty-boy?"

The voice emanated from the air where the figure's mouth should have been. It held a mocking edge, and although Scott couldn't see it, he knew the man was smiling….

LIKE DEATH

TIM WAGGONER

LEISURE BOOKS NEW YORK CITY

A LEISURE BOOK ®

January 2005

Published by

Dorchester Publishing Co., Inc.
200 Madison Avenue
New York, NY 10016

ISBN 0-8439-5498-1

The name "Leisure Books" and the stylized "L" with design are trademarks of Dorchester Publishing Co., Inc.

Printed in the United States of America.

Visit us on the web at www.dorchesterpub.com.

LIKE DEATH

Chapter One

He's huddled beneath the kitchen table, knees drawn to his chest, hands balled into fists, jammed against his ears, kneading them, as if he might cut off the screams by grinding cartilage and flesh to a pulp. It doesn't work; the screams come through just fine.

He keeps his eyes open, doesn't seem to be able to close them, even to blink. Which is too bad, because he'd give anything to shut out what he's seeing. At nine, he's too young to make useless bargains with God—*If you take away the cancer I swear I'll be faithful to my wife, I really mean it this time*—and he's too old to think he can make it never-was merely by wishing hard, hard, *hard!* All he's got are those fists of his grinding, grinding. . . .

A woman falls to the kitchen floor with a wet smack. Her face is turned toward him, and like his, her eyes are wide open. The difference is she's never going to close hers again, not on her own. An image flashes through his mind, a composite drawn from hundreds of movies and TV shows: a hand (sometimes belonging to a cop, sometimes a coroner) passing over the open-eyed face of an actor pretending to be dead. The fingers are straight, and there is no obvious contact between the hand and the mock-corpse's face. Yet when the hand has finished its pass, the eyes are closed, almost as if it were some sort of magic trick. The boy wonders if he were to reach out and pass his hand an inch or so over the woman's face, if her eyes—those terrible, empty eyes—would close. He doubts it. Life is never as good as TV.

The front of the woman's flower-print sundress is covered with blood, so much and so thick that it's almost black. The dress itself is shredded, and he realizes that what he first took to be blood on the fabric is really gore smeared on her flesh. He stares at something round with a little nub in the middle, and he understands that he's looking at his first naked breast. At least, the first he's ever seen outside the pages of a purloined *Playboy*. It looks so much different than the pictures he's seen; it sags a bit, for one thing. And of course, it's slick with blood. Miss June after she's been through a meat grinder.

Someone else is screaming now. Or maybe the screaming has taken up residence inside his skull despite his efforts to keep it out, and it's echoing in there, bouncing around, becoming louder and shriller with each pass, and soon it'll get so loud that his head can't possibly contain it anymore and it'll explode, splattering the underside of the table with blood, bone, and brain.

He wants to look to see who else is screaming, but he can't move (besides his fists, of course, those he can move just fine, still grinding, grinding), not even to turn his head, so he keeps staring at the dead woman's face—*name, name, name, he knows her name, knows who she is, but he can't*—and he watches as a pool of dark blood spreads out from beneath her, the leading edge of it sliding toward him slowly, as if he were sitting on a beach watching a crimson tide come in.

Gotta move. If he doesn't, the blood will reach his sneakers within seconds, stain them, and his mother—*that isn't his mother on the floor, staring, mouth gaping open like a dead fish, it isn't!*—will get mad at him for getting them dirty. She just bought them last week. But if he moves, he'll draw attention to himself, and that would be a Very Bad Thing, because . . . because . . . He's not sure why, really. Just because.

So when the blood touches his sneakers, his legs tense, but he doesn't move, and when it rolls on, touching the bottom of his shorts, starting to soak through at once, warm as fire against his skin, he grits his teeth and a soft keening sound starts deep in his throat, but he doesn't move, doesn't *dare.* Only now he's punching his ears with fast jabs, left-right, left-right, left-right, and his head starts to ring, but it's not loud enough to cover the screams, not nearly.

A shuffle of feet, and the table gives a jump. The sound startles him, breaks his paralysis, at least for a second, and he's able to turn his head, sees a pair of hairy legs, men's legs, feet in brown leather sandals. There's blood on those legs, streaks and splatters, though they seem to be undamaged. *Dripped from above,* the boy thinks, the observation as cool and rational as any made by the cops in the TV shows he likes, *Starsky and Hutch, Baretta, The Streets of San Francisco,* and the coolest of all, *Hawaii Five-O.* Drums, that wave, Jack Lord's hair.

There's another pair of legs beyond the hairy ones; these are covered by blood-dotted khaki slacks, feet encased in crimson-speckled black shoes. Under those shoes are red smears, and the boy wonders how either of these men have managed to maintain their footing with so much blood all over.

He hears the sound of what he guesses is a knife plunging into flesh—*chuk, chuk, chuk*—but it's a terribly ordinary sound, like when his mother slices a cantaloupe (though he can't see it from here, he knows there's one on the counter, Mother bought it before they left home, they were going to have it for supper, but he knows they aren't going to have it now, no one's going to have an appetite after *this*).

Chuk-chuk-chuk.

Those hairy legs buckle, the sandaled feet slip out from under them, and the man crashes to the floor, causing the table to slide back a couple inches. He falls next to the wide-eyed woman, a hairy arm draped across her leg, almost as if he were purposefully posing for the crime-scene photos to come. His blood pools, runs, mingles with the woman's. The boy experiences an urge to reach out and try to separate the blood, smear it apart, because if it gets all mixed up there's no *way* anyone'll be able to tell whose is whose, and then how will the doctors be able to put it back? But he doesn't move, keeps pounding his ears until he realizes something.

The screaming has ended.

He stops hitting himself, draws his fists away from red, raw ears. Listens through the ringing, hears harsh breathing, tired but excited. Looks at the khaki legs still upright, standing patiently. A hand hangs next to the right leg; it's holding a wicked-looking hunting knife, metal coated with wet red.

"Come on out, Scotty." This is breathed more than said, the words drifting forth when the speaker exhales. The boy tries to place the voice, almost can, but fails.

A pause, and he senses a smile accompanying these next words.

"It's your turn."

The boy sighs, closes his eyes (since he still can), and waits for the hands to reach for him.

Scott Raymond took a drag on his cigarette and let the smoke drift out of his mouth of its own accord. He cracked the car window so the smoke wouldn't obscure his view of the apartment building, and more specifically, the entrance. The radio was on—the cassette player didn't work and he couldn't afford a car with a CD player—tuned to an oldies station, though the songs they played didn't seem all that old to him. Mostly seventies and eighties stuff, with a bit of early nineties thrown in for the hell of it. A song by Soft Cell was playing, "Tainted Love," the one that had a series of tones that sounded like the beeping of a medical monitor. It felt almost as if the radio were keeping track of his pulse, making sure he stayed calm.

Oh, he was calm, all right. Relaxed. Just fucking great. Least he would be if Gayle would deign to make an appearance sometime this century, the goddamned bitch.

Easy, boy. Don't want to get the radio all worked up, do we? He took another drag on his cigarette and pretended not to notice his hand was trembling. It had been three weeks since he'd seen her last, almost twice that since she'd let him see their son. He'd talked to David on the phone a couple times—*How you doing, are you eating enough, we'll go to a Reds game this summer, how's that sound?*—but it wasn't the same as being able to see him, stand close enough to touch him, to smell the lingering odor of Doritos and Ho-Ho's on his breath, a scent finer than any rose.

He looked at the door to building 203. He knew he had the right place; her Taurus was parked just a few spaces down from him. He scowled, focusing all his willpower on the door, as if he hoped to force it open through sheer mental effort. And then, sonofabitch, it *did* open, and out walked Gayle carrying a plastic laundry basket full of clothes, and David behind, lugging a blue laundry bag. His breath caught in his throat at the sight of them, and he felt his sinuses go hot and moist, his eyes begin to tear up.

Keep it together, man. You might not get a second chance at this.

He opened the car door, stepped out of his Subaru and into the slight chill of an early April afternoon. He closed the door and let his cigarette drop to the ground. Gayle hated the things, and he didn't want her to see him with one in his hand. He crushed the cig out with a quick step and twist of his foot, then hurried toward his wife and child, only barely managing to keep himself from running.

David saw him first. T-shirt, jeans, running shoes. Thin and tall like his father, unkempt brown hair that refused to stay combed, like his mother's. Blue eyes from somewhere back in his genetic ancestry. Sky blue, ocean blue, break-your-goddamned heart blue. Those eyes widened in what Scott hoped was surprise, and then David grinned. "Dad!" But he didn't drop the laundry bag, didn't come running over to give his old man a hug. No biggie, Scott told himself. The boy was ten, too big for hugs. He understood, but that didn't mean it didn't hurt like . . . like a hunting knife in the heart.

Gayle turned her head, saw him, but aside from a flicker of something in her eyes, a flicker that was gone before he could name it, her expression remained neutral. Not the best of signs, but at least she wasn't yelling at him. Not yet, anyway.

That ratty brown hair: he knew its scent, texture, taste. Mud-brown eyes she insisted were really hazel. Full lips, and oh Jesus what he could remember about them. She wore an oversize gray Ohio State sweatshirt to conceal the fact she was ten pounds overweight, but she wasn't fooling anybody; you could tell by her round cheeks. He didn't care. She looked damned good to him, always had.

"Hi." He continued toward them, smiling, hands in the pockets of his jeans. He wanted to look as non-threatening as possible. He stopped, making sure to keep six feet between them. Out of arm's reach.

"What do you want?" Gayle said. No *hello, it's good to see you, we've missed you, David especially.* Not that he really expected any of that. Still, it would've been nice.

He shrugged, still making sure to keep his hands in his pockets. "Just to say hi." For the last several days he had mentally rehearsed what he would say once he saw them, but now that he was here, he couldn't think of anything. All he could think to do was look at them and hope they sensed the love he was broadcasting.

"You already said that."

Scott smiled. "I guess I did." He turned to David. "How do you like your new place?"

Now it was the boy's turn to shrug, and from the corner

of his eye, Scott saw his wife scowl. The gesture must've looked a little too much like his father's for her comfort.

"It's all right. My room's smaller than back home, and I don't have a good view out my window, just the parking lot."

Scott glanced at the building, saw four windows, two lower, two upper. David's was one of those.

"I've told you before, hon, this *is* our home now." A hint of irritation on *is* but otherwise Gayle managed to keep her tone even. Scott knew she had seen him look at the building, knew she probably didn't like the idea of his knowing too much about where they lived.

David let the duffel bag touch to the ground and studied his Nikes. "I liked the house better." Almost too soft to hear.

Gayle gave Scott a look that said, *See what you started?* "I liked the house too, sweetie, but we don't live there anymore. We sold it. You and I live here, and Daddy lives in an apartment in Cedar Hill."

"Actually, I don't. Not anymore." This wasn't the way he wanted to tell them, it would've been so much better to make some small talk first. But now that he'd started, he couldn't turn back. "I just moved into a place on the other side of town. Not as nice as this," he took a hand out of his pocket and gestured at their building, "but it's not bad."

David looked up from his shoes and grinned. "Really? That's great!"

From the way Gayle's eyes narrowed, it was obvious what she thought about it. "We had an understanding."

He took a deep breath, stalling for time to think of a way to phrase his explanation that would mollify her. It was so much easier when he was writing; there was time to think, time to reword, rework. Never in real life. The air smelled of cut grass, and chlorine from the pool over by the rental office. Birds sang, calling to potential mates. He wished he could remember whatever song he had sung that had attracted Gayle to him in the first place. He'd sing it at the top of his lungs, if he could.

"We did. But I just . . . wanted to be closer to you both. In case you needed anything. I know we've had some troubles"—*yelling obscenities, fingers pressing the soft flesh of upper arms, leaning forward, thinking how easy it would be to fasten his teeth onto her nose and just riiiip*—"but that doesn't mean I don't still have a responsibility toward my wife and son. Besides, you said you were willing to try to work things out."

"I said I'd think about it." Her voice was cold now, and he knew that if David weren't here, she'd tell him to fuck off.

"Okay, but how can we do anything if we live an hour and a half apart? Besides, a dad should at least live in the same town as his son." He looked at David. "Right?"

David nodded, smiled, but in his eyes Scott saw he was remembering the yelling and the grabbing. Scott looked away, ashamed. If he didn't love them both so much, *need* them so, he wouldn't have been able to face them.

There was another reason he had moved to Ash Creek, one that had nothing to do with either of them, but he wasn't about to mention it, not now, not with how Gayle felt about his work, how she blamed it for . . . the bad days.

"Look, Scott, we really need to get going. We've got clothes to wash, and the laundry room is always busy, so we're heading off to a laundromat." David looked up at her. "And we *don't* need any help," she hastened to add.

Scott nodded. "Sure. Maybe we can get together for dinner sometime? My treat? You know, just so we can . . . be together for a while?"

Gayle looked at him for a moment, then set her basket down on the sidewalk. She fished her keys out of her jeans and handed them to David. "Go get in the car, honey. I'll be there in a minute."

"But, Mom—"

"Go on." Gentle, but firm.

David made a face, but he did as his mother said. On the way to the Taurus, he turned, waved once at Scott, then kept going.

He turned to Gayle. "Look, I'm sorry I didn't call, but—"

She took a step toward him, then stopped as if she were afraid to get too close. "I told you I needed to be alone for a while so I could have some time to think, and I meant it. *Alone*. Without you. Get it?" She glanced at David, who had climbed in the Taurus and was sitting on the passenger side, watching them. "And he needs time, too. He doesn't talk about it much, but I know it's eating at him. I need him to talk to me, I need to find out just how badly he's hurt inside."

Scott could barely hold back the tears now, but he had to. Gayle hated it when he cried, accused him of using tears as manipulation. "I'm so sorry. If I could take back—"

"But you can't, so don't even bother to say it." She paused, took a breath. "If I have to get a lawyer and take out a restraining order on you, I will. If that's what it'll take to keep you the hell away from us, I'll do it, and don't think I won't."

She sounded as if she were trying to convince herself as much as him, but he knew better than to say it. "I understand. But can I at least call soon, just to see how you're doing?"

"You saw us today; we're doing fine. There's no need to call." She picked up her laundry basket and walked to her car without giving him a backward glance. Scott watched as she got in, started the Taurus, and drove out of the lot. David watched him without expression, and when Scott waved, he started to hold up his hand, but then he stopped, as if thinking better of it, and turned and looked forward. Scott was still standing on the sidewalk when they pulled onto the street and drove off.

"Well," he said softly to himself, "that didn't go so well." He started back to his car. He needed a cigarette, and more, he needed something to take his mind off Gayle and David and the complete cock-up he'd made of his marriage. And he knew just the thing: her name was Miranda Tanner. She was the other reason Scott had moved to Ash Creek, Ohio. Maybe, in the end, the real reason.

He got in his car, lit a cigarette, started the engine, and backed out of his parking space. It was time to make Ms. Tanner's acquaintance.

Chapter Two

Scott drove to the Ash Creek Community Recreation Center, pulled into the lot, and slowly drove around the small traffic circle where people could drop off their children before parking or, more likely, getting the hell out of there for the hour or so their swim class or ballet lesson would last. It really wasn't much to look at from the outside. Brown brick, narrow, rectangular windows, large glass doors like a department store. The lawn was neatly mowed and the hedges trimmed. Ash Creek wasn't a ritzy community, but that didn't stop folks from trying.

He drove back into the lot, found a space that afforded a good view of the front of the rec center, and parked. He sat and finished his cigarette while he watched people in sweats and shorts come and go—old, young, in singles and pairs. Some talking and laughing, others quiet and expressionless, as if they were husbanding their energy for the physical exertions to come. *Busy for a Sunday afternoon,* he thought. But then the citizens of Ash Creek seemed determined to keep the good times rolling, no matter what. He stubbed out the nub of his cigarette in the ashtray and got out of his car. He locked the doors, then strolled up to the rec center's entrance.

He didn't go in, though, didn't even bother peering through the glass doors to see what it looked like inside. He wasn't here to sign up for an aerobics class. Hell, the way he smoked, he'd have a heart attack before the warm-up was over. No, he was here to get to know Miranda Tanner.

He looked around, taking in the scene. Trees, grass, sky, cars. . . . He tried to imagine what it must have been like on that day in May. The twelfth, to be exact.

It was warm, warmer than this for sure, though maybe not hot yet. Spring and summer in balance, the scales just starting to tip in favor of the latter. Cloudy? Maybe some leftover April showers that hadn't quite gotten around to bringing May flowers. A punch line to a stupid kids' joke drifted through his mind. *And what do Mayflowers bring? Pilgrims!*

He smiled. Good, good. That's the mind-set.

Sunny, he decided. *Clear blue, a few clouds, the kind of sky that looks like a gigantic painting stretched across the heavens, too beautiful to be real. She would've started here, headed down the sidewalk.*

He began walking. He'd come back to pick up his car later. No notebook this time, no tape recorder. Not yet. He'd document eventually; right now he just wanted to experience.

Six-year-old Miranda Tanner had finished her after-school gymnastics class and headed straight home. Like Little Red Riding Hood's mother, Miranda's mom had always cautioned her not to dawdle on the concrete path. Ash Creek was a safe enough place, but even so, it didn't pay to take chances. School would let out for the summer in a few days, and Miranda was looking forward to vacation. She'd been asking to go to Disney World for what seemed like *forever*, and her mom and dad had finally given in. They were due to leave for Florida after Memorial Day.

Did she skip down the sidewalk, singing softly to herself? Scott decided she probably had. Still, excited as she was, she wasn't distracted enough to miss her street. When she came to Poplar, she stopped, looked both ways just as her mom had taught her, then crossed.

Scott did the same.

Once she was on Poplar, things became sketchy. That Miranda had left the rec center and started walking down the sidewalk was clear. There were witnesses. She'd said good-bye to a friend inside the center, and her instructor had gone outside not long after Miranda, and she'd seen the girl walking away. And while there were no witnesses to attest to whether or not Miranda had made it to Poplar, it seemed a likely enough supposition. James, the road the rec center was on, was the only way in or out of the parking lot. She wouldn't have been taken on James. It was too busy, too much of a risk.

But Poplar . . . ranch homes in rows on either side of the street, only slight variations in their designs, color schemes, and landscaping marking them as different from their neighbors. Not many kids outside playing, if any. Cable TV, video games, and the Internet would've kept most inside. Those adults who were home—mothers, primarily—were tending to the needs of younger children, doing housework, getting dinner ready. They didn't have time to be looking out their windows to see what was about to happen to Miranda Tanner.

So it was uncertain exactly how far Miranda had gotten, but one thing was clear: she'd never made it to 4560 Poplar where her mother had been sitting on the couch, watching *Oprah*, and giving Miranda's baby brother a bottle. That had been almost a year ago. Since then, despite the largest police investigation in Ash Creek's history, despite a blitzkrieg by the local media, despite tearful pleas from her parents for the abductors to bring their little girl home, despite nearly twelve months' worth of HAVE YOU SEEN THIS GIRL? posters plastered all over town, inside the lobby of every business, in display windows, on telephone poles, despite faded yellow ribbons tied around the trunks of oak, elm, and yes, poplar trees, no one had the first clue as to what had happened to Miranda Tanner. It was as if she had been swallowed up by that beautiful May day, as if summer couldn't wait for her to come to it, so it had reached out, engulfed her, and kept her close to its bright, warm bosom.

Scott continued walking down Poplar, senses open, drinking in sights, smells, sounds, hoping they'd stimulate his imagination. He didn't consider himself psychic or anything, but sometimes, when he was physically present at a crime scene, he received . . . impressions. A reviewer had once called them "unfounded speculations," but these impressions allowed him to write about crime, to make it come alive for his readers. After all, what was the hoariest advice given to writers? Write what you know. In his case, because he often wrote about *un*knowns, speculation was the only way he had of knowing.

Scott kept walking, gaze lowered to the sidewalk. Step on a crack, break your mother's back.

Torn flower-print dress, pool of blood, crimson-slick breast.

He stopped, squeezed his eyes shut as a lance of pain speared his head. He didn't need this now. Hell, he didn't need this *ever*.

Deep breath, count to ten, think about Miranda, about the book he wanted to write on missing children, with Miranda's case as the centerpiece. He already had the title— *Lost.* Simple, almost childlike, which was of course the point. He even knew how he'd begin. He'd start with pulling into the parking lot, his walk here . . .

The pain subsided, though it didn't go away entirely. Sometimes he wondered if it ever truly went away, or if it were always there hovering in the background, waiting for its next chance to sink its teeth into his brain.

He opened his eyes. He was looking down at a jagged crack on the sidewalk through which grew a half dozen blades of grass, and he suddenly knew that this was *the spot*—the place where Miranda had stood when her abductor approached. He didn't know how he knew, told himself that the feeling ·was probably nothing more than imagination mixed with a desire to be distracted from the pain. But a deeper part of him, the part that knew rationalizations and explanations and any other-ations were just so much bullshit . . . that part *knew*.

This was it.

He inhaled through his nostrils, as if some trace of little girl scent might linger in the air even after a year. Then he turned slowly in a circle, looking at the houses across the street, the gray-black surface of the street itself, sighted along the vanishing point of the sidewalk as if he were taking aim at the horizon, more houses—halfway down the block would be Miranda's, but he'd save that for next—more trees, lawns, sidewalk again, street, then back to where he'd started. These were the things Miranda had seen that day. Sure, there might've been a new mailbox here, a new coat of paint on shutters there, but essentially, it was the same.

How had it happened? Had he (Scott assumed it was a *he*, it almost always was) parked down the street and approached her on foot? Unless it was a neighbor, he had to have had a car, would've needed a way to get her off the sidewalk fast, take her someplace where he wouldn't be rushed, where he could go slow, do everything he wanted without fear of interruption.

Scott's fingers tingled, and he almost sensed the smooth, unmarked, sweet skin of a child beneath his hands.

He made fists, dug nails into his palms, told himself his breathing hadn't become heavy with excitement, that his forehead really hadn't broken out in sweat. Identification with his subject was one thing, but there were some dark corners of the human psyche that he wasn't willing to plumb, not even in the name of art.

He forced a chuckle to break the mood. Right. As if true crime writing could be considered art. One of the harsher reviewers accused his first book, *Forty Whacks: The Riverton Ax Murders,* of being "tabloid trash that gives pornography a bad name."

He'd stood here long enough. Time to look at Miranda's home.

He started walking again, and nearly stopped when he saw someone approaching from the other direction. At first he had the impression of a group clustered shoulder to shoulder, a huddle of indistinct, shadowy figures moving slowly toward him. They seemed not so much to be walking as drifting forward, their feet not quite touching the ground. He blinked; his vision blurred, cleared, and now all he saw was a lone woman on the sidewalk. His damn imagination again.

A breeze kissed the back of his neck, too cold for April. More of an October wind, the kind that whispered *winter's coming.*

She was too far away to make out her facial features, but she was around five-and-a-half feet, a good five inches shorter than he. Black top, long sleeves, low neckline but not *too* low. Purple skirt, hem at mid-thigh, black tights, black shoes, the kind with thick, cumbersome heels that women always seemed to be able to walk on in apparent defiance of the laws of physics. Straight blonde hair, cut short. Hard to tell her age from here; given the style of her clothes, he'd guess late teens, early twenties.

Nothing remarkable about seeing someone else on the sidewalk. That's what it was for, right? Walking. Still, there was something about the way she moved. Purposeful, focused, as if she had somewhere important to be. She didn't look around, instead kept her gaze trained forward—on him.

His imagination again, or maybe wishful thinking. What

interest would a nearly forty-year-old man who dressed like he'd just gotten out of rehab hold for a pretty young thing like her? And she *was* pretty, he could see that now. Not jaw-dropping, erection-inspiring sexy, though she did have a tawdry little postmodern Lolita thing going. Her lips were small, delicate; her nose thin and narrow with just the slightest upturn. Her eyes . . . her eyes . . .

He'd never been good with colors. To him, the world was painted in primary shades—simple reds, blues, yellows. After that, he was hopeless. Sure, he could spell *burnt sienna*, but that was about it. But those eyes were a very specific color, and he could even name it: amber. Like thick, golden-brown honey, her pupils black insects trapped inside. He'd never seen anything like it.

As she drew close, he realized he'd stopped walking and was staring at her. She stopped, cocked her head, gave a wry half smile.

"It's the eyes, right?"

"Huh?"

Her smile finally reached the other half of her mouth. "My eyes. People are always staring at them. They're kind of unique, I guess."

I'll say. They were the sort of eyes a cat might have, or maybe a wild fairy, the sort that tempted unwary travelers into ancient barrows from which they never emerged.

"I have to admit, they are striking." As soon as he said it, he felt like an idiot. He sounded like someone *trying* to sound charming and adult, like an overly bright high school kid desperate to impress his prom date.

She narrowed those amber eyes as she scrutinized his face. "You're here to get a look at her house, aren't you?"

A cold tightness gripped his gut, and he felt ashamed and dirty, like when he'd been fourteen and his grandmother had caught him masturbating in the bathroom. She hadn't yelled, hadn't scolded, hadn't acted all prudish and scandalized. Instead, she merely closed the door and later, at dinner, said, "Remember what I've always told you, Scott: be good. In everything you do, in all your thoughts and actions." Then she smiled kindly (which was somehow worse than if she'd looked at him with disappointment or disgust), and that was all she said on the matter.

He wanted to lie to the girl, but the memory of his grandma wouldn't let him, so he nodded.

"I thought so. We used to get a lot of you curious types around here after it first happened. Not so many come around anymore, but we still get one or two a month." She sounded alternately amused and derisive. "What's your story? You don't look like a private detective—the family's hired more than a couple over the last year. Maybe you're just another sick twist who gets off on imagining a little girl getting snatched." She grinned. "And maybe imagining what might have happened afterward. Is that it?"

She was too close to the mark for comfort, so much so that he felt a need to explain himself. "I'm a writer. I do true-crime articles and books. I'm thinking of doing one on missing children. People have come to take child abduction for granted over the years. I hope to remind people to take it seriously again." He knew he was babbling, but he couldn't stop himself. There was something about this girl that made him nervous. Maybe it was those eyes, or maybe it was the knowing, adult tone in her voice, the mocking edge to her smile that would've been more suited on the face of someone far older.

It didn't help that he had the impression they were being watched, and not merely by stay-at-home moms peeking through their blinds. He kept seeing movement on the edge of his peripheral vision, shadows that melted into nothing whenever he tried to focus on them directly. His imagination again, he told himself, but that didn't help unravel the cold knot of unease in his gut.

She stepped closer, and he saw that her nipples were erect beneath the fabric of her shirt. No bra. A scent came to his nose, a faint sticky-candy smell, like the bubblegum lip gloss girls had worn when he'd been in junior high. And underneath that smell, the rich, heady musk of a vagina after sex.

"You know what I think?" She was almost whispering now. He felt her breath on his face. It was cool, and smelled of moist earth. "I think you're here because you're drawn to the darkness within yourself, but you're afraid of it."

Before he could respond, she stood on her tiptoes, gave him a quick peck on the cheek, and whispered, "Be good." Then she stepped past him and continued on down the sidewalk.

He turned and watched her go, the smell of bubblegum, sex, and soil lingering in his nostrils, pain nibbling at the base of his skull. And if he had a momentary impression of shadows drifting along behind her, he told himself they weren't real, merely a trick of his eyes; that, or simple fancies conjured by his overly active writer's mind. And he believed it.

Mostly.

Chapter Three

"Mom?"

"Hmmm?" Gayle kept her attention focused on the towels she was folding. David hadn't said much since they'd gotten to the laundromat, but she knew what was coming. It had only been a matter of his working up the courage to ask her.

"Why can't we go to dinner with Dad?"

She sighed, folded one last towel, then placed it on top of the others. She wished they'd done their wash at the apartment complex's laundry room, but there were *so* few washers and driers, and they were always *so* busy. But if they had, they might not have run into Scott, and she wouldn't have been forced into having this conversation with her son. A conversation she wished like hell she could avoid—especially in public.

Not that anyone would likely care all that much if they did overhear. The others customers in the laundromat—a half dozen or so—stood or sat, staring blankly into space while they waited for their clothes to finish. And when they did move, to add softener to the wash or more quarters to the dryer, it was with the listless shuffle of zombies from cheap horror flicks on late-night TV. They didn't look as if they were much interested in their own lives, let alone anyone else's.

Gayle turned to her son, working to put a smile on her face and keep it there. "Honey, I know it's hard for you to understand"—*hell, it's hard for me to understand sometimes*—"but your father and I need time apart for a little while. We have some problems that we need to work out. Problems that have nothing to do with you." She brushed a stray lock of hair off his forehead. The fluorescent light directly above him flickered, casting a wavering, liquid shadow across his face. "We both love you as much as ever. You know that, right?"

David nodded, but she wasn't sure he meant it. She'd gone over all this with him at least a dozen times, but that was okay. She was a social worker, and while that didn't make her a trained therapist, she knew that a kid in David's position needed as much reassurance as he could get. Just as much as he needed to be kept away from a man who the last few months had yelled too much, too loudly, and had started grabbing too hard. There'd been no hitting, not yet, but Gayle had worked with too many abused and battered women to know that it would come sooner or later. Probably sooner.

Damn you, Scott, she thought. Things had been good between them once. Maybe not great, but then what marriage was? But he'd let his work take over his life—*their* lives—let the darkness he wrote about contaminate him, as if he were someone who worked with hazardous substances but failed to take the proper safety precautions. But instead of getting jabbed with a dirty hypodermic or spilling a corrosive chemical on himself, his mind, his spirit had been affected. No, *infected* was a better word for what had happened to Scott. She still loved him; at least, she thought she did, and she wished things could go back to the way they were, but she didn't see how they could. If anything, she thought Scott was just going to keep getting worse.

She felt sorry for him. She knew about his past and all,

about what had happened to his family that summer at the lake, and she sympathized, she really did, but she couldn't let his mental problems destroy her life or that of her son. And it wasn't like she hadn't tried to help him, tried to talk him into getting some help, but he had a deep distrust of mental health workers after having seen so many as a child.

So she had done everything she could think of, had stuck it out as long as she could, but now she had to do what was necessary for her own sanity, and for David's. And if that meant they had to leave Scott behind, then that's what it meant. And if that made her a failure as a wife, then so be it. She'd rather fail as a wife than as a mother.

"Mommy? Why are you crying?"

She wiped her eyes, forced another smile. She was getting good at it; she'd had a lot of practice over the last few weeks. "I'm not crying, honey. There's just a lot of dust in here, that's all. It bothers my eyes."

She looked down, saw David's eyes were watery. "Mine, too," he said softly.

She knelt and hugged her son and told herself that whatever happened, the two of them would be all right. And that was all that mattered: the two of them.

I'm sorry, Scott.

Then the dust got to her again, bringing tears once more, and if any of those tears were for Scott, she pretended they weren't.

Scott leaned on the metal fence, cigarette burning in his hand, and stared at the empty pool. He had no idea when the manager of the apartment complex would have it filled. Probably within the next few weeks, certainly in time for Memorial Day. Right now it was uncovered, curved blue bottom slick with an oily mixture of rainwater and decaying leaves. A dead sparrow lay in the middle—there wasn't enough water for it to float—along with a crushed cigarette pack (not his) and a crumpled fast food wrapper. The bird was just another piece of discarded trash. God might note the fall of every sparrow, but that didn't mean he cleaned up the mess afterward.

Scott took a drag on his cigarette and contemplated how he might be able to use the image of the pool in his new book. Draw a parallel between the refuse in the muck and the way children are cast aside and forgotten by too many adults? Maybe. Then again, it might be too obvious. He'd have to think about it.

"Hi, neighbor."

He turned, half expecting to see the Lolita he'd run into this afternoon near Miranda's house—he'd never finished his walk, hadn't been able to bring himself to go past the girl's home after what Lolita had said to him. But instead he saw a redheaded woman a couple years older than he. She was heavier than she probably should've been, but she carried the weight well. Her face was pretty, though her features seemed exaggerated: big eyes, big nose, big smile. She wore a bit too much makeup for his taste, but then he'd always preferred the natural look. She wore a white turtleneck, white sweater, black slacks, black shoes. She carried a sack of groceries that was stuffed too full and looked as if it might explode any moment. He wondered if she'd bagged them herself and decided she probably had.

"Hi." He lowered the cigarette to his side in case the smoke bothered her. He was tempted to toss it into the muck at the bottom of the pool, let the water extinguish it, but he couldn't bring himself to heap further humiliation on the dead sparrow.

"I'm Laura Foster. I live in 4A, just a couple buildings down from you."

"Sure. I'm Scott Raymond." He didn't want to give her his name, didn't want to talk to her at all given how his day had gone—the less-than-enthusiastic greeting from his wife and son, the weird encounter with the teenage tart— but he couldn't think of a way to get out of this gracefully so he stood his ground, smiled, and pretended to give a damn.

"You just moved in, didn't you?"

"Yeah, about a week ago." It had taken him that long to work up his courage to go see Gayle and David. Now he was wondering if it had been a mistake to move to Ash Creek, if they all wouldn't have been better off if he'd continued to do the long-distance hubby and daddy thing.

"I've been here for a couple years. It's not the most elegant place to live"—she nodded toward the pool—"but at least it isn't too expensive."

Expensive enough on a freelance writer's income, he thought. "They can't exactly charge us extra for atmosphere, can they?"

She grinned. "So what do you do, Scott?"

He glanced at her left hand, saw she wasn't wearing a wedding ring. *Try to figure out how the hell to get away from manhunters like you.* "I'm a journalist." It was easier than saying *writer*. The latter led to *Oh, really* and *Tell me all about it* and *I have a great idea for a book; I'll tell it to you, you write it up, and we'll split the money fifty-fifty.* He wanted to get out of this conversation as quickly as possible. Not that Laura was unattractive, and there was a certain confidence about her that made Scott think she'd be good in bed, but he was still married and he hoped to stay that way. Not only didn't he have the emotional energy for a little on the side, he wasn't about to do anything that would screw up his chances of getting back to being a real family with Gayle and David again.

"You mean like newspaper writing, that sort of thing?"

"Kind of." He tried to imagine what the skin beneath the cloth of her turtleneck was like. Not as smooth and soft as when she'd been in her twenties, he guessed, but she no doubt used body wash instead of harsh soap, was careful to moisturize, too, all on the off-chance she'd run into someone who might be interested in touching her. *Fingers enclosing her throat, linking behind her neck; thumbs pressing on her windpipe. Harder . . . harder . . . Skin breaking, blood gushing over fingers, flesh shredding, bone snapping . . .*

He blinked, swallowed. Where the hell had that come from? Christ, he'd almost *felt* his hands around her throat, almost smelled the tang of fresh blood. He struggled to thrust the image aside, told himself that a morbid imagination was a natural side effect of writing about crime and death so much. That's all.

She waited, probably hoping he'd elaborate on being a "journalist," but after a few moments passed without him saying anything more, she jumped in to fill the silence. "I'm a drama teacher at the high school, and over summer break I direct community theater. Do you like live theater?"

Only when it's done by professionals, he thought. "Love it. Look, I hate to be rude, but I'm on a deadline, and my editor can be a real jerk if I get behind schedule."

Disappointment passed over her face like a cloud, but she fought to conceal it. "Even on a Sunday?"

"Yeah. It blows, but what can you do?"

She nodded. "Well, I'll see you around."

"Sure thing."

She didn't move, and Scott knew he had to leave the pool and go back to his apartment to make his lie look good. He smiled one last time, moved past her, and started down the narrow walkway to his building.

Laura called out after him. "Maybe we can get together for a drink sometime?"

Scott waved without turning to look at her, hoping she'd take the gesture as friendly but noncommittal. And as he walked the rest of the way to his apartment, he tried not to think about hands tightening on soft, sweet throats.

Miranda Tanner was like any other six-year-old girl. She liked Barbies, gave her stuffed animals tea parties, dreamed of playing soccer like Mia Hamm, and was already wondering what it would be like to kiss a boy. She was a modern child, had never known a world without CDs, DVD players, and the Internet. To her, the word "chat" was a virtual place where real friends met to type messages to each other instead of talking on the phone, and she'd seen enough presentations at school to know enough to JUST SAY NO! to drugs, and to be careful of STRANGER DANGER. Perhaps if she'd paid a bit more attention to the last, she might not have vanished on that fateful day in May.

Scott stopped typing and read over what he'd written on the monitor. A bit too melodramatic, but then his editor told him that's what true-crime readers liked. But Heysoos Christ, that last sentence stank worse than a plugged-up toilet in a frat house. Fateful day in May? He shuddered and hit the BACKSPACE key. . . . *might not have vanished in the broadest of daylights.* He nodded. Better. He kept typing.

She might not have huddled beneath a kitchen table, pissing

*herself, listening to screams that echoed long after the vocal
cords that made them had stilled.*

He jerked his fingers away from the keyboard as if he'd
been burned. He re-read the sentence once, again. He had
no memory of writing it. Hands trembling, he reached for
his cigarettes, but he couldn't manage to steady his fingers
long enough to get one out, so he dropped the pack onto
the card table he was using as a desk. He looked at the sentence for several minutes—how long exactly, he didn't
know—before reaching for BACKSPACE. His index finger
touched the key, depressed it enough to reduce *stilled* to *sti*,
then he lifted his hand. He read the sentence one more
time, restored the letters he'd just deleted and made one
more change: turned *She* to *He*. He then highlighted the
sentence, copied it, opened a new file and saved it under
the file name CABIN. When he was finished, he returned
to his original document, deleted the sentence, then saved
that file as well.

Then he shut down his computer, picked up his cigs,
and walked from the bedroom—where his computer was
set up on a card table in one corner—down the short hallway to the living room. He plopped down on the Goodwill
couch, scrounged a match from his pants pocket, and was
finally able to control his shaking hands enough to light a
cigarette.

Scott was nine when his family had been viciously
slaughtered. His dad, mom, older sister, grandmother,
aunt, and two cousins—all dead, hacked up as if they'd
been run over by an industrial-size lawn mower. Only he
had survived, completely untouched. The family had been
on vacation at Lake Hopewell, what was supposed to be a
week of hiking, fishing, swimming, and just lazing around
in the sun. Scott remembered the first four days well

enough, but the evening of the fourth day, when *it* had happened, wasn't even a blur. It just . . . wasn't there. His next memory was waking up in a hospital and hearing someone screaming. It was several minutes before he realized the screaming was coming from his own throat.

The police questioned him, and later, when it was clear that he'd been so traumatized that he'd blocked out that night, he was questioned by doctors who wanted him to make drawings, to role-play, to tell them how he *felt* today. Nothing any of them did succeeded in prying out more than the most fragmentary of memories. He'd remembered a few more bits and pieces over the next couple decades, give or take a few years, but he'd never been able to recall the two most important things: whodunit and *why*.

There had been a time when Scott feared *he'd* done it, gone crazy, sliced his family into cold cuts, then blocked out the event. It took a number of years and even more psychologists to convince him that the evidence the police had gathered made it clear that the murders had been committed by an adult. But that was the last help the police had been: They'd never been able to identify the killer, had never even been able to come up with any serious suspects.

He'd gone to live with his grandma, his only close relative who resided in Ohio. He had an uncle in California as well as a few other relatives scattered around the country, and the psychologists had hinted that maybe he'd be better off with them, since they were all younger. But his grandmother took care of him just fine, showered him with love and kindness mixed with unwavering (but never unfair or dictatorial) discipline. She passed away during his freshman year in college from a heart attack at the well-seasoned age of ninety-one. Sometimes Scott thought she'd held on as long as she had just to make sure that he made it to adulthood okay.

He'd majored in journalism in college, where he met Gayle, who was studying social work. They fell in love and were married after graduation. He landed a job right away, working for a Cincinnati paper on the city beat, eventually moving up to the police beat. He'd . . . *enjoyed* wasn't the right word for how he'd felt about the work. He'd found it fulfilling, in a way, like when you scratch a maddening itch. But it was an itch that never quite went away. At first Gayle found his attraction to crime writing fascinating. She'd called him *dedicated* then, seemed to view him as some sort of heroic figure, like Sam Spade or Batman. But after they'd been married a few years, and their son David came on the scene, *dedicated* became *obsessed*, and she started hinting that maybe he should look for a new line of work, one that wouldn't keep him out of the house at all hours of the night, when she'd be up tending the baby alone. A job that wouldn't leave him depressed and moody so much of the time.

Eventually, he caved in, but only partway. He went free-lance, doing articles, starting work on a book. Since he could set his own hours, Gayle was mollified for a while, but it didn't last. He became even more obsessive as the years went by, and the horrors of human cruelty that he wrote about began to affect him, sink deep into his soul, began to poison him. He started drinking, *seriously* drinking, and soon after the yelling started—and the grabbing, the shaking. . . . It wasn't too long afterward that Gayle moved out, and took David with her.

Of all the crime stories he'd written, though—and it didn't take even a psych intern to diagnose why he'd been

attracted to that particular field of journalism, did it?—
he'd never written about his own up close and personal
encounter with murder. He'd always told himself it was
because he couldn't remember enough specifics to do a
good job, even though he had police reports to fall back
on. And of course, since the killer had never been identified, let alone caught, there was no resolution, no ending.

And there was truth in all of that. But the deeper
truth—the *truer* truth—was that he was damn scared of
digging deeper, of unearthing those buried memories. He
was afraid of finding out who did it, of course, but even
more, he was afraid of finding out why he, of all of them,
had been spared.

Survivor guilt, the docs had called.

"I need a goddamned drink is what I call it." He stabbed
his cigarette out in an ashtray on the coffee table, and rose
from the couch. He grabbed his keys off the kitchen
counter and headed for the door, determined to seek out a
place that sold cheap booze and lots of it.

It was reeeeeaaally late, about, about . . . he struggled to
read his watch in the fluorescent light of the parking lot,
the glare so bright that not even the dipping and darting
mass of insects surrounding it could blunt its harshness.
But he couldn't make out the numbers and said fuck it. He
knew he shouldn't have driven here—he giggled, hell, he
shouldn't have driven *anywhere*—but he just had to be
close to them. David's window was dark, but that was
okay, just fine and dandy-do, because at least Scott knew
his son was in that room, snug under the covers, breathing
deep in that way he had, almost a snore but not quite.

He remembered checking on David when he was a baby,

standing over the crib, listening to him breathe, holding his own breath so he wouldn't wake the boy.

"Shit." Tears rolled out of his eyes, down his cheeks, over his chin, and dripped onto his beer-stained shirt, soaking it further. He gripped the steering wheel tight, as if he might start the ignition, hit the gas, ram the front of the apartment building, break down the door, hop out of the car, rush upstairs and get his son back.

He was still gripping the wheel when he fell asleep.

She was blonde and thin, her breasts too big for her tiny waist and small ass. Implants, probably. He'd enjoy finding out, like looking forward to the prize at the bottom of a cereal box.

She was in front of him at the self-scan check-out at the supermarket. She had six items: milk, yogurt, chocolate-chip granola bars, tampons, a tennis magazine, and a greeting card with a photo of a shirtless, well-muscled hunk on the cover. Birthday card for a girlfriend, he guessed. He had only two items: a roll of duct tape and an X-acto knife. He didn't need anything else.

He'd first spotted her browsing the magazines. She was standing before the sports section, checking out the golf and tennis magazines. He stood in front of the more lurid tabloid section, flipping through a copy of *True Detective*. When she tucked her magazine into the plastic basket and walked off to continue her shopping, he waited a moment, put his magazine back, and followed. She didn't notice him, of course. He was far too experienced at being not noticed. He wore his hair short in a simple, forgettable style, dressed in plain clothes—black suede jacket, white shirt, black pants, black shoes—so that no one would give him a first look, let alone a second. He moved with mid-dling speed, not too fast, not too slow, and he kept his ges-tures economical and to a minimum. He was a chameleon, able to move freely and almost invisibly as he went about his work.

As the blonde scanned her groceries one at a time and put them into white plastic bags, he watched her move, enjoying the easy, confident way she did everything. No hesitation, no pondering. She picked up an item, scanned it, put it in the bag and picked up the next. No nonsense. He liked that.

He found her breasts fascinating. No matter how she moved, bent over, stretched her arms, stood up, they didn't jostle in the slightest. It was almost as if she were wearing a form-fitting armored plate underneath her blouse. Oh, he'd had women with implants before, many times. But none quite like this. It wasn't the breasts them-selves he found so interesting as it was the entire effect. She was model thin, almost waifish, and yet her breasts were straight out of a 1960s B movie. But she didn't dress provocatively: a simple white blouse, blue jeans, sandals. No rings, no earrings. Lipstick, eye shadow, and blush minimal. Everything—including her motions—worked to create an image of a practical, mature woman who felt no need to draw attention to her beauty. Everything except those goddamned breasts, that is. If she truly was the kind of woman she seemed, she wouldn't have gotten implants, wouldn't have felt the need to buy a twin pack of self-esteem. And she sure as shit wouldn't have bought a pair so big!

How would she react once he had her? Would she con-tinue to be strong, struggle to stay in control, or would she reveal the shivering, frightened thing she was on the inside, the girl who thought she was ugly and unlovable, even with her store-bought boobs?

He couldn't wait to find out.

She finished scanning her items, ran her debit card through the reader, punched in the proper code, waited a moment for her receipt to print, then tore it off. She picked up her groceries (she'd managed to fit all the items into two bags) and headed for the door.

He debated. If he took the time to pay for his items, he might lose her. Especially since he'd have to feed cash into the self-scanning machine. He knew better than to use plastic. He'd been taught to be smarter than that.

The door opened and the blonde walked outside. Who knew how close her car might be? She could be in it and gone before his receipt printed. And he'd have to wait for the receipt; he couldn't very well leave it behind. Not if he was going to be smart.

Better to change your plan than to miss out, boy.

It was good advice when he'd first heard it, and it was still good now. He put the duct tape and X-acto knife down on the metal counter next to the scanning area and walked after the blonde. He'd have a harder time getting at those implants without the blade, but then again, he'd have more fun too.

Grinning, he stepped out into the night.

Tap-tap-tap.

Light stabbed into Scott's eyes, and he immediately shut them again. His head throbbed, his mouth was drier than sandpaper, and he had a crick in his neck that felt like someone had jabbed a knitting needle in there while he'd been sleeping.

Sleeping. He remembered the dream. Jesus, that had been a weird one! He'd been stalking some big-breasted blonde at the supermarket. But it hadn't been him, exactly. He'd been someone else in the dream, someone who—

Tap-tap-tap! Faster, more insistent this time.

His brain felt as if it were wrapped in several dozen layers of wet cotton, but it finally managed to produce a coherent thought: Someone was tapping on his window.

Just what he needed. It was probably the apartment complex's security guard. Or worse, it was Gayle, who'd spotted his car on her way to her own vehicle. Maybe if he just kept his eyes closed, whoever it was would give up and—

TAP-TAP-TAP!

He sighed. It had been worth a try. He opened his eyes, slowly this time so the light wouldn't come as quite a shock. He turned his head to see who it was.

Short blonde hair, small lips, thin nose, and of course those amber eyes.

Lolita.

Chapter Four

The girl smiled and made a motion with her hand, indicating he should roll down the window. He stared at her for a moment, transfixed by those amber eyes. They seemed cold, distant, untouched by the smile on her lips. They were eyes carved from unearthly jewels, the strange treasure of some faraway planet.

She motioned again, quicker this time, smile falling

away in irritation. Scott snapped out of his trance and
rolled the window down. The smell of early spring night
drifted into the car, mingled with a trace of what smelled
like honeysuckle, though it was too early in the season for
it. Her perfume? The night air held a chill and he shivered.

"It must have been a big one," she said.

Scott frowned. As sluggish as his brain felt, she might as
well have been speaking Urdu. "What must have?"

She grinned. "The truck that hit you."

He couldn't help smiling. "I look that good, huh?"

It should have struck him as weird, her being here, their
chatting like old friends. But for some reason it didn't; it
seemed the most natural thing in the world. *That* was the
weird part. He wondered if he were still dreaming.

"You sleep in your car often?" she asked.

"Stayed out too late, had a bit too much to drink. That's
all." Which was true enough, as far as it went, but he
wasn't about to tell her the real reason he was here. *I'm
stalking my estranged wife and son. No biggie.*

The fluorescent lights of the parking lot gave her skin a
bluish-white cast that made her look as though she were
ready for the autopsy table. She wore the same outfit she
had on when he'd met her earlier, only now she had a
khaki backpack slung over her left shoulder. Her nipples
were stiff from the night air, and strained against the fabric
of her shirt. She obviously wasn't wearing a bra.

"Normally, I might suggest you take a picture, it'll last
longer. But considering what you're staring at . . ." She
sounded more amused than angry.

Scott tore his gaze away from her breasts. He felt like a
first-class perv; he was old enough to be her father, if just.
"Sorry," he mumbled. He wondered what time it was,

checked out the dashboard clock. 1:24. Jesus, last he remembered, it was sometime after ten.

He turned toward Lolita. "Kind of late for you to be running around on a Sunday, isn't it?" As soon as he said the words, he regretted them. They made him sound old, like he really *was* her father, checking up on her. At least he hadn't added, *Don't you have school tomorrow?* He held up a hand in apology. "Never mind. It's none of my business."

She shrugged. "I like the night. All the best things happen at night."

Like running across a drunken middle-aged man sitting in his car outside his wife's (maybe soon-to-be ex-wife's) apartment?

He was waiting for her to ask him what he was doing here and wondering how he would respond. He couldn't tell her the truth. Not only because he didn't know her well enough, but because he didn't want to come across as a head case. He was a writer; he ought to be able to come up with some sort of plausible lie. But his brain was still too numbed by alcohol to be creative. When he was young, not much older than Lolita, he'd bought in to the romantic image of the writer as outsider who worshipped the trinity of muses called sex, drugs, and alcohol. He'd learned long ago that recreational substances didn't enhance one's creativity, didn't unlock previously closed doors of the mind. They just made you even more stupid than you already were.

"I know who you are."

He stared at her for a moment, not quite comprehending what she'd said. "Excuse me?"

"I thought I recognized you this afternoon, but I couldn't place your face. I had to think about it for a while, but eventually I remembered." She reached around to her backpack and brought out a paperback book. "I picked this up at the library. I'd already read it, but I wanted to double-check the author picture." She held out the book for him to inspect.

Though the colors of the cover were muted grays and blacks in the white-wash of the parking lot lights, Scott knew the title letters were a garish blood red. *Forty Whacks: the Riverton Ax Murders*. It was *his* book, the first he had published. The forty whacks of the title was a reference to Lizzie Borden, though she had nothing directly to do with the Riverton killer. Merely a bit of poetic license on his part. How he'd had to fight the editor to keep the title. At the time he had thought it artistic, but now it struck him as overly precious.

Lolita turned the book around and opened the back cover. There he was, a bit younger and thinner, gaze intense, left hand folded into a fist and propped against his chin. He'd always hated the ubiquitous hand-on-the-chin author photos, had never seen any purpose in that damn hand being there. But then his editor had told him that the hand had a definite purpose: to hide a double chin. Since then, Scott had made sure to always put his hand on his face whenever he had an author photo taken.

"You're Scott Raymond," Lolita said. "Right?"

He felt a momentary urge to deny it. It wasn't that he felt ashamed of his work. Despite the rather lurid cover—a stylized silver ax with blood dripping from its edge—he thought it was a good book of its type, and he was proud of it. But he had never been comfortable dealing with the enthusiasm some people displayed when they found out he was a published writer. They always wanted him to give them the secret of becoming published, as if it were merely a matter of knowing the proper trick and good writing had nothing to do with it. Or worse, they started telling him in excruciating detail about the book they wanted to write, but which Scott knew damn well they'd never even start.

But in the end, he nodded.

"This is so cool!" Lolita ran around to the passenger side and opened the door. Scott was surprised it wasn't locked. He *always* locked doors, in his car, his apartment, everywhere. Being a crime writer had made him cautious to the point of being paranoid, at least to hear Gayle tell it. He supposed he'd forgotten to lock the doors in his alcohol-induced haze.

The girl tossed her backpack onto the seat and slid into the car, closing the door behind her with a solid *chunk!* Scott glanced at the backpack and was surprised to find himself feeling a pang of disappointment that there was something between them. It was the sort of feeling a horny adolescent boy might have over losing a chance to get close and rub legs with a pretty girl. His mind began to consider ways of getting rid of that backpack, of excuses he might make for putting it in the backseat.

What the hell's the matter with you? She's a kid, for Christ's sake! And you're a married man, at least for the moment.

Still, he couldn't help being aware that she was alone with him in his car in a deserted parking lot at 1:30 in the morning. If this wasn't the sort of situation that adolescent fantasies—and perhaps more than a few middle-aged ones—were made of, he didn't know what was.

And she wouldn't have been the first female to come on to him because he'd written a book about murder and death. He was light years from being famous, but he'd done several book signings over the years, and he'd encountered more than a few women who'd flirted with him, and sometimes outright propositioned him, because they were turned on by what he wrote about. He was a true-crime writer, and to some women, that made him "danger-ous" and "edgy." He'd never taken advantage of any of those offers, had never told Gayle about them because she had a tendency to get jealous. He wondered if Lolita was going to turn out to be another of these women, and he wondered how he would react this time if she did.

His grandmother's voice whispered through his mind: *Be good, now.*

I'll try, Gammy.

"That's what you were doing on Poplar Street today, wasn't it?" she asked. "You were researching another book."

"Yes."

She shifted on the seat, turned so she could better face him, and Scott noticed how her skirt rode up. Enough thigh was exposed to make him wonder if she were wear-ing any underwear.

"One about Miranda Tanner?" she asked.

"It's going to be about missing and abducted children in general, but Miranda's case is going to be a large part of it." He sounded too formal, almost professorial. He was sure she saw him as some stuffy, pedantic writer, but he couldn't help it. Despite himself, she was making him ner-vous. Her physical proximity, her un-self-conscious sexu-ality, hell, the very *smell* of her, was gnawing at his nerves. He felt a line of sweat trickle from his right armpit and run down his side. He ran his fingers across his brow and found it moist. His window was still rolled down and a breeze drifted in, but if anything, the air made him feel even warmer, as if the coolness drew attention to how hot he really was.

Lolita nodded. "That's cool. People find it too easy to forget about things like that. It's good there's people like you to remind them. Writers, I mean."

Scott was pleased. It wasn't often that someone understood why he did what he did. Too many readers—not to mention critics—viewed his work as a form of pornography, existing only for base titillation.

"So did you like it?" He nodded to the copy of *Forty Whacks* that she still held in her hands.

She didn't answer right away. She looked at the cover for a few moments, ran her fingers over the raised letters of the title. When she finally spoke, she didn't look up. "Yeah, I did." Her tone was noncommittal.

"Do I sense a 'but' somewhere in there?"

She didn't answer.

He smiled. "You can be honest. After all the reviews I've gotten during my career—some good, some not too good—I've developed a pretty thick skin."

"It's hard to explain. I mean, it was interesting and well written and all, but there was something . . . missing." She turned to look at him. "It's like you were writing about death and darkness from the outside. You know, like one of those guys on the nature shows on TV? The ones that stand back and tell you about the animal while the video guy shoots footage? Even when they get close to the animals— touch them, pick them up, handle them—they never really seem *close* to them. Never really *understand* them. You know what I mean?"

Despite his assurance that her criticism wouldn't bother him, Scott found himself bristling at Lolita's critique. He worked goddamned hard to get inside his research and make it come alive for his readers so his books weren't merely dry recitations of criminal reports.

As if she sensed his feelings, she hurried to add, "Don't get me wrong; it's really good!" She looked down at the book, which she now held tight in her hands. "I suppose no one can really write about the kind of things you do as if they lived them. Most people can only stand to get so close to darkness."

Blood-slick floor, dead eyes staring at him, the soft whisk-whisk *of someone cleaning a knife blade on their pants* . . .

Oh, he'd been close to darkness, all right. He just didn't remember, not all of it.

He almost told her that, but he didn't. The absurdity of the situation struck him then. Here he was, sitting in his car in the middle of the night outside his wife's new apartment, still at least partially drunk, with a teenage girl whose name he didn't know, playing lit crit.

"How about you?" He fought to keep the defensiveness out of his voice, but failed. "Nothing personal, but you don't seem old enough to have experienced much darkness in your life."

She looked at him, expression neutral, but her tone was almost accusatory. "It all depends on the life, doesn't it?" She held his gaze for a long moment before turning and gesturing toward the night outside her window. "Besides, there's darkness all around us, all the time. People just don't see it, that's all. They don't want to."

As attractive as he found the girl, he was beginning to get tired of their little tête-à-tête. His mouth was dry, his throat sore, his head was beginning to throb, and he could really use a cigarette. He decided to put an end to this.

"Not that this hasn't been fun—"

Before he could finish, she got out of the car, closed the passenger door, and ran around to his side of the car. She opened his door and grabbed his hand.

"C'mon."

She started pulling him out of the car, and he was so surprised that he let her. Her hand was cool, almost cold, but the flesh was soft and smooth. It had been a long time since he'd touched the skin of a girl this young, and he'd forgotten how it felt. Gayle's skin had been like this when they'd first started dating, but over the years it had gotten rougher, almost leathery in a way. Not unpleasantly so; after all, it was just the years catching up with her, as they did with everyone. But this skin, this flesh was full of life, full of promise, full of energy and vitality that time hadn't had a chance to leech away yet. Just touching it sent an electric shock through him, straight down into his testicles, and he could feel his penis begin to harden.

She pulled him all the way out of the car and onto the sidewalk in front of the apartment building. Then she released his hand—and didn't he feel a pang at that?—and walked back to the car to close his door.

She came back to him, but she didn't take his hand again, and Scott couldn't help feeling a wave of disappointment. His erection didn't subside, though. If anything, it got harder.

"Let's go," she said.

"Go? Where?"

"Like I said, there's darkness all around us, and I'm going to show it to you. At least a little bit of it."

She started walking away from him, but he didn't follow. She stopped, turned, and smiled at him.

"What are you afraid of? C'mon . . . it'll make you a better writer."

He hesitated another moment, and then, knowing he was probably going to regret it, he started walking.

* * *

The girl led him out of the apartment complex's parking lot and onto the sidewalk. He felt a pull from her, an attraction, as if she were a ship surging through water and he was being borne along in her wake. He had the impression she was tugging him by the hand, could almost feel her smooth, cool flesh clasping his. But her hands were at her sides, his in his pants pockets.

Distantly, he wondered what the hell he was doing, walking the streets of Ash Creek in the middle of the night, trailing along behind a girl whose name he didn't know—and didn't seem to care enough to ask; wasn't that odd? Part of it was because he was still drunk, of course. Nowhere near as bad as he'd been when he'd driven to the complex—and hadn't he been lucky not to wrap his car around a telephone pole on the way over?—but still drunk enough. Part of it was his damnable writer's curiosity. Periodically, he'd step outside the narrow pattern of his life, do a Lou Reed and take a walk on the wild side, for no other reason than to see what it was like, to *experience*, all so he could have something to write about.

When he'd been sixteen, younger than Lolita, he judged, he'd gone to the country fair. That year, they had a mechanical bull, and the operator was offering one hundred dollars to anyone who could stay on for five minutes. Scott had never ridden anything more dangerous than a ten-speed before, but on impulse, he'd decided to give the bull a try. He'd gotten on, the operator flipped the switch, and thirty seconds later Scott was lying in the dirt with a broken clavicle.

There'd been other incidents. The time he'd visited a prostitute when he was nineteen, and paid her fifty dollars just so he could talk to her about why she did what she did. They'd spent so much time talking that her "business manager" had shown up and threatened to gut him with a switchblade if he didn't get the hell out of there so his woman could make some goddamned money.

And the time in college when, despite the fact he never touched the really hard drugs, he'd taken a couple of buddies (who were really more acquaintances) on a heroin run, and they'd all nearly been caught by an undercover cop posing as a dealer.

So given his track record, he had no reason to believe this nocturnal hike would end any other way than badly. Still, he continued trailing after Lolita, and he knew he'd follow wherever she led, whatever she led him into. Just because.

Besides, she'd made him a promise. *Like I said, there's darkness all around us, and I'm going to show it to you. At least a little bit of it.* She was probably just blowing smoke up his ass, but what writer could resist a line like that? Maybe he could steal it and work it into a book sometime.

The night air was cool on his skin, so much so that he started to shiver. It felt more like late November than it did April; he wouldn't have been surprised to see snowflakes falling. This section of Ash Creek was mostly residential. Apartments, houses, a gas station slash convenience store or two. It wasn't the poorest part of town, but it wasn't money street, either. Trash dotted the grass at the side of the road—crumpled fast-food wrappers, cigarette butts, unidentifiable bits of plastic and metal. The sidewalks were cracked and buckled, with tufts of grass poking through fissures in the concrete.

Fluorescent streetlights lit their way, but there was something wrong about the light. Instead of the familiar blue-white glare, their illumination seemed to be tinged yellow, and it felt . . . greasy, as if the light were somehow coating his skin. He had to resist the urge to rub his hands on his face, neck, and arms to get the gunk off. *Light doesn't leave residue,* he told himself. What he felt was probably just a layer of sweat. He could use a shower, that was all. Still, he looked up at the streetlight, shading his eyes with his left hand. He squinted, trying to make out the shape of the bulb. It looked almost like the abdomen of a large insect, a gigantic firefly with its head jammed into the socket and its ass pointing toward the ground, shitting light.

He smiled at the ridiculous thought. But his smile died when the bulb shifted position with the gentle movement of filament-thin legs.

Just the booze coupled with a generous portion of imagination. That's all. Besides, he thought, his mental voice tinged with a hysterical edge, *it's too early in the year for lightning bugs.*

But now the night didn't feel so cool anymore. It felt hot as hell, and beads of sweat started to ooze from his pores. He looked away from the light and focused his gaze on Lolita's back. He blinked in surprise. She was naked, and across her shoulders and lower back was a tattoo of a dragonfly. The tattoo pulsated and bulged as if it were trying to tear free of the prison of her flesh. One leg broke the skin with a soft tearing sound, and a line of blood trickled down her back, rose and fell over the swell of her ass, dripped to the sidewalk with an almost inaudible *plap-plap-plap.*

She stopped, turned, gave him a smile. "Something wrong?"

She was clothed again, the tattoo—if it even existed—concealed.

He shook his head. "I'm fine."

She held his gaze for a moment longer before turning

and continuing to walk. He followed, noting the small splashes of blood, rendered black in the greasy yellow glare of the streetlight, dotted on the sidewalk.

And that's when he began to hear the voices.

Chapter Five

Whispering, taunting, accusing . . . words shapeless and slippery, dancing into his ears and out again, leaving only a hint of meaning.

He looked around. There was no one on the sidewalk besides the two of them, no cars on the road. Ash Creek wasn't exactly New York; it definitely was a city that slept.

The whispering increased in volume, though he still couldn't make out any of the words. The emotions behind the nonsensical syllables were crystal clear, though. Pain, anger, sorrow . . . so strong and sharp they cut through his soul like a straight razor. He felt tears well up and he fought to keep from crying.

"Do you hear that?" he asked.

Lolita didn't bother turning around. "No. Do you?" An edge of mockery in her voice, but tempered with sympathy.

Despite his efforts, a tear ran down his left cheek. Scott was terrified. Not because he believed what he was seeing and hearing was real. He was an intelligent man; he knew better than to believe in insectine streetlights and phantom voices. No, he feared that *it* was happening again, that he was losing his fragile grip on what the rest of the world laughingly called sanity.

After his family's murder, he had spent years in therapy, and his doctors had never been shy about prescribing meds to keep him on an even keel. Large segments of his youth were fuzzy, drug-clouded blurs—and not in the fun way. But thanks to his doctors, and far more, thanks to his grandmother, he'd slowly gotten back at least a semblance of mental health, and he'd managed to maintain it ever since.

But now . . . the violence against Gayle and David—*I never hurt them, not seriously. A few bruises, that's all.* But that was enough, wasn't it? More than enough. And there were the flashes of memory from the day of the killings—and the dreams, don't forget those. Dreams of stalking, of killing, of wallowing in blood like some kind of god-damned animal. Now this. Hallucinations, both visual and auditory. If he were smart, he'd turn around right now, ditch Lolita—assuming she was really here and wasn't just another manifestation of his mental illness—head back to the car, go home, sleep off what was left of his drunk, and in the morning pull out the yellow pages and start looking up psychiatrists.

Then Lolita was standing in front of him, smiling, head cocked slightly in a way that was both endearingly child-like and sexy as hell. She took his hand, whispered something that might have been, "It's all right," but might not, and pulled him forward. He almost yanked his hand away, almost turned and ran, but he didn't. He allowed her to lead him as if she were his mother and he a small, confused child.

They walked another block like that, moving from one circle of greasy-yellow light to another. At one point, Scott looked into the street and saw a shadowy form standing on all fours over a bloody lump of roadkill. Instead of a possum or groundhog, the dead thing had pink, smooth skin with tiny fingers and toes. The creature worrying the small corpse was shaped like a canine, but when it looked up and turned toward Scott, he saw that it had the head of a crow. The beast cawed once, then lowered its beak back to its meal, digging into the sweet, soft contents of the infant's skull.

Scott felt his stomach lurch, and for a moment he thought he was going to spew alcohol and bile all over the sidewalk. But then his nausea subsided. What was there to be upset about? It was just another hallucination. Nasty as hell, sure, but not real, so there was no use getting worked up over it. All he had to do was ignore the sounds of the creature's beak *chukking* into wet meat and the excited, heavy breathing as it eagerly gulped down the morsels it tore free, one after the other. All he had to do was that, and he'd be fine and dandy.

The whispering had faded into the background, but it hadn't receded entirely, had instead melded with the sigh of the breeze, the rustling of the trees—*and don't forget the delightful sound of crow-dog chowing down.* Chuk-chuk-chuk! *Nummy-num!*

They approached a twenty-four-hour convenience store, gas pumps lit so brightly it might have been daylight where they stood. There were no cars parked at the pumps, no late-night drivers filling their tanks. Ash Creek was so small, Scott didn't see the point in having a twenty-four-hour *anything* here. How could such a business make enough money overnight to pay for the electricity it used to stay open? Sure, people liked the idea of twenty-four-hour convenience stores; they slept better knowing that if the urge for a pint of Cherry Garcia struck in the middle of the night, they could hop out of bed, throw on some clothes, and drive on down to that ever-so-convenient twenty-four-hour Gas and Gulp. But how many people ever actually *did* that? Besides drunks, burnouts, and freaks, that is? And did they spend enough on microwave burritos, chocolate-coated snack cakes, and cigarettes to make staying open worthwhile?

Lolita glanced at the convenience mart as they drew near. Did she have a look of concern on her face? Maybe, or maybe he'd just imagined it. She increased her pace, pulled him along after her.

The glass door of the convenience mart opened, and a woman stepped out carrying white plastic bags in each hand. She was blonde, with large breasts and a small waist. She wore a white blouse, blue jeans, and sandals. Scott recognized her. She was the woman from the dream he'd been having before Lolita woke him by tapping on his car window. The woman who had been his prey.

But only in the dream. He'd never hurt anyone in real life; the closest he'd come was with Gayle and David, and even then he'd never seriously injured them—not that that was any excuse, and he knew it—but there had been no cuts, no broken bones. Just harsh words, shoves, hard grabs, shaking. All bad enough, all reprehensible, inexcusable, but not even close to the level of violence he'd intended to do to this blonde in his dreams.

As the blonde headed toward them across the parking lot, making her way between the empty gas pumps, her sandals *thwopping* on the blacktop, Scott began to relax. He'd been disturbed by the barely audible whispers, the firefly streetlight, the tattoo on Lolita's back, the crow-dog (and the baby, don't forget the baby), had begun to fear his brain was melting down for good this time. But now that the blonde had appeared, he understood what was really happening: he was still in his car outside Gayle and David's new home, drunk and asleep. His dream about stalking the woman hadn't ended; instead, as in a cheesy Hollywood horror flick, the dream had only *seemed* to end, but in reality it had morphed seamlessly into a new sequence, one involving the girl he had met while researching his book that afternoon. The only difference between this and a movie was that he had figured it out early, without the need for a "second" awakening to bring home the realization that, after all, it had been Just a Dream. So he could calm down, wait for whatever was to come, and simply let it run its course.

He stopped and Lolita tugged his hand.

"C'mon," she said through gritted teeth. "I have something to show you."

Scott nodded toward the blonde, who was halfway across the parking lot now. "Why don't we wait and see what she wants? It's obvious she's coming toward us."

"Because," and now Lolita sounded frustrated, so much so that he wouldn't have been surprised if she stamped her foot on the sidewalk like a little girl, "she's not part of the plan!"

Twenty more feet until the woman reached them. Scott shrugged. "Looks like she is now."

"Fuck," Lolita swore, though it was more of a sigh than a curse. She released his hand, and he felt a sudden loss deep in the core of his being. He wondered if it was the same sense of loss that babies felt when the umbilical cord was snipped.

The blonde stopped five feet from them, not quite on the sidewalk. Her eyes blazed with anger and pain. Her hands trembled—with fury? fear?—making the plastic bags she held shake and rustle.

Scott frowned. Now that she was closer, he could see there was something wrong with her skin. It was paler than he remembered in his dream, and it seemed to sag, almost as if she were a wax figure that had been left out too long in the sun.

"You sonofabitch," she hissed, the words more breathed than voiced. A stink of rotting, spoiled meat wafted from her mouth, and he felt his gorge rise again.

Lolita stepped between them and glared at the woman. "This isn't the time or place."

"I disagree. This is the perfect time and place." Her words sounded wet, as if her throat were clogged with mucus—or worse.

The whispering—which had faded into the background but never truly left, like insect song on a summer night—increased in volume again, and this time he could make out the words just fine.

Time and place, time and place, time and place, time and place, time and—

Lolita glanced at him, but he couldn't interpret the expression on her face. She turned back to the blonde, her voice tense. "We decided—"

"Wrong. You and the others decided. I missed the discussion." She looked at Scott and smiled, revealing teeth slick with blood. "See, I'm too new."

She dropped her bags, and they fell to the ground, half the contents spilling onto the blacktop. He remembered the items from his dream—or rather, from the earlier sequence of this larger dream: yogurt, tennis magazine, box of tampons. And still in the bags: milk, granola bars, greeting card.

The woman bent down and picked up the tampons. "Thanks to you, I never had a chance to use these. 'Course, by the time you were finished with me, I would've needed a truckload to soak up the blood."

"I'm warning you . . ." Lolita's voice was almost a growl now, and suddenly she was no longer desirable in her jail-bait way, she was . . . dangerous. He took a step backward.

A fissure opened on the blonde's cheek, widened, grew longer. Blood began trickling forth from the wound, slowly at first, then faster, thicker, until it ran from the cut as if it were a faucet. More cuts opened up on her face, neck, arms, legs, blood gushing from each. It struck the ground, splattered, droplets striking Lolita's legs, but if the girl noticed, she didn't care.

"There's no need for this sort of cheap theatrics." Lolita sounded more irritated than anything.

The blonde ignored her, looked at Scott as blood ran from a dozen wounds—no, two dozen, three, more. . . . She reached down and gripped the hem of her blouse. "You wanted to know what was inside my breasts so badly. Couldn't wait to get cutting." She lifted the hem up to her chin, and two pieces of red flabby meat tumbled onto the ground. They hit, bounced, quivered, and grew still. Inside the ragged things, covered with knife and—Christ help him, *teeth* marks—no sign of implants was visible. The damn things were natural after all.

Her grin was so wide, the corners of her mouth split, adding two more rivulets of blood to the rivers streaming downward. "Like what you see?"

Dream or no dream, Scott had had more than enough of this shit. He turned and ran down the sidewalk, back toward the apartment complex that was now home to his wife and son, back toward his car, back, he hoped to God, toward some semblance of sanity.

* * *

The girl and the blonde watched him vanish into the darkness. Other forms had joined them, shadowy, indistinct, more sensed than seen, but they were there, and they watched too. Only now, they watched silently, their whispering stopped. For the moment.

"Too much?" the blonde asked.

The girl who Scott thought of as Lolita sighed. "The point isn't to scare him," the girl said. "It's to awaken the darkness within him. Slowly, carefully, in a controlled manner. So we can use it."

The blonde's form was beginning to go fuzzy around the edges. "We can't afford to go too slow." Her voice grew faint, like the sound of wind skirling across a snowfield. "We aren't the only ones who want to awaken his darkness."

The blonde had become just another shadow, and she drifted off to join the others.

Lolita peered into the night, wishing she could see where Scott had gone, wishing she knew what he might encounter out there, on his own. Wishing she could go to his aid, knowing that she couldn't. Not now.

Scott ran, a refrain sounding over and over in his head.

Not real, not real, not real, not real . . .

It was the closest thing to true prayer that he had engaged in since he'd been a child, and while he fervently hoped it would be answered, he was beginning to fear it wouldn't. Because dreams *ended*, dammit! They didn't just go on and on, getting worse as they went. You *always* woke before you hit the ground, the bullet struck you, the knife plunged into your flesh. That was the way it *was*, those were the *rules*! In dreams, your body wasn't coated with sweat, your stomach didn't clench tight like a fist, your bladder didn't ache, your bowels weren't all watery. And you sure as hell didn't have the stench of blood clinging to your nasal passages, so thick and strong you were afraid you might never stop smelling it. Dreams just weren't that *real*!

Feet pounding on sidewalk, lungs struggling to pull in one searing breath after another, heart pumping jack-rabbit fast . . .

Not real, not real, not real, not real, not, not, NOT!

He reached the apartment complex, left the sidewalk, and ran across the lot, heading for his car. He tried reaching for his keys, but he couldn't get into his pants pocket while he was running. He slowed to a jog, dug for his keys, managed to finally fish them out.

He looked up, saw that someone was sitting behind the wheel of his car. Not Lolita. Bigger than her. Much bigger.

Scott stopped, stared, trembled. Seconds passed . . .

The car door opened.

A heavy work boot clomped onto the blacktop, followed by another. Worn jeans covered tree-trunk legs, a plaid flannel shirt stretched across a barrel chest and broad shoulders. Black belt, big silver buckle shaped into the head of a rearing horse. The left hand was free; the right held a wooden-handled ax. Head silver, edge sharp. The face—

Scott couldn't make out the figure's face. Whoever it was *had* a face, he was sure of that. But even though the parking lot was well lit and he was looking straight at the man, Scott saw . . . nothing. Not a blur, not a shadow. Nothing. While he felt sure his eyes *saw* the face, it was as if his mind refused to register its features.

The man without a face closed the car door with a solid *chunk!* He stood for a moment, gripping the ax with both hands, slowly turning it around and around. The fingers on the hands were thick and callused, the flesh covered with coils of black hair.

Scott felt an icicle of fear stab into his spine. He recognized the man. At least, he recognized his basic shape, his clothes, his weapon. He'd never been caught, and the only victim to survive long enough to describe him to police hadn't gotten a good look at his face.

It was the Riverton Ax Murderer. The killer Scott had written about in *Forty Whacks*. The man had never been positively identified, let alone caught. During the course of the investigation, the prime suspect had committed suicide and the killings—after a final tally of eight—had stopped. Still, the case remained officially open to this day.

"This hasn't been a good night for you, has it, Scotty-boy?"

The voice emanated from the air where the figure's mouth should've been. It held a mocking edge, and although Scott couldn't see it, he knew the man was smiling.

And there was something else about that voice, something familiar . . .

Come on out, Scotty. It's your turn.

"You're pathetic." Faceless took a step forward. "Mooning over that cow you married . . . getting tanked . . ." Another step. "Lusting after that little piece of teen poon, and then pretending to yourself that she doesn't give you a stiffy." A third step. Only a few feet separated them now.

Scott wanted to run, but he was frozen to the spot by that voice. It was as if his nervous system had shut down and refused to pass along the commands his brain was issuing to get the fuck out of there.

"Then Poon-Girl takes you for a little stroll and what happens? The blonde with the big tits shows up, and you turn pussy at the first sign of a little blood." Scott had the impression the man shook his invisible head. "I taught you better'n that, boy."

Despite himself, Scott felt ashamed by the tone of disappointment in Faceless's words.

"I'm sorry." The voice that came out of his mouth was that of a little boy.

"Damn straight you are." Faceless took a last step toward Scott and raised the ax high. "I think it's high time for a *corrective measure,* don't you, Scotty?"

Before the scream could escape his throat, the ax came down.

Chapter Six

Light stabbed his eyes, setting his head to throbbing. He squinted, trying to keep as much of the light out as he could and still see. There was a coating of sweat on his face that made his skin feel greasy and tight, and the inside of his mouth felt like it was coated with beach sand—after the tide had gone out. He shifted in the seat and a jolt of pain shot through his neck. He'd gotten a crick from sleeping sitting up. He reached up to rub his neck, though all he accomplished was to make it hurt worse. Still, he kept rubbing; the pain helped to clear his mind.

He was inside his car. He glanced at the dashboard clock, but he couldn't quite get his eyes to focus enough to make out the time. It was morning, he guessed. Light out, but not too bright yet. He looked around. He was in a parking lot.

Fragments of memory came tumbling back. The bar . . . driving across town to Gayle and David's . . . sitting in their parking lot, feeling sorry for himself . . . Was he still . . . No, this was his apartment complex. Evidently he had made it home okay last night, though he had no memory of driving here.

He couldn't believe he'd been so stupid. It was bad enough that he got drunk. Drinking too much had been one of the factors that led him to—*Go ahead, admit it, at least in your own thoughts: led you to physically abuse your wife and son.* Ever since Gayle had taken David and left for Ash Creek, Scott had stayed away from alcohol. Until last night, that is.

And to top it off, after he'd gotten drunk, he'd climbed behind the wheel of his car and driven to their place—which he at least had some memory of doing—and then he'd driven back to his place in a blackout. He'd never had a blackout before, at least, not of the alcohol-induced variety. He wasn't a stranger to having gaps in his memory, not after what had happened to his family at the lake when he was a kid. But that was different; there was a goddamned good reason why he didn't remember any of *that* shit. But there was no excuse for last night. It was nothing but stupidity, plain and simple. He was lucky he hadn't gotten in a wreck, killed himself or worse, someone else.

Driving around town drunk was hardly the way to convince Gayle that he'd changed, that everything was all right the three of them could be a family again the way they used to be. If he wanted to rebuild the life he had torn apart—and he did, Jesus Christ, he did—he needed to straighten the hell up.

He noticed the keys were still in the ignition. At least he'd had the presence of mind last night to turn the engine off. He removed the keys and put them into his pants pocket, and out of the corner of his eye, registered something sitting on the car seat next to him. He turned and saw a khaki backpack. Lolita's backpack.

He didn't remember everything, but he remembered enough. Lolita tapping on his car window, showing him the book she'd gotten from the library, taking him for a walk, something about . . . a tattoo? A dog? He wasn't sure. Going past the convenience store. . . . That's when things really started to get fuzzy. He remembered a blonde woman—had she been hurt? He seemed to recall she'd been bleeding. And then . . . then . . . As near as he could remember, he'd started dreaming about the Riverton Ax Murderer. But exactly what he'd dreamed, he couldn't say.

He supposed it didn't matter. Where the dream had come from was clear enough: Lolita had brought a copy of *Forty Whacks* with her. Seeing the book and talking about it with her had caused him to dream about it later. Simple enough. If it hadn't been for the backpack, he might have thought Lolita's visit had been just another element of his alcohol-sodden dreams.

He reached out and touched the backpack. It was solid enough. Evidence that she really had been there, that they had talked about his writing, and then she had . . . what? Offered to show him something. It was at that point where his memory started to get mushy. He wondered for a moment if her offer had been some sort of come on, if they'd gone off somewhere to have sex. He couldn't deny that he'd been attracted to Lolita, despite the fact that he loved Gayle and was determined to get back together with her. He supposed it was possible they'd done it, but he felt fairly confident that even though he'd had a lot to drink, he'd remember if he'd had sex with Lolita. What man ever forgot getting laid? Besides, the idea just didn't *feel* right. It wasn't quite a memory, but more like an echo of a memory that told him they hadn't made love.

Part of him was relieved. After all, he wanted to patch things up with Gayle, and starting an affair with another woman wouldn't go very far toward that end. Plus, he had no idea how old Lolita was. It was possible she was under eighteen, in which case she was hands-off, for that reason if no other. Part of him—the animal part that was only concerned with having its appetites satisfied—was disappointed that he hadn't nailed her.

She left her backpack, a voice inside him whispered. *You've got an excuse to see her again. After all, you should return it to her, right? You're a good guy, and a good guy would make sure she got her property back. Nothing sleazy about that.*

As Scott looked at the backpack, he thought he heard a soft, distant sound, almost like wind whispering. But that wasn't possible; the car windows were still rolled up. He put the sound down to his hangover, just a different version of ringing in the ears, and forgot about it. He touched the backpack, rubbed his fingers lightly over the fabric.

"Nothing sleazy about that at all," he said.

After a shower, a cup of coffee, and a handful of ibuprofen, Scott was ready to take a look at the backpack.

He'd put it off, telling himself that it wasn't any big deal, that he'd get around to it when he could. After all, it was Monday morning. He needed to get his shit together, clear away the beer-soaked cobwebs from last night, and get some work done on his new book. Plus, he had laundry to do, and he needed to go grocery shopping and return some videos. But the truth was, he was dying to get into the backpack. His writer's curiosity was gnawing at him, and the longer he put off looking, the more his anticipation built. It was almost like a form of foreplay.

He'd left the backpack on the kitchen table, clearing away the stacks of notes, books, and unopened bills that he'd left cluttered there. It was almost as if he'd wanted to create a special place for the backpack, as if it were a holy object that deserved its own altar.

He sat before it now, just looking at it, almost as if he were afraid to touch it. Afraid of what he might find out about Lolita—and himself?—once he looked inside. Fingers trembling (from his hangover, he told himself), he undid the buckles and pulled back the flap. There was something almost sexual in the action, as if he were undoing her belt, unsnapping her fly, unzipping her pants.

Stop it! he told himself. *You're just opening a backpack, for chrissakes.*

The first object he found was the copy of *Forty Whacks* she'd taken out of the library. The cover was crinkled at the edges, the pages a bit yellowed, showing that it had been handled by a number of people. Scott was ambivalent about that. On the one hand, he was glad people were reading his book; on the other, he wished they'd buy copies of their own so he could make a few bucks in royalties. He set the book on the table and returned to his exploration.

He found a half-empty pack of cigarettes—Kools—and the smell of tobacco made him want a cigarette of his own. He was tempted to go get one and light up, but Gayle had never approved of his smoking, and he wanted to at least cut down, if not quit entirely. So he resisted. Besides, he didn't *need* a cigarette now. He was satisfying an entirely different craving.

He found a full bottle of spring water, the kind with a fancy label that sold for a buck or more. He wondered why people—women, especially, it seemed to him—bothered to pay for what they could get for free from any tap. Some marketing executive somewhere was probably laughing until he pissed himself. He set the water next to the Kools.

Next came a few grooming items: hairbrush (no strands of her hair between the bristles, though), eye shadow, lipstick . . . He opened the latter. The color was some trendy variant of purple. He held it up to his nostrils, inhaled. It smelled like candy. He looked at the nub of lipstick, wondered if it had touched Lolita's lips. She hadn't been wearing lipstick the two times he'd seen her. Maybe she saved it for special occasions, like kissing—or other activities involving lips. He was tempted to touch the tip of the lipstick to his tongue, to see if any taste of her lips lingered, but he put the cap back on and set the lipstick on the table next to the other objects.

Next he found a plastic baggy. From the feel of it, his first thought was he'd located her marijuana stash. But when he pulled the baggy out into the light, he saw that instead of herbs, it contained the dried bodies of a dozen or so spiders. The big brown kind that always sneak into the house when it's cold outside. He stared at the spiders for a moment, then shook the bag to see if any were alive. They weren't.

Odd. Up to this point, he hadn't found anything that was different than what a normal teenage girl might be expected to carry in her backpack. True, there were no CDs of pretty-boy singing groups, no *Seventeen* magazines, no journals, no notes from friends or pictures of cute boys. But their omission didn't mean anything. He'd never been a girl, and unless he and Gayle got back together and had another child, he'd never be the father of a girl. For all he knew, the stereotypes he imagined had little bearing on the reality of a modern teenage girl. But he felt fairly confident that most didn't consider a bagful of spiders to be a vital fashion accessory.

Maybe it's some sort of science project for school, he thought. *Some kind of nature study.*

And maybe it was something else. He lay the baggy on the table—suppressing a shudder at the dry, rustling sound the creatures made as they settled against each other—and dug around in the backpack one more time. He hadn't found any sort of ID—no wallet, no name and address written in magic marker on the outside or inside flap. And the pack felt empty now. It looked like he wasn't going to find anything that would help him locate Lolita and return—

His fingers closed around a slip of paper. He pulled the paper out, unfolded it—maybe it was a note from a friend after all, a *Meet me after school and we'll go the mall* message—and held it up to his eyes. Her handwriting was neat, the letters small and rounded. He wasn't surprised to see that the *I*s had been dotted with tiny smiley faces.

> Scott:
> Man, were you out of it last night! After you blew chunks all over the sidewalk (gross!) I thought you were going to pass out! It was all I could do to get you back to your car! I had to half carry you (and you're heavier than you look, you know that?), and I had a hell of a time getting you into the car, since you were pretty much asleep by then. I almost took your keys (maybe I should've), but I figure you'll probably sleep it off until morning.

*Too bad our "date" was cut short, but I know it wasn't
your fault. That's just the way things go sometimes, right?
How about we try it again tonight? Meet me at the Orchard Street Park at 11 P.M. You have to—you've got to
return my backpack!*

Love,

Miranda

Scott couldn't help smiling. He felt like a teenage boy
who just discovered confirmation that the girl he had a
crush on dug him back. It was pathetic, he knew that, but
he couldn't help it. *She wants to see me again.* Would he go?
He knew he shouldn't, but he *did* need to get her backpack
to her.

He was confused by the note's reference to his throwing
up. He had no memory of that, nor did he remember the
girl walking him to his car. Of course, his memories of last
night were fragmented and jumbled at best. He'd be better
off accepting Miranda's version of events at face value—
after all, *she'd* been sober. He felt a wave of embarrassment
at the thought of her witnessing him—a sad, almost
middle-age man pining for his wife and son—crouched on
the sidewalk, heaving his guts out. He was surprised she
wanted anything more to do with him after that. But she
did; her note testified to that.

And she'd signed it *Love, Miranda.* She probably signed
all her notes that way, it didn't mean anything. Still, he
kept looking at that word, at "love," and wondering—

A thought struck him then, something he might have realized earlier if he hadn't been hungover. She'd signed her
named "Miranda." Miranda Tanner was the name of the
missing girl whose case he planned to make the center-

piece of his next book, *Lost*. It was near Miranda's house where he had first met the teenage girl who up to this point he'd mentally referred to as Lolita. Was it some sort of a joke, a sly reference to where they had met? Or by coincidence, was Miranda her name too?

A thought drifted across his mind, then. A quiet little thought, all the more disturbing for being so.

Maybe it's more than a joke, more than a coincidence. Maybe . . .

The thought refused to complete itself. Scott's head began throbbing anew; the ibuprofen had done little to blunt the pain of his hangover. Wherever the thought had been leading, he knew it was ridiculous. All right, so he had first encountered "Miranda" on Poplar Street, where the other Miranda had lived and, presumably, been abducted. And teen Miranda was blonde, as was kid Miranda. And, now that he thought of it, there was a resemblance between them. He had plenty of pictures of the missing Miranda culled from newspaper and magazine clippings, and of course he had a copy of her HAVE YOU SEEN ME? poster.

He put the note down on the kitchen table and walked down the hall to his bedroom. His computer rested on a card table in the corner, his notes and research files for *Lost* in a cardboard box beneath. He sat in the metal folding chair and rummaged around in the box until he found his photocopy of Miranda's poster. He'd found the original hanging on a bulletin board at the Ash Creek library when he'd first started his research. Even though he doubted the poster would do any good after all this time, he couldn't bring himself to take the original, so he'd taken it down from the board, made a photocopy, then put the original back up. Just in case.

He took his copy back to the kitchen, sat and examined the six-year-old face of Miranda Tanner (she'd be seven now, he reminded himself, assuming she was still alive) and compared it with his mental image of teen Miranda. They were both blonde, of course, though it was possible teen Miranda dyed her hair. Their faces were a similar shape, as were their mouths. The biggest difference—besides the fact that there was over a decade's difference in their ages—was the eyes. Though it was a little difficult to tell from the photocopy, six-year-old Miranda's eyes appeared normal, and there had been nothing in all the articles he'd read to suggest otherwise. If she had possessed eyes as striking as those of teen Miranda, such a detail would surely have been mentioned by police as an identifying characteristic to help trace her.

He also knew from his research that Miranda didn't have a big sister. Ash Creek was a relatively small town, though. It was possible she had a cousin living here, and his research hadn't been so thorough as to delve that far into her family tree.

He read over teen Miranda's note again. Now he had even more reason to meet her tonight. Was Miranda her real name? What connection, if any, did she have to the missing girl named Miranda? Why did she seem interested in him—and exactly what was the nature of that interest? (He knew what he *hoped* it was.)

And why the hell should he wait until tonight? He'd planned to spend the day working on his new book, but he knew he wouldn't be able to concentrate on it now. Besides, if teen Miranda did have some connection to the other Miranda, he might well have found a new angle on the girl's case.

And, though he didn't want to admit this to himself, he

wanted to see his Lolita again. To apologize for last night, if nothing else.

He grabbed his wallet, keys, a pack of cigarettes, and headed out the door. But he left the backpack on the kitchen table. He wanted to save it for tonight.

It was closing in on noon by the time Scott reached the high school. The sign out front read ASH CREEK HIGH SCHOOL: HOME OF THE FIREBALLS. There was a picture of a cartoonish devil beneath the word *fireballs*. Probably a play on the "ash" in Ash Creek, he thought. Although who wanted their sports team to be named after the burnt residue of a fire? Seemed awfully defeatist to him, but then he hadn't grown up around here. He was sure no one in town gave it a second thought.

The school buildings were anonymous blocky structures the color of orange sherbet. Entirely bland and without personality, but so many buildings in small Ohio towns were like that. He wondered if it was part of some statewide building code, that any structure over a certain size had to be boring as hell to look at.

He found the entrance and pulled in, wondering as he did if his son would still be living in Ash Creek when it came time for him to go to high school, and if so, whether he'd be living with both parents again. He felt a sudden, deep need to see his wife and son. To do something to make him feel like there was at least a chance that they could all be together again. He resolved to call Gayle at work when he was finished here and see if they couldn't have dinner—just dinner, that's all, no pressure, no strings—soon. Maybe tonight.

But he was supposed to meet Lo—to meet Miranda to-night. But that wasn't until 11 P.M. Plenty of time for dinner before that, assuming he even kept the . . . appointment. (He couldn't bring himself to think of it as a date; he wasn't *that* pathetic.)

The student lot was full, but there were a couple open spaces in the teachers' lot. There were probably visitors' spaces somewhere, but he hadn't seen any, and he didn't want to waste any more time looking for them. A teacher's space would do fine. Besides, what would they do if they caught him? Send the high school parking police after him? Make him serve a week's detention? Ban him from going to the prom?

Scott parked and got out of the car. But after he closed the door to his Subaru, he just stood there for a long moment, looking at the building and wondering what to do next. It wasn't like he could just go to the office and ask the secretary if they had any students named Miranda who might or might not be connected to the missing girl of the same name. She'd probably think he was some kind of nutcase, call the police most likely. *There's a suspicious man here asking about the missing Tanner girl. I think you should get over here right away!*

And he couldn't just wander the halls, peeking into classrooms to see if Miranda was in one of them. He'd most likely be challenged by a teacher before he got twenty feet, asked who he was and what he was doing there. And when he couldn't give a satisfactory answer, there'd be that call to the cops again.

He supposed he could go to the principal and tell him about his book *Lost*, say that he was here doing research. That might fly. Then again, it might not. It hadn't quite been a year since Miranda Tanner's disappearance, and the fine citizens of Ash Creek were bound to still be upset by it. Too upset to like a stranger poking around and asking questions. It had happened to him on the other books he'd written, and he knew it would happen again here when he got around to the personal interview stage of his research. He wasn't in any hurry for that. Besides, the more he thought about it, the more he doubted the principal would buy it. Why do "research" at the high school when the girl who'd disappeared had been six?

He was on the verge of deciding that coming here had been a stupid move and getting back into his car—he'd even fished out his keys to unlock his door—when a bell rang. Several seconds later teenagers poured out of the exit nearest him. Some ran, most walked, but all were talking and laughing as they pulled packs of cigarettes out of jacket and pants pockets.

Scott smiled. Lunchtime. And just as when he'd been in high school, it seemed some kids preferred an alfresco all-nicotine meal. In his school days, the outside smoking area had been off-limits to "good" kids. Only the "hoods" went there. From the look of the students passing by—black concert T-shirts, trench coats, facial piercings, tattoos—it seemed it was the same here and now. Good. This looked like the sort of crowd his Lolita would hang with.

He fell behind the line of teens and followed them to the smoking area. They didn't look back at him, didn't cast sideways glances, frown or smirk at each other. *Check out the old fuck. Man, how many times do you think* he *got left behind?* Nothing. It was strange. In his teen years, kids had been extremely territorial, especially when it came to places they designated as No Adults Allowed. At the very least, he should've received a resentful look or two. But these kids acted as if he weren't there, and not in the "I know you're there, but I don't want you to *know* that I know you're there" way. It was as if he literally didn't exist for them.

The teens stopped, formed a lopsided circle on the grass and began pulling out cigarette packs, passing around matches and lighters, firing up, inhaling, exhaling, all with the exaggerated motions of kids trying way too hard to look like smoking wasn't any big deal. It almost made Scott smile, but he knew that it would be deadly to give any hint that he found them amusing—assuming any of them were paying attention to him. Instead, he took out a cigarette of his own and lit it. *Might as well act like one of the tribe*, he thought. Besides, after the night and morning he'd had, he sure as hell could use a cig.

He pulled the smoke into his lungs, held it there for a sweet, long moment, then released it. It was then, when the tendrils of smoke first began curling out of his mouth, that every head turned his way. Brows furrowed, eyes narrowed, lips curled into almost-sneers.

"What do you want?"

The boy who spoke was taller than Scott. His skin was pale and pockmarked, but relatively clear, thanks most likely to the wonders of modern acne medications. His greasy black hair spilled onto the shoulders of his black trench coat. A black T-shirt, black jeans, and black shoes completed his *ensemble*.

I sense a theme here, Scott thought.

"I just want to ask you guys a couple questions." He considered quickly, decided to gamble. "I'm a writer," he added.

The boy grinned, showing nicotine-yellowed teeth that seemed somehow too small, too sharp, like tiny shark's teeth. The sight of them almost made Scott take a step back, but he held his ground. Maybe the kid had filed them down that way as an extreme fashion statement. Hardly a good choice in the dental health department, but not unheard of.

"You're a writer, huh?" The kid glanced at the others and smirked. "Too bad none of us can read."

Their laughter was brittle, hollow bones falling down stone steps.

Scott felt his face go hot, and his jaw clenched. He hadn't been big man on campus during his high school days, but he hadn't been a geek, either. Just one more kid in a sea of kids, no more or less special than all the rest. So he hadn't been picked on too often, and then not badly. Called a name here and there, received a flick on the earlobe, maybe a punch to the upper arm or the occasional wedgie, but that was the extent of it.

His anger didn't come from some deep well of long-repressed high school trauma. He wasn't exactly sure where it came from. All he knew was that this kid was seriously pissing him off, and if this kept up much longer he'd—

Knuckles smashing into the soft flesh of the kid's cheek, driving lips against sharpened teeth, points cutting, blood gushing hot and thick onto his hand. Grabbing the back of the kid's head to steady him, ignoring his cries, his beating hands as he tried to fight Scott off. Pressing his fist harder against the kid's lips, working them back and forth, around and around, using those teeth like a saw. Cutting . . . cutting . . .

He blinked, gave his head a shake, actually glanced down at his right hand to see if it was covered in blood, saw that it wasn't. He turned his gaze back to the boy.

Scott's anger hadn't left him, but experiencing the—vision? imagining?—had taken the edge off of it.

"Any of you know a girl named Miranda?"

They didn't answer, just looked at him.

"Blonde, petite. Dresses in black." Like that was a distinguishing feature among *this* crowd. "She has a tattoo of . . ." In his mind, he saw Miranda walking on the sidewalk in front of him, the dragonfly's leg tearing free from her skin, blood dripping. *Plap, plap, plap.* He swallowed, his throat suddenly dry. "A tattoo on her back," he finished, his voice less steady than he would've liked.

The teens looked at each other, unspoken messages passing among them, eyes filled with dark amusement.

The kid with the sharpened teeth grinned again. Scott wondered how the hell he managed to keep from tearing his lips to shreds when he ate. "How'd you get to see her tat? She flash you a little skin?"

"More than a little, I bet," said another boy.

"Probably charged him, too," added a girl.

"Only way a raggedy-ass fucker like him's gonna get any," said yet another boy.

More laughter, more rattling bones. Sharp pain flared behind Scott's right eye, and his vision blurred. He blinked, eyes watering, until his sight cleared. But the pain remained and began to grow worse.

Screw this. The last thing he needed right now was another of his goddamned headaches.

"Thanks for nothing," he mumbled and started to turn away, but he stopped when Sharp-Teeth sniffed the air like an animal, pulling air through wide, pulsating nostrils.

"Hey, you carrying, man?"

Scott frowned. "What, you mean drugs? No."

Sharp-Teeth stepped closer, sniffing like an excited dog, gaze fastened on Scott's eyes. "Don't give me that. I can smell it on you, and so can everyone else."

The others began scenting the air then, making a circle around Scott and Sharp-Teeth and closing ranks until they were shoulder to shoulder. Their eyes burned with the same intensity as the leader's, and they smiled, revealing teeth just as small and sharp as his.

Flashes of last night's dream sparked in his mind. A dog with the head of a crow, beak smeared with crimson. A blonde woman standing before him, blood running from a dozen wounds. An ax rising, falling.

He remembered now; it hadn't been a dream, not exactly, but some kind of hallucination. And he was having another one right now. The realization should've reassured him. After all, he was in no danger from Sharp-Teeth and company because they weren't real, not a one of them. Or at least they weren't as sinister as he was perceiving them. No teeth, no sniffing, no burning gazes. But this knowledge, instead of comforting him, set him on the verge of panic. It was happening again, he was losing control of his mind, and there wasn't anything he could do about it.

He squeezed his eyes shut so tight that he saw flashes of light against the darkness. *This isn't happening,* he told himself, trying to make his thought-voice sound strong, confident, commanding. *When you open your eyes, they'll just be regular teenagers. Sullen, mocking, disinterested, and irritating, but no teeth, no sniffing, no blazing eyes. Just kids out for a smoke during lunch, that's all.*

"I smell it on you," Sharp-Teeth whispered, his breath cool on Scott's right eye. He felt the boy's nose press against his cheek as he took another deep breath. "But you don't have any on you right now. The scent would be stronger. You handled some, though, didn't you? In the"— a deep sniff—"the last couple hours."

Scott kept his eyes closed as he asked, "Handled what?"

Sharp-Teeth chuckled. "Spiders, of course. What the fuck else?" Another sniff. "Some good shit, too, from the smell. Real primo."

Scott felt wetness on his cheek, and he knew that the kid was licking him.

Furious, he reached out, intending to grab the fucker. He was going to rip his goddamned head off and then piss down the neck-hole. But his hands found only empty air.

He lost his balance, stumbled and fell. His eyes flew open as his hands hit the grass. He looked up. Sharp-Teeth was with the other kids, and they weren't in a circle anymore, just standing around. Their eyes looked perfectly normal, though they were now filled with a mixture of confusion and disgust.

"What the hell's your damage, man? You drunk or high or something?"

The kid's teeth, while perhaps in need of a good orthodontist, were no longer sharp.

The pain in Scott's head had lessened to a dull ache. He got to his feet, feeling a combination of relief and embarrassment. He might have a made a fool of himself, but at least the hallucination was over.

"Why don't you go sleep it off somewhere else?" the boy said. "We told you, we don't know no Miranda."

Several of the other kids muttered agreement, adding a few *assholes* and *dumb fucks* for seasoning.

Scott nodded. He turned and started back toward his car. As he walked, a breeze kicked up, bringing to his ears the sound of whispered laughter.

Chapter Seven

Scott drove toward Walnut Hills elementary school, hands tight on the steering wheel, teeth grinding together so hard it was a wonder that bits of enamel didn't come shooting out of his mouth.

I really don't think it's a good idea, Scott.

But it's just dinner. Hell, it's not like the three of us haven't eaten a meal together before.

I know. But we're just not ready yet. Give us some more time.

How much more goddamned time do you need? Assuming that you aren't just blowing me off, that is. You do intend on giving us—the three of us—another chance, don't you? Gayle? Answer me . . . please.

But she'd just hung up.

After leaving the high school, he'd stopped at a convenience store and called Gayle at work from a pay phone. After all the strange things that had been happening to him recently, he really needed to see his wife and son, to be together with them as at least a semblance of a family, if only for a couple hours.

Maybe she was right; maybe it was too soon. He needed to be more patient, give them more time. She'd come around in the end. Sure, they'd had some problems in their marriage, but underneath it all, they loved each other, and they both loved David more than they loved their own lives. They'd be a family again. They would.

He calmed down a little, but he still gripped the steering wheel too tightly, and his jaw remained clenched.

So patience would be his new watchword. That was cool; he could do that. But while he was being patient, he needed to see his son, if for no other reason than to touch base with the normal part of his life (he almost thought the *sane* part, but he didn't want to go down that particularly nasty road, no way, José). After all the weirdness of the past couple days, he needed to get grounded again, get *real* again, and he couldn't think of any better way to do that than to see his son and give the kid a big ol' bear hug.

He reached the school and pulled into the parking lot— the second school he'd visited in less than an hour. He had no trouble finding a space, which wasn't a surprise since the students weren't likely to be riding their big wheels to school, and he parked. As he got out of his Subaru, it occurred to him that this was the school where Miranda Tanner had gone. Even though it had been May, classes had still been in session when she'd disappeared, and she had been here that day, struggling to pay attention to her teacher (even though she was kind of boring), gossiping with her friends at lunch, going to her gymnastics class at the rec center after school, and then . . . nothing. She was just gone.

Though he had come here to see David, the writer part of him was glad for the opportunity to do a little recon before he did any actual research here. He had no idea if the principal or any of the teachers would talk with him about Miranda. They would be reluctant at best, that was for damn sure. Maybe the fact that his son went here might give him an in with them. Yeah, it might be worthwhile to stop by the office, say hi to the principal, maybe do the same with David's teacher. Lay some groundwork for when the time came for him to return to Walnut Hills and start asking questions about Miranda.

And as for the other Miranda . . . he didn't want to think about her right now. He decided to put her out of his mind, pretend she didn't exist, at least for the moment. Better to concentrate on seeing David and, strictly as a side benefit, picking up bits and pieces of the school's atmosphere for his book. Working, even in such a minor fashion, was another way to reconnect with normalcy.

As he approached the side door, he saw a sign taped to the inside of the glass. *All visitors must stop by the office after entering the building.* The message didn't elaborate on the reasons why, but he could guess: It was a security precaution to prevent noncustodial parents from pulling their kids out of class and taking off with them. He realized then that he was a noncustodial parent, in fact if not in the legal sense. The thought depressed the hell out of him.

He pushed open the door and walked inside.

The smell hit him first, a miasma of crayon, construction paper, glue, and paint, combined with an indefinable scent that he could only think of as child. The hallway seemed narrow, cramped, the walls too close together, the ceiling too low. It hadn't been that long since he'd been in an elementary school—he'd gone to the open house last year at the school in Cedar Hill where David had gone— but in some ways it felt as if he hadn't been back since his own childhood. A series of sensory images flashed through his mind: sitting at a desk, trying not to squirm in his seat though his body desperately wanted to move for no other reason than the sheer joy of it, trying to keep his mouth closed though his throat ached to give voice to the thoughts tumbling and jumping in his brain, trying to focus on what the teacher was saying when all he wanted to do was pick up a pencil and draw pictures of dinosaurs and spaceships.

Thirty years or so ago. A long span on the calendar, maybe, but only an eye-blink away as the heart reckons time.

Scott started down the hallway, realizing as he walked that he had no choice but to check in at the office. Not because he was a stickler for following rules, but because he didn't know which classroom was David's. He suddenly felt like a Bad Daddy. What kind of parent didn't know the name of his child's teacher? Back in Cedar Hill he'd known. But here, in this place where Gayle had run to (to get away from him, let's face it), he didn't have a clue. He wondered what it was like for David, coming to a new school, getting a new teacher and new classmates so close to the end of the school year. Probably hard as hell. Damn Gayle for not staying in Cedar Hill, at least long enough for David to finish out the school year. If she'd just—

No, not damn Gayle. Damn *him*. It was because of him that she'd left, that she felt she *had* to leave. He couldn't forget that, not if he hoped to make things right between them again. He had to own up to his part in it and take responsibility if he truly wanted to change.

He heard his grandmother's voice whisper through his mind: *Be good.*

I'm trying, Gammy. Trying like hell.

As he continued down the hall, he noticed that all the classroom doors were shut. He'd expected the doors to be open, the hall filled with the sounds of teachers talking and children working on various projects. But the hall was silent. If the doors hadn't had small square windows embedded in them, he wouldn't have been able to tell if there was anyone behind them or not. He saw teachers, saw students, but he couldn't hear them. It was as if a veil separated them, as if he were looking into a world from which he was forever separated, a ghost spying on the living. The thought was a disturbing one, though it might make an interesting image for his book. He mulled it over as he walked.

From the pictures taped to the walls, it was obvious that this section of the school housed the kindergarten and first-grade classes. Crayon renderings of people with overlarge heads and sticklike limbs were etched above the black magic marker words *My family is . . .* The teachers had written the first part of the sentence, and the students, after presumably drawing their families, had completed the thought.

My family is . . . fun!

My family is . . . cool!

My family is . . . a rotting chunk of maggot-ridden meat!

Scott stopped, blinked, gave his head a shake to clear it. Surely he hadn't read that. But there it was, in blocky crayon letters of blue, red, and green. The picture above the words showed a mommy, a daddy, two children, and a pair of cats. One of the children had torn a cat's head off with her teeth and red-crayon blood dribbled down her chin. The other child had ripped open the second cat's belly and had wrapped coils of intestine around his neck and was strangling himself. His face was colored a pale blue. The parents were the worst. They were naked, lying on the ground in a sixty-nine position, faces buried in each other's crotches, sprays of red crayon splashing forth from where they chewed.

Pain lanced through his skull, and he knew he was having another hallucination. He *had* to be; there was no way in hell this atrocity could be real. No teacher would allow it to be drawn, and she surely wouldn't have posted it on the wall if it had. She would have taken one look and immediately contacted the school nurse, who in turn would've called child services. Psychologists and social workers would've descended en masse on the school like a battalion of military commandos.

He started to reach out, intending to touch the picture, hoping that physical contact would break the illusion and he'd be able to see the picture as it really was. But he hesitated. What if after his fingers touched the picture it stayed the way it was? What if it were real?

Nonsense. It couldn't be real, not in a billion years.

But what if?

He hesitated several more seconds before finally lowering his hand to his side. He turned away from the drawing—and the crayon figures who were *not* starting to writhe and moan in bloody ecstasy—and continued down the hall. He was no longer interested in finding the office. He wasn't at all confident that he could manage to pull off the "I'm Not Crazy, Don't Call the Cops" thing right now. David was in fourth grade. Better to just keep walking until he found the wing where the fourth-grade rooms were housed and peek in the windows until he spotted his son. Once he'd located David, he could make up some bullshit excuse why he needed to see him. A few minutes talking to his son, touching him, reconnecting with the best part of himself—the part that had nothing to do with murder and madness—and everything would be okay again. Right as fucking rain.

He wandered the halls, unchallenged by teachers or staff. He passed the office, picking up his pace and being careful not to look through the open doorway so he wouldn't be noticed by the secretary and summoned inside. He then passed the gym, which doubled as the cafeteria. Lunch was over and the maintenance workers were folding up the tables and returning them to the storage room. Scott inhaled the greasy scent of school food. The smell took him back to his own childhood, to a time when his family had been alive, before his life had become an endless series of talks with psychologists. This last thought made him doubly determined to keep the patchwork quilt that was his sanity intact. He'd do anything to give David as normal a childhood as he could—the kind of childhood Scott himself had lost forever one blood-smeared evening at the lake.

The hallway came to an end and branched to the right and left. He flipped a mental coin and went left. Here, the metal plates below the room numbers and the teachers' names all read *fourth grade*. Bingo. He slowed down, peered through the small windows set into the doors, moved from one side of the hall to the other as he searched. He saw kids sitting at desks, writing, reading, working in groups, looking up at the teacher standing at the chalkboard. But he didn't see David.

Finally, in the second-to-last classroom on the right, Scott found him. The nameplate next to the door identified this as Ms. Miller's class. Now that he knew the teacher's name, he searched his memory for any conversation he might've had with Gayle or David in which the teacher had been mentioned, but he couldn't find any. The thought that his son had a life that he was so shut out of—he'd never seen the apartment where the boy now lived, had never seen the room where he slept, hadn't even known the name of his *teacher*, for Christ's sake—filled him with sadness.

David, like the other children, was sitting at his desk, writing. Occasionally he'd look up at the teacher, then look back down at his paper and write some more. A spelling test, Scott guessed. He debated whether or not to interrupt. On the one hand, he didn't want to disturb the class while they were taking a test, but on the other, he didn't know how much longer he could lurk in the hall before someone saw him and wanted to know what he was doing here.

He lifted his hand to the door, hesitated one last moment, then knocked softly.

As one, the class—including the teacher—turned to look at him. But Scott didn't pay them any attention; he kept his gaze focused on David, wanted to see the boy's initial reaction to his surprise visit. He was afraid (so very afraid) that David's eyes would widen in fear—or worse, that his face would show no reaction at all. But David broke into a wide, happy grin that filled Scott's heart with high octane joy. Any doubts he'd had about coming here in the middle of the school day vanished. He already felt a hundred percent better after seeing that grin.

The teacher, a tall blonde in her late twenties wearing a white blouse and a black skirt, moved out from behind her desk and started toward the door, brow furrowed in irritation. David said something as she passed his desk. Scott couldn't hear it, but he could guess what the boy said. *That's my dad.* And did he say it with a measure of pride? Scott hoped so.

Ms. Miller opened the door a crack, just enough for them to talk.

"Mr. Raymond, while I normally encourage visitors to my classroom, we're in the middle of a test at the moment. If you wouldn't mind waiting in the office, I'll be happy to send David down to fetch you when we're finished, and you can visit all you like after that."

Her tone was pleasant enough, but it contained a rigid

"I'm the teacher and I know best" quality that set Scott's teeth on edge. He'd never responded well to people attempting to wield authority over him, which had made his life difficult on more than one occasion when he'd been a crime reporter. Dealing with police—who used their authority as often and casually as a cook used a spatula or a plumber a wrench—had never been easy for him. That was one of the main reasons he'd gone freelance.

"Thanks, but I just need to talk with David for a couple minutes. Family matters." He hoped Ms. Miller wouldn't press him for further details. Not only didn't he want to lie to her, he wasn't certain he could pull it off in his current state of mind.

The furrow between her brows grew more pronounced as her scowl deepened. "If it's an emergency—"

"No, nothing like that. Something's, uh, come up, and I just need to let David know about it." That sounded lame as hell, but it was the best he could do at the moment. *And you call yourself a writer.*

"As I said, Mr. Raymond, we're in the middle of a test. I suggest you either wait in the office or, if you don't have the time, you can give me the message and I'll pass it along to David for you."

A wave of anger surged through him, coming on fast and strong, taking him by surprise. No, not merely anger; this was *way* past that. It was *fury*, pure and unadulterated. White-hot rage, liquid magma racing through his veins, hands itching to grab flesh and squeeze, teeth aching to bite down on skin and tear . . .

Ms. Miller's face was streaked with blood, her cheeks chewed red and raw, the skin of her forehead hanging down in a wet flap over her left eye, revealing white bone. Her teeth were smeared crimson, and when she spoke next, pinkish streams of blood and spittle rolled out of the corners of her mouth.

"Well, which shall it be, Mr. Raymond? The children are waiting to finish their test."

He could smell the sweet coppery tang of blood, could practically taste it hot and thick on his tongue. For an instant, he experienced an urge to step forward and lick the blood from Ms. Miller's face, and he might have, too, but she was standing before him whole and uninjured once more.

"Sorry," he mumbled. "Just, uh, just tell David that I—" *that I love him like crazy and I wish to hell we were a family again.* "Tell him I'll see him later."

The teacher scowled, as if to say, *You interrupted my class for that?* But she nodded, then closed the door. Scott watched as she returned to the front of the class. The kids were still looking at him, but he didn't care about that. He only cared about David.

He smiled and waved. After a moment's hesitation, David returned both the smile and the wave, and then the teacher was calling for the class's attention, and David turned around to resume taking his spelling test.

Scott watched for a moment more, earning another sharp glance from Ms. Miller, and then he turned and walked back the way he came. As he passed down the kindergarten and first-grade halls, he heard the crayon figures in the pictures taped to the walls whispering softly. He didn't bother to look at them, partly because he was afraid of what he might see, partly because he no longer gave a damn.

"Fuck off," he muttered, but the whispering didn't subside, and it followed him outside, all the way to his car.

Chapter Eight

Scott stopped at a McDonald's for lunch, ordered a quarter pounder with cheese extra value meal, let the drone behind the register talk him into supersizing it, then he hardly ate any of it. Afterward, he went to the library under the pretense of doing some research for his book, but despite spending a couple hours there, he got little done beyond skimming through back issues of the town newspaper—all of which he'd read before—and viewing some missing children sites on the Internet. He tried calling Gayle at work from a pay phone in the lobby a couple times, but all he got was her voice mail and he hung up without leaving a message. He thought he stood a better chance, slim as it might be, of getting her to agree to have dinner if he could talk to her in person.

After leaving the library, he drove around for a while, finally driving down Poplar Street, past Miranda Tanner's house. He wasn't sure why . . . maybe he was hoping to get a glimpse of the other Miranda, the one he still occasionally thought of as Lolita and with whom he had a "date" tonight.

But there was no sign of her, no sign of anyone, for that matter. The sidewalks were deserted. School was still in session, of course, but even so, Scott bet the parents of Ash Creek didn't let their little ones wander around the streets by themselves much since Miranda Tanner had disappeared, and he couldn't blame them. He wondered if

Gayle knew about the missing girl. For the past couple years, Gayle hadn't wanted him to talk to her about his writing, so he hadn't mentioned anything about the book he was working on. He hoped she knew, hoped she was keeping a close eye on David. *Of course she is,* he told himself. *She's his mother.* Still, Gayle wasn't exactly the most detail-oriented person in the world, and she did have a tendency to believe that bad things happened to other people, never to her or her family. But Scott knew otherwise, both from personal experience and from the articles and books he'd written over the years. The most unspeakable, most unimaginable things could happen to anyone at anytime, for no reason whatsoever—just because. In a world like that, you had to be on your guard every moment of every day. Otherwise, you were nothing more than a cute furry little animal waiting your turn to fill a predator's belly—a turn that was going to come around a hell of a lot sooner than you thought.

Maybe he should call Gayle, tell her about the Tanner girl's disappearance. At the least she'd be irritated, at the most seriously pissed off, but she might keep a closer watch on David after that.

As he pulled into the parking lot of his apartment complex, he decided he'd give Gayle a call at work, tell her about his concerns for David's safety, and while he was at it, see if he couldn't pin her down for a day and time when the three of them could have dinner together. After that, assuming he was still in the mood for it after talking with Gayle, maybe he'd try to get some work done before—

He'd been about to think: *before his date with Miranda.* Which was stupid, because not only wasn't it a date, he wasn't planning on going, even if he did need to return her backpack. He'd find another way to get it to her. Hell, maybe he'd drop it off at the police station and let them deal with it—and her.

He parked, got out of his car, and headed past the stagnant miniature swamp that was the swimming pool on the way to his apartment, telling himself that he was going to take Miranda's backpack to the police, but knowing he wouldn't.

Gayle still didn't pick up at work, and he wondered if she were screening her calls in order to avoid talking to him. He tried to write then, but after about an hour pecking futilely at his keyboard, he went outside to have a smoke. He could've smoked inside—after all, he lived alone now— but Gayle had always insisted that, if he was determined to "kill yourself slowly with those damn things" that he go outside, and the habit, like the smoking itself, was hard to shake. And by going outside, maybe he was trying to delude himself that he still lived with someone who gave a damn about his health, about whether he lived or died.

So he found himself standing by the pool again, cigarette smoldering between his fingers, listening to the sound of the wind, when Laura came walking in from the parking lot.

Scott swore beneath his breath. He'd forgotten all about her. The last thing he wanted right now was to have another conversation with that man-hungry teacher. He dropped his cigarette—only a third of it smoked—to the sidewalk, ground it beneath his heel, and started back toward his apartment.

"Scott!"

He swore again, this time more audibly than before,

though if Laura heard him, she gave no sign as she came toward him, trying to look as if she wasn't hurrying and failing dismally.

He considered making a run for it, but decided against it. As determined as she was, she'd probably tackle him before he got halfway to his apartment. He stopped, turned, and tried to force a smile.

"Hi, Laura."

She grinned, probably in delight that he'd remembered her name, and he couldn't help feeling a wave of sadness for her. He wondered how many men she'd met over the years who'd forgotten her name as soon as they'd learned it.

"Taking a break?" she asked.

For a moment, he had no idea what she talking about. Then he remembered: yesterday, he'd told her he was a journalist. She was asking if he were taking a break from writing.

"Yeah. Just trying to gather my thoughts, you know?"

"I sure do. Before I became a drama teacher, I was an actress for a few years. Nothing big, just some parts in regional theatre productions, though I did play the lead a few times. I know how important the right frame of mind is when it comes to being creative."

Scott almost laughed. He hadn't been in the "right frame of mind" for some time now. But he nodded agreement as he tried to figure out the fastest way to disentangle himself from this conversation before it—

"So have you managed to stave off your deadline long enough to have a drink with me?"

He groaned inwardly. He supposed he should be flattered that she was being so persistent, but he knew it had nothing to do with him. She'd be the same way with any man who demonstrated the slightest bit of interest in her. In a way, he admired her for it. At least she wasn't sitting around her apartment, waiting for Prince Charming to knock on the door and ask her to try on a glass slipper. She was out there, trying to make things happen, going for it, reaching for the stars—banal clichés, sure, but that didn't make them any less true. He just wished she wasn't "going for it" with him.

"Maybe tomorrow night?" As soon as the words escaped his lips, he wished he could take them back, but it was too late. "I'm close to finishing what I'm working on, and I don't want to lose momentum, you know?" He cursed himself for not being able to come up with a better lie— one that would've allowed him to avoid making a date with her.

But he couldn't go tonight, could he? Tonight he had a date with Miranda.

Laura nodded knowingly, one creative person to another. "I understand completely. How about five tomorrow night? We could meet at Alexander's. It's a little bar in a shopping center just a few miles down the road from the high school."

Scott knew the place she was talking about. He'd driven past it during his explorations of the town. "Five o'clock tomorrow sounds fine." And then, for reasons that he wasn't clear on, he added, "I'll look forward to it."

Laura smiled a smile that wouldn't have been out of place on the lean and hungry muzzle of a wolf. "Me too."

After finally getting away from Laura, Scott returned to his apartment and locked the door, putting the chain in place as well, as if he feared Laura might change her mind about waiting until tomorrow night and attempt to break in. He didn't know what he was going to do about her, and he decided not to worry about it right now. He was still ragged out after last night's bender, and if he was going to keep his eleven o'clock . . . *appointment* . . . with Miranda, he could use a nap.

He went into the bedroom and lay down without bothering to take off his clothes or throw back the covers. He stared up at the ceiling, feeling suddenly wide awake and wondering if he were going to be able to fall asleep, when he did.

Scott crouched in the dirt on the edge of his grandma's property. The grass didn't grow here, thanks to the shade from the large elm trees looming over the backyard. Gammy had tried sowing grass seed, putting down sod, watering it every day, but nothing helped, and eventually she'd given up in disgust. Which was fine with Scott. He liked having the dirt to play in. It made a great battlefield for his army men, and a wonderful martian landscape for his spaceman. But today he was playing a different game. One far more exciting than moving around tiny plastic figurines.

He'd found the cat in a ditch a ways down the road next to a cornfield. A white Persian, unmoving, fluffy fur matted with blood, thin, bright pink length of intestine protruding from its tiny, pinched rectum. Scott guessed that it had been hit by a car—that happened a lot out here in the country—and had crawled into the ditch to die. Scott had been on his bike, a ten-speed that Gammy had bought used from the Jenkins in town. His grandma made money cleaning folks' houses, folks like the Jenkins, as a matter of fact, but she didn't make so much that she could afford to get him a new bike. Still, the ten-speed worked well enough, used or not, and after staring at the dead cat for several minutes (several minutes during which a warm, tingling sensation spread through his lower abdomen and into his privates), Scott pedaled that bike as fast as he could back home, hopped off before the ten-speed had come to a complete stop, and ran for the house. The bike fell over and slid to a halt in the gravel driveway, and he knew the paint had just gotten all scratched up, but he didn't care. He had more important business to attend to right now.

He banged open the front screen door and ran down the hall and into the kitchen. Gammy stood at the stove, wearing a housedress that fit her like a powder-blue tent and a pair of raggedy pink slippers that looked as if they'd fall to pieces if she so much as twitched her toes. Upon seeing her, a small knot in his stomach relaxed. Gammy had heart trouble and took all kinds of pills for it. Once, not long after he'd moved in with her, she'd had a heart attack and he'd found her lying on the kitchen floor, eyes wide, mouth opening and closing like she was trying to say something, but no sound came out. He ran to the phone and called 911, then held her hand and cried while they waited for the life squad to arrive. It seemed like it took forever, but the paramedics made it in time, got Gammy to the hospital, and after a few days she was okay. Since then, she made sure to take her medicine regularly and hadn't had another attack, but every time he came into the house—especially if she was working in the kitchen—he feared he'd find her like he did that day, lying on the floor, eyes staring, mouth working silently.

Gammy was stirring the contents of a large pot. The smell of hot, bubbling homemade applesauce filled the kitchen. Normally, Scott would've stopped and begged for a taste, even if the applesauce wasn't ready yet. But not today. Without slowing or saying a word, he ran straight to the sink and opened the cupboard beneath. His grandmother was something of a pack rat, and the cupboard under the sink was crammed full of coffee cans and wadded-up plastic grocery bags. Scott pulled a bag loose from the mass, managing not to cause a landslide of plastic and metal in the process.

"Want a taste, Scotty?" Gammy asked without turning away from the stove. She continued stirring with slow, constant, economical motions. Precise and without any wasted effort. No machine could've been any more exact.

It wasn't like her to offer. Usually she forbade him to taste anything she cooked or baked until it was finished to her satisfaction, which meant he often had to wait to be called to the table. On any other day, an opportunity like this would've been too good to pass up. But today he had other, darker appetites to satisfy.

"Maybe later, Gammy." He knew he was too old to call her that—he was almost thirteen—but he couldn't help it. She'd been "Gammy" for as long as he could remember. "I'm kinda busy right now."

He opened the plastic bag he'd chosen and examined it for tears. He didn't want the bag splitting apart on the way back. Satisfied that the bag was suitable, Scott headed out of the kitchen, but before he reached the hallway, Gammy stopped him with a look.

He'd never been able to figure out how she did it. It was like she had some sort of magic power or something. But all she had to do was train her gaze upon him, frown slightly, and he was always frozen in his tracks like a tiny bird caught in the mesmeric gaze of a serpent.

"What?" he said, sounding defensive despite himself.

"Just wondering what you're up to." Her voice was calm, almost disinterested, but she was still frowning.

"Just . . . you know . . . playing." He shrugged, trying to make the gesture look casual.

Gammy looked at him for a few moments longer, and he knew she was trying to decide whether or not to press the issue. He put all his willpower into looking innocent. Finally, she turned back to the stove and resumed stirring the applesauce.

"Off with you, then. But try not to get too filthy, you hear?"

"Yes'm." Scott walked out of the kitchen, but as hard as he tried not to, he was running before he was halfway down the hall.

Outside once more, he hopped on his bike and pedaled back to the cat, holding the bag up and letting the air fill it so it trailed behind him like a plastic flag. He was half afraid someone else had stolen his treasure while he was gone, but it still lay in the ditch, just as dead. Maybe a few more flies had gathered, but that was the only change. He knew the flies were laying eggs, and that eventually maggots would hatch and feed on the cat's dead meat. The thought excited him, though he wasn't sure why, and he felt his penis grow warm and twitch in a way it never had before. He suddenly felt feverish, but it wasn't a sickish sort of feeling; rather something altogether new, something he couldn't name.

He knelt next to the cat and opened his bag, then paused, almost as if he expected the dead thing to give forth one last spasm of life and fling itself into the bag for him. But of course it didn't, which meant he would have to maneuver it into the bag himself. And since he didn't have gloves or tools or any sort, he was going to have to *touch* it.

He hesitated, feeling stupid, but unable to help it. *Of course* he would have to touch it. Wasn't that one of the main reasons he wanted the damn thing, so he could *do* things to it, and experience whatever feelings the doing would spark inside him? But now that the time had come to actually put his hands on the cat, he wasn't certain he was going to be able to. He'd never touched anything dead before. Not unless you counted—

Blood sliding across the floor, a crimson slick rolling toward him . . . Mother's eyes, staring . . . staring . . .

—and he didn't want to count that, didn't even want to think about it, so he didn't. He gotten really good at not thinking about things in the past few years since he'd come to live with his Gammy, and though it always gave him a headache whenever he pushed the bad thoughts away, it was worth it, every single time, and right now was no exception.

He reached a hand toward the cat, let his fingers brush its fur. The hair felt drier, stiffer than a live cat's, more like straw than fur. He set the bag on the ground next to the cat, then grasped the animal around the middle with both hands. He was mildly surprised to find the flesh beneath the fur felt hard like marble, though it still had a little give to it. He lifted the cat several inches, then gently—not that there was any need for gentleness anymore—put the animal's head and shoulders into the bag. Then he set the cat down and pulled the bag the rest of the way along its length, until most of the animal was inside. The tail stuck out, stiff, not wanting to bend, and he felt more than heard small cracking sounds as he tucked the tail inside the bag. He held the bag by its handle holes and stood. The cat hung at his side, its dead weight somehow heavier, he knew, than the animal would've felt if it had still been

alive. Everyone always spoke of death as if it took something away, the spirit or life force or whatever you wanted
to call it. But it seemed to Scott right then that death had
added something to the cat, and that it was this added
thing, whatever it might be, which had made the animal
heavier. He wondered what new dark gift now resided in
the hidden depths of the dead cat. He couldn't wait to take
it somewhere and find out.

As he mounted his bike, he thought he heard whispering: a soft, mournful sound of a chorus of sad women.
Frowning, he looked up and down the road, but he saw no
one. He turned his head toward the cornfield. The tops of
the stalks waved gently in the breeze, like undersea plants
stirred by the ocean current. Could there be someone hiding in the rows of corn, watching him? Someone who
guessed why he wanted the cat, who knew what he
planned to do with it?

He shook his head. There was something wrong here;
there shouldn't be any whispering. There hadn't been any
the first time.

First time? What a strange thought. He'd never found a
dead cat before, had never stuffed it in a bag, had never
done what he was going to do as soon as he got his treasure
someplace where he could be alone with it. Had he?

The whispering grew louder, and he could make out
some of the words now. Not all, but a few.

*Put it back . . . don't do this . . . wrong, so very wrong . . .
blood and death . . . blood and death . . .*

Whatever these whispers were, Scott knew they were in
the same category as Bad Thoughts, so he squeezed his
eyes shut, gritted his teeth, and pushed them away with all
his might. Pushed . . . pushed . . . His head began to
throb, but that was okay, that was cool, because the pain

obscured the voices, made them grow fainter, and so he kept pushing and pushing until the whispering was gone.

He sighed with relief and opened his eyes.

He was kneeling in the dirt at the edge of Gammy's property. The cat lay on the ground before him, split open from throat to pubis, its innards pulled out and placed neatly on either side of the dead animal. Scott held an X-acto knife in his hand, the blade smeared crimson, both hands slick with the same sweet wetness. And was the same copper-sweet smeared on his lips and dancing on his tongue? Yes.

He heard footsteps behind him, a shuffling sound as of house slippers moving through grass. His grandma, come to interrupt his fun, right on schedule. He knew what came next: He was supposed to turn around in surprise and shame, drop the X-acto knife to the ground, begin babbling excuses as Gammy hauled back and smacked him hard across the mouth, the only time she ever had or ever would strike him, her face contorted by warring emotions: disgust, sorrow, fear, concern, and above all, love.

So he began to play his part. He turned, the first excuse rising to his blood-slick lips, but it died unspoken, for Gammy was coming slowly toward him, not rushing as she was supposed to. And she was smiling, though it was a sad smile, and her eyes . . . they were full of sorrow, too, but they also looked . . . old, somehow, far older than could be accounted for by her years. They were the eyes of someone who had seen many secret and hidden things, and who desperately wished she hadn't.

"Hello, Scott. It's good to see you again." Her voice was weary, but still full of love.

Like an actor who's suddenly realized his co-star has begun deviating from the script, Scott didn't know how to react. "You . . . you're supposed to hit me now."

She nodded. "Yes, when this really happened, that's what I did. And while ultimately that might have done you some good, I went to my grave wishing I'd never done it. But this"—she gestured, taking in the yard, the house, the sky, and above all, the cat—"is just a memory, just a dream you're having. You're an adult, Scott, sleeping on a bed in your apartment. You're separated from your wife, and you miss her and your son something awful. You write books about the terrible things that people do to one another. Do you remember?"

His head began to throb, and this time he wasn't grateful for the pain, wished like hell it would go away.

"No matter. It'll all come back to you when you wake up. The important thing is that this dream has given me the opportunity to warn you."

"Warn me?" The voice that came out of his thirteen-year-old mouth belonged to a grown man, though the tone remained that of a confused boy.

She nodded. "There's a battle going on, Scott. A war between what is and what-might-have-been."

Out of the corner of his eye, he saw the cat's legs twitch. He felt a strong urge to turn his head and look at it, but he was too afraid of what he might see, so he kept his gaze fastened on Gammy. "I don't understand."

If his grandma took note of the dead cat's movement, she gave no indication. "Once you pass on, you can see things that you couldn't when you were alive. You can see that each individual's existence is like a road stretching out before them. Sometimes this road is straight, sometimes it's curvy and twisty, and sometimes it takes unexpected turns.

But these roads have . . . well, I suppose you could call them side roads that branch off from the main one. These branches represent all the different paths a person's life might take, if only one or two things were changed."

The birds singing in the trees sounded more like whispering women now, and the cat was twitching and jerking, claws scrabbling in the dirt. Scott tried to ignore it, tried to push it all away just like he pushed away those bad thoughts whenever they came, but no matter how hard he pushed, the whispering didn't decrease in volume, and the cat, dead though it was, didn't stop moving. Its exposed organs began to pulse and writhe like the tentacles of some soft, boneless undersea creature, and it *mreowed*: a fierce, angry cry which sent foul air wafting forth from dead lungs. The *mreow* sounded almost like words to Scott's ears—words spoken in a man's voice.

Don't listen to her, Scotty-boy. The dried-up cooz is trying to unman you, use her words like a pair of gardening shears to snip off the old between-the-legs tube steak.

"Sometimes, though, the branching off points are so close together, the circumstance that makes one or the other of them become *real* so minor, that both exist. And that's what's happened to you, Scott. You've become two different people living two different lives at the same time. But in the end, only one life path, one *you* can be the real one. And that's what we're fighting for—to see which one of you survives."

She means she's trying to kill you, Scotty. Kill the real you. But don't worry; I'll save you. All you have do to is turn and look at me.

"Don't listen to him, boy! He's filled your head with so many lies, taught you so many awful things . . . monstrous things." Gammy held out her hand and smiled. "You come with me. You be good."

Be dead is what she means. Look at me, Scotty . . . Look at me before it's too late.

Scott reached for his grandma's hand but stopped short. Her plump, old-lady flesh had gone gray and leathery, the parchment skin rotted away in places to reveal yellowed bone.

The birds in the trees, the breeze blowing through the yard, the blood rushing through his veins, all whispered the same refrain. *Take her hand, take her hand! Take it, take it, take . . .*

He hesitated, looked up at her face, and saw . . . saw . . .

"Ish okay," the dead thing said through lipless jaws. "Ish shtill me, shtill your old Gah-ee!"

Scott screamed, turned toward the cat, saw coils of intestine whip toward him, felt them wrap around his wrists, his neck, pull him face-first toward the deep, endless darkness inside the animal's body cavity. As he plunged into shadow, he saw the cat's eyes had changed, become human. They were eyes he recognized, eyes he had looked into many times. Eyes filled with glittering dark desires that had no name. But desires which Scott knew all too well.

He heard his Gammy scream. "No!" Heard the other voice say, *That's my boy.*

And then the blackness took him.

Chapter Nine

The darkness was cold, though that word hardly did it justice. He felt as if he were adrift in a frozen, lightless galaxy, his individual atoms slowing down one by one, surrendering to the cold, becoming inert. In a strange way, though, the darkness felt comforting. Familiar.

But he wasn't alone in the darkness. The voice was with him.

You made the right choice, Scotty-boy. I'm proud of you. Always have been.

Who are you?

A hint of a mocking smile in the reply. What, you don't recognize my voice? I'm hurt, wounded to the very quick. *A dry chuckle, a smoker's brittle, truncated laugh.*

An image flashed through Scott's mind then, a faceless man dressed in a flannel shirt, holding an ax easily in large, powerful hands. The ax-head was crusted with dried blood, the same rusty-red lodged beneath the man's fingernails.

Not quite, Scotty. You're not ready to "face" me yet, but you will be soon enough. In the meantime, I have things to show you. Marvelous things, wondrous wet secrets. Worlds of blood and shit and piss. At the risk of sounding pretentious . . . behold!

Sights, smells, tastes, sounds, and tactile sensations flooded his mind. Parting flesh and welling blood, glistening organs and voided bowels, shrill screams of agony and soft exhalations of final breaths.

Welcome to the first day of school, Scotty. I know you're going to be an A student.

The universe of darkness became an endless sea of blood. Scott felt hot coppery liquid rushing into his nostrils, pouring down his throat, filling his belly to the bursting point.

And he liked it.

Chapter Ten

Scott sat behind the wheel of his Subaru, window cracked to allow cigarette smoke to escape, backpack resting on the seat beside him. The dashboard clock said it was 10:48.

This is stupid, he thought. No, stupid was an understatement. This was insane.

His stomach felt hollow and it ached, though the sensation wasn't intolerable, was actually pleasant, in a way. Combined with the nicotine buzzing around in his system, the hunger gave him an edge. He had a feeling he'd need an edge tonight, though why he felt this, he wasn't sure.

He'd slept until a little after ten and had awoken nauseated. No surprise after the dreams he'd had. He couldn't recall them all, especially whatever came after he'd fallen into the body cavity of the dead cat—a macabre variation on Alice's rabbit hole. But he remembered enough to make the thought of food unpalatable to say the least. His skin had been slick with night-sweat, and he took a quick shower, taking extra care when washing his pubic hair and genitals. He told himself he just wanted to feel clean, that he wasn't making any special preparations for meeting Miranda, but he knew better. By the time he was finished, his penis was half erect, and he had to suppress the urge to masturbate.

Don't want to waste it; you're supposed to meet her in less than half an hour.

It was a stupid thought. He wasn't about to risk his already fragile marriage to Gayle—*There's no way she'd find out*—and if he *were* tempted to stray, it wouldn't be with some piece of Goth jailbait—*You don't know how old she is. Besides, remember what they say: Old enough to bleed . . .*

That last thought dredged up images from his dreams, images of torn flesh and gushing crimson. He'd spent five minutes dry-heaving over the toilet before finally regaining control of himself.

Now here he was, at Orchard Street Park, sitting in the parking lot, smoking and wondering if a patrolling cop would drive by and pick him up, suspicious that he was a drug dealer, or maybe a married man out looking for anonymous gay sex under the cloak of darkness. *Not me, Officer. I'm just here to return this backpack to a teenage girl I met yesterday. All perfectly innocent.* There were no other cars in the lot, so if Miranda was already here, she hadn't driven—assuming she was even old enough to drive.

Old enough to bleed . . .

This was a mistake. He wasn't exactly in the pink of mental health, not after the strange dreams and outright hallucinations he'd had the past couple days. The last thing he needed now was any more stress. Maybe he should leave Miranda's backpack on the ground for her to find, get the hell out of here, go home, crawl in bed, and try to hold onto whatever meager scraps of sanity he had left.

He got so far as putting the key in the ignition and turn-

ing over the engine, but before he could put the car in reverse, there was a *tap-tap-tapping* at his window. He
turned, saw Miranda smiling at him.

The driver's side window was still cracked, and he could
hear her plainly when she said, "Chickening out?"

Hand still on the key, he hesitated. But then he smiled
back and turned the car off. He stubbed his cigarette out in
the ashtray, then took the keys from the ignition and
climbed out of the car, Miranda backing up to give him
room. He started to shut the door, remembered the backpack, and reached back inside to retrieve it. He closed the
car door, the metallic *chunking* noise sounding loud as a
cannon blast in the still night air. He held the backpack out
to her without a word, awkward as a teenage boy offering
flowers on a first date.

"Thanks." She took the pack and slipped her arms
through the straps. "You didn't look through it, did you?"

"Of course not," he lied.

She grinned. "Then how did you find my note?"

He opened his mouth to answer, but he couldn't think
of a reply.

She laughed and elbowed him lightly in the belly. "It's
okay, silly. I *wanted* you to find it. That's why I left my
backpack in your car in the first place. I figured it'd give
you a reason to see me again."

"You thought I'd need a reason?" A second ago he'd been
tongue-tied; now suddenly he was Mr. Smooth.

"A girl has to cover all her bases." She said it like it was a
line she'd memorized from an old movie on cable, but that
just made it all the more effective. Sexy, in an endearing
kind of way.

Now that the backpack had been returned, Scott wasn't
sure what to say next. The natural question to ask was,

Why did you want to see me again? but he wasn't ready to ask that yet, wasn't sure he was ready to hear her answer. Instead, he asked, "Why here, of all places?"

She shrugged, the backpack nearly sliding off her thin shoulders. "Why not? It's as good a place as any other."

He was disappointed by her answer. He'd been hoping she'd say, *Because it's dark, it's quiet, and it's private: a perfect place for the two of us to screw each other's brains out.*

"Besides . . ." She smiled, her teeth a slash of white in the dark. "I've got something I'd like to show you."

He arched an eyebrow. "Oh?"

She swatted him on the arm. "Perv! I'm not talking about *that* kind of showing!" She cocked her head then, as if considering. "At least, not yet." She took him by the hand, just as she'd done last night, and started pulling him after her. "C'mon."

And just like last night, he let her lead him into the dark.

She took him to a playground not far from the park's entrance. Scott had been mildly surprised when he'd pulled into the parking lot to discover that there was no barrier to prevent anyone from entering afterhours. Either the citizens of Ash Creek were trusting as hell or naïve beyond belief—probably a little of both. An open, unguarded park like this was an invitation to all sorts of trouble: drug trade, prostitution, mugging, rape . . . hell, even murder. Paranoid? Maybe, but after what he'd lived through as a kid and all the true-crime articles and books he'd written over the years, he preferred to think of himself as realistic. Still, here he was with teen Miranda, allowing her to lead him into who knew what, and he wasn't worried, wasn't nervous. All he felt was anticipation of what she had in mind for him. Her hand seemed to be sending a low-level electric current into his, a charge which ran up his arm, down through his chest and belly and straight into his cock. He felt himself grow hard. He couldn't remember the last time he'd gotten an erection from merely holding hands—probably not since he'd been a teenager himself.

The night sky was clear, the stars bright and sharp overhead. The moon was only half full, but it provided more than enough illumination to see by. His eyes had adjusted especially well to the darkness, almost as if they were used to spending a lot of time away from the light. The air was chilly, but not uncomfortably so, and a mild breeze stirred the leaves in the trees, causing a rustling sound that was too much like whispering. He had the impression that shadowy figures hid among the branches, clutching limbs for balance as they peered down at the couple walking hand and hand into their domain. But of course there was nothing in the trees except maybe birds and squirrels, and the rustling of leaves was just that, and nothing more.

The playground was covered with cedar chips designed to help blunt the impact if children should fall while playing. The chips were fresh, and the cedar smell was strong, nearly overpowering. His Gammy had possessed a cedar chest full of old clothes that smelled like this, though that scent had been combined with the musty-funk of moth balls. The smell curled into his nostrils and clung to his nasal passages and throat, thick as tree sap. Scott felt his stomach lurch, and he thought he might start dry-heaving again, but he managed to control himself.

The first piece of playground equipment to welcome them was a swing set. Three kid-sized swings, two for babies or toddlers. Atop the crossbar from which the swings dangled were three metal heads set at regular intervals.

Dorothy's friends from the *Wizard of Oz*: the scarecrow, the tin woodsman, and the cowardly lion. The heads had faces on both sides, as if they were sentinels designed to keep watch over the entire play area. Their paint was flaking, bright yellow and metallic silver scoured away by decades of wind and rain to reveal gun-metal gray beneath.

As Scott and Miranda walked past, the heads appeared to swivel in their direction, dead metal eyes narrowing, mouths stretching open wide as if to speak.

No yellow brick roads here, no Emerald Cities. Better watch your ass, Scotty-boy. There's worse than witches here. Way worse.

Scott felt his guts twist into a cold knot. He glanced at Miranda. She smiled, eyes full of knowledge beyond her years, but she said nothing. He turned back to the swing set, saw the heads had returned to their original state, facing forward, features frozen, keeping watch blankly over the play area.

Without realizing it, he gripped Miranda's hand tighter. *It was just a trick of the night and my imagination,* he told himself. The thought did nothing to reassure him.

They came to another swing set, smaller, but the bars were heavier, sturdier. The metal was rusted, as if it hadn't been used for a long time. A sign bolted to one of the legs proclaimed that this swing set was FOR WHEELCHAIR USE ONLY. The seat was a wide platform hanging from the upper crossbar by thick chains, like a smaller version of a ferris wheel car. Scott had never seen anything like it before, and he tried to picture how the contraption was supposed to be used. It looked as if you rolled the entire wheelchair onto the platform. There was a front panel designed to close and lock once the passenger was on board, and you'd probably have to lock the wheels of the chair so you wouldn't roll back and forth as you swung. There wasn't a lot of clearance between the seat and the ground, so it wouldn't be a very exciting ride, but it looked as if it would get the job done.

For some reason, he found this more eerie than the Oz swing set and its talking heads. The design was clunky and awkward, seeming more like a medieval torture instrument than a piece of playground equipment. When he was a little kid—probably no more than four or five—he remembered his parents taking him to a mall, where he'd gotten his first look at a man in a wheelchair. He'd been confused and a little frightened, and when his mom noticed, she'd said, "There's nothing to be afraid of, Scott. Some people use their legs to get around; other people use chairs with wheels. But the important thing is that we all can get to where we want to go, right?"

He'd sensed that she wanted him to agree, so he nodded, though he wasn't sure he understood. Of course, his mother hadn't explained to him why the man was in a wheelchair, and Scott's overactive imagination conjured up images of babies being born with tiny wheelchairs growing out of their backsides and legs. He wondered if they could roll right away or, if like regular babies that crawled before they could walk, they had to learn to use their wheels. Later, when he'd asked his mother, she'd looked at him strangely and told him it wasn't nice to make fun of handicapped people. Scott didn't know what "handy-cap" meant, but his mother's disapproving tone made him feel ashamed, and he asked her no more questions about wheelchairs.

Even as an adult, he still felt uncomfortable around people in wheelchairs. They seemed some sort of amalgamation of human and machine, the vanguard of a new species whose evolutionary path would someday lead to the elimination of the flesh altogether. He knew better, of course, but childhood imaginings run deep, are as hardwired as any genetic trait, maybe even more so, and he'd never been able to completely banish the image of babies with metal protruding from their smooth, pink butts and legs.

Miranda continued pulling him along, past slides and monkey bars. They came to a piece of climbing equipment that was built like a spider—round, smooth black body with painted-on eyes and smile; eight thin metal legs protruding from the black abdomen, rising up, angling down into the earth. It wasn't large enough for older kids to climb on, but little kids would probably get a kick out of it, if they weren't afraid, that is.

Scott blinked, and suddenly the spider was no longer a child's plaything but a huge, hairy arachnid crouched atop cedar chips, rows of tiny black eyes glistening with hunger, chelicerae opening and closing, eager to grasp prey. Scott felt an electric jolt shoot through his hindbrain as the monkey part of him—a part of all humans unchanged for millennia—recognized a predator. He froze, fearing that the spider would sense his fear and scuttle forward, eight legs kicking up cedar chips as the arachnid surged toward him, fangs dripping venom.

But the creature made no movement other than continuing to slowly open and close its chelicerae. An ambush predator, then, one that depended on camouflage to lure its prey. Miranda continued leading him forward, and they walked past the spider, Scott keeping his eyes on the creature as they went. The arachnid quivered with excitement as they walked by, but it made no move toward them. When they were a half dozen yards away, the air around the spider shimmered, like heat distortion, and it became—or at least *seemed* to become—just another piece of play equipment again.

Scott wondered how many playgrounds around the world were hunting grounds for such predators; how many jungle gyms and swing sets were in truth traps designed to ensnare unwary children.

"Less than you'd fear; more than you'd believe," Miranda said, as if she'd read his thoughts. She sounded suddenly more adult, the light, girlish tone she'd affected in her speech up to now gone.

Scott was beginning to feel light-headed and dizzy, as he had the night before. It was as if he'd somehow slipped into a dream state while still awake. Nothing seemed real, or rather, everything seemed hyper-real. Too intense, too sharp, too *too*, as if the elementary building blocks of matter were finely honed razor blades instead of atoms, and with every step you took through the world, every action, every thought, you were cut, and cut deep.

"Don't be afraid," Miranda said. "You're just starting to see things as they really are."

Scott wasn't sure what she was talking about. He felt feverish and confused. Part of him felt that he was wandering through the sinister, alien landscape of nightmare, but another part viewed his altered surroundings as comforting and familiar, as if they were exactly the way things should be. As if he were finally home.

As they reached the far side of the play area, Scott heard voices. Miranda crouched down behind a teeter-totter and pulled him after her. The paint had long ago flaked off the teeter-totter, and its wooden surface was frayed to fine threads by the weather. But if Scott squinted at the teeter-totter, it appeared that—instead of wood—it was constructed of lengths of human bone bound by raw, glistening cords of muscle.

He blinked and it was wood again, but he made damn sure not to touch the thing just the same.

Beyond the play area, a grassy field was cut by a paved walking path that wound between large oak and elm trees. At various places along the path rose shoulder-high poles with what appeared to be baskets formed from lengths of chain and solid metal bottoms attached to the top half. These baskets were open at the top, making the whole construction look something like a miniature, landlocked crow's nest. Scott recognized them from his youth: It was a set-up for frisbee golf. The object was to stand a certain distance away from the "hole," throw the frisbee at the pole, and hope the plastic flying disk would bounce off and into the basket. He couldn't recall how the scoring went, couldn't remember if he and his friends had ever kept score.

"It's my turn!"

"Like hell it is! You just went!"

Figures emerged from the darkness, walking toward one of the frisbee golf holes. Three . . . no, five of them. Scott couldn't make out their features from where he and Miranda were hiding—though they weren't exactly hiding all that well, were they? A teeter-totter didn't provide a whole lot of cover, but it was all they had. From the sound of the voices, he could tell they were young men, teenagers, probably. And there was something familiar about one of the voices . . .

"Fuck that! I did not! It's my turn, and there's nothing you can do about—"

A fist raised, came down—once, twice, a third time. My Turn fell to the grass and lay still.

Evidently there *was* something the boy's companion could do about it.

"Asshole," he muttered, and Scott recognized the voice. It belonged to the skinny, pale kid in the black trench coat whom he'd spoken with earlier today, when he'd gone to the high school in search of Miranda. The one with the mouthful of tiny sharp teeth.

No, the teeth were just a hallucination. Don't forget that. It was bad enough to see that kind of shit, but it'd be a whole hell of a lot worse if he actually started to believe in it.

"Dickhead's gonna miss out, isn't he, Jamey?" said another boy.

"Gonna miss out big time," echoed a fourth. The fifth youth remained silent, not having anything to add to the conversation, it seemed.

"Aw, he'll probably come to in time, the dumbass. Not that he deserves to. Now c'mon, I wanna finish the game before it's time to get started."

The boy Scott had thought of as Sharp-Teeth—whose name, it appeared, was the much more mundane *Jamey*—continued walking toward the nearest frisbee golf hole, his four remaining (and conscious) companions trailing along behind. Scott tried to focus on them, to penetrate the darkness so he could see them more clearly. But despite the illumination provided by the moon, he couldn't. It was almost as if they were cloaked in shadows that followed them wherever they went. He could make out little beyond simple, broad silhouettes. It didn't help that he felt like shit. His fever felt worse, and he was beginning to tremble. His gut cramped and roiled as if his stomach were collapsing in on itself.

He sensed more than heard Miranda moving, and he turned to look at her. She had quietly reached into her backpack and withdrawn a plastic baggy. She opened it, took out a small, dry object and pressed it into Scott's palm. Then she leaned close to his ear and whispered, her lips brushing against the soft, sensitive flesh of his lobe, almost as if she were nibbling it as she talked. Despite his fever and nausea, the touch of her lips on his ear made his balls ache.

"Take it. It'll make you feel better, and you'll be able to see more clearly."

Take it? What, like medicine? He opened his mouth to ask, but she touched two fingers to his lips to shush him. She drew her fingers across his lips, circling them once before pulling her hand away. His cock throbbed in time with his pulse.

His head was throbbing now, too, and he felt like he was on the verge of throwing up. If there was any chance that whatever Miranda had given him would help, then he'd take it and not ask any questions.

He popped the dry, light object into his mouth, and just as it touched his tongue, he remembered the baggy he'd found in Miranda's backpack when he'd explored it in his apartment—a baggy filled with the dry husks of what looked like dead spiders with more than eight legs apiece. His stomach heaved and hot bile splashed the back of his throat. He opened his mouth to spit the damn thing out, when he felt a feather-touch on his tongue. Just a tiny tickle at first, but it was followed by more, much more, and he realized with a cold wash of disgust that whatever he had put in his mouth wasn't dead—at least, it wasn't dead *anymore*—it was alive and crawling around on his tongue. He turned away from Miranda and bent over the ground, fully intending to empty the contents of his stomach onto cedar chips, when he felt the spider or whatever-the-fuck-it-was scurry to the back of his tongue and pause before beginning to crawl down his throat.

His abdominal muscles bucked and the cords of his neck pulled wire-tight as his digestive system prepared to initiate an emergency purge. But before he could bring anything up, he felt the gentle touch of spiderlegs making their way deeper inside him, and with each inch farther they traveled, the need to vomit subsided a little more. Within moments, he no longer felt the urge to puke at all. His stomach muscles unclenched, he stopped trembling, and his temperature returned to normal. More, he felt a growing sense of well-being. Not only was he all right, but the entire universe and everything in it was hunky-dory, a-okay, and peachy-keen.

He turned toward Miranda again, and her smile nearly blinded him. He had to half close his eyes against the luminescence that poured from her mouth like a fount of glowing water. It was as if she were some sort of deep-sea creature, the kind that lives its entire life in total darkness and has to manufacture its own light from whatever chemicals its body can produce.

She pressed her lips to his ear again and whispered once more, though now the words sounded like symphonic tones. "It hits you pretty hard at first, but you should adjust before long."

He heard the boys yelling again, turned to look at them. He could see them clearly now, all five, and yes, they had been among the kids he'd seen at the high school smoking area today. And Sharp-Tooth, now Jamey, their leader at school, was still their leader here.

The others stepped back—except the one Jamey had knocked out; he lay on the ground, still as stone—while Jamey planted his feet and lifted his arm, silver disk in hand, preparing to throw. Now, thanks to whatever the hell Miranda had slipped him, Scott could see that the object Jamey held was no ordinary plastic flying disk. In fact, it wasn't made out of plastic at all, but rather gleaming metal with jagged teeth around the circumference. And then he recognized it for what it was: a rotary saw blade.

Scott's gaze tracked to Jamey's intended target, and instead of a chain-basket frisbee golf "hole," a twisted length of wood protruded from the ground, like a tree root growing the wrong way, and upon the tip of the root was a severed human head. A woman's head, but not just any woman: it was the blonde who had confronted Scott last night outside the convenience mart during his night-time promenade with Miranda. Despite being bereft of its body, the head appeared very much alive, its eyes moving back and forth, opening and closing, its mouth gawping wide like that of a fish.

"FORE!" Jamey shouted, and with a flick of his wrist, he sent the saw blade hurtling toward the woman's head.

The whirling disk flew straight toward the woman's mouth, and she opened wider, as if eager to receive it. Then, almost faster than Scott's drug-enhanced vision could detect, her jaws snapped together on the saw blade, her teeth striking the metal with a loud clanging sound. Blood trickled from the corners of the woman's mouth where the saw blade had bit into her flesh, but she had managed to stop the disk before it could cut any deeper.

Jamey whooped. "Hole in one!" he shouted.

His compatriots weren't so thrilled. "Fuckin' lucky shot," muttered one. "Big deal," said another. "Shoulda cut her in two."

As if struggling to add his two cents, the boy on the ground began to stir and moan.

"Aw, you bastards are just jealous, that's all." Jamey walked over to the "hole," carefully gripped the saw blade and tried to work it out of the blonde's mouth. But although the blade had to hurt like hell—it had sliced into her cheeks, had probably done some damage to her tongue—she refused to release it.

"Stupid bitch." Jamey pressed the knuckle of his index fingers against the hinge of the woman's jaw and began turning it back and forth, hard. The head began to tremble in pain, but still it didn't release the saw blade.

"Goddamn it!" Jamey let go of the blade, made a fist, and slammed it into the head's temple. The blonde canted to the side, as if she might fall off her stake, but she maintained her grip on the blade. "I want to get another hole in before—"

"Too late, Jamey." A woman's voice, the *clack-clack-clack* of high heels on blacktop. Scott turned to see who the newcomer was, though he needn't have bothered. Her voice had already told him.

It was his man-hungry neighbor, Laura Foster.

Chapter Eleven

Laura led the five boys deeper into the park, the others trailing behind like obedient hounds, talking, laughing, occasionally taking a swing at one another, sometimes connecting, sometimes not. They kept their voices at a low volume, though, as if they didn't want to upset her. Scott and Miranda followed at a distance—Miranda still holding his hand, though he barely took note of this now. Spider juice surged through his veins, more intoxicating than any drug he'd ever ingested. It felt as if each one of his cells was burning energy at an incredible rate and he might burst into flame at any moment.

As Laura and her puppies walked across grass and between trees, other teenagers joined them, girls and boys both, detaching from the shadows as if born from them. Soon Laura led a dozen, two dozen, three dozen kids through the park. They fanned out behind her in a V shape, like a flock of geese heading south at the beck of instinct they didn't understand but couldn't deny.

They passed a number of severed heads on wooden poles; all women, all somehow familiar to Scott, though he couldn't attach a name to any of them. Laura and the kids ignored the heads for the most part, though one of the boys—Jamey, usually—would cuff one as he walked past. The head would invariably snap at him, and he'd laugh as if it were the funniest thing he'd ever seen.

As Scott and Miranda walked by each head, the woman's

eyes would fix on Scott and she'd open her mouth and whisper, though he couldn't make out any of the words. Sometimes the head would attempt to swivel toward him, ragged meat and blood shifting moistly on the stake, and it would tilt and teeter, in danger of slipping off and falling to the grass below. Numb as he was from the chemicals jangling through his system, he felt little reaction as they passed by, though the mix of emotions in their gazes— anger, fear, concern, anticipation—disturbed him some- what, though he couldn't have said why, but within seconds the drug washed away even that minor vestige of feeling, and everything was a-okay again. He was out for a moonlight stroll with his new girl (and wasn't she a piece?) and all was right with the world.

Finally, they reached what Scott presumed was the cen- ter of the park: a circular concrete fountain. Water sprayed upward from a nozzle in the middle, arced down, splashed into the basin only to begin the journey all over again. Laura stopped in front of the fountain, and her followers spread out in a circle around it, quiet now, as if waiting for their mistress's next command, the only sound was the hush of falling water, a hush that sounded like the whis- pers of women. Miranda pulled Scott behind a tree less than a dozen yards away. He didn't see why they needed to hide. It looked like some kind of party was going on, and Scott figured the more, the merrier, right? But then Laura stepped up onto the edge of the fountain, turned around to face her entourage, and raised her hands toward the night sky. The kids grinned and Scott saw their mouths were filled with the same rows of tiny sharp teeth that Jamey had, and he decided that he was cool with the idea of hiding. *Very* cool.

"Attention everyone! It's time for the show to start!"

More than a few of the kids giggled. Laura ignored them.

"You all know your parts . . ." She grinned. "Or perhaps I should say, *part*."

More laughter, with a nasty hyena-edge this time.

"Let's see if we can keep it together a little longer than last time, okay? After all, you want to make sure to *satisfy* your audience."

They were all laughing now, voices sharp and cutting as a bag full of razor blades. Still laughing, they began to disrobe. Laura did too, removing her clothes—sweater, blouse, skirt, shoes, hose, panties—tossing each article to the ground in turn. The moonlight, along with Scott's spider-juice enhanced vision, highlighted every curve of her body. *Lush* and *Rubenesque* were the words he would've used if he were being polite; *doughy* and *fat* if he weren't. Still, she wasn't all that heavy, and somehow the extra weight made her seem even more sexy. Maybe it was the way the night shadows caressed her thick arms and legs; tiny hands and feet; large, lax breasts with dark aureoles like wide, staring eyes. Maybe it was the way she stood, chin up, head tilted slightly, hands resting comfortably on plump hips, feet planted apart, vagina open to the air. Powerful, commanding, like some sort of ancient earth goddess. Or maybe it was simply that it had been too long since the last time Scott had made love to his wife, and he was horny as hell.

The teens were all lean and lithe as young wolves, their bodies strong, hard and glowing with health and life. Scott tried to remember a time when he'd possessed a body like that, but he couldn't. It was as if he'd never been that young, had been born at exactly the age he was now.

Scott felt his cock getting stiff, and he glanced at Miranda, afraid she'd notice and be disgusted, and at the same time *hoping* she'd notice and be turned on. But she was watching the scene play out before them, eyes shining with an emotion he couldn't name—lust? glee? terror?—all of these and yet none. Her mouth opened, her breathing deepened, and her tongue extended. It flicked up and down, once, twice, almost as if she were tasting the air like a snake, then she licked her lips slowly, her saliva leaving behind a trail of glowing fluorescence. His penis throbbed and strained painfully against his jeans, feeling as if the erectile tissue were stretched to its limits and might tear any moment.

He turned to watch Laura again and saw that she had stepped into the fountain. The night air was chilly and the water probably freezing, but if it bothered her, she didn't show it. She ducked beneath the falling spray, turned and sat down with her back against the fountain's inner column. She spread her legs wide and began to—there was no other word for it—*grow*.

Not proportionally, not increasing in size from a normal woman to a giantess. Rather, her vagina flowed outward and upward, billowing open like a great flesh-colored tent. Her pubic hair blossomed like time-lapse photography of forest undergrowth pushing through soil. The hair rustled as it coiled and writhed toward the stars, becoming a wiry thatch of curly black weeds. And still her genitals grew until they eclipsed Laura, who presumably was still attached to them, and the fountain against which she lay. A large mound of quivering flesh, topped by strands of pubic hair at least six feet tall. It was like an X-rated version of the cheesy old monster flicks Scott used to watch on TV when he was a kid: *Attack of the Fifty-Foot Quim*.

The lips of the vagina spread open, and a thick, redolent musk wafted forth, as if it were a sideways mouth exhaling. The scent was both rank and sweet, and it hit Scott's nasal passages like a jolt of lightning, making his already painfully stiff cock jump. He thought for a moment that he would come like a shotgun in his pants, sperm jetting onto his leg, soaking into the fabric of his jeans. But he managed to control himself, if only just.

The sound of falling water changed to a thick, sludgy gurgling, and Scott saw that the fountain—the uppermost arc of its jetting liquid still barely visible above the grotesque thing Laura had become—was now pumping out a clear gooey substance that looked for all the world like KY jelly. It landed with moist plaps onto the vagina, matting down the pubic hair, sliding along the lips, falling into the opening. Several of the naked teenagers rushed toward the fountain, laughing, and scooped up great gobs of the stuff in their hands.

The other teens had formed a column of three rows before the vagina and now began to embrace one another. At first Scott thought that an orgy was in the offing, but he quickly realized that wasn't the case. There was no kissing or fondling, no insertion of cocks into pussies. The kids were fitting their bodies one to another, molding together, hands clasping ankles, arms wrapping around torsos, legs intertwining, heads tucked snugly beneath armpits until they had become a single unit of flesh and bone, with no visible space between the individual bodies to tell where one left off and another began. Most of the teens were lifted into a horizontal position, but a goodly number remained with their feet firmly on the ground to support the others. At the rear, a large base formed of the biggest, strongest males—Jamey included—stood shoulder to shoulder, arms interlocked, breathing fast and heavy like a team of weight lifters getting ready to go to work.

The teenagers who had gone to the fountain now ran up and down the flesh-column formed of their companions, laughing as they smeared goo over bare skin, returning to the fountain for more handfuls when they ran out. It took five, maybe ten minutes to lube the column, but when they were finished, the remaining teens climbed aboard, folding and twisting their bodies into prearranged positions until they melted into the giant shaft they'd created.

Because that's what it was, wasn't it? Scott thought: a giant penis for the giant vagina. The movie had morphed into *Super Cunt vs. Monster Cock.*

Laura's voice echoed from somewhere in the mound of flesh and hair that she'd become, almost seeming to drift from inside the dark depths of the vaginal canal itself.

Let's get to it, kiddies. It's rude to keep a girl waiting when she's in the mood.

No laughter, no sound at all, save for a large intake of air, and a group grunt from the boys at the base as they began to move forward with small, load-laden steps. As the head of the column touched the vagina and began to slide inside, those teens who had their feet on the ground for support pulled them up as their section of the group-cock disappeared into the dark folds of flesh. They kept going, one slow step at a time, until the entire shaft was in Laura up to the base. They paused a moment, and then began backing up.

Oh, yeah . . . that's sweet. So sweeeeeeeeet . . .

Laura's transformation aside, this wasn't possible. There was no way the kids could blend their bodies together so seamlessly, no way they could hold together as they did, manage to move without their phallic column breaking apart. Scott was a writer, not a physicist, but he knew enough to know that. Besides—and this was a pretty goddamned big *besides*—even though Laura's vagina had grown nearly as big as a house, there wasn't enough depth to house the length of the monster cock the kids had created. As far as they were pushing in, they should have ripped Laura wide open, not to mention breaking the fountain she leaned against. But neither happened. Somehow, Laura was able to take the whole thing as the kids pushed in, then pulled out with loud, moist sucking sounds . . . in and out, in and out, each time with increasing dexterity and speed.

Laura was moaning and gasping all the time now, the soundtrack to every bad porno movie that Scott had ever seen. A number of the kids were keening as well, but whether from ecstasy, fatigue, or a combination of both, he couldn't have said.

Miranda's lips were suddenly against his ear. "Pretty sexy, huh?" And before he could reply, her hand was on his crotch, squeezing his rock-hard penis through his pants. It was his turn to gasp, and he knew he should tell her no, he was a married man, he loved his wife, wanted more than anything to get back together with her, and besides, you're probably jailbait, but he said nothing as her fingers found his belt, undid the buckle, pulled down zipper, jeans, then finally underwear, his penis bobbing erect, stiff as a ship's mast in the night air.

He felt Miranda's fingertips gently brush against his foreskin, and where the spider juice had numbed his senses before, now his nerve-endings flooded with sensation, and his penis jerked away from her touch as if burned. Scott looked down at her, but she hissed, "No, keep watching them," so he turned his attention back to the cluster-fuck, watched it continue, imagined the teens mentally chanting *Heave ho! Heave ho!* as they reamed their transformed drama teacher.

Miranda's hands wandered up and down the length of his cock, stroking here, lightly pinching there, gripping, kneading, working his penis as if it were a musical instrument and she were a virtuoso determined to wring every bit of sound she could out of it. Scott had never had the endurance of a porno film stud, but he'd never been prone to premature ejaculation, either, but the spider-drug, the scene playing out before him, and Miranda's expert manipulation—an almost preternatural skill far beyond her apparent years—combined to send him racing toward the edge of orgasm.

As if sensing this, Miranda began pumping his member hard, matching her rhythm, whether by accident or design, to the strokes of the gigantic group-cock as it slid in and out of the impossibly huge vagina that had once been Laura Foster.

He could hear Laura's voice, little more than a whisper, and it seemed to be coming from within his own head. *Almost there, almost there, almost . . .*

His own orgasm came hurtling near, and he gritted his teeth, reached out for Miranda, found her head, entwined his fingers in her hair, and then he was coming, Christ Jesus, he was—

He looked down at the moment of orgasm, saw fluid jetting forth, not viscous white, but rather dark wine-red, heard Miranda cry out in pain. She jerked her hand away, and he saw that blood gushed from her palm, fell to the grass in dribbling lines. He looked down at his penis and saw not a glistening head, round shaft, nest of pubic hair. Instead, protruding from between his legs was a wicked knife blade, ten inches long, blood smeared on its stainless steel surface.

Miranda looked at her bleeding hand, the expression on her face not so much one of pain now as of irritation. "Shit, I didn't think *that* would happen."

Scott didn't reply. He couldn't take his gaze off the cruel metal object jutting forth from where his cock had been. He concentrated, flexed muscles in his trunk, and the knife blade jerked upward in response, flinging a dollop of Miranda's blood into the air.

"Hey! Who's there?" It was Jamey's voice.

Scott looked up. The boys who formed the base of the group-penis were looking in his and Miranda's direction. Many of the teens who formed the shaft had turned their heads and were looking too, and while he couldn't see Laura's face, obscured as it was by her vast, mutated vagina, he sensed that her attention had been drawn as well.

He looked down between his legs once more and saw that the knife had become a rapidly deflating cock, cum-pearl welling at the slit, though the flesh was still slick with blood. He turned to Miranda, saw she had wrapped her wounded hand in the fabric of her shirt, exposing her taut belly.

"I think it would be a really good idea if you pulled your pants up and we got the hell out of here."

He looked back toward the fountain. The gigantic group-penis had withdrawn from Laura and was beginning to break apart. Some of the teens—Jamey among them—were already starting to head in their direction, scowling, mouths open, shark teeth glinting in the moonlight.

Scott bent down and reached for his pants as the first of them began running.

Chapter Twelve

This isn't happening . . . it can't be happening . . .

Scott ran, Miranda at his side. He held her hand—the one that hadn't been sliced open by his cock-knife—as they wove between trees, followed by the sounds of angry, shouting voices and bare feet pounding on grass. If they could just make it back to his car, they could get in, drive away, and he could begin the hard work of trying to convince himself none of this had happened.

If.

The first of them caught up just outside of the play area. Scott felt a hand grab his arm, stop him, pull him away from Miranda and spin him around with surprising strength. The boy—not Jamey but still one of the kids he'd seen at the high-school smoking area, he thought—was still naked, his body slathered with fountain-lube and vaginal fluid, making him smell like a combination pharmacy and whorehouse. His hair was plastered to his skull, eyes wild, teeth bared.

"So you like to watch, huh, freak? How 'bout I chew your goddamned eyes out so you can never watch again?" He grabbed Scott's head, and with a snarl lunged for his face.

The kid's hands were too slick to maintain a grip, though, and Scott was able to pull away before he could connect. Scott looked around frantically and saw one of the severed-head frisbee golf holes not more than ten feet away.

The boy lunged for him again, but Scott sidestepped, grabbed the kid's forearm, and—holding onto the slick flesh as best he could—spun his attacker toward the head. The boy stumbled toward it, slipped in the grass, and fell face-first toward the woman's head. She . . . it . . . snapped her teeth onto his ear, and he howled in pain as he fell to the ground, pulling the head—which was busy chewing his ear to ragged meat—off the stake and down with him. The head, propelled by whatever muscles it still controlled, flipped off the ear and went to work on the kid's neck. His shrill screams sounded more animal than human and, God help him, they were the sweetest of music to Scott's ears.

His gut churned, and he imagined he felt the spider he'd ingested flailing around, stung by stomach acid. He clamped his jaw shut tight and told himself that he couldn't afford the time it would take to throw up. He looked for Miranda, hoped she'd had the presence of mind to keep running, saw she hadn't, and he grabbed her hand and pulled her toward the play area as more kids drew near.

Only a handful, though, not more than a half dozen. Perhaps the others had scattered after realizing they'd been discovered, or maybe they'd remained behind to attend to their mistress. Whatever the case, Scott was grateful. There was no way Miranda and he could've survived if the entire mob had come after them. Even so, there was a damn good chance they weren't going to survive as it was.

The second attacker, a girl this time, caught up with them just inside the play area. She went for Miranda first, slamming into her and knocking her down onto the cedar chips. The girl, matted wet hair clinging to her back, screamed in fury as she clawed at Miranda's face. Miranda raised her hands to protect herself, exposing her wounded palm, and the girl fastened her teeth onto it like a dog latching onto raw meat.

Miranda shrieked in pain, the sound causing an explosion of white heat inside Scott's skull. He stepped forward and grabbed the girl's hair, twisting it around his fingers so they wouldn't slide free. Then he yanked the wild thing off Miranda—mouth smeared crimson with Miranda's blood—turned and, without thinking, spun her toward the nearest object: the spider climber. He released his grip on her hair as she fell toward it, and the air around the metal object shimmered and it was a child's plaything no longer. The spider scuttled forward eagerly, fangs dripping venom. The girl hit the ground but before she could attempt to rise, the spider was on her, plunging its fangs into her shoulders and injecting its poison. The flesh around the fangs began to swell and blacken, and the girl thrashed about as if she were having a seizure. The spider held her down and continued pumping its killing fluids into her, and within seconds her movements became less violent and then ceased altogether.

Serves you right, bitch. The voice inside Scott's head was and wasn't his own, at once alien and familiar. The spider, fangs still embedded in the flesh of its prey, began dragging the girl toward the hedges surrounding the play area, presumably so it could dine in solitude. *Bon appetit*, he thought, then he grabbed Miranda's hand once more and started pulling her in the direction of his car.

He heard footfalls behind them, Miranda yelling, "Scott, look out!" but before he could turn around, pain burst at the base of his skull and an explosion of white went off behind his eyes. He let go of Miranda's hand and stumbled forward, though he didn't fall. He turned, head throbbing, to see another naked teen, a boy this time, holding a good-sized tree limb. The end had been broken off, probably just now when the sonofabitch had hit him.

Miranda ran toward the boy, but he swung the tree limb as if he were the mighty Casey himself and connected with the side of her head. The sound of wood striking flesh and bone made a muffled, hollow thump. Miranda's eyes rolled white and she fell to the cedar chips, her body folding on itself like a suddenly stringless puppet. Casey turned to Scott and pointed the splintered end of the limb toward him, obviously intending to use it as a stake. He snarled, displaying his shark teeth, and then attacked.

Scott held his ground for a second . . . two . . . then just as the boy was about to jam his makeshift stake into Scott's chest, he jumped aside. The boy tried to stop and turn, but momentum was not on his side, and he fell in a tangle of arms and legs into a rusted metal contraption that bore the sign: FOR WHEELCHAIR USE ONLY.

The boy tried to pull himself free, but the crossbar snapped shut, and the swing—whether due to the boy's momentum or under its own power—began to sway, forward and back, forward and back. The letters on the sign seemed to grow clearer, sharper, as if they were trying to draw attention to themselves. Then the boy screamed and arched his back, the ridges of his spine bulging hideously beneath paper-thin flesh. Skin tore and blood ran as the first segment of bone emerged, an awful butterfly crawling free of its grisly cocoon. Bone jutted out, bending and twisting with horrible popping sounds. The seam that had opened along the length of his spine continued down both his legs and more bone juddered free and knotted itself into strange shapes. And then it was finished, the boy slumped forward, dead, sitting in a wheelchair formed from his own blood-slick bones, swinging back and forth, back and forth.

Part of Scott was terrified by the nightmarish tableau before him, while another part appreciated the irony. After all, the sign *did* say the swing was for wheelchair use *only*. He turned away and walked over to Miranda, who still lay on the cedar chips, groaning and rubbing her head with her wounded hand, groggily smearing blood all over her face.

Scott pulled her bleeding hand away, the sight of her blood-covered skin at once sickening and exciting him. He imagined licking the blood off her, wondered how it would taste when mixed with the salt of her sweat.

"You okay?"

She nodded, though from her expression, she didn't seem too sure. Scott helped her to stand and kept an arm around her shoulders to steady her as they continued toward the parking lot. Miranda shuffled more than walked, and the same part of Scott that had been amused by the wheelchair-boy's fate whispered that he should leave her behind if he wished to escape the park with his life. His grip on her shoulder loosened, just for an instant, but then he tightened his grasp, ashamed at himself. There was no way he was going to abandon her, not even if it meant his own death.

You have a wife—at least until she gets around to filing for divorce—and you have a son. You owe it to them to live. You don't owe this little cooz anything. Hell, you just met her yesterday!

He ignored the voice, kept firm hold of Miranda, and continued for the parking lot. They drew near the Wizard of Oz swing set, and Scott saw the faces of Dorothy's companions that adorned the top were more detailed now, more lifelike, the swings swaying as if in a breeze, though the air felt still and stagnant.

"You motherfucker! I'll tear off your balls with my teeth and swallow them whole!"

Scott recognized the voice as Jamey's. The pack leader had finally caught up to them.

Scott pushed Miranda aside, and wobbly as she was, she fell. He turned, intending to take the brunt of Jamey's attack. Before tonight, he'd never been in a fight in his life, had never struck another human being in anger—*Oh, yeah?* came the voice. *You weren't above getting rough a time or two with the wife and kid, were you?*—and had no idea what to do. He prayed that some buried instinct, some remnant of survival skill passed down the evolutionary ladder over thousands, perhaps millions of years, would come to his rescue.

Yeah, right. Get ready to say good-bye to your balls.

Jamey, naked skin glistening with vaginal fluid and lubricant, came pounding across the cedar chips toward him, hands outstretched, teeth bared, eyes wild, the embodiment of that primitive fury that Scott so desperately wished he could summon forth.

Jamey's clawing hands were less than ten feet away . . . seven feet . . . four . . . two . . .

Without thinking, Scott sidestepped, grabbed Jamey by the wrist—the vaginal fluid coating his skin cold, thick, and rank as hell—and used the boy's own momentum to spin him toward the Oz swing set. Jamey stumbled, tripped, and fell forward. The swing nearest him lashed out cobra-swift and coiled around the boy. A second, then a third wrapped around him, their chains stretching impossibly long to reach. Jamey struggled and thrashed, shrieking like a mad animal, gnashing his teeth in frustration, tearing his lips to bloody ribbons, but the swings held fast, and soon the boy stopped fighting and hung limply, swaying back and forth, toes dragging in the cedar chips. He let out a low, mournful sound, almost but not quite a wolf's howl, and the noises of his pack ceased. Scott sensed them pausing, listening, and then came the sound of bare feet padding on grass as Jamey's sharp-toothed clan retreated into the night.

It—whatever in the hell *it* was—was finally over.

"Not quite, Scotty-boy."

He turned and saw the faceless face of the Riverton Ax Murderer. He was leaning against one of the swing set's legs, arms crossed casually.

"You can't let this one go. He's the leader, and you've not only defeated him, you've humiliated him." He kicked out with a lumberjack boot, caught Jamey in the side. Air whooshed out of the boy's lungs and he began spinning around.

"He'll come after you and your little cooz again, and you know damn well he'll bring his playmates along. You were lucky to escape them tonight, but you might not be so lucky next time."

Gagging sounds came from the tin woodsman. Scott looked up just in time to see the funnel-capped head vomit forth a gout of black oil. Washed along by the viscous tide was a long metallic object which fell to the ground with a solid thud. It was an ax, covered with oil.

The Riverton Ax Murderer's face was invisible, but from the tone of his next words, Scott knew he was smiling. "To quote the Queen of Hearts, off with his head, Scotty-boy."

Scott looked at the ax. The oil was sliding off the metal, almost as if it were retreating, and the surface gleamed silver in the moonlight.

"It's the only way to make sure you and Miranda are safe. It's self-defense, really."

The ax head looked solid and heavy, the edge keen and sharp.

"He's just hanging there. It'll be easy." A grin in the voice. "Like chopping firewood."

Miranda mumbled something, but Scott couldn't make out the words. A whispering breeze moved through the trees, the sound of a chorus of women, but he couldn't hear what they were saying either. He couldn't take his eyes off the ax. Sweat dripped from his forehead, ran down his sides and along his spine. He imagined what the ax would feel like gripped in his hands, imagined standing over Jamey, lifting the ax high, pausing for a delicious eternity of a moment before bringing the ax down on his neck. Heard the sweet sounds of flesh parting, of metal striking bone, of screams ripping free of a throat in the process of being severed.

He let go of Miranda and took a step toward the ax. He felt himself coming erect, and an image flashed through his mind: his penis a knife blade, Miranda's palm sliced open. A wave of disgust moved through him, and he tore his gaze from the ax and looked at the Riverton Ax Murderer with the too-familiar voice.

"No."

The faceless apparition uncrossed his arms. "You fought against the boy only a moment ago. You would've gladly killed him then if you'd been able."

"That was different. I only wanted to protect us, give us

a chance to get away. He's caught in the swings; there's no need to kill him now."

"No need?" Amusement in the voice. The Riverton Ax Murderer stepped toward the tin woodsman's gift, bent down and picked it up. "Scotty-boy, there's nothing else in the universe but *need*. And the greatest need of all is the need to kill." He stepped around Jamey's body until he stood over the boy's head. He lifted the ax high, just as Scott had imagined himself doing a moment earlier.

"No!" Scott stepped forward, intending to stop the faceless killer, but Miranda grabbed his arm and held him back.

The ax whooshed down, the blade bit into flesh and bone. Jamey screamed, but only for an instant. Then his head thunked to the ground and lay in a widening pool of his own blood. The boy's mouth gawped open like a fish's, though his teeth were no longer those of a shark, just ordinary blunt kernels.

"Easy enough, eh?" the faceless man said. "But hardly satisfying. No hunt, no struggle, no risk. No goddamned fun." He drew back his boot, then kicked Jamey's head off into the darkness. He looked at them, them—at least, it looked as if he were looking at them; without a face, it was hard to tell.

"That little cooz has been causing all sorts of trouble for you, boy. I'd be happy to take care of her for you. Hell, we could do her together, cut her up good and chew on her intestines while we fucked the juiciest wounds. Whattaya say? After all, it wouldn't be the first time." He laughed and started toward them, silver ax gripped in both hands.

Miranda mumbled something that sounded like *run*, and Scott thought that was a damn fine idea. He grabbed her hand—the wounded one this time, but he didn't care, not now—and they ran like hell for the car, the faceless man's laughter slicing through the night air, the footfalls of his lumberjack boots heavy on the ground as he came after them.

Chapter Thirteen

"Not too hard, now. You want to cut, not tear."

Scott nods and tries not to look afraid. Sometimes his teacher merely corrects him with words. Sometimes he does . . . other things. Scott doesn't look up at the teacher, knows better than to take his eyes off his work. He learned that particular lesson some time ago.

He continues with the knife—a huge hunting knife, the kind used to dress deer, though he and the teacher are using it for prey of a different sort—carefully peeling soft, unblemished skin from red, wet muscle.

They are deep in the northern California woods, in a clearing surrounded by spruce and pine trees. This is the teacher's special place, a place where they can work undisturbed. The teacher has brought him here before. Many times.

Scott kneels over the prey, while the teacher stands back and watches. Sometimes the teacher breathes heavily while Scott cuts, and sometimes there's the soft sound of a zipper being drawn downward, then a rough, callused hand sliding along flesh. There's no sound this time, though. This time the teacher just watches.

Scott finds it hard to cut so slowly. He wants to rip into the prey, plunge his hands into the cavity, smear the sweet juices all over his naked body. Sometimes his teacher lets him. But not to-day. Today is about control.

"There are pleasures to be had in denial," his teacher says, "and in restraint."

Scott has heard this before, but he nods anyway to show that he is listening. He is almost finished with the belly. Next he will begin on the arms, starting with the left, he thinks. Shoulder down, this time.

"When a wave comes toward shore, you can dive into it, let it wash over you, toss and turn you about in its churning. Or you can mount a surfboard and ride the wave. Mind you, riding does not make you the wave's master, for the ocean is too strong, too wild to ever tame. But you can use its power, if you know how."

Scott lifts the knife toward his face, sniffs the blood smeared on the blade. He longs to taste it, but he knows he'll be punished if he does. He lowers the knife to the prey's shoulder, makes his incision with a surgeon's skill. Cut, not tear, he reminds himself. He hears the words in his teacher's voice. He hears his teacher's voice in his head quite often, more so than he hears his own, it seems.

Scott is naked, his clothes folded neatly a half dozen yards away. His teacher taught him long ago that it's better not to get your clothes messy. Blood washes off skin more easily than it washes out of cloth.

"Good, good, keep going . . . nice and easy."

Scott's penis dangles between his legs, limp and small.

"Tell you what: If you manage to peel all the skin off without getting an erection, I'll let you have first pick of the organs to do with as you please. How's that sound?"

It's an extremely generous offer, for the teacher always has *first choice. Scott knows why the teacher has said this, though. It's part of the test. Part of learning control.*

Scott continues his work, concentrating on technique and doing his best to avoid thinking about which organ he'll choose— the heart? the uterus?—and to avoid imagining all the things he'll do with his warm, wet prize, should he win it.

His penis twitches, the merest of spasms, so mild he barely feels it. He hopes the teacher hasn't noticed, but knows he has.

The sound of boots crossing the clearing, coming fast. Scott grits his teeth against the blow he knows is about to fall. He wonders where the teacher will strike this time. The back? The head?

Light bursts against his optic nerves, a bright flare quickly swallowed by darkness.

The head.

Scott slumps forward onto the partially flensed body of his prey, her blood smearing slick and hot on his flesh. Too bad he's unconscious and can't feel it.

The darkness shifts, changes from the cold nothingness of unconsciousness to the warm, drifting tides of sleep. In this new darkness—a darkness which should be more comforting but somehow isn't—Scott hears his Gammy's voice.

Be good.

Scott opened his eyes with an effort. The lids were gummy and stuck together, and it took several seconds for his vision to clear. When it did, he found himself staring at the ceiling. At first, he thought it was the ceiling of the house in Cedar Hill, and he reached for Gayle, expected to find her rolled over on her side, most of the covers wrapped around her, snoring softly. But her side of the bed was cold and empty, and he remembered that the house in Cedar Hill had been sold, that he and Gayle weren't together at the moment, and he now lived in a one-bedroom apartment in Ash Creek. Sadness whelmed into him then, and he closed his eyes. Why bother to get up? Why bother to do anything?

He almost drifted back to sleep, but then he remembered. His eyes snapped open and he sat up, the sudden movement setting his head to throbbing.

Miranda.

The nightmarish events of the previous night washed back into his memory in a confused torrent of images and sensations. Everything was clear enough up to the point where he met Miranda in the park, but after that things got weird. *Really* weird. She'd given him some kind of drug (*not* a spider, probably just a pill or something), and he'd started hallucinating. Not that he needed any chemical help in that department; his ability to perceive reality was screwed up enough all by itself, thank you very much. He thought for a few moments, trying to strip away the surreal window dressing from last night's events and separate fact from fantasy.

He decided the core incidents were probably true enough. He and Miranda had met in the park, and she had led him close to the fountain to watch some teenagers screwing. An orgy of some sort, maybe, though he doubted Laura Foster had been there—that was probably just a detail added by his imagination. Miranda had jacked him off, though his cock hadn't turned into a knife blade. Scott was dressed only in his underwear now, and he had to resist the urge to draw back the covers and check to make sure his penis was flesh and not steel. The teens had noticed them (maybe Scott had made too much noise when he'd climaxed, though he didn't recall doing so) and they'd come after them. There was a chase, and he'd had to fight off several of the teens. All the rest—the giant vagina, the group dildo, the cock-knife, the bizarre playground equipment, the faceless man—were nothing more than delusions conjured by his fucked-up brain, with the aid of whatever drug Miranda had given him.

Still, he was fuzzy on what had happened after the park. Obviously, they'd gotten away, but he wasn't quite sure . . .

He remembered. He drew back the covers, looked at the other side of the bed, saw brown smears of dried blood on the sheet. Blood from Miranda's cut hand. They'd come back here after the park in order to treat her wound (but if his cock hadn't become a knife, then there wouldn't have been any wound, would there?). He'd offered to drive her to the hospital, but she'd refused, said the cut wasn't bad enough, all she needed was to clean and bandage it. In his bathroom, washing the wound with soap and water, applying hydrogen peroxide, Miranda's hissing intake of breath as the chemical frothed along the length of her cut. Putting a gauze pad on (hurrah for first-aid kits!), wrapping tape around it, Miranda kissing his hands, his neck, his lips as he worked.

When it was done, they went into the bedroom, got under the covers and . . .

Scott couldn't remember any more. Maybe that's because there *wasn't* any more. It had been late, his system was clogged full of some drug, and however much of the experience had been real, it was fairly certain they'd been through some sort of battle in the park. Most likely, he'd fallen asleep as soon as his head hit the pillow.

Real smooth, loverboy. I bet Miranda was really thrilled by that.

Part of him was relieved. Bad enough that she'd jerked him off in the park when he was high; it would've been worse to compound the mistake by having more sex with her once they got back to his place. Not only was there a chance that she was underage, he didn't want anything to screw up his chances (however slim they might be) of getting back together with Gayle. But another part of him was disappointed that he hadn't had a chance to discover the warm, tender secrets of Miranda's flesh.

An image flashed through his mind, his hand holding a knife, using it to carefully peel skin from muscle.

He remembered his dream. Remembered the woods, the teacher . . . realized the teacher possessed the same voice as that of the faceless man in the park last night. The dream had been intense, vivid, more like a memory. But he'd never done anything like that. The closest he'd ever come was mutilating the dead cat at his grandma's when he was a kid. He'd never had a "teacher," had never harmed a human being, let alone skinned one.

Jesus Christ, was he completely losing his mind?

Pain stabbed through his gut; it felt as if his intestines were tying themselves in knots. He got out of bed, hobbling across the bedroom floor, hunched over, holding his abdomen, gritting his teeth against the pain. It felt like he needed to shit his guts out, but he bypassed the bathroom, walked down the short hall and into the living room.

"Miranda?"

The living room was empty, as was the kitchen. He looked for a note, didn't find one. The door was locked, though the chain hadn't been latched. It seemed Miranda had let herself out sometime during the night—probably not too long after her almost middle-aged lover had conked out on her.

His gut spasmed again, and this time he knew he wouldn't be able to put off the inevitable any longer. He hobbled to the bathroom, yanked down his underwear (relieved despite himself to see that his penis was still made of meat), and squatted on the toilet. His bowels voided themselves with such noise and stink that he was glad Miranda wasn't around. Bad enough to have fallen asleep on her during the night; it would've been worse to completely disgust her in the morning.

It seemed to take forever, but eventually the cramps subsided and he was finished. He wiped, stood, pulled up his underwear, and turned to flush the toilet.

And there, floating atop the brown sludge, was the small, curled-up body of a spider.

Scott flushed the spider and, trembling, took a quick shower. Moving on automatic, he dressed, grabbed his keys and wallet, and headed out the door. His nightmare had woken him early, and it wasn't quite 7 A.M. yet. He might be able to catch them, if he hurried.

He got in his car—ignoring the dots of dried blood on the passenger seat—and put his key in the ignition. Moments later, he was pulling out of his apartment complex's parking lot, and heading down the road. Ash Creek wasn't a big city, and the streets weren't crowded this early on a Tuesday morning. Still, he drove carefully, concentrating on every single move—making sure to allow enough distance between himself and the car ahead, braking well in advance of stoplights, hitting his signal every time he intended to turn—as if he were a drunk doing his best to avoid being picked up by the police. His head was clear enough, though he did feel hungover. He was terrified of losing control, of not being able to get where he so desperately needed to go, and so he drove like a student driver, obeying the speed limit and yielding to other drivers when necessary. No matter, he was going to reach his destination because he had to, simple as that.

He pulled into the parking lot of Gayle and David's apartment complex and parked as close to their building as he could get. He got out and walked up to 203. He knew the door was locked before he reached for the knob, but he had to give it a try anyway. He waited a few moments, hoping that a resident would either come out or go in, allowing him to slip inside, but no one came. Finally, he began pressing buttons on the intercom next to the door, saying, "It's me," whenever anyone answered. He'd written an article once about a rapist who'd used this technique to gain entrance into apartment buildings.

As expected, most of the residents ignored him, but he only needed one to buzz him in, and sure enough, someone did. He opened the door quickly before it could lock again and stepped into the building's lobby. Score one for the rapist. He walked over to the mailboxes and looked for Gayle's name. Not all the mailboxes had names on them; some just had numbers. He didn't relish the idea of going from door to door and knocking, but he would if—then he found it. O'Neil. Gayle's maiden name.

He supposed it could've been a coincidence, could've been some other O'Neil, but he knew it wasn't. Seeing the name hit him like a physical blow. It was a small thing, to be sure, nowhere near as serious as taking their son and moving to another town, but somehow, it was all the worse for being so minor a change. It was as if Gayle were reshaping her identity, casting him off for good, as if he'd never been a part of her life. Erasing him as if he'd never existed.

The number on the mailbox was 2B.

He took the stairs two at a time, found the door, hesitated for a half second and then knocked softly. Three raps with a knuckle. He waited a moment, then gave three more raps.

Please, Christ, let them be here. He needed to see them. Not merely because he loved and missed them, but because they were a touchstone to reality—a touchstone he needed if he were to have any chance of holding onto whatever sanity he had left.

The door opened a crack; the chain was still hooked. A sliver of Gayle's face appeared: an eye, nose, part of her mouth, a shock of brown hair. Scott took it as a good sign that she'd opened the door even this far. Surely she had looked through the Judas hole to see who it was first. Then again, maybe she hadn't. This *was* Gayle after all. She forgot things like that all the time.

"What are you doing here? I thought I told you to leave us alone."

From behind her: "Mom, who is it?"

She ignored their son. "Get out of here or I'll call the cops."

"Mom?"

Scott caught of glimpse of David behind his mother. He waved and the boy waved back.

"I have to get him ready for school. The bus picks him up at ten to eight."

"I thought . . ." Now that he was here, now that he could see both of them, he wasn't exactly sure what he had been thinking. He'd just wanted to be in their physical presence again, wanted that reassurance. Wanted to know that there still were good and normal things in the world, things untouched by death and madness. But there was no way he could explain this to them, even if he could somehow find the words. No way he would want to.

"I thought maybe I could treat the two of you to a quick breakfast. There's a McDonald's over by the school." He'd eaten there yesterday. "We could drive separately, eat, and then you could drop David off at school before the first bell."

She opened her mouth, but before she could protest, Scott held up his hands. "No pressure, no expectations. Just the three of us having breakfast, that's all."

"Please, Mom!" David said. "There's plenty of time. It's just a few minutes after seven. Please!"

Gayle looked daggers at Scott, but she said, "I don't know," and he could tell from her tone that she really didn't.

"It won't even be an hour," Scott said. Then he lowered his voice almost to a whisper. "Isn't what we had, what we still might have, worth at least that?"

She looked at him for a long moment before finally sighing.

"Give us a couple minutes to get ready."

They found a booth by the window. Gayle and David sat on one side, Scott on the other. He was hurt that his son didn't want to sit next to him, but he decided not to show it. It was enough that the three of them were together again, even if it was only for a fast-food breakfast. Gayle's hair was mussed and she didn't have any makeup on. Most likely she had planned on getting ready for work after David left school. Scott knew how much she hated going out in public without looking her best, and he wished he could tell her that he was grateful, that she still looked damn good to him, makeup or no. But he sensed that any such talk might break the tenuous truce she'd granted him, so he decided to say nothing, not now anyway. But maybe, someday in the future, when they were a whole family again, he could tell her. *Remember that day we went to breakfast at McDonald's? The day you didn't have time to put on any makeup?*

Even though he wasn't hungry—his gut was still churning from expelling the (*not* a spider!) whatever it was Miranda had given him last night—Scott had gotten an egg mcmuffin, hash browns, and coffee. He sipped the thick, acidic brew and hoped he could keep it down. David had gotten an order of pancakes and sausage, with OJ to drink: the same breakfast he'd gotten at McD's ever since he'd been a toddler. Just hearing him order it at the counter had been a balm to Scott's soul, the familiarity comforting beyond words. Now, Scott watched his son take a bite, chew, and swallow, each movement a step in a ritual that pushed the madness of the world back a little bit more. Was there anything as primally satisfying as watching your child eat? he wondered. He doubted it.

Gayle had just gotten coffee, perhaps out of defiance to show that she wasn't fully committed to Scott's breakfast plan. On the other hand, maybe he was just being paranoid; she'd never been a big breakfast eater.

They didn't talk much. Scott had been waiting for Gayle to say something about his visiting David at school yesterday, but she hadn't. Maybe the boy hadn't told her about it. Or maybe she was just waiting for a chance to get him alone, so she could let him have it without David hearing. Whichever the case, he was glad that he didn't have to deal with it now. He wanted no conflict, no stress. Just a little time alone as a family, or at least a reasonable facsimile of one.

The restaurant was crowded for this early in the morning, though most people were getting their orders to go. There were a few people sitting alone, reading newspapers while they ate. Some of these were dressed in business suits; others in uniforms denoting blue collar trades. There were more of the latter than the former, which was to be expected in Ash Creek. It wasn't exactly a white-collar town. Groups of senior citizens in jogging suits, sweats, or flannel shirts and jeans filled out the rest of the tables and booths, mostly men but there were a few women present. Talking, laughing, enjoying the morning and each other's company. These were people who believed that life was good, that things made sense, that everything would work out all right in the end if you just maintained a positive attitude, kept the faith, and ate enough fiber.

Scott knew better, of course, but this morning, he wanted to believe otherwise. He felt like lifting his coffee toward the oldsters and giving them a salute. *God bless you all. The Reaper's pounding his bony fist on your door, and you're determined to ignore him for however long you can.* He wished he could engage in the same sort of self-delusion. Life might not be any more easy that way, but it sure as hell would be more tolerable.

"How's your writing coming?"

Scott turned toward Gayle and tried to keep the surprise he felt from showing. It wasn't like her to ask about his work, considering that she blamed it for a great deal of the problems in their marriage.

"Pretty good. I started a new book, and it's coming along. Still in the early stages, though."

She nodded and took a sip of her coffee. He knew she wouldn't ask anymore about his project, not with David present. She wouldn't want to upset him with any talk of crime or murder, and that was cool with Scott. Just because he wrote about the darkness in the human soul didn't mean that he wanted to inflict that darkness on others, especially his son. Lord knew it had slopped over into his wife and son's lives often enough in the past, and there was no need for it to do so now, not on Family Busting Their Asses to Act Normal Day.

"How about you?" he asked. "Work going all right?"

She shrugged. "I suppose. Could be better, could be worse. But it pays the bills, you know?"

Scott wondered if that was a dig at him. His freelance income, while steady enough over the years, had been erratic, waxing and waning with no easily predictable pattern. It made it hard to budget their money, something that had increasingly become a sore point with Gayle as time went by. He almost said something about it, but kept his mouth shut. Breakfast was going well enough so far; why screw it up by revisiting an old argument?

"I know what you mean." He took a sip of coffee and felt his gut roil in response. *Just keep it down until Gayle and David leave for school,* he thought. *You can run to the restroom and throw it up then if you have to.*

The conversational possibilities exhausted, Scott glanced around the restaurant again. Two tables over, a clean-shaven man in his mid-twenties was reading a copy of *USA Today*. He wore a navy-blue suit that looked freshly dry-cleaned and a too-thin yellow tie that hadn't been in style for several years. As Scott watched, Suit Boy turned the page, his fingers brushing the sharp edges of the paper.

Deep-red jewels of blood welled forth from his fingers and spattered onto his half-eaten bacon, egg, and cheese biscuit. The man continued reading as if nothing had happened.

Sweet Jesus, no . . . not now . . .

Suit Boy reached down, picked up his bloody breakfast sandwich and took a big, juicy bite. Crimson dribbled down his chin as he chewed, but he didn't take his eyes off the newspaper. He swallowed, and then a black amphibian tongue flicked out and began to clean the blood from his chin as he read.

"Is something wrong?"

Scott turned toward Gayle and forced a smile that felt more like a grimace. "No. Well, kind of. I was up late last night. Working." He tried to ignore the moist sounds of that frog tongue *flick-flick-flicking* as it cleaned. "I guess it's catching up with me."

She frowned at him for a moment, as if she were trying to decide if he was lying. Finally, she broke eye contact and turned to gaze out the window.

Scott looked down at his coffee. He was having breakfast with his family. Everything was okay. Everything was normal. He lifted his gaze, looked in another direction.

At one table, senior citizens were peeling strips of flesh from their faces and exchanging the raw, red flaps, pressing their new skin in place and giving it a couple pats so it would stick. At another table, a mother barely out of her teens was scouring her baby's syrup-coated fingers with barbed wire. The baby shrieked in pain, but no one—least of all the mother—paid any attention. At the table next to them, a man in a white coverall was talking on a cell phone, undisturbed by the infant's screams. As he spoke, tiny segmented legs extruded from the phone and latched onto the man's ear. The phone scurried out of the man's hand and burrowed into his aural canal, digging and shoving until it was gone. The man stopped talking and stiffened. His eyes glazed over and his mouth fell open to emit a ratcheting, electronic busy signal as he sat staring into space.

na-na-na-na-na-na-na-na-na-na-na-na-naaaaaaaa . . .

"Dad?"

Scott started, sloshing coffee onto his lap. It was hot, but no longer hot enough to scald.

"Goddamnit!" Scott put his coffee on the table, which was good considering how his hand was trembling. He grabbed a napkin and began blotting his crotch.

"I'm sorry, Dad." David sounded as if he might cry. "You looked kinda weird for a minute, and I thought . . . I don't know. I'm sorry."

"Don't worry about it." Scott meant for the words to come out reassuring, but they were more an angry snarl.

Gayle glared at him and checked her watch. "It's getting late. David and I—"

Before she could finish, a sixtyish woman in a McDonald's crew uniform came walking over. She was short and heavy, with thick-lensed glasses. Still, behind those Coke-bottle lenses, her eyes were bright and her smile friendly.

"Can I take you folks's trash?"

For a moment, Scott had no idea what she was talking about, and he thought the woman was another in his latest round of hallucinations. But then he realized that she was the lobby hostess and it was her job to go from table to table, be pleasant, and check to see if the customers needed anything.

Gayle quickly piled the remains of their breakfast,

Scott's coffee included, onto the plastic tray and held it out to the woman. "Thank you very much."

The woman smiled. Scott half-expected her to reveal a mouthful of tiny incisors, but her teeth were normal. She continued smiling as she said, "You folks hear the news?"

Scott felt a cold pit open up in his stomach.

"What news?" Gayle asked.

"It's awful, just awful." Still smiling, as if she were a mannequin with a painted-on grin. "A boy was killed last night in the park. Local kid. Head cut clean off." Smile unwavering, she shook her head. "I tell ya, the world's a funny place, isn't it?"

She turned and walked off to throw away their trash, Gayle and David staring after her in shock.

Scott felt as if he might vomit any second. "Yeah," he said, throat burning with stomach acid. "It's a fucking laugh riot."

Chapter Fourteen

Gayle left with David shortly after that. The boy was clearly disturbed by the lobby hostess's news and seemed on the verge of tears. Gayle shot Scott a dark look before walking out of the restaurant, as if she blamed him for what the woman had said. And maybe she was right to do so. He was a magnet for darkness, had been ever since his family had been murdered that summer at the lake. He never should've gotten married, never should've had a kid. It was irresponsible for people like him to try to have normal human relationships. Their weirdness spread to the people in their lives like some sort of awful communicable disease. Better to be a spiritual leper and isolate one's self in order to keep from infecting anyone else.

Scott left the restaurant, got in his car, and drove to a convenience mart. He looked for a local paper, one that might have a story about Jamey's death, but the bored teenager behind the counter told him the *Ash Creek Citizen* only came out once a week, on Wednesdays. It wouldn't be in until tomorrow. The closest big city was Cincinnati, but Scott doubted the *Cincinnati Enquirer* would have anything. Miranda and he had left the park around midnight, so Jamey's body had to have been discovered after that, perhaps quite a bit later. He didn't think any Cincy reporters would've had enough time to get anything about the boy's death into their paper. Still, he bought an *Enquirer*, just in case, and skimmed through it while sitting in his car in the parking lot. Sure enough, there was nothing about Jamey in the paper, and he tossed it into the backseat and drove off.

He returned home to his apartment and turned on the TV, hoping there might be something on the local news. Most of the network affiliates were airing national daytime talk shows featuring grinning automatons with perfect hair, perfect faces, and perfect clothes. But Scott eventually found a channel where a twenty-something reporter in a brown leather jacket stood holding a microphone before a *Wizard of Oz* swing set.

He turned up the volume.

"—still no word on any possible motive for the slaying. No weapon was recovered at the scene, but sources speculate that the killer or killers used an ax."

Behind the reporter, a handful of police stood around.

Some talking, some examining the cedar chip–covered ground for clues, others just staring off into the distance as if they intended to solve the crime through the sheer force of their concentration. It was a scene doubly familiar to Scott: not only because he had been in the park last night, but because of his years working as a crime reporter for a newspaper. How many times had he visited similar murder scenes and interviewed police? Too many.

The reporter—a round-headed kid with thinning hair that put Scott in mind of a grown-up Charlie Brown—went on.

"To bring those of you just joining us up to date, the decapitated body of a teenage male was discovered in Orchard Park early this morning by a pair of joggers. Police have removed the body and cordoned off the scene as they continue to investigate this grisly murder. Authorities say it's too early for any leads, though they hope to have more information for us by noontime. This is Arthur Shaugnessy reporting for Action News Live."

Just before the picture cut back to the newsroom, Scott saw the Tin Woodsman's head on the swing set swivel around and wink at the camera.

Scott stood by the pool, smoking a cigarette and staring into the brackish water. At first, he was afraid to come here, afraid that Laura would show up again as she always seemed to whenever he came out for a smoke. But it was a school day, and even if they dismissed classes early because of Jamey's death, she'd probably stay at work, at least for a while. He figured he was safe enough. Besides, part of him didn't want to avoid the pool just because he might encounter Laura. Doing that would be acknowledging that he was afraid of her. And being afraid of her would mean acknowledging that what he saw last night—*all* of it—had been real.

Clearly, a good part of what he'd experienced in the park had been nothing more than a hallucination conjured up by his less-than-stable mind under the influence of whatever drug Miranda had slipped him. And despite the fact that he had seen (or *seemed* to see) the curled-up body of a spider in his toilet bowl this morning, he refused to believe that what she had given him was anything more than a normal, if powerful, drug.

Most of the therapists Scott had seen in the years since his family's murder hadn't been a great deal of help. They'd been more interested in listening to him recite the lurid details of that night and talking about whether he could get an erection or not than with helping him. But one psychologist, a Dr. Brownbach, had given Scott a piece of advice that had stuck with him.

There's nothing that's completely unreal, Scott. Even the most impossible-seeming events have a core of reality to them; the trick is determining exactly what that core is. When you can do that, then you'll know what to believe in.

Easy enough to say; hard as motherfucking hell to do, but Scott was determined to give it a try. For Gayle and David, if nothing else.

All right. So out of everything that had happened last night, what *was* real?

He'd already decided that Miranda had been real. He had met her at the park, and she'd given him some sort of drug that he'd been stupid enough to ingest. She'd taken him to see something . . . maybe some high-school kids engaging in group sex? Maybe even with Laura, though her presence might've just been his imagination's contribution to the scene. Still, she wouldn't be the first teacher who'd become sexually involved with her students. Why Miranda had wanted to show him that, he wasn't sure. Maybe to turn him on? It certainly had, and she'd jacked him off as they watched. Of course, his penis hadn't turned into a knife blade, which meant that her hand hadn't been cut. At least, not cut right then. Perhaps she'd somehow cut it later, when they were fleeing from their pursuers. She *had* fallen a couple times. Though why he would imagine she was cut before she actually was . . .

He shook his head, then took a drag on his cigarette. He didn't need to sort it all out perfectly. There was simply no way the cock-knife could be real, so Miranda hadn't been cut by it. That meant she had to have been cut by something else.

Miranda and he had been seen by the youths and chased. It made sense, especially if Laura had been there: They would've wanted to protect their secret. Scott didn't think that having sex with a bunch of students in the park in the middle of the night would look good on Laura's next faculty performance review. He doubted the kids had really wanted to kill them, though. More likely they'd just wanted to scare the two of them off.

He wasn't sure whether or not there'd actually been any fighting. Maybe a scuffle or two. He hadn't taken any blows, at least, he didn't feel like it and he didn't have any bruises. The playground equipment hadn't come alive, of course, but maybe some of the kids had tripped over it or gotten entangled in the darkness and confusion. It would've been easy enough to do.

Miranda and he had gotten away, driven back to his place where they'd cleaned and bandaged her wound and then spent the night together. He was fairly confident they hadn't had any more sex. He'd been so tired that he could barely keep his eyes open, let alone get an erection. Sometime before morning, Miranda had awakened and slipped out of the apartment without leaving a note.

In the clear light of day, brain jazzed by caffeine and nicotine, it all seemed clear enough. Except for one thing: how the hell had Jamey died, and who had killed him? It was the one thing that didn't make sense no matter how he looked at it. Jamey's murder had been one of the most hallucinatory events of last night, and yet, according to the news, it was real. Scott knew that there had been no faceless man, no ax vomited forth by the Tin Woodsman (and by the way, the latter had *not* turned around and winked during the newscast; that was just a little leftover weirdness from last night, that's all). No killer, no ax, no beheading, right? Except the kid's goddamned head had gotten chopped off anyway.

Scott's cigarette was almost gone. He took a last drag, then flicked it into the pool to join the rest of the detritus. Jamey had been killed, and despite the hallucinatory trappings, it seemed Scott had witnessed his murder.

Witnessed? Or committed?

He shook his head. It wasn't possible. He'd never hurt anyone in his life.

Oh, yeah? said a voice inside him, a voice that sounded too much like that of the faceless man. *What about your wife and kid? You used to manhandle them pretty good.*

That wasn't the same. Inexcusable, yes, but grabbing and yelling were hardly in the same league as decapitation.

And that cat you dissected in your sweet Gammy's backyard . . . and all those special lessons in the clearing . . .

There *were* no lessons, not in real life. It was just a dream.

Capable of murder in dreams, maybe capable in life? Especially if you thought Jamey was a threat to you and your new piece of ass.

No. Despite everything, Scott was confident of one thing: He didn't kill Jamey. He *didn't*.

A mental shrug. *If you say so.*

There was one other person who knew what had really happened last night, one other witness to Jamey's death. Miranda. She could clear everything up.

You mean reassure you that you aren't a killer, don't you?

All he had to do was find her.

He started toward the parking lot.

Scott drove around town until nearly lunchtime. He tried the convenience store near Gayle and David's apartment and went past Orchard Park, though he didn't stop in case the police might still be working there. He cruised past the high school, but he didn't stop there either. He wasn't prepared to see Laura Foster just yet. With no other idea where Miranda might be, he drove aimlessly through the town, up and down streets, through business and residential sections, head swiveling back and forth, gaze sweeping sidewalks as if he were a police officer himself, on patrol. He saw mothers pushing strollers and old people walking slow, but no Miranda.

There was one other place he could try: Poplar Street, where Miranda (the other Miranda) had lived, and where he'd first encountered *his* Miranda, the girl he'd mentally dubbed Lolita. He did a U-turn at the next intersection he came to and headed in the direction of the rec center, where Poplar was. When he reached the street, he turned onto it and parked. He got out of his car, feeling shaky, jittery, and weak. Last night was catching up with him big time. He knew he should go home, eat something, and crawl into bed for a few hours and give his body a chance to recuperate. But there'd be time enough for that later; right now, he needed answers. He started down the sidewalk.

Poplar was as deserted as it had been on Sunday: no strollers, no senior citizens, and certainly no Miranda. Well, what had he expected? That she'd be standing around waiting for him, hand on her hip, wry half-smile on her face, as if to say *What took you so long?*

He was about to give up and head back to his apartment when his gaze fell upon a particular house. There was nothing special about it on the surface; it looked much the same as every other ranch on the street. But this one had the number 4560 on the mailbox. Miranda Tanner's house.

Before Scott realized what he was doing, he was striding up the walkway to the front porch, pressing the doorbell, waiting.

A few seconds later, the door opened and a brunette in her mid-thirties was looking out at him, frowning slightly. She was shorter than Scott, but not by much. She was dressed in a white blouse that she wore untucked and a pair of loose jeans. She was one of those women who carried her weight in her hips and thighs, something her baggy pants couldn't conceal. Her hair was tousled, and her eyes were red, the skin beneath them puffy and discolored. He wondered if she'd been crying recently, if she cried every day for her lost child.

A barefoot toddler boy in T-shirt and shorts stood close behind her, holding onto a sipper cup with both hands. He looked as if he were afraid to stray too far from his mother, and considering the kind of world the boy lived in, Scott didn't blame him one bit. He had a chubby face and blonde hair, and he looked so much like his sister that just seeing him made Scott's heart ache for the missing girl. A part of her remained here, mirrored in the face of her brother. Maybe the only part that still existed.

"Yes?" the woman said, her tone flat.

She's depressed, Scott thought. Probably clinically. He wondered if she were on meds. If so, they didn't seem to be doing her a lot of good. From the articles he'd read on Miranda Tanner's case, he knew the mother's name was Phyllis. If he'd ever known the boy's name, he'd forgotten it.

Scott had planned all along to interview the girl's family for his book, but now he was here for a different reason, and he wasn't sure how to proceed. All that came to mind were research questions. *When did you first realize something had happened to your daughter? Do you still hold out hope for her return? How do you manage to make it through the days?* Awful questions, questions that would cut as deeply as any knife, but which had to be asked if he were to do Miranda Tanner—and all the other missing children he was writing about—justice in his book. But they were questions for another day.

"I'm . . . I'm looking for someone. A teenage girl." He gave a quick description. "I think she might live around here." He didn't want to say her name, didn't want to speak the word *Miranda,* not if he could avoid it. He'd interviewed enough witnesses and survivors during his years as a true-crime writer to know how hearing her daughter's name would affect the woman.

Phyllis Tanner's frown deepened and turned into a scowl. "Why are you looking for this girl?"

Great, Scott thought. *She thinks I'm some kind of pervert.*

He remembered the feel of Miranda's hand on his cock

and decided that maybe Mrs. Tanner wasn't far from the truth.

Explanations tumbled through his mind: she'd skipped school and he was the truant officer, she'd lost something and he needed to return it to her, he was a friend of the family with an important message to give her, she'd won the goddamned Publisher's Clearinghouse sweepstakes and he was here to deliver her check.

"I . . . just have to find her. It's important."

Phyllis Tanner began closing the door. "There's no one like that in this neighborhood."

He put his hand on the door to stop it. "Please . . . I really need—"

Her eyes blazed and she spoke through clenched teeth. "If you don't take your hand off my door this instant, I will start screaming and I won't stop until everyone on the block has heard me."

He knew she wasn't kidding. Besides, what could he do? It wasn't as if he could make her talk with him.

He pulled his hand away. "Sorry."

She slammed the door shut before he got out the second syllable of his apology.

He stood there for a moment longer, unsure what to do next, but then he realized he'd better get moving. There was a good chance Mrs. Tanner was already on the phone to the police.

He headed back to his car, hurrying while trying to look like he wasn't. The last thing he needed was for the cops to pick him up for questioning. He wasn't worried that they'd think he'd had something to do with Miranda Tanner's disappearance. Once they verified that he was a writer, they'd turn him loose. But the fact that he'd bothered Mrs. Tanner, as well as wasted their time, would create a lot of ill will with Ash Creek's finest, making it damned difficult to interview them—let alone the Tanners—when the time came.

If he didn't want to screw up this part of his book, he needed to get out of there fast. And that's just what he did.

Once back at his apartment, he ate a ham sandwich, an apple, and a handful of potato chips. The food was tasteless, and chewing and swallowing were an effort, but he managed to choke it all down. After his less-than-sumptuous lunch, he decided to try working a little. He didn't feel like it, but now that he'd met Phyllis Tanner, however briefly, he knew that it would be best to write down his impression of her while it was still fresh in his mind.

He fired up his computer and was about to open his word-processing program when he noticed a tiny envelope icon flashing at the bottom right of his screen. He had e-mail. It might be from an editor, or maybe his agent, eager to see the first few chapters of *Lost*—chapters he hadn't written yet. Sighing, he clicked on the icon and waited while his e-mail program opened.

He had only one message, from Miranda512. Five twelve. May 12 . . . the date Miranda Tanner had disappeared.

> Scott:
> Sorry to cut out on you last night/this morning but I was really ragged out after everything that happened in the park (I bet you were too, huh? <g>). Besides, I had to be at work early today. If you want to see me, you can find me at Martindale's Grocery on Schoenharl Street.
> Love,
> M

Scott read the message over several times, a number of thoughts jumbling in his mind. Chief among them was this: how the hell had Miranda gotten his e-mail address? In the end, he decided he didn't care. All that mattered was that he knew where to find her.

He shut off his computer, grabbed his keys and wallet, and headed out the door.

Chapter Fifteen

Scott had never been to Martindale's Grocery before. He usually picked up whatever odds and ends he needed from convenience marts and, when he absolutely had no choice, went to the Kroger only a few blocks from his apartment. As soon as he pulled into the lot, he recognized that Martindale's was a throwback to an earlier, simpler time of commerce, when grocery stores actually carried groceries and not toys and appliances and CDs ad nauseum. The parking lot was small, the store facade simple: brick walls, glass windows, MARTINDALE'S spelled out in large red plastic letters above the entrance.

As he walked inside, he was passed by an elderly woman being followed by a teenage boy pushing a cart laden with groceries. For a moment, he was shocked back to his childhood, when grocery employees brought your purchases to your car, helped you load them, all for a thank-you and a quarter tip, maybe fifty cents if they were fast, cheerful, and careful not to smash the eggs and mush the bread.

Once inside, he was hit by the smell. Not unpleasant by any means, but it was a different odor than the corporatized cookie-cutter shop-o-ramas that predominated in most American towns of any size. They always seemed to him to smell something like hospitals. A bit *too* clean, too antiseptic, as if they were hosed down every night with chemical foam sprayed by men in hazmat suits. But the air in here smelled of fruits, vegetables, and freshly baked bread, the way a grocery should smell. It was almost like being in someone's kitchen. For no good reason, Scott found the smells cheering, and he practically had a bounce in his step as he headed deeper into the store in search of Miranda.

He'd considered stopping at the customer service counter and asking for her, but decided against it. He was no longer afraid she was jailbait—she wouldn't be working this early on a weekday if she was still in high school—but it might raise a few eyebrows among her coworkers if a nearly middle-aged man came sniffing around for her. A nearly middle-aged man who didn't even know her last name. No, better to cruise the aisles and see if he couldn't locate her himself. After all, the store wasn't that big. As long as she wasn't in the back, he shouldn't have any problem finding her.

He wandered through the store, accompanied by the sound of muzak coming through the ceiling speakers. "Raindrops Keep Falling on My Head." Ordinarily, he hated such tinny, soulless so-called music, but it fit the retro atmosphere of the place, and he soon found himself humming along. He had to repress an urge to inspect the items on the shelves and mentally compare prices with those of the Kroger where he usually shopped. As he made his way through the pasta aisle—boxes of vermicelli, spiral noodles, shells—he passed a sixtyish woman whose face looked as if someone had grabbed the corners of her eyes from behind and pulled backward. He stopped and turned to look at her. It was like her picture had been scanned into a computer and then stretched horizontally a few clicks. It couldn't be some sort of deformity, could it? Plastic surgery, maybe a botched face lift?

The woman noticed Scott staring and scowled, the expression making the distorted, taut flesh of her face bend and twist as if she were her own funhouse mirror.

A sharp ice pick of pain jabbed into the base of his skull, and his gut roiled as if his stomach were shrinking in on itself. He looked away and quickly moved on to the breakfast aisle. There, he found a man in a business suit standing before the toaster pastries, shaking his head and muttering, "No, no, no, no, no," to himself. The man didn't pick up a box, didn't take a step forward or a step back as he tried to make up his mind which kind to buy. He just stood there, shaking his head and murmuring, as if he were a Disney animatron with a glitch in its program.

Scott's head was throbbing now, as if a legion of tiny men were chipping away at the inside of his skull with miniature hammers—or axes.

In the dairy aisle, he saw a bearded man with a gauze bandage over his left eye. There was a wet patch in the middle of the bandage, and as Scott watched, it widened, as if the eye—or whatever was behind the bandage—was seeping something fierce. And it appeared the gauze pulsated slightly, like the skin on top of a newborn's head where the skull hasn't grown together yet. The man looked at Scott, opened his mouth to speak, but Scott hurried on before he could hear what the man had to say, keeping his teeth clenched against the rising tide of vomit that threatened to gush forth at any moment.

As he continued searching for Miranda, the muzak died

away, and he became aware of a different sound coming over the store's speakers. A hiss, almost like the white noise an old-fashioned vinyl album made when the needle got to the end and the disc continued spinning. But then he realized that what he was hearing was whispering. Women whispering, of course. Unlike the other times he'd heard it, though, now he could make out what they were chorusing, if only just.

Aisle seven . . . aisle seven . . . aisle seven . . .

"You've got to be shitting me," he mumbled to himself. But he decided "what the fuck?" and headed for aisle seven, and there she was, stocking jars of baby food on the shelves, open cardboard boxes on the floor around her. Miranda looked much the same as last night, hair and makeup no different, only now she wore a light brown uniform shirt, blue jeans, and sneakers. The outfit made her look more normal, less exotic, and he was surprised to find himself feeling disappointed. A woman like Miranda wasn't supposed to be just another working-class drone. She should remain a woman of mystery, of cryptic statements, shadowy midnight rendezvous, of unannounced and unanticipated comings and goings. Otherwise, she was just . . . a girl stocking baby food.

Idiot, he told himself. *You've been craving normal for the last couple days like you're starving for it, and now here it is in front of you, and you're complaining. You really* must *be insane!*

She looked up as he approached and smiled. "I see you checked your e-mail today."

Scott wasn't in the mood for banter. He didn't reply as he walked up to Miranda. She stopped working and looked at him quizzically for a moment, jars of baby food in each hand, head cocked to the left, as if she wasn't sure how to take his lack of response. But her eyes were calculating and full of knowledge.

"What the fuck happened last night?" Scott demanded. "I mean, what *really* happened."

"Going for the tough guy approach, huh? It doesn't suit you."

His hands balled into fists, knuckles whitening as nails bit into the flesh of his palms. Miranda noticed.

"What are you going to do? Hit me in the middle of the baby aisle?" Her tone was mocking but calm, as if she didn't give a damn what he did one way or the other.

Suddenly self-conscious, Scott relaxed his hands. "Of course not, but I have to know." Even though they were the only two in the aisle, he looked around to make sure no one was listening, and even then he spoke the rest in a near whisper. "They found him this morning . . . the boy who got his head cut off. It was real."

"I know." Voice still level, as if she were discussing matters of no more import than the weather. She held up her right hand to display a large adhesive strip covering her palm, a wet spot in the middle from seepage.

Scott stared at her bandaged wound, almost reached out to touch it in order to confirm its reality.

"It's not possible. Look, something awful happened to me—or at least my family—when I was a kid, and it messed me up pretty bad. I've lost track of how many shrinks I've seen, and I've been on so many meds since childhood that I have the residue of several pharmacies' worth of antidepressants and antipsychotics pumping through my veins. I thought I'd made some real progress over the last few years, so much that I didn't need the doctors or the pills anymore. But it's obvious that I've had some sort of regression and started hallucinating. The things I saw last night . . . they just *can't* have been real." He gave her a weak smile. "Hell, half the time, I don't know if you're real."

Miranda put the jars she was holding on the shelf then leaned forward to give him a light kiss on the lips. When she pulled back, she smiled and said, "Did that feel real?"

He nodded.

"Well, there you go, then. You've been proceeding under a faulty assumption, Scott. You presume that what you perceived before we met was reality. But like most people, you've spent your entire life walking through the world wearing mental blinders, completely unaware of the true nature of existence." Miranda sounded different now: no longer playful and far more mature than her apparent years. "I . . . removed those blinders, and now you've begun to see things as they really are. That's all."

"*That's all*? If what you're saying is true—and I'm not saying I believe it—then how could you do such a thing? More to the point, *why* would you?"

She seemed to consider for a moment, then stepped forward and took his hand. "Follow me."

She led him away from the baby food, past the meats, then down the magazine aisle. As they walked, people turned to stare—no doubt wondering why a sweet young thing like Miranda would be holding the hand of a grizzled old bastard like him. He knew he should let go of her hand; they were in public, after all, and despite the "manual assist" she'd given him last night, he was still determined to patch things up with Gayle. But right now he felt so unsafe, so untethered from reality, that holding onto her hand provided an anchor for him.

They walked past garish magazine covers that screamed
Lose Weight Now! or *Discover the Sexual Secret That Will
Drive Your Guy Wild!* or *Double Your Income in Less Than a
Month!* Looking at the magazines, Scott experienced a sudden wave of vertigo accompanied by a powerful sense of
déjà vu. Though he'd never been inside Martindale's grocery before, he felt as if he'd been down this aisle before,
seen these magazines . . .

He remembered a woman. Blonde, large breasts, tiny
waist, perfect ass. He could see her flipping through a tennis magazine, deciding to buy it, moving off with her basket of groceries toward the self-checkout. Him following,
anticipating . . .

It came back to him then: the dream he'd had when he'd
fallen asleep in the parking lot of Gayle and David's apartment complex. A dream of hunting. It had been a dream
he'd never finished, for Miranda had interrupted it, tapping on his car window and waking him.

But the dream wasn't the only place he had seen the
blonde, was it? He half-remembered walking with Miranda
after she'd woken him, heading down the sidewalk,
seeing . . . something . . . on the road. Stopping in front of
the convenience mart on the corner. Women coming toward them. The blonde . . .

Agony blossomed behind his eyes and he let out a moan
of pain.

Miranda stopped. "Something wrong?"

The pain seemed to be blocking his memory, allowing
only bits and pieces to get through. He knew from his
years of therapy that this was probably a protective measure on the part of his mind, but he didn't care. He wanted
to know. He closed his eyes and tried fighting through the

pain to get at whatever memories lay on the other side, but all he managed to do was make his head hurt worse. Flashes of white light sparked along his optic nerves and the pain intensified to the point where he feared he might pass out.

"Scott!" Miranda was tugging on his elbow. "Whatever you're doing, stop it!"

Good advice, he thought. Especially since it seemed he didn't have any choice. He stopped fighting, let the memory of the convenience mart fade back into the mental fog it had emerged from. Immediately, the pain began to subside.

He opened his eyes, managed a weak smile. "I'll be all right. Just a little headache."

Miranda frowned. "Little? For a minute it looked like your head was going to pop like a goddamned balloon. You want to go lie down? I could take you to the employee lounge. There's a couch there."

"No, I'll be okay." Not that he believed it. He was light years away from okay, maybe even a galaxy or two. "What were you going to show me?"

She looked at him a moment longer, as if trying to decide if he really were going to be all right. Then, evidently deciding his brain wasn't going to explode any time soon, she turned and led him past the magazines to the books. There weren't that many; after all, this was a grocery, not a bookstore. Five rows of paperbacks, most of them romance novels. But there was a sprinkling of true-crime books, and Scott was pleasantly surprised to see a couple of his among them: *Forty Whacks* and *The Boy Next Door*. The former was his book on ax murderers, and seeing it after what had happened last night gave him a chill. The latter book was a collection of interviews with neighbors of killers, the kind of people who always showed up on the TV news saying things like, "We were shocked. He seemed like such a nice, quiet fella. Who knew he had thirty bodies buried in his basement?"

He had to resist the urge to reach out and pick a copy up. No matter how many times he touched one of his books—ran his fingers over the cover, lifted it to his nose so he could inhale the sweet smell of fresh paper and ink—he never grew tired of it. But that was a private act, something not be done in the presence of others, like self-pleasuring. There was nothing wrong with it, as long as no one caught you.

Miranda released his hand and removed a copy of *The Boy Next Door* from the shelf. The cover was black, the letters of the title blood red. Beneath the title was an image of a house with a silhouette of a man standing at an upstairs window, looking out. The picture was supposed to present a sinister image of a next-door neighbor, but Scott had never liked the cover. He thought it too cartoonish, but then the book had sold well enough and was still in print, so what the hell did he know?

Miranda began flipping through the book, as if searching for a particular page. Finally, toward the end, she stopped and marked a specific passage with her finger. "Here it is. Listen to this." She began reading aloud.

"To say that the houses that surround us—the homes that belong to those others that we call our neighbors—are only facades is to state the obvious. *Facade*, of course, means *face*, and just like we never truly know what lies behind the faces of other people—the dreams, hopes, desires, and secrets—even those who are closest to us, so too are we forever uncertain what lies behind the face of a house. We see the outside, note that the lawn is well kept, the yard nicely landscaped, grass mowed and edged, gutters clean, front walk swept, and we assume that the inside is just as neat and orderly. But it might not be. If we were to step over the threshold, we might find piles of old newspapers, decades of dust, and several dozen cats using the carpet as their litterbox. The point isn't just that we don't know: it's that we can *never* know. And maybe in the end we're better off not knowing, just making our assumptions and going about our lives, deluding ourselves that our neighbors are all nice people, that everything makes sense, and the world is ultimately a safe place. For if we were to learn otherwise, how could we go on?"

Miranda closed the book and looked at him. "You've glimpsed the true nature of reality before, Scott. That passage shows it, but it's only a partial glimpse. The facade isn't just the outside of a house or even the impenetrable mask of a person's face: It's *everything*. Everything we see, taste, touch, smell, or hear. Our senses lie to us constantly, insulating and protecting us from the truth of what surrounds us. Because if we could perceive reality as it truly is, we couldn't handle it. At the very least, we'd go insane. At the worst . . . well, let's just say there are states of being that make madness seem like a blessing."

Scott wasn't certain he fully understood, let alone believed what Miranda was talking about. "So you're telling me that you've done something to my senses so that I can see beyond this . . ." He waved his hand in the air as he searched for the words . . . "sensory fog and perceive the *real* reality?"

"Exactly."

"Assuming for a minute that what you are saying is true—*and* that you somehow possess the ability to do this—why *would* you? And why to *me*?"

Miranda sighed. "It's difficult to explain, but I suppose the simplest way to look at it is—"

"Giving one of our customers a little extra attention?"

Scott turned to see a tall, broad-shouldered man coming toward them. He wore a white shirt, blue tie, blue slacks, and black shoes. A plastic name tag on the left side of his chest read MANAGER, but the letters below were too small for Scott to make out the man's specific name. He had a round, clean-shaven face, and what hair he had left was black, short, and plastered to his head by some sort of gel. The expression on that face was by no means a happy one.

"I was just helping him locate a book." Miranda turned away from the manager and put *The Boy Next Door* back on the shelf. Though she didn't seem afraid of the man, there was something wary in her manner, as if she didn't trust him.

The manager reached them and stopped. "I thought you were supposed to be stocking baby food."

Scott felt a need to jump in. "She was, but I—"

The manager glanced at him. "When I want to hear from you, Scotty-boy, I'll speak to you directly."

Scott started to say that he didn't appreciate being spoken to like that, but the words died in his throat.

Scotty-boy.

The manager glared at Miranda. "Well?"

She glared back for a moment, and Scott had the impression that a battle was being waged on a level that he couldn't perceive. Finally, she lowered her gaze and said, "All right." She turned to go, stopped, gave Scott a last look and a weak smile. "We'll talk later." Then she started walking up the aisle, Scott watching her go. Within seconds she was gone.

He turned to the manager and felt nausea twist his gut, for now the man had no face, just a swirling, roiling void. Scott looked at the man's name tag. Below MANAGER was a tiny picture of an ax.

"You shouldn't trust her, Scotty-boy." His voice had become suddenly familiar. "You're kidding yourself if you think she cares about you. You're nothing more than a tool to her." His tone changed as if he were grinning. "And I don't mean *tool* in a sexual sense, though maybe that applies as well, eh?"

"And I suppose *you* have my best interests at heart?" Scott surprised himself by sounding more strong and defiant than he felt.

"Believe it or not, I do. I want to preserve your life; she wants to end it."

Scott didn't know what to say to this. Miranda hadn't done anything to harm him directly, but if she were responsible for the hallucinations he'd been having—though according to her they weren't hallucinations, but rather the opposite: glimpses of true reality—then she'd been messing with his mind and getting him into potentially deadly situations, like in the park last night. But then Faceless didn't exactly strike him as a saint, either.

"That boy . . . the one you attacked last night. He's dead."

The faceless man let out a bark of a laugh. "Well, he sure as shit ought to be! I chopped the little fucker's head off!" He laughed again. "If the bastard had lived, you can bet he was going to track you down and kill you and your little cooz, just as soon as he got untangled from that swing. I saved both of your lives by doing him first. Think about this: She got you into that mess, but *I* got you out."

It was true. The ax man hadn't tried to harm either of them, only Jamey.

Scott glanced at the bookshelves and saw the cover of *Forty Whacks*.

"Are you . . . him?" He pointed to the book. "The Riverton Ax Murderer? Or maybe his . . . I don't know . . . his ghost or something?"

The faceless man took a step forward and put his right hand on Scott's left shoulder. The grip was firm, but not painful. It felt almost comforting somehow. Reassuring.

"No. This is just how you need to see me right now." With his free hand, he gestured toward the void that was his face. "At least, as much of me as you're ready to see. But don't worry about it. When the time comes, you'll know me for who I really am."

Scott stared into the swirling emptiness only a couple feet from his own face. He tried to penetrate its depths, tried to see what lay inside, what lay beyond. But he couldn't. The effort made his head throb anew.

"Like I said, give it time." The faceless man paused, and when he spoke again, his voice held a sinister edge. "Tell me, did it feel good last night?"

"Did what feel good?"

"The moment when you came . . . when Coozie was jacking you off and your cock turned into a knife." He tightened his grip on Scott's shoulder, squeezed, released, squeezed again, as if he were massaging it. "Did you enjoy feeling her flesh slice open? Her warm wet blood jetting onto you, almost like it was she coming instead?" He leaned forward until the vortex of nothingness was only inches away from Scott. "You can tell me," he whispered. "After all, if you can't share secrets with family, who can you share them with?"

The faceless man laughed then, long and loud, and as he laughed, the emptiness that was his face began to take on form and grow solid as human features emerged.

Somewhere deep in his subconscious, Scott knew that he really, really did *not* want to see this. He pulled free of the man's grip and ran past him toward the grocery's exit, laughter echoing behind him all the way.

As he passed the checkout lanes, he saw that the registers—all of them—were staffed by women. Every one was naked, her pale skin criss-crossed by deep, wicked-looking cuts, hair matted with blood, eyes open and staring. He stopped, unable to keep running. There were customers in their lanes: men, women, some with kids, some not, but none gave any sign that they were aware of being served by corpses. The women passed item after item over the price scanners—one of the few modern touches in the store, along with the self-checkout near the exit—leaving bloody fingerprints on cereal boxes, bananas, and plastic jugs of milk. Sometimes a gobbet of flesh would fall off a face, a chest, or an arm onto the scanner, and the woman would pause to sweep it onto the floor with her hand before continuing to scan items.

Then, as if responding to some inner signal, the dead women turned in unison toward Scott and opened their mouths. He expected to hear whispering, but instead they screamed. Screamed so loud he thought the windows at the front of the store might shatter, thought his eardrums would burst. They kept on screaming, eyes no longer dead but alive and blazing with hatred. Hatred, he sensed, of him.

He balled his hands into fists, jammed them against his ears, and ran sobbing for the exit. He plunged into the open air of the parking lot and kept running. He didn't head to his car, had in fact forgotten that he even owned a car. He was focused on one thing only: getting away from those screams.

But no matter how far he ran, he still heard them. And that's when he realized the screams were coming from inside his own head.

Chapter Sixteen

Water rushed by, thick and sludgy brown. It had rained a lot last week, and the river was still swollen and full of silt. Scott stood at the bridge's railing, looking down at the turbulent, churning water and resisted thinking it was an appropriate metaphor for how he felt inside.

His car was parked just beyond the north end of the bridge, on the shoulder so it wouldn't block traffic. Not long after he'd run out of the grocery, his mind had cleared enough to remember it, and he'd returned to the parking lot, afraid that more weirdness awaited him there, but nothing happened, and he got in his car and drove away, just like any other customer. *Any other customer with recurrent psychotic episodes,* he thought.

He liked listening to the sound of the water surging beneath him, at once quiet and powerful. The brown hue made it look as if the water would be warm, but this early in April, it would most likely be cold. Not that it mattered: No one would be foolish enough to go swimming, not with the river this high and moving this fast. It would be suicide.

Now *there* was a thought. A good, solid thought that a man could get his hands around.

It wasn't as if he were a stranger to such notions. Given his precarious mental state over the years, he'd contemplated—sometimes seriously, sometimes less so—taking his own life on numerous occasions. In his teens, he'd even gone so far as to cut his wrists a few times, but these had been faux attempts, designed more to get attention from his therapists than to end his life. The cuts had been shallow, and he'd always made them when he knew someone was around so they could discover what he'd done and get him medical attention quickly. Pathetic, really.

But here . . . should he climb over the railing (easy enough to do; it was only waist-high) and jump, there would be no turning back—after all, gravity wouldn't change its mind at the last minute and let him go. And there was no one around to go into the water after him (not that anyone would be dumb enough to try, fast as the river was flowing) or call 911. And even in the unlikely event someone did drive by, see him, stop and phone for help, it would take at the very least several minutes for rescuers to arrive, and by that time the river would have done its work.

It would be so simple.

After he'd left Martindale's, he'd driven aimlessly for a time. He found himself going past David's school, wondering what his son was doing right then. Working on a math problem? Maybe checking a book out from the library that he'd have to do a report on later? There'd been a time when he'd known everything that was happening in his son's life: what he was learning in school, who his friends were, what TV shows he liked to watch, what he dreamt about the night before. Now he was cut off from David, and the days and weeks of his son's life were going by, changing him bit by bit, making him less of a kid every day. What kind of a father was he—and could he even call himself David's father in anything but the crudest biological sense—if he wasn't there for the boy day in, day out?

He'd thought about what Miranda had told him, not that he was certain he believed any of it, but if what she'd said was true, then what sort of world had Gayle and he brought their son into? A place of gossamer-thin illusions that could be ripped apart any second to reveal the awful truth: that there was no order or rationality to existence, only chaos and madness.

He'd found himself weeping for David, and he prayed the boy would live out his life in blissful ignorance, a state Scott himself deeply wished he could return to. But then, his innocence had been murdered along with his family in a cabin by the lake that long-ago summer night, and nothing could ever restore it.

He'd driven past the office building where Gayle worked, and was tempted to stop, but he kept going. He'd driven past the high school then and wondered how the students were taking the news of Jamey's death. If they were all part of his sharp-toothed pack, maybe they didn't give a damn. Or maybe they were filled with fury and lust for revenge. But there were likely some students who were normal, who still clung to their illusions of reality. These kids might take the death of a fellow student hard, even if they hadn't known him personally. Jamey's murder would be one more crack in the mental armor that shielded them from the true nature of existence, one more bit of their in-

nocence lost. Lose too much, and you had nothing to protect you against the madness of the world.

He wondered if Laura Foster was inside, consoling her
students in a very special way.

He'd driven past the park again, though he wasn't about
to stop, not if the police were still there investigating
Jamey's death. He drove past Miranda Tanner's house,
again not stopping, then past the library where he'd done
research for his latest book. The whole notion of writing
seemed quaint to him now, of no more lasting import than
a child scratching chalk drawings on the sidewalk. An
amusement to occupy one's time, nothing more.

With nowhere else left to go, he'd driven home to his
apartment. His computer had been still on, but he wasn't
about to check his e-mail, not after the last one he'd received. The message light on his answering machine was
blinking, and he stared at it for some time, debating, before
finally pushing the PLAY MESSAGES button.

The first message was a hang-up; a telemarketer, no
doubt. But the second message was from his wife.

"Scott, this is Gayle. It's just about lunchtime." Silence
for several seconds. "I want to say that I appreciate what
you tried to do this morning. I know you still love David
very much and want to be a good father to him."

Scott knew he wouldn't like what was coming next.
When Gayle had something really bad to say, she always
started off by sounding as if she were on your side.

"But it was obvious to both David and myself that you
weren't . . . with it today. Seeing you like that just confuses
and upsets him."

And what about you? Scott thought. *How does seeing me
make you feel? Assuming you feel anything at all, that is.*

"I really think it would be in David's best interests if you didn't see him for a while, Scott. I mean it this time. I made an appointment to see a lawyer this afternoon, and I'm going to get the paperwork started on a restraining order. I'm not sure how it's going to work or what all the details will be. I guess the lawyer will contact you about that. But I want you to stay away from David. From both of us."

More silence, longer this time.

"Get some help, Scott. Go see a therapist, start taking medication again. Do whatever you have to, okay? Just . . . get better."

No *I love you* or even a simple *Good-bye*. Merely a pause, and then a click as the connection was broken—in more ways than one, Scott thought.

Images flashed through his mind, then. Gleaming knives; soft pink skin; bright red blood. He felt an urge to pick up the answering machine and dash it against the wall, then run through his apartment destroying everything he could get his hands on. But then his fury drained away, leaving behind only cold, empty despair.

And so he had left his apartment again, and without thought or plan, had driven here, to this bridge outside of town, where he stood looking down at the water, a bargain-basement Hamlet trying to decide whether or not to jump.

He lifted one leg over the rail, then the other, and sat looking down at the water, dangling his feet in the air, kicking them back and forth like a child. It had been too easy to do. Whoever had designed the damn bridge really should've given more thought to the height of the rails. Then again, given what Miranda had shown him of the true nature of Ash Creek, maybe the architect had purposefully made the railing low to encourage suicides. After what he'd seen the last two days, it wouldn't have surprised him a bit.

He knew he hadn't moved much at all from where he'd been standing a moment ago, but psychologically, it was a universe of distance. The breeze seemed stronger here, colder, the rushing water louder. It felt almost as if the river were exerting its own gravitational pull, trying to suck him down into its mud-brown depths. He experienced a wave of vertigo, and despite his reason for climbing up here in the first place, he gripped the railing tight with both hands to steady himself. He couldn't help smiling. It seemed his body was reluctant to leave this world, however fucked up it might be.

Nothing but blind, animal instinct, he told himself. It could be fought.

He forced his right hand to relax and let go of the metal railing, then he forced his left to do the same. Now the only thing keeping him from plunging downward into the river was his sense of balance. All he had to do was lean forward a bit, and let gravity do the rest.

He remained sitting upright. Despite the coolness of the breeze, sweat beaded on his brow. He could feel his heart slamming against his rib cage, knew that if he hadn't been wearing a shirt, he would be able to see it make his left pectoral throb as if the muscle were spasming. He began trembling.

What's David going to think? a voice inside him said. *All his life, he's going to wonder why his daddy jumped off a bridge, wonder if maybe it was because of something he did, or something he didn't do. He'll hate you, and he'll grow to hate himself, too.*

He's young, Scott thought. He'll get over it. Kids can adjust to almost anything. In a few years, he won't even remember me. I'll be just a face in old pictures—pictures he never even looks at.

True, he might forget the details of your face, the specific sound of your voice. But he'll remember how you ended your life, you can bet on that. You know what it's like to suffer through a traumatic childhood event: You lost your entire family in one blood-soaked evening. Do you really want to do unto him as was done unto you?

It's not the same, Scott thought. My mom and dad were good parents, not psychotic headcases. David's better off without me.

Better off without you living in the same house with him and his mother? Maybe. Better off with you moldering in the ground after dying a coward's death? No.

"I didn't deserve to live." The words were whispered, and as soon as they were out, tears streamed down his face. "I should've died along with everyone else."

Let me clue you in on a little secret, Scott. No one deserves to live, and no one deserves to die. They just do. It isn't a matter of morality or some divine plan; it's nothing more or less than simple mathematics. The cold equations, my friend. When you run the numbers and hit the equal sign, sometimes the answer is life, and sometimes it's death. That's all there is to it. Any guilt or self-loathing you feel for being a survivor you brought to the party. Shit, after all the years you've spent writing about death and murder, you think you would've learned that by now.

Scott looked down at the water. It didn't seem so inviting anymore.

He let out a sigh, wiped the tears from his face, and climbed down from the railing. He started walking toward his car, but he only got halfway when he saw a silver Lexus approaching. It drove past his car, onto the bridge, and slowed as it drew near.

The driver pulled up next to him, stopped, and rolled down the window. He half-expected it to be Miranda, though how she could afford a Lexus on a grocery clerk's salary, he had no idea. But it wasn't her.

"Out for a walk?" She smiled, though from her puffy red eyes, he knew she'd been crying.

It was Laura Foster.

Chapter Seventeen

Hot breath in his ear, hands on his back, nails digging into skin. His tongue on her neck, licking slowly upward, tracing her jawline, now passing over her chin, moving around to the other side of her neck, pausing along the way for a quick nibble of her earlobe. When he bends to the neck, his chest brushes her large breasts and his left nipple slides against her right—engorged, thick, seeming almost as rock-hard as his penis inside her. An electric jolt shoots from his nipple straight down into his cock, and he surprises himself by not coming there and then.

She moans deep in her throat as her pelvis rises to meet his thrusts, and for a moment he pauses, thinking that she made a similar sound last night in the park. An image flashes through his mind: a mammoth vagina being penetrated by a gigantic dildo formed from the tightly packed bodies of naked teenagers slick with lubricant. He feels his penis soften, and a new image forms before his mind's eye: her cunt yawning open, stretching wide to pull him in and swallow him whole. He sees himself falling, tumbling through a darkness without end, his only companion the musky smell of vaginal juices—a scent which grows increasingly rank the farther he falls, until it's become the odor of an open, suppurating wound, then the stench of a swollen, flyblown corpse.

He finds this last smell intoxicating, sweeter than any flower, more heady than the finest wine, more powerful than any pheromone manufactured by nature, and his cock stiffens again, harder than before, painfully so, as if the skin has stretched to its limit and is going to tear. But it's a *good* pain, and he resumes thrusting, forgetting about the park, the teenagers, the Freudian cliché of the infinite cunt in his vision. All he cares about is sheer sensation, feeling the jangle of nerve endings and the bright pulse of firing neurons. So close was he to death before that now he wants only to touch life, taste it, fuck the holy living shit out of it.

"I can't believe it. I mean, things like this just don't happen in Ash Creek."

A bar outside of town, close to the county line.

"Jamey wasn't the best student in the world, Lord knows." She takes a sip of her double vodka, grimaces at the taste, takes another. *"And he was a real discipline problem. I had him in English lit last fall, and he and another boy in class got into a fight. I don't mean a name-calling, chest-puffing, foot-shuffling show for the girls. The real thing, hitting, kicking . . . hell, they were even biting. Some of the other boys in class tried to separate them, but in the end I had to run down the hall and get Bob Garrety, a social studies teacher who lifts weights and coaches track. Big guy, doesn't take any shit. And even he had trouble pulling Jamey and that other boy off each other. I forget how long Jamey got suspended for that."*

Her eyes are tearing up. He's seen them do that a lot over the last hour or so.

"He barely squeaked by in my class with a C, and he probably cheated to get that, but I didn't give a damn. I was just glad
to get rid of him." She shakes her head, starts to take another
sip of her drink, but stops as if thinking better of it. "But none
of that means dick now. No one should have to die like . . . like
that. No one."

He mumbles something sympathetic. He's done that a lot
during the last hour, too. He's watching her eyes, listening to the
tone of her voice, trying to detect the least hint of insincerity in
her words. He finds none.

She hooks her heels around the backs of his legs, as if
she's trying to hold on, or perhaps gain better leverage for
her own thrusting. He senses she's restraining herself,
holding back. Maybe she's trying to turn him on by playing submissive, or maybe she's not letting go for a different
reason. After all, she's a drama coach; she knows how to
act.

He thinks about facades.

But his thoughts are quickly banished by the sound of
her breath coming short and rapid—*huh-huh-huh-huh-huh-
huh-huh-huh*—and he thinks she's close to orgasm. He
hopes so. He doesn't think he can keep from coming himself much longer.

But then she stops thrusting, unhooks her legs from
around his, pushes him gently but firmly off her.

She sits up, says, "Let's change positions." Her voice is
husky, and he sees her skin is dotted with red patches from
where he's bitten her—at her request. So many it's almost
as if she has a rash. The skin is broken in a couple places,
nothing major, but blood has collected around the tiny
wounds, already in the process of drying and crusting
over. He feels an urge to lick the blood, to taste yet another
element of her body—he's tasted so many already—but an

image of bloody women standing at grocery registers flickers through his mind, and he resists.

"Sure." Changing positions is fine with him. It'll give his cock a chance to rest, even if only for a few moments, so he can pull back from the edge of orgasm and keep going. He wants to make this last as long as he can, make it last forever, if possible. And in this new world that he's somehow slipped into, a world where such quaint notions as rules and consequences seem to no longer apply, it might just be possible to go on fucking forever. At least he damn well intends to try.

She scoots around on the bed, gets on her hands and knees, feet dangling over the side of the bed, ample ass raised for him. He steps off the bed onto soft carpet, turns, and places his hands on her hips, lets his fingers settle into her flesh before moving forward to enter her. At the last second, he thinks he sees her vagina opening and closing as if it's a mouth eager to be fed: a hungry infant's, a starving baby bird's, the opening of some carnivorous plant oozing sweet fluid to attract insects. He hesitates, isn't about to shove his cock into *that*, but then the mouth reaches out, actually extends from her pubis like a pseudopod and surrounds his penis, grips it, pulls it toward her, retracting as it goes.

He tries to pull away, but he can't, not unless he wants his dick ripped off, and panic swells inside him. But then her vagina—or whatever the hell it is—begins massaging him, its inner walls rippling along his flesh like waves of warm water. Every nerve ending in his cock is flooded with physical sensation beyond anything he's ever experienced, whether natural or chemically induced. There are no words for it. *Ecstasy* is laughably inadequate, as are *rap-*

ture, euphoria, bliss . . . Ugly, harsh syllables that come nowhere near capturing the merest fraction of what he feels. The experience is primal and transcendent, like birth, like death.

Unable to stop himself, he begins pounding into her flesh, no longer in control of his body, his consciousness nothing but a distant observer as orgasm rushes toward him.

She looks back at him and smiles, eyes shining, mouth full of tiny sharp teeth.

They've progressed to holding hands like a couple of teenagers. She's had a few more vodkas, he's had a few beers. He's trying to decide what, if anything, to say about last night. She's given no indication that she was at the park, and if she was, no hint that she's aware he was there, too, watching as she had monstrous sex with the Amazing Human Dildo. He's beginning to think that maybe Miranda is wrong—if she even exists at all, that is. It's not the world that's fucked up; it's just him, just little Scotty Raymond who's never been able to get over the brutal slaughter of his family. He finds this thought comforting. If he's—go ahead and think the word, he tells himself—insane, then the world is the same semirational, semisafe place it's always been. A hard, unforgiving place to be sure, but not the vast open-air asylum Miranda would have him believe it to be. If the madness is confined to his own skull, if the world is just the world and not a nightmarish landscape of faceless taunting killers, blood-smeared apparitions, and behemoth vaginas, then David is safe.

And as for Gayle . . . *it's clear she doesn't give a damn about their marriage anymore, so why should he give a damn about her?*

"You'll probably think I'm some sort of slut, but would you

like to go back to my place?" Her speech is thick, her words mushy from too much vodka. "I just don't want to be alone right now, you know?"

He knew all right. "I'd like that."

He doesn't care about the teeth, closes his eyes so he doesn't have to see them. All he cares about is riding the climax that's coming, and it's here and his body jerks and spasms as if in the throes of an epileptic fit. A guttural animal cry bursts from his throat, and sparks of white flash against his optic nerve. He feels dizzy, numb, about to lose consciousness, and he does gray out for a moment, but he manages to steady himself by sinking his fingers into her fleshy hips and holding on tight, and then it passes, and he's still coming inside her, as if he's a machine with an endless reserve of semen that just keeps pumping and pumping and . . .

Something's wrong. Fire explodes inside his cock, like something is worming its way up into him. When he was a teenager, his appendix burst and he was in the hospital for the better part of a week. While he was recovering from emergency surgery, a nurse ran a catheter, and it was one of the most painful, humiliating experiences he ever had. It feels like that now, as if a long, thin, hard tube is jamming into his penis.

He opens his eyes, tries to pull away from her, but he can't. She's laughing, and he sees those teeth again, and this time he cares about them, cares *a lot*. He looks down at his penis, sees that the vaginal pseudopod that gripped him has retreated, and extending from between her legs is a long black tube that looks like an insect's stinger.

When he was in first grade, he was a voracious reader. Fiction, nonfiction, it didn't matter. He read it all. One day,

Join the Leisure Horror Book Club and
GET 2 FREE BOOKS NOW—
An **$11.98 value!**

— **Yes! I want to subscribe to** —
the Leisure Horror Book Club.

Please send me my **2 FREE BOOKS**. I have enclosed $2.00 for shipping/handling. Each month I'll receive the two newest Leisure Horror selections to preview for 10 days. If I decide to keep them, I will pay the Special Members Only discounted price of just $4.25 each, a total of $8.50, plus $2.00 shipping/handling. This is a **SAVINGS OF AT LEAST $3.48** off the bookstore price. There is no minimum number of books I must buy and I may cancel the program at any time. In any case, the **2 FREE BOOKS** are mine to keep.

Not available in Canada.

NAME: _____
ADDRESS: _____
CITY: _____ STATE: _____
COUNTRY: _____ ZIP: _____
TELEPHONE: _____
E-MAIL: _____
SIGNATURE: _____

If under 18, Parent or Guardian must sign. Terms, prices, and conditions subject to change. Subscription subject to acceptance. Dorchester Publishing reserves the right to reject any order or cancel any subscription.

he took a book about crickets out of the school library. It had been interesting enough, but the section that fascinated him most was the one on how the insects reproduced. He fixated on a series of pictures showing a female cricket depositing her eggs in a hole: a long tube protruded from her rear and dangled down into the hole, and the eggs—long, narrow things—came out the end.

He thinks about those pictures now as he feels something coming through the tube, going up inside him, and it hurts, sweet Jesus, hurts as much as his orgasm felt good before, and she laughs and goes on laughing until he can't hear her anymore.

David sat cross-legged on his bed, reading a book about the moon he'd gotten out of the library at school. He was supposed to do a report on it, but he had until next Monday—almost a whole week!—so he wasn't paying that much attention. He was too busy thinking. Mom said he thought *too* much, though he didn't quite understand what she was talking about. After all, if thinking was a good thing, how could somebody do too much of it? Sometimes, though, he had trouble falling asleep at night because of all the thoughts tumbling through his mind. Maybe that was what she meant.

Tonight he was thinking about this morning's breakfast at McDonald's with Dad—and about what had happened in the park last night.

He closed the moon book, placed it on his nightstand, then lay back on the bed, hands folded across his chest, and looked up at the ceiling. He didn't like this room. He didn't think of it as *his* room and he never would. *His* room was back at the house in Cedar Hill, though since Mom and Dad had sold it, that one wasn't his anymore, not really, but that's how he felt about it: *his room*. And this one? It was just the place where he slept.

It was bigger than his old room—at least, that's what Mom said. If it was, it didn't seem *that* much bigger, not to him. He had most of his stuff here, though some things, like his bike, remained locked up in their storage space in the basement. On his dresser sat the big glass jar containing the marble collection that had been left to him by his grandfather on his mother's side. He didn't have any grandparents on his father's side; they'd all died somehow before he was born, though neither his mom nor his dad had told him how. Whatever had happened to them, he figured it must've been pretty bad if grown-ups wouldn't talk about it to a kid.

He had an upright set of shelves for all his books, most of which he was too big for now, like *1-2-3 Sesame Street* and *The Poky Little Puppy,* but he kept them anyway because Dad had bought them. His father was a writer and books were very important to him, and he wanted them to be important to David, so they were. At least, David tried real hard to think they were important, but the truth was he liked playing computer games better. He could only play those at school and at the library now. The only computer they'd had belonged to Dad, and he'd taken it with him when he moved out.

When Mom made *him move out, you mean.* The thought was followed instantly by a wave of guilt. David loved his mother and knew she loved him and only wanted what was best for him. At least, that's what she told him (it seemed like she told him that all the time), and she wouldn't lie, right? Not Mom. Still, if she wanted what was best for him, he couldn't see why she didn't want them to live with Dad—or at least buy him a new computer.

Grown-ups sure are confusing sometimes.

At the foot of his bed was a cedar chest filled with toys. He didn't play much with them anymore, didn't really feel like it these days. It was nice to know they were there, though, just in case he needed them. He liked the chest better anyway. Dad had gotten it at a garage sale when David was a baby and even though he wasn't the handiest man around, he refinished it and put on new brackets and screws. Sometimes David liked to lie on his belly, face toward the foot of the bed, hand dangling over the edge so he could brush his fingers over the smooth surface of the toy box. Sometimes he'd do that for a few minutes, sometimes for the better part of an hour. And sometimes he'd cry as he stroked the box, though not so often anymore.

The ceiling wasn't much to look at. The ceiling of his room back home in Cedar Hill had been decorated with glow-in-the-dark stars and planets that Dad brought home from the Dollar Store. After Dad had put them up, David had never been afraid of the dark. He loved it whenever Mom or Dad turned out his lights at night, because then he'd get to look up at the glow of his very own night sky until he fell asleep. But the ceiling of this room was a boring, blank white. He thought about asking Mom if they could go to the Dollar Store—if Ash Creek *had* a Dollar Store, that is—and get some more stickers. But she was touchy about his mentioning anything to do with the old house and with Dad since they'd moved, and he wasn't sure if he'd upset her by asking. He'd have to think some more about it.

He'd liked having breakfast with Dad this morning, even if it had been kind of weird. No one had said much of anything, David included. He'd tried to think of something to say, but he just couldn't come up with anything. The strangest thing was that in one way, it was like they were a family again, but in another, it was like Dad was a stranger, somebody David had seen in photographs or on a home video but had never met in person before. He hadn't liked feeling that way, but at least the three of them had been together. Dad had gotten nervous toward the end, looking around the restaurant and shivering like he was cold. That hadn't bothered David too much, though. Dad just got that way sometimes.

Then that creepy old lady had come over and told them that some kid had gotten killed in Orchard Park last night. That had really scared David because Mom took him there sometimes. It seemed like such a nice place: children running, swinging, sliding, laughing. He couldn't imagine someone getting *killed* there, let alone having his whole head chopped off! He'd wondered if maybe the old lady had made it up just to scare them, but later at school, some of the other kids told him that they'd heard about the murder too, so he figured it must be true.

He tried not to think too much about the dead kid, though. He was sorry the boy was gone and all, but he'd rather concentrate on today's breakfast. Dad had always told him it was important to try to focus on the good things in life and not the bad things, and that's what he tried to do. He wasn't stupid; he knew that his mom and dad still might get a divorce. He knew lots of kids, both back in Cedar Hill and in Ash Creek, whose parents had gotten divorced. He also knew that just because Mom and Dad had breakfast at McDonald's one morning didn't mean that everything was suddenly all right and they were going to get back together again. But that didn't mean he couldn't hope, did it?

He looked up at the ceiling, thoughts continuing to buzz in his mind like bees drifting aimlessly through a field of flowers. *I gotta ask Mom for some stickers*, he decided. *First thing in the morning.*

He sat up, retrieved his moon book from the nightstand, opened it, and pretended to pay attention as he read.

Dusk. Shadows growing longer, thicker. Night's foreplay.

He stood in the parking lot of the apartment complex, leaning against a Dodge Omni that wasn't his and smoking a cigarette. His gaze was fixed on one of the buildings, in particular on a rectangle of yellow light. The boy had left his curtains open. He probably thought he didn't have to bother closing them, that he was safe on the second floor. But the Watcher knew better. No one was safe—ever.

He continuing staring at the window until full night fell and the light finally went out. He imagined the boy's mother saying good night as she left the room, and he wondered what she smelled like. He'd find out soon enough, but not tonight. Tonight he had other work to do.

He spit his latest cigarette onto the ground, then turned and started walking toward the street.

Chapter Eighteen

Scott sat at Gammy's kitchen table, despite the fact that she had died from heart failure when he was in college and he had sold her house a few months after the funeral. He wasn't a child, but rather his normal almost-middle-aged self. That meant this wasn't a memory; this was happening now. Dream? Hallucination? He supposed it didn't really matter anymore.

Gammy stood at the stove—it seemed she was always there—stirring the contents of a small pot. Other pots of various sizes sat on the remaining burners, and a pumpkin pie was cooling on the counter. The oven light was on, and though he couldn't see past Gammy well enough to make out what was cooking inside, he could tell by the smell that it was turkey. Gammy wasn't wearing her usual housedress. Instead, she had on a white blouse, red vest, blue slacks, and black shoes. Her hair was done up, and Scott knew she had just been, as she always put it, to the "beauty parlor." The signs were unmistakable: It was Thanksgiving.

She turned and gave him a smile. "Glad to see you could make it. Want to help me check on the turkey?"

Scott was dressed for the occasion: light blue shirt, tie, navy slacks, and dress shoes. He pushed back his chair and stood, grimacing as a cramp hit his lower gut. It hurt to stand all the way upright, but if he leaned over it was a little better. He hobbled to the stove, feeling older than his grandmother.

Her smile fell away. "I'm sorry to see you pained, Scott, though you did bring it on yourself." She sounded disappointed, just like the time she had found his secret stash of *Playboy*s. She pointed to the cupboard over the stove. "Be a dear and get a couple pot holders for me."

Since sixth grade, the year he became officially taller than Gammy, it had been his job to do all the high reaching around the house. Scott stepped to her side and saw the pots on the stove were filled with corn, sweet potatoes, mashed potatoes, lima beans—all his favorites from childhood. He stretched his hand toward the cupboard, the cramp clenching in protest as he straightened, but he gritted his teeth against the pain and managed to get the pot holders. He doubled over then, and the pain eased, though it didn't subside entirely.

Gammy frowned. "I don't think you're in any shape to take the bird out yourself. Tell you what: you give me the pot holders and open the oven door, and I'll do the rest. And don't try to tell me it's too heavy. You know I always get a small turkey for the two of us."

Ever since the lake, it had been just Scott and Gammy for Thanksgiving, Christmas, birthdays . . . He still had some relatives on his father's side—an uncle in California, a few distant cousins scattered around the country—but Gammy was all the family he had in Ohio. But that was okay; she was all the family he needed.

He did as she asked—handed her the pot holders and, after she taken a couple steps back, opened the oven door. Heat wafted out, making his eyes ache, and he had to turn his face away from the stove. The smell of cooked meat drifted into the air, and his mouth watered in response, though there was something not quite right about the scent, as if it wasn't turkey Gammy was cooking but some other animal.

Protecting her hands with the pot holders, Gammy reached into the oven and lifted out a gray metal cooking pan. She walked it over to the counter where she had already laid out two trivets, set the pan on them, and then removed the lid and put it to the side. She leaned over the pan, closed her eyes, and inhaled.

"Smells done to me, Scott. What do you think?"

He didn't answer. Inside the pan was the charred body of a disemboweled cat. The same one that Gammy had caught him mutilating when he was a kid. The pain in his gut intensified, and he bent over, hands clasped to his belly as if he were trying to hold his own bowels in.

"Still, we should probably give it the fork test to make sure." She walked over to the silverware drawer, got a fork, and returned to the counter. She stuck the fork into the cat and pulled away a greasy black chunk of meat. She held it up to her face and inspected it closely while she blew air on it. After a moment, she popped it into her mouth and chewed. She swallowed, then smiled.

"Tastes done to me." She got another forkful and held it out to Scott. "Want to check for yourself?"

He couldn't speak, could only shake his head.

She shrugged. "Suit yourself." She ate his portion as well, then put the fork down on the counter. "Doesn't look like you're too hungry. Well, that's okay. We're not really here to eat anyway. We're here to talk." She turned to the "turkey," reached into the open cavity of its abdomen with her bare fingers—despite how hot it still was—and rooted around inside for a few moments before finally pulling free a wishbone.

"Here it is!" She held it up for Scott's inspection, her fingers burnt and swollen. If she were aware of the injury, it didn't seem to bother her.

He stared at the grease-slick wishbone, not comprehending.

"I know, I know . . . cats don't have wishbones. Well, this one does. Or did, I guess I should say." She grinned. "C'mon, now. It's getting late." She turned off the oven and the burners, then walked past him, across the kitchen and toward the back door.

She obviously expected him to follow, so he did, keeping up as best he could with his cramp. "Where are we going?"

She opened the back door, then turned to him, a look of surprise on her face. "Don't tell me you've forgotten our Thanksgiving tradition! I haven't been dead *that* long, have I?"

Despite the pain in his gut, he smiled. "Of course not." He remembered now: every Thanksgiving, when he and Gammy were finished eating, they'd take the wishbone outside, along with a hand spade, walk to a tree—a different one every year—snap the wishbone, and whoever got the larger half would silently make a wish. Then they would bury the two halves at the base of the tree so the wish would come true by spring, when the leaves grew out. He had no idea how the tradition had gotten started; Gammy had simply told him that was how her family had always done it, so that was how the two of them had done it. Some years Gammy got the larger half, but most years Scott did. He'd always suspected that she knew just how to hold the bone so that when they pulled, he'd get the larger half, but he'd never been able to figure out how she did it. He'd tried doing the same thing with David over the years, but he'd never gotten the knack. One more of his failings as a parent, he supposed.

The hand spade—a rusty old thing with a weathered wooden handle—sat on the outside windowsill. Gammy walked down the back steps, picked it up, then started out into the yard. Scott walked slowly behind her, cradling his aching abdomen. There were numerous trees in Gammy's backyard. Most of their limbs were bare, the grass covered with red, brown, and yellow leaves that crunched beneath their feet as they walked. Scott looked down, saw they weren't stepping on leaves but rather the dried bodies of spiders, just like the kind Miranda had given him. There were hundreds . . . no, *thousands* of the dead creatures.

"Don't you mind those," Gammy said sternly. "He's just trying to get to you. Same as with the cat."

"*Who's* trying to get to me?"

Gammy didn't answer. She led him to a sycamore tree at the southwest edge of the property. "This one'll do, I think." She turned to him and held out the wishbone. "Go ahead, give 'er a yank."

"Gammy, I don't want to do this. Whatever's going on here, I need to—"

"*After* we do the wishbone, Scott. Not before."

He sighed. "You know, you're just as stubborn dead as you were alive."

She smiled. "Just take hold of your side and pull."

He did so, carefully watching how Gammy gripped her half, but he could see nothing special about how she held the bone. They pulled, twisting this way and that, and the bone snapped in two. As usual, Scott got the larger half.

"I guess I should make a wish."

Gammy shook her head. "Not this time. Save it for when you need it."

He had no idea what she was talking about, but said, "All right," and held out his half to her so she could bury it.

"Keep it. We'll just bury my half this year." She knelt at the base of the sycamore, brushed away dead spiders, then dug in the earth with her rusty spade. When she'd made a hole big enough, she dropped her part of the wishbone in. She then scooped dirt back over the hole with her hand and patted it down with the spade. She stuck the spade into the earth point-first and left it there as she stood and wiped dirt from her hands.

"There, that's done."

Scott held up his half. "What am I supposed to do with this?"

"Put it in your pocket. Don't worry about it getting your pants all greasy. It's dry now."

Scott looked at the splintered half of the wishbone and saw Gammy was right. There was no more grease, no tiny shreds of meat clinging to the bone. It was dry and smooth, almost as if it had been polished. With a mental shrug, he stuck in into his pants pocket, expecting to feel the broken end poking into his skin, but he felt nothing. It was like the wishbone fragment had disappeared as soon as he had put it away.

"*Now* do we get to talk?" he asked.

"We do, but only for a minute." Her eyes filled with love and she reached up to touch his cheek. "It's not fair, you know. You had a hard stretch of road to travel to get where you are now, and there's an even harder stretch ahead of you, and you've done nothing to deserve it—nothing at all." She sighed. "That's just the way of things, I suppose, but that doesn't mean we have to like it, right?"

Scott wasn't sure what she was talking about, but he smiled. "Right."

She patted his cheek before lowering her hand. "Now I want you to listen to me very closely, Scott. What I'm going to tell you might just save your life and the lives of a lot of other folks as well, so work hard to get it fast in your mind so you remember it when you wake up, hear?"

He nodded solemnly. "Yes, ma'am."

"Good boy. Very soon there's going to come a moment when you have to make a choice. A hard choice. And when that moment comes, it's important that you—"

"Now, now. We don't want to give it away too early, do we?"

He stepped from behind the tree, bent down, grabbed the rusty hand spade, and in a single fluid motion, straightened and swept the metal end across Gammy's neck. Despite the spade's dull edge, there was enough strength behind the movement to tear open the old woman's throat. Blood geysered forth and Gammy fell back against the sycamore's trunk with a gagging sound, hands clasping her wound, trying to hold her life in. But it was like trying to hold back the ocean with a sieve. Blood ran through her fingers, over her hands, spattered onto her white blouse. Drops fell onto the ground, hitting several of the desiccated spiders. The blood revived them—bodies swelled, legs uncurled—and the arachnids began scuttling around excitedly, looking for more to drink.

Scott could only stare in shock as Gammy's eyes began to glaze over. Her mouth gawped like that of a fish too long out of water. He had the sense that she was trying to tell him something, to impart one last message, but the only sound that came out was a soft bubbling. From the way her lips moved, he thought she was trying to say *Be good*, but he wasn't sure. Then her mouth stopped working and she slid down the base of the tree and collapsed onto her right side. Instantly, the spiders her blood had revived swarmed over her, with more spiders swelling to life, eager to join in on the fun. Within moments, her body was covered by a blanket of squirming brown arachnids.

Numb, Scott turned toward his grandmother's killer and looked into the void of his nonexistent face. He wore his usual flannel shirt, jeans, and work boots. He held onto the spade, its tip still coated with Gammy's blood, and as

Scott watched, a spider scurried up the faceless man's leg, sprang onto the small shovel, and began to feed.

"I thought about manifesting in a pilgrim costume given the season, but I decided it would be a bit much. I think I made the right choice, don't you? I've always believed there's a certain elegance in simplicity."

Scott's shock began to turn to rage. "You motherfucking sonofabitch—"

"Such language! It's a good thing your grandmother's dead—again—and can't hear your potty talk. And don't think she's going to come back to give you advice the next time you go to sleep. I've taken her out of the game permanently this time."

Scott detected motion out of the corner of his eye. He turned to look at the house and saw that it was fading, becoming less real with each passing second. It was the same for the sky above them, the trees, and the spider-covered ground beneath their feet. Whatever this dreamscape was, it seemed that with Gammy gone, it wasn't going to last much longer.

Scott turned back to the killer, soul awash with grief and fury. "Why? Goddamn you to hell, *why?*"

"Simple. She and that little cooz you've hooked up with have been trying to destroy my Scotty-boy. And I won't let that happen." He raised the hand spade to his face, shook off the spider that clung to it, then touched the metal to the place where Scott presumed his mouth was. Bits of crimson vanished from the spade as if they were being licked off.

"After all, blood is thicker and all that." A grin in the voice. "Tastier, too."

Scott had no idea what the man meant by Gammy and Miranda intending to harm him. Miranda, maybe. Scott hadn't figured out what her agenda was, but ghost or not, there was no way his grandmother would ever try to hurt him. But he didn't give a damn about the faceless man's words. He grabbed a handful of the bastard's flannel shirt, made a fist with his other hand, pulled back his arm, ready to pound the holy shit out of the fucker. The sudden movement intensified the cramp in his gut, but he ignored the pain, was actually grateful for it; he could use it as further fuel for his rage.

"Whoa, there, boy!" He sounded amused. "If you're going to do this, do it right." He held the hand spade out to Scott. "After all, it would only be fitting to do me with the same tool I used to do in your sweet old Gammy, right?"

Scott hesitated, then let go of the man's shirt. He took the spade and gripped the handle so tight his knuckles ached. He'd never killed anyone before, but then he'd never been so angry before, either. Besides, this faceless thing wasn't a person, but whatever the hell it was, Scott knew one thing: It sure as shit deserved to die.

The world around them was beginning to fade completely, leaving behind a hazy grayish white fog, only somehow not as substantial. Scott knew he had only seconds to strike before the dream ended and his chance to avenge his grandmother had passed.

He raised the spade and prepared to bring it down smack in the middle of the swirling void the apparition had instead of a face.

"Before you do it, wouldn't you like to see who I am?" He gestured at his clothes. "And I don't mean this Riverton Ax Murderer get-up your psyche has clothed me in. I mean the *real* me."

Scott hesitated. He knew it was probably a trick, but the man's voice sounded so damn familiar . . .

"All right. But hurry it up." The nothingness was all around them now.

"It isn't up to me. I'm not hiding my face. You are. If you want to see me, you have to really *want* to see me."

Scott closed his eyes and pictured the void that concealed the killer's face fading like the dreamscape around them. Dissipating like a cloud of smoke in a strong breeze, burning off like early-morning fog scoured by sunlight. Only instead of leaving nothing behind, he imagined the man's features slowly being revealed.

He opened his eyes and saw the round, ruddy face of a man in his mid-fifties. Straight, greasy black hair, receding hairline, bald spot on top. Dark brows, thick nose, puffy skin under the eyes, thin lips, face covered with salt and pepper stubble, the beginnings of a double chin.

Scott knew that face. He'd seen it mostly in photographs while growing up, though he'd had occasion to be in its physical presence a few times over the years.

The thin lips stretched into a grin. "Well, aren't you going to say hello to your uncle?"

Laura Foster stretched languorously on the bed, like a cat lazing in a patch of warm sunlight. The musk of sex still hung heavy in the air, and she inhaled deeply, enjoying the pleasant ache between her thighs. She toyed with the idea of masturbating, but decided against it. Her experience with Scott had been so good that she didn't want to diminish it with a lesser, secondary orgasm.

She smiled as she thought of how he'd looked just before he'd stumbled out of her bedroom, his expression a mixture of physical satisfaction, confusion, and pain—and the latter was going to get a hell of a lot worse before it got better.

Serves him right, she thought. Especially after he'd interrupted last night's fun in the park and caused the death of several of her sweet, sweet children—including Jamey, her absolute favorite. She'd knocked on his apartment door early this morning, but he was gone, and she'd spent the rest of the day trying to track him down. She knew his scent, had since first meeting him on Sunday, but she'd still had the devil's own time finding him. It was as if another scent had interfered, one that was almost the same as Scott's, but not quite. She'd criss-crossed the town without luck, until she'd finally found him on the bridge, getting ready to do the good-bye cruel world bit. She'd almost let him, but that wouldn't have been nearly as much fun as what they'd ended up doing. Besides, she needed to replace those who were lost last night, and Scott was going to help her.

Can you say "poetic justice"? she thought, and grinned.

She was considering getting up and taking a shower when the bedroom door opened.

Surprised, she rolled onto her side and propped her chin on her hand.

"Back for more? I didn't think you'd be up to it right now."

He smiled, but there was no mirth or warmth in it. It was the smile of a predator baring its teeth.

"Oh, I'm up for all sorts of things."

She saw the knife in his hand. Watched him close the bedroom door and come walking slowly toward her. She didn't know whether to purr with delight or scream in terror.

Before it was all over, she did both.

Chapter Nineteen

Scott opened his eyes and immediately closed them again as pain twisted his gut. He reached for his lower abdomen and gingerly probed it with both hands, keeping his eyes closed so he could better focus on physical sensations. After several moments, he decided that everything felt normal enough, at least from the outside. Maybe he just had a touch of indigestion or constipation or something. Not that he'd had a lot to eat yesterday. In fact, he couldn't remember having any food since breakfast with Gayle and David.

He opened his eyes again, looked around, saw he was in his own bedroom. He knew he must've been completely ragged out when he came to bed, because normally he couldn't fall asleep with the light on. He threw back the sheet, then rolled onto his side and pushed himself up into a sitting position so he wouldn't have to use his abdominal muscles any more than he had to. He was naked and—he sniffed—he smelled funky. He remembered breakfast at McDonald's, the lobby hostess telling them about Jamey's decapitation, going home and watching a news report about the boy's death, getting that e-mail from Miranda, going to the grocery store in the hope of getting answers from her, being confronted by her manager (her *faceless* manager, he recalled), seeing all those dead women at the registers, running out of the store, driving around town confused and upset, and then . . . and then . . .

There's no need to pretend you're having trouble remember-ing, he told himself. *You just don't want to remember, do you?*

All right, then: listening to the phone message from Gayle about the restraining order, driving to the bridge outside town, parking, walking to the middle and climbing up on the railing. Preparing to jump and take his own life.

Don't avoid the word—it's spelled S-U-I-C-I-D-E.

He felt a certain distant shame at the thought, mingled with a touch of regret that he hadn't gone through with it, but that was all. Right now, he was more concerned with what had happened afterward. Laura Foster had driven up and talked him down from the railing. They'd gone to a bar, talked some more, had a few drinks (all right, more than a few), and had ended up driving separately back to their apartment complex, after which he'd gone to her place and they'd screwed like a pair of rabid weasels. To-ward the end, he'd had another hallucination—he winced as he remembered the spine protruding from her cunt and jabbing into his penis. It might have been an illusion, but it had *felt* real enough at the time, so much so that just the memory of it made him wince now.

Maybe that's why your gut hurts so bad, a voice whispered. *Maybe Laura put something inside you, just like the momma cricket in that book you read as a kid used her spike*—called the "ovipositor" he now recalled, and wasn't *that* just a lovely name?—*to put her eggs into the ground.*

Bullshit.

He remembered what Miranda had told him at the gro-cery. *Like most people, you've spent your entire life walking through the world wearing mental blinders, completely un-aware of the true nature of existence. I removed those blinders, and now you've begun to see things as they really are.*

If what Miranda said was true, then maybe—

His gut spasmed and he doubled over, sucking air through his teeth. He remained like that for several moments until the worst of the pain passed. Then he straightened and rubbed his hand lightly across his abdomen.

After leaving Laura's, he'd obviously come back here, though he had no memory of it. He did, however, recall the dream he'd had—Thanksgiving at Gammy's, the wishbone, her saying she had something important to tell him, being interrupted by the faceless man before she could impart her message, whatever it was.

At the thought of the wishbone, he reached into his right pants pocket, almost expecting to feel it there, but of course the pocket was empty.

He remembered the faceless man picking up the hand spade, using it to kill Gammy. Even though it had been a dream—but if what Miranda had told him was true, maybe it wasn't *just* a dream—the shock and grief he'd experienced at witnessing his grandmother die a second time had felt all too real. He remembered the faceless man becoming faceless no longer, revealing himself to be Scott's uncle from California. Uncle Leonard.

In some ways, that had been the weirdest part of the dream—weirder than feeling that he really had been somehow communicating with Gammy's spirit, weirder than her cryptic half-warning, than the yard covered with dead spiders and all the rest. Leonard Raymond was the only sibling of Scott's father, and he'd moved from Ohio to California before Scott was born. Scott had seen him only occasionally while growing up, a Christmas here, a birthday there. The last time he'd seen him was at his family's funeral, before Scott had gone to live with Gammy. Gammy had never said much about Leonard, though Scott had the impression she didn't like the man. A few years back, Scott had gotten a call from a lawyer informing him that Uncle Leonard had died from pancreatic cancer, and as his only living relative, he was due to inherit the man's estate, a whopping $3,563 dollars, all of which Scott and Gayle had put in David's college fund.

As to why an uncle whom Scott had barely known should figure so prominently in his dreams and hallucinations (he could almost hear Miranda say *Not hallucinations!*)—and why he should be tied at least superficially to the Riverton Ax Murderer—Scott had no idea. Just another kink in his completely distorted psyche, he supposed.

He glanced at the clock on his night stand. It was 6:06 on . . . he had to think for a moment. Wednesday morning. He wasn't sure what time Laura had to be at school, or even if there would be classes today after Jamey's death. But if she had to go into work, there was a good chance he still had time to catch her. He could confront her, demand that she tell him the truth about what had happened between them yesterday. Or, if he chose to be less insane about it and behave like a rational person, he could apologize for not spending the night with her, let her know he'd had a good time, that he hoped she had too, and maybe they could see each other again.

He went into the bathroom and relieved himself, and while washing his hands, he examined his reflection in the mirror over the sink. His hair was greasy and matted, and he was in desperate need of a shave. His mouth felt like it had been upholstered with cotton, and he was sure his breath smelled like the stench from an open dump. He didn't have time for a shower, not if he wanted to catch Laura before she left, so he stripped off his clothes and tossed them to the floor. He brushed his teeth quickly, then used a cloth to wash his face and underarms. He put on deodorant, then looked at his hair in the mirror and tried to decide what to do with it. He broke down and gave it a quick wash in the sink, banging the back of his head against the tap several times in the process. When he was finished, he dried it with a towel, brushed it, and decided he looked like a drowned rat with a faceful of stubble. It would have to do, though.

He went into the bedroom, put on fresh underwear and socks, a white button shirt and jeans. He found his tennis shoes in the living room, slipped them on, then grabbed his wallet and keys from the dining table. He checked the clock on the microwave: 6:27. It might be too late, but he was still determined to try. He walked out of his apartment, locked up, and started toward Laura's place.

It was the sort of morning that belonged on a calendar: the warm pinkish-orange of the rising sun coloring the east, the rest of the sky a bright, almost glowing blue. All the colors of the world seemed sharper, clearer, as if he were truly seeing them for the first time. *Of course. You're not wearing blinders anymore.* The thought didn't disturb him, though, and despite it—and despite the muted but still present ache in his gut—he felt almost cheerful as he reached 4A, Laura's apartment. He hesitated, then knocked.

No answer.

He figured he was probably too late, that she'd already left for school, but he knocked again anyway, a bit harder this time in case she was still getting ready, had the water running, maybe a radio going, and hadn't heard the first time.

The door opened a crack.

"Laura?"

Nothing.

He pushed the door open, realized it hadn't been closed all the way. In his drunken, sex-addled state, had he failed to shut the door on his way out last night? It looked that way, and evidently Laura hadn't noticed. She'd probably stayed in bed and slept through the night herself—after all, she'd had plenty to drink yesterday too. He felt awful. Ash Creek appeared to be a safe enough town on the surface, but he'd known ever since that night at the lake that surfaces could be deceiving. He hadn't needed Miranda to show him that.

She's all right, he told himself. She'd slept soundly and now was getting ready for work, because if she'd left, she would've shut and locked the door. This was a good thing; it meant he wasn't too late to talk to her.

He thought of the park, thought of the grotesquely bloated thing she'd become, thought of the ovipositor protruding from between her legs, and he wondered if maybe—just maybe—she'd purposely left the door open as some kind of trap for him.

He felt a strong urge to turn and walk away, to start running and keep running until he was miles from here, miles from Ash Creek, miles from everything and everyone, and even then he wouldn't stop running, he'd never stop, not even after his lungs caught fire and his heart exploded.

But he didn't run. Instead, he pushed the door open the rest of the way and stepped inside.

He listened for the sound of the shower running, the whirr of the bathroom fan, music blaring from a clock radio, early-morning chatter of local TV news. But the apartment was silent.

"Laura?" Again, no response.

Her apartment was laid out the same as his, though it was furnished more nicely, and there were paintings on the walls—prints of French Impressionists: Monet, Manet and the like, alongside framed theatre posters for *Cabaret, Sweeney Todd* and others—fresh-cut tulips (how very spring!) in a vase on the dining table. Her kitchen was clean, a few dishes in the sink, but that was all. The air smelled of potpourri and scented candles. Everything was as he remembered it from last night. Perfectly normal, if somewhat artificial, as if Laura had purposely staged her place to look like the apartment of a single high-school drama teacher.

He moved through the living room and down the hall toward the bedroom.

There was a new smell in the air now, one that he couldn't immediately identify, but then he recalled his dream of crouching naked in the forest before the equally naked body of a dead woman, the faceless man—no, *Uncle Leonard*—standing back and giving instruction. He remembered skinning the woman to his uncle's specifications, remembered being punished for getting an erection.

He knew the smell now: It was the stink of blood.

The bedroom door was half closed. He pushed it open and stepped inside.

Laura lay on her bed. From the tip of her chin down to her rectum, she'd been sliced open with surgical precision, her organs removed—though in many cases still attached—and placed to one side or the other of her body. Heart on the right, stomach on the left, a lung on each side, coils of intestine outlining her hips, legs, and feet. Her eyes were open and glassy, mouth wide as if she were still silently screaming. The bedclothes were drenched with so much blood it looked as if they'd been dyed crimson.

And as awful as all this was—and it *was* awful, Jesus bloody fucking Christ, was it *ever*—there was something worse yet. Sticking out from the open cavity between Laura's legs was the sharp tip of her ovipositor.

Scott's abdomen twisted in agony, as if whatever was inside him was responding to the violations done to its mistress. He bent over, stomach heaving, but all that came out was a thin drool of bile that dripped to the floor and made a tiny puddle that quickly soaked into the carpet.

He straightened and looked at the tableau before him, trying at once to both deny and accept the horrible reality of it.

"This is great . . . just great." The voice oozed sarcasm.

He turned with a start. Standing in the doorway, leaning against the jamb, arms folded across her chest, right hand wrapped in gauze, with a look of disgust on her face, was Miranda.

"You know something, Scott? You really are a pain in the ass sometimes."

Chapter Twenty

"Stop for a minute; I need to get a better . . . there! Okay, let's go."

Scott duck-walked backward, holding one end of a dead high school drama teacher wrapped in a blood-stained sheet, feeling as if his fingers were sinking through the cloth and into the flesh of the woman's shoulders. Miranda had hold of Laura's ankles—again; she kept losing her grip thanks to her wounded hand. Scott thought Miranda had the better part of the deal. The feet were far

enough away from the head that you could fool yourself
into thinking you were carrying something other than the
remains of a human being, like maybe a side of beef. But
Laura's head, hidden by the sheet though it was, was only
inches away from his crotch. Less than twenty-four hours
ago, her mouth had been all over his body, his genitals one
of her main stopping points. If he wasn't careful, the top of
her head would actually bump into his crotch as they carried her down the sloping path toward the river. He imagined her head swiveling on its neck to a degree impossible
in life, teeth tearing through cloth, gnashing at the air, eager to sink themselves into his pants and the soft flesh underneath.

Other than wobbling a bit in response to her bearers'
motions, Laura didn't stir beneath the makeshift shroud
kept tight on her body by a belt around her legs, another
around her waist—hands and wrists tucked underneath to
keep her arms from flopping about—and the sash of a robe
cinched around her chest. Being a true crime writer had its
advantages: Scott had written about so many killers over
the years that he knew dozens of ways to dispose of bodies. But that hardly meant he was comfortable with what
they were doing.

"We can't just 'get rid of her' like she's a troublesome piece of
trash! She's been murdered; we have to call the police!"

"And tell them what? That you slept with her yesterday, went
back to your place, woke up, decided to come back here to say
hi, and found her gutted on the bed? Who do you think is the
first person they'll suspect? I'll give you a hint: the man whose
DNA is all over her."

"But I didn't do it!" He didn't sound as confident as he
would've liked. He had been having dreams of stalking, killing,

and mutilating over the past few days. But he hadn't dreamed anything about killing Laura, he was sure of that. Besides, dreaming something and actually doing it were two different things. At least, they had been before he met Miranda.

She touched her hand to his cheek. "I know that. But believe me when I tell you this: If the police investigate, they will find only evidence that you were here—no one else. They will arrest you and charge you with the crime, and given your history of mental health problems—along with the fact that you've made a career out of writing about murder—prosecutors will have little trouble convincing a jury of your guilt. They might even manage to pin Jamey's death on you too."

Scott's abdomen still ached, but he ignored the pain. He grabbed Miranda by the shoulders and gave her a violent shake. "Everything in my life might not have been exactly normal before you came along, but it was a hell of a lot closer than it is now! You know what's going on, so tell me, and please skip the obscure mystic pronouncements for a change and give it to me in plain English, all right?"

Miranda glared at him and knocked his hands away. "I'm not God. If I knew everything, I would've come over here yesterday and stopped you before you climbed into bed with the Amazing Colossal Cunt. You gave them an opportunity"—she gestured at Laura's violated corpse—"and they used it against you." She slapped his abdomen and he grunted in pain. "And you managed to get yourself knocked up in the process! Smooth move, Scott. Don't you see? They want to frame you for Laura's murder, want you put away where you won't be a threat to them anymore."

His hands tightened into fists and he imagined them pounding into Miranda's face, breaking her jaw, crushing her cheekbones to powder. Hitting, hitting, hitting until she finally told him the complete truth. He actually raised his right hand a few inches, but then Miranda noticed the gesture, looked into his eyes, and he saw that she knew what he intended to do—despite her claim that she possessed no divinity—and she just stood there, waiting for him to make a decision.

He lowered his hand and relaxed his fingers. "Who are 'they,' Miranda? For that matter, who the hell are you?" He almost added, which Miranda are you: teen Lolita or little lost Miranda Tanner—or are you somehow both?

She looked at him for a long moment, as if trying to decide how much, if anything, to tell him. "You already know who one of them is. You saw him at your car the night we went for a walk, and it was he who killed Jamey, and who stopped me from talking to you at the grocery store. He's been walking in your dreams as well, trying to confuse you, to keep your Gammy and I from helping you."

Scott supposed he should've been surprised that Miranda knew about his dream visits from Gammy, but he wasn't. "At first he appeared as a faceless man dressed like the Riverton Ax Murderer, but in my last dream, I finally saw who he really was: my Uncle Leonard, my dad's brother. But what he has to do with the madness my life has become, I have no idea."

"It's simple," Miranda said. "He started it all."

Scott looked at her, not comprehending.

"It was him, Scott. That night at the lake. Your uncle was the man who murdered your family."

While it had been Scott's idea, Miranda did the actual work of replacing Laura's organs back in her body and crudely stitching her together with needle and thread from a sewing kit they found in the closet. Scott watched numbly as she worked with the calm, steady hand of a surgeon, finishing the job by putting staples all along the seam. When Miranda was done, she examined her handiwork with a critical eye.

"It won't last forever, but it'll do."

"We'll have to get rid of those, too," Scott said, nodding toward Miranda's tools.

She tossed the needle, thread, and stapler onto Laura's stomach, then went to the bathroom to wash, bringing back the wet, bloody hand towel to add to the items for disposal.

Scott knew there was no way they could clean everything up—the blood-soaked mattress would have to stay behind, and if they were going to leave it, there was no reason to do anything about the stains on the carpet.

"The point isn't to make it look like her murder didn't happen," Miranda said when he raised the issue, "but to destroy any evidence that might connect you to the crime."

His gut throbbed and he had trouble concentrating through the pain. But he was more than clear-headed enough to ask how she expected to carry Laura's body to his car in broad daylight without anyone seeing them.

"Remember how I told you most people are unaware of the true nature of existence? How they literally don't see the real world around them? At least, not the complete world."

"Blinders," he said, and she nodded.

"I can . . . help us move through a level of reality that most people refuse to perceive. We won't exactly be invisible, but we'll be something people prefer not to notice, so they won't."

Scott didn't intend to ask how such a thing was possible. He'd witnessed this other level of reality for himself over the past few days, though he desperately wished he hadn't. What he did want to ask was how *she* was capable of doing it. But the pain in his gut was too distracting, and besides, he was just grateful that Miranda was here, helping him, and that she knew what to do.

He remembered Uncle Leonard's words (Uncle Leonard the family-killer, and wasn't *that* a revelation he needed time to absorb?) regarding Gammy. *She and that little cooz you've hooked up with have been trying to destroy my Scotty-boy. And I won't let that happen.*

Maybe he shouldn't trust Miranda. She had fucked up his life in a major way since they'd met, and it was clear she had a *very* hidden agenda that she refused to share with him. True, she hadn't taken any direct action against him, but she'd placed in him dangerous situations, like the other night in the park. And for all he knew, Laura's death was just another part of whatever plan Miranda had, and his uncle—or his uncle's ghost or whatever the hell Leonard was now—had nothing to do with it.

But in the end he decided to trust her again for a simple reason: He didn't know what else to do.

So they had wrangled Laura's body into the trunk of his Subaru, as near as he could tell without anyone seeing them, and then Miranda returned to Laura's apartment to wipe away any fingerprints. When Miranda returned, she directed Scott to drive out of town to the river, not far from the bridge where he had tried to kill himself yesterday.

And now here they were, carrying Laura's body down a crude path toward the river, trying not to drop her, lose their footing, or both.

It was midmorning, and although the sun was well up in the sky, it did little to warm the early-April air. Scott wore a windbreaker, and even with the physical exertion of lugging Laura's body down the path, he was chilly. Miranda was dressed in her usual black, the outfit so familiar to Scott by now that he was beginning to think of it as a kind of uniform. She wasn't wearing a jacket and didn't seem bothered by the cool air, though from the way her nipples pressed stiffly against the fabric of her blouse, he knew she felt it.

Jesus Christ, here you are carrying the dead body of a woman you fucked yesterday—with the intention of finding a safe place to dump her—and you're checking out the stiffies on the teenager helping you! It was this, more than anything else that had happened so far, which made him think he had finally gone completely and irrevocably bug-fuck. He almost laughed, but he was afraid once he started, he'd never stop, so he bit his lower lip and kept shuffling backward, trying not to look at Miranda's breasts.

At least she hadn't noticed his scrutiny. She was too busy looking around, scanning the trees, the ground before them, glancing right then left, her gaze sweeping the area like a searchlight, and although her face was for the most part without expression, the way her eyes had narrowed and her lips pressed together made Scott think something was bothering her. But when he asked her if everything was all right, all she said was, "You bet. I always carry corpses down to the river on Wednesdays."

The trees were covered with leaf buds, but the limbs were still too bare to provide much concealment. They were far away enough from the bridge now that they shouldn't have to worry about anyone driving by and seeing them, though if what Miranda had said about her ability to "cloud men's minds" that shouldn't be a concern. Still, he felt more comfortable with every step they took farther away from the bridge.

Birdsong drifted on the air. Not a lot; spring was still a

few weeks away, after all, but what birds there were sang as enthusiastically as if the season were already here. They were accompanied by the sound of rushing water. The river sounded even more swollen and angry than it had yesterday when Scott had been preparing to jump into it, but perhaps that was only because he was closer to it now. And somewhere in the mix of sound, he thought he detected the strident drone of cicadas, but he knew that wasn't possible. It was way too early; the insects wouldn't be out until the beginning of summer, at least.

All in all, it was a pleasant morning to be disposing of a body, he thought, and he had to bite his lip even harder this time to keep the laughter at bay.

But the urge to laugh quickly died as fresh waves of pain pounded into his gut. He grunted and released his grip on Laura's shoulders. The top half of her body thudded to the ground as he doubled over and cradled his abdomen. Miranda shouted, "Hey!" as Laura's legs slipped out of her hands. The sheet-covered body began to slide down the path, and she grabbed for the feet before it could get too far away. She needn't have bothered, though; after sliding only a few feet, Laura's head came in contact with a large rock protruding from the earth—hitting with a nasty hollow sound like someone thumping a watermelon with their first—and although the head bounced up and over the rock, the left shoulder caught on it, stopping Laura's downward slide.

Scott was in too much pain to give a damn. Laura's corpse could shoot all the way down the hill like it was riding a goddamned log flume, flip up into the air and do a double gainer into the water for all he cared. His abdomen had hurt all morning, but that sensation had been nothing compared to this. It felt as if something were inside him, clawing at his organs with talons of flame. No, worse; it was like his intestines were possessed of their own separate life and were trying to tear themselves free of the body that had imprisoned them and forced them to process waste for so long.

He remembered what Miranda had said about allowing himself to get "knocked-up," and he thought he might scream. And then the pain doubled, and he did scream—long and loud.

Miranda was in front of him, her hands frantically working at his belt. A thought flashed through his mind—*This is hardly the time for that sort of thing*—and he tried to push her away, but he was in too much agony to put any real effort into his shoves, and she easily resisted. She got his belt undone, unsnapped his fly, pulled down the zipper, then yanked his jeans down around his ankles. She then grabbed the band of his underwear and pulled it down too.

Exposed to the air, his cock swelled like a puffer fish, instantly becoming rock-hard and purple. It felt like all the blood in his body had rushed to engorge his penis, and he wouldn't have been surprised if the damn thing popped like a blood-filled balloon any second. And if such an explosion would ease his pain, he would've welcomed it.

"It's all right," Miranda said. "You'll be okay in a couple minutes, just hold on."

He tried to focus on her, but his eyes were filled with tears, and her face looked like a watery pink blob with equally watery blonde hair on top. She took his hand, and his fingers tightened convulsively around hers. She gasped, and he knew he was hurting her, and he was sorry, but there was nothing he could do about it. He was no longer in charge of his body, had been reduced to nothing but a spectator. No, a passenger who had no choice but to go along for the agonizing ride, wherever it took him.

His penis began twitching, bobbing up and down in time with his pulse. His heart rate increased, and his cock responded, keeping pace until it was nearly a blur. And then the first spasm hit.

It wasn't orgasm, nothing even remotely like it. There was no pleasure, no rush of electric sensation flooding upward from his testicles, washing along the length of his penis until it exploded outward in a spray of semen. It was more like passing a kidney stone—something Scott had unfortunately experienced in his late twenties—but only if the stone was the size of a bowling ball and covered with spikes.

Blood jetted forth from the tip of his penis and something fell to the ground with a wet plap! He tried to look to see what it was, but another spasm hit, and he squeezed his eyes shut against the pain and bellowed like a wounded animal. He had to endure four more such spasms before consciousness mercifully fled, taking the pain with it.

But he wasn't out long. His awareness came swimming back almost at once, and he found Miranda was at his side, one arm around his back, another around his waist, supporting him. The pain was still there, but muted now, subdued. A distant dull throbbing instead of the sensation that someone was trying to ream his cock from the inside out with a fistful of broken glass.

"It's over," Miranda said, sounding relieved.

Scott's vision cleared enough for him to see a red pearl of blood well forth from the tip of his penis, grow larger, and then fall. His gaze followed the blood drop's descent into the mouth of a wriggling white creature the size of his thumb. It looked something like a maggot: pulpy white and legless, but it had a mouth filled with miniature shark teeth and its eyes . . . its eyes looked like those of a tiny doll. No, not a doll. A baby. A *human* baby.

The thing had five siblings that were busy cleaning up the blood that had accompanied their birth. It didn't take long, and when they were finished, they crawled down the path, toward the sheet-covered body of their mother.

For an awful moment, Scott thought the creatures were going to begin feasting on Laura's corpse, but they merely nudged her feet with their little round heads, then turned to look back up the path. It was impossible to tell, of course, for their eyes were so small, but Scott had the impression that the six wormlike things were giving him an accusing look. Then each emitted a tiny wail that sounded far too much like an infant's cry before leaving the path and crawling off in six separate directions. Despite their size they were fast and soon lost to view.

Scott turned to Miranda and struggled to say something, anything, but the best he could manage was, "Help me pull up my pants, would you?" before he passed out for real this time.

Chapter Twenty-one

"Too bad those things didn't eat her. It would've saved us some work."

They sat cross-legged on the ground, side by side, their backs to Laura's body, which lay ten feet away. While Scott didn't exactly agree with Miranda's sentiment, it *had* been quite a chore getting Laura's corpse this far, especially after . . . what had happened. The abdominal pain had diminished after he'd expelled the maggots (or whatever they were) but he was left feeling weak and nauseated, and they'd had to alternately drag and push the body the rest of the way down the trail. After what she'd done to him, Scott would've been more than happy to give Laura a good, hard shove and let gravity do the rest, if he'd had the strength.

But in the end they made it, though not to the river's edge as he'd first thought. Before they reached the water, Miranda directed him to turn onto a smaller side path that eventually led to a boggy area hemmed in by trees. They sat at the edge of the tree line now, looking out at the flat, wet, muddy ground and waiting, but for what, Scott didn't know, and for once, he really didn't want to ask. He was just grateful for the chance to rest.

The crotch of his jeans was damp with blood, but after he'd regained consciousness, Miranda had assured him that he didn't need medical treatment.

"You'll be sore as hell and piss blood on and off for the next few days, but you'll be okay."

Okay. The concept was laughable to him now. There was no okay, not for him, and there never would be again.

After a bit, when his nausea had subsided and he felt somewhat stronger, he asked, "What was she?"

He expected Miranda to give an evasive answer, if she answered at all. But she said, "A broodmother," then wrinkled her nose in disgust. "Nasty things, but quite common, really."

Scott resisted the urge to look over his shoulder at Laura's sheet-wrapped corpse. "Common?"

She gave him a small smile. "In the circles I travel in, yes."

"You mean that hidden dimension of existence you keep talking about."

She nodded. "Ever wonder why there are so many bad people in the world? People are who are just plain rotten through and through? Creatures like her make them. Not all of them, of course, but a lot."

He thought of the first time he'd encountered Jamey and his friends in the smoking area at the high school, thought of their sly, dangerous manner and of their tiny shark teeth. The same sort of teeth as those of the maggots he'd given horrible birth to.

"Those kids in the park . . . they were her children?"

"Yes. And she used you to replace the ones who were lost that night."

Scott shuddered as the image of a bloody gob ejecting from his penis flashed through his mind. "Why would anyone want to bring such awful things into the world?"

Miranda shrugged. "It's a broodmother's nature. Their children are parasites that feed on reality, break it down bit by bit in order to increase the sum total of entropy in the universe."

"That's horrible."

"They do what they do." She turned to look at him. "Besides, everything we do increases entropy, even just sitting here talking. There's nothing we can do about it."

"You make existence sound so hopeless."

"Oh, I believe in hope, or I wouldn't be here right now."

For a moment, he thought she said *couldn't* be here. "If broodmothers and their children are so dangerous, then why did you take me to the park the other night?"

She didn't answer right away. Instead, she turned to look out across the marsh once more, her foot tapping impatiently—or perhaps nervously—on the ground. "For the same reason I took you for that walk the first night after we met, and the same reason you've been having such strange dreams lately. It's important that you understand there's more to existence than what our five senses usually reveal to us. It's also important that you come to know the true nature of the darkness that infests reality."

"You make it sound like reality has a bad case of lice." When she didn't respond to his joke, he went on. "All right, you wanted to remove the scales from my eyes, and you've done so. But that still doesn't answer the ultimate question of *why?*"

She turned to face him once more, and for an instant, he thought she was actually going to tell him everything, but then she said, "I'm sorry, but you're not quite ready yet. You'll just have to trust that there's a good reason for everything that's happened to you."

Scott was incredulous. "Miranda, everything that you've done has been designed to teach me *not* to trust my perceptions, so how am I supposed to trust *you?*"

"Well, if you don't—or can't—trust me, then trust your grandmother."

"So you're telling me that Gammy really did visit me in my dreams?"

"Her spirit did, yes. We were . . . working together, I guess you could say. I was in this level of reality, she in hers. But she won't be of any further help to us now, not after what your uncle did to her."

He saw the hand spade slice through Gammy's neck, saw her blood fountain into the air.

"Is she dead? I mean, *really* dead. Hell, I don't know what I mean."

"The aspect of her spirit that allowed her to enter your dreams was destroyed. I'm afraid that's the best answer I can give you." She smiled. "Like I said before, I'm not God."

No, you just play with my life as if you were. "And Uncle Leonard is a ghost, too, right? So how can he be in both my dreams and in the real world?"

"He's a stronger spirit than your grandmother. During his life, he became aware of the dark side of existence and learned to walk there. He's very good at it."

"Better than you?"

Miranda didn't answer.

"I suppose I'm not surprised. Anyone who can murder his entire family would know more than a little about darkness." Ever since Miranda had told him that it had been Uncle Leonard who'd hacked his family to death that summer at the lake, Scott had been exploring that memory, trying to fit Leonard into the blank spaces the killer occupied, but no matter how hard he tried, he couldn't do it. It seemed that merely knowing Leonard was the murderer wasn't enough to restore his fragmented memory.

"So my uncle killed Laura."

She glanced sideways at him. "Not exactly."

He gritted his teeth in frustration. "Then who *exactly* did it? And don't tell me I'm not ready to know yet!"

Miranda said nothing.

"Jesus Christ!" Scott got to his feet. "You can't drag me into this . . . this"—He waved his hands in the air as he searched for the words—"existential cesspit and then only tell me what you think I should know! After everything that's happened—the dreams, the hallucinations, the deaths, the blood-drinking maggots shooting out of my cock—I deserve to know it all, and I deserve to know it right now!"

Miranda didn't look at him; she kept gazing out over the

bog. "You're right, you do deserve to know it all, and you will. But not now. If you knew the full truth too soon, it might . . . mess things up. You'll just have to—"

"Trust you, right. We've been over that. I'm fresh out of trust these days. I mean, shit, I tried to kill myself yesterday, and I probably would've succeeded too, if Laura hadn't come along. Was that part of your plan too? Did you want me to commit suicide? Or maybe you wanted me to go bed with Laura the Broodmother and end up fathering a litter of her wormy little children."

Miranda was silent, but a single tear rolled down her cheek.

"Nice touch. Tell me, is it real or just another trick to help 'expand my perception of reality'?"

She pressed her lips together and sniffed back more tears.

Scott came to a decision. "Look, whatever's going on here, I've had more than enough. My wife and son think I'm crazy, I almost jumped off a bridge, I'm in danger of becoming the number-one suspect in at least one murder and maybe two, and today I ejaculated a half dozen monster maggots. I'd say it's *way* past time to bring down the curtain."

The thrum of cicadas, which had been rising and falling in the background ever since they'd gotten here, now suddenly increased in volume and pitch. Except it didn't sound much like insect song anymore; it sounded more like whispering. Angry whispering.

Miranda jumped to her feet and took his hands. She looked alarmed and kept glancing from his face to the bog. "You can't do that, Scott! It'll ruin everything!"

He yanked his hands away. "I don't give a damn. I have to get out while I still have a few meager shreds of sanity left. I'm going to go home, pack my bags, get in my car and start driving until I run out of gas, at which point I'll fill the tank again and keep going, and I won't stop until I find a place where I can be as blissfully unaware of all the weird shit you call 'the dark side of existence' as every other poor schmuck on the planet!"

He turned to go, but she grabbed his arm and stopped him. "What about your grandmother? What about her sacrifice?"

He remembered her last attempt at words. *Be good.*

"Assuming what you told me is true, and not a load of metaphysical crap, I'm sorry for what happened to her, and I'm grateful for what she tried to do. But I can't believe she'd want me to continue suffering through this nightmare." He tried to pull away again, but Miranda held him fast with surprising strength.

The whispering was quite loud now, so much so that he had trouble hearing Miranda, had to focus on her mouth and half lip-read what she said.

"What about your uncle? Don't you want to confront him, find out why he killed your family? And more to the point, why he spared you?"

He did, actually. Those were the two questions that had haunted him for the last thirty years. But he wasn't going to let that change his mind. "Fuck him. And while we're on the subject, fuck you, too."

Out of the corner of his eye, he saw shapes rising forth from the murky substance of the bog. Human shapes, covered with mud and slime. The whispering was nearly deafening now, and he make could out two words being repeated over and over.

Stop him, stop him, stop him, stop him, stop him, stop him, stop him, stop him, stop . . .

"Then what about me?" Tears ran from her pleading eyes. "Don't you want to find out who I really am—learn what connection I have to the missing little girl whose name I share?"

He told himself not to look at the bog, not to look at the figures that were stepping free of the muck and beginning to stride toward them. Figures that looked like naked women, a dozen or more . . . and one that looked smaller, almost the size of a child. He especially didn't want to look at that one.

"No." He struggled to free himself, fighting harder than before because the women (and the smaller one he didn't want to think about) were coming closer, and they were raising their arms, reaching toward him, fingers curling and uncurling like the legs of some hungry crustacean.

Stop him, stop him, stop him, stop him, stop him!

And had Laura sat up and begun to claw at the sheet that covered her? He wanted to tell himself no, but he couldn't. With a last mighty heave, he managed to win free of Miranda's grasp, though he had the impression she had finally relented and let him go.

He turned to run, but before he could take a single step, Miranda shouted, "What about Gayle and David?"

He turned to face her once more, the advancing woman, their whispering, and Laura momentarily forgotten.

"What about them?"

"If you run away, they'll die, Scott." Her tears had stopped and she looked deadly serious. "They'll die in ways more hideous than you can imagine, and before they're gone they'll experience levels of agony and terror beyond human reasoning. If you stay, there's a chance you can save them. But if you leave, they're as good as dead."

Fear and fury surged through him in equal measures.

Fear for the safety of his wife and child, fury that Miranda would drag them into her twisted, dark game. He took a step toward her, intending to grab her, shout at her, hit her by God if he had to, whatever it took to make her tell him what he needed to know to keep Gayle and David out of all this.

But then he heard the sound of tearing cloth and Laura's corpse was free of its temporary shroud. The others had closed to within a few yards, and the hatred that blazed in their eyes was like a glimpse into the core of the sun.

Miranda turned to them. "It's all right, he's not going to go! He's going to stay and help us!"

The women—including Laura now, who approached from the opposite direction with puppet-jerky motions as if she were having trouble learning how to work her newly dead body—ignored her.

Stop him, stop him, stop him, STOP HIM, STOP HIM, STOP HIM!

Miranda ran toward Scott, and he thought at first that she had decided to join in the attack, but she pressed her hands on his chest and shoved him away.

"Run! I'll hold them off!"

Scott hesitated. Despite his earlier anger at Miranda, he didn't want to leave her alone with these apparitions.

As if sensing the reason for his reluctance to flee, Miranda said, "They won't hurt me, but if you don't go right now they'll tear you apart!"

That did it. Scott turned and ran like hell, barely managing to avoid a swipe from Laura as he went. His crotch throbbed as his feet pounded the ground, but he ignored the pain and kept going. And he didn't look back, not once, not even when he heard Miranda start screaming.

Chapter Twenty-two

His suitcase lay open on his bed, sitting lopsided atop mussed covers and sheets. The linens gave off a faint odor of sex and sweat, the aftermath of his time spent with Laura and the disturbing dream he'd had afterward. But Laura was dead now—a mental flash of her corpse clawing at him as he ran past—and his dreams didn't matter anymore. Whatever metaphysical psychodrama was playing itself out in Ash Creek would just have to go on without him. The legion of shrinks he'd seen over the years would no doubt accuse him of avoidance, and they'd be right, but that was fine and dandy with him. Sometimes avoidance was just another word for survival.

Underwear, socks, an extra pair of jeans, a half dozen shirts, toilet kit containing deodorant, toothpaste, toothbrush, floss, shampoo, electric razor, shaving lotion, aftershave . . . He'd changed his clothes after getting back from the river—they'd been filthy, the jeans especially—so that counted as another clean outfit. Good enough, he decided. There was no way he could take everything he owned— not that he had that much to his name. He only needed the bare essentials, and if he never came back to get the rest of his stuff (and right now he'd rather go skinny-dipping in a lake of molten fire than return to Ash Creek) so what? Material possessions could be replaced, but sanity wasn't so easily purchased.

He shut the suitcase, pressing on the top so he could

zip it closed. The suitcase was part of a set of luggage Gayle's parents had gotten them as a wedding present. This had been the only piece he'd taken with him when he moved out. Gayle had suggested he take a couple more pieces, but he'd refused. She had David to think about, and besides, she always took more stuff on trips than Scott did anyway.

He ran his fingers across the surface of the suitcase. The fabric was rougher than it appeared. Funny how he always forgot that, how he was always surprised when he touched it. There was probably a metaphor for his marriage in there somewhere, but he didn't feel like looking for it. Instead, he thought of what Miranda had said about Gayle and David.

If you run away, they'll die, Scott. They'll die in ways more hideous than you can imagine, and before they're gone they'll experience levels of agony and terror beyond human reasoning. If you stay, there's a chance you can save them. But if you leave, they're as good as dead.

More than one book critic had accused him of indulging in lurid prose, but he'd never overwritten anything that badly. Miranda really could use a good editor.

More avoidance, Scott?

Maybe. But whatever Miranda's ultimate goal was, it was clear it involved keeping Scott in Ash Creek until the bloody end, so to speak, so of course she'd say and do anything to keep him from leaving. As near as he could tell, she hadn't out and out lied to him yet, but she'd withheld the full truth from him, doling bits and pieces out as she thought appropriate. For Christ's sake, he didn't even know who—or what—she was. How could he trust her?

She told you to run, put herself between you and those women . . .

If he closed his eyes and listened, he could still hear the sound of her screaming.

Despite all the misery Miranda had caused him, Scott was worried about his Lolita. He told himself that she'd be okay, that whatever abilities she possessed would protect her. But he couldn't help fearing for her.

All right, so maybe Miranda had saved him—perhaps at a terrible cost. But that didn't mean she had told the truth about Gayle and David. Maybe they were in danger, maybe they weren't.

Do you want to take that chance? You love your son, don't you?

"More than my own life," Scott whispered.

And despite everything that's happened between the two of you, Gayle—for the moment, at least—is your wife, and while you might prefer it otherwise, you still love her too, right?

"Yes."

Then if there's even a chance that Miranda told you the truth, how can you run out on them?

Scott looked at his suitcase, tried to force himself to reach out, grasp the handle, and lift it off the bed. But he stood motionless.

So far as he knew, none of the weirdness that had infected his life had touched his wife and son yet. Yesterday at breakfast, they hadn't noticed the strangeness swirling around them. Their blinders were still intact and functioning perfectly, and he was thankful for that. No, *he* was the magnet, the focal point, the main attraction for whatever the hell was going on. And if he left, maybe all of it—Miranda and her zombie chorus, Uncle Leonard, and who knew what else—would follow him. He might not be able to escape the darkness, but at least he could draw it away from Gayle and David.

So we've chucked avoidance and moved on to rationalization now, have we?

Scott picked up his suitcase and walked into the living room. He stopped before his computer, which was still on. The icon in the bottom corner of the screen indicated that he had e-mail, but after yesterday, he wasn't about to open it. He grabbed the mouse and quickly went through the process of shutting down and turning off the machine. He hated to leave the computer behind. He always grew attached to the tools he used to write. In high school, it had been an expensive pen and pencil set Gammy had gotten for him one Christmas; in college, it had been a leather-bound journal that he'd purchased at the campus bookstore so he could feel self-consciously literary whenever he wrote in it. After that it had been an electric typewriter he'd used when he first started at the newspaper, then a computer, though one not as nice as this.

But there wasn't any point in taking this computer with him. It was bulky, and he had the feeling that he'd need to be traveling light from now on. Besides, he didn't think he'd be doing any writing soon. Thanks to Miranda, he'd had his fill of death and darkness for a while—maybe for his entire life. And after everything he'd experienced over the past few days, writing about ordinary rapists and killers seemed almost childish.

He debated whether to take his backup disks with him, though. Those several dozen floppies contained the text of every article and book he'd written as a freelancer: his life's work so far. And even though writing held no attraction for him now, it might again someday.

He stood before his computer for several minutes before finally deciding screw it. If he ever wrote again, he'd start fresh, maybe even write about something other than crime for a change.

He started for the door, but out of habit he glanced at the answering machine and saw the message light was blinking. He decide to ignore it. The last thing he needed right now was a message from Miranda or worse, from the ghost of Uncle Leonard. But if Gayle needed to get in touch with him, she'd use the phone. After her message yesterday about the restraining order, he doubted she'd call again, at least not so soon. But just in case . . .

He walked over to the machine and pressed the message playback button.

"Mr. Raymond? This is Stewart at Showcase Video. Our computer shows that you have several tapes overdue. If you could return them at your earliest convenience, we'd appreciate it. Thank you."

The machine clicked off. He'd had only the one message.

Scott felt a bit let down at the mundane message, and he laughed at his own reaction.

"You're pathetic. You should be happy it wasn't another cryptic pronouncement about hidden forces and unspeakable dooms."

He didn't give a damn about the videos. There were only three, all true-crime documentaries he'd rented late last week for research, before all the weirdness with Miranda had begun. He hadn't had a chance to watch them, and now he never would, not that he cared.

But he'd paid for them with a credit card that he still shared with Gayle. He'd meant to get his own card after moving out, but he'd never gotten around to it. The card was in her name, so the bill would be mailed to her. He'd planned to give Gayle a check to cover the items he'd charged to the account, but he hadn't yet. That meant if he didn't return the videos, the late fees would keep racking up, and Gayle would end up responsible for them.

This is so lame. You're about to flee for your life and sanity, and you're standing here worrying about late fees?

He supposed it *was* kind of dumb, but it was comforting in a way, too. Maybe there were things like broodmothers and their sharp-toothed children in the world, but there were also boring, everyday things like video rental late charges.

It was out of a need to connect to such ordinary, safe things—if only for a moment—that led Scott to walk over and pick up the videos off the top of the television.

The first was called *World's Slickest Cons and Scams*; the second was *Blood on the Highway: Carjackings, Road Rage, and Vehicular Manslaughter*; and the last was *Killers in Shadow: The Worst Serial Murderers in U.S. History*. The cover of the latter showed pictures of four of the serial killers profiled in the tape: John Wayne Gacy, Jeffery Dahmer, Ted Bundy and . . .

Scott stared at the cover of the video box. The fourth killer was supposed to be Ed Gein. It *had* been Gein when he'd rented it. But now there was another picture in Gein's place.

A picture of Scott Raymond.

He fast-forwarded through the tape until he reached the segment he was searching for. He watched it once, then he watched it again. When he finished, he turned the TV off and sat on the couch for almost an hour, staring at his reflection on the blank screen. Finally, he turned the set back on and watched·the segment a third time.

Images and words struck him, seeming even less real now than they had the first two times.

A photo of him and Uncle Leonard. Scott was thirteen, maybe fourteen. The announcer's voice that of a cooly dispassionate woman with a slight English accent.

Raymond's grisly career began under the tutelage of Leonard Raymond, his uncle, who—although authorities have never been able to prove so conclusively—is believed responsible for a string of serial killings in California during the nineteen seventies. Dubbed "the Surgeon" by the press because of the precise, clinical incisions made on his victims, this killer took the lives of at least fourteen women, and perhaps many more, before the last of the Surgeon's victims was discovered in nineteen seventy-eight: the same year that Scott Raymond came to live with his uncle. Many authorities believe that Leonard Raymond gave up his solo career at this point and took on his nephew as a protégé, schooling him in the dark art of killing. And Scott Raymond proved to be an eager and talented pupil indeed.

A snatch of home video of a young woman in her twenties, walking across a college campus in a white sweater and plaid skirt.

This woman—Nancy Miller—is believed to be the first of Scott Raymond's victims. She disappeared in September of nineteen eighty and was found a month and a half later in the forest by a pair of hikers. While the county medical examiner would later determine she died of strangulation, her corpse was discovered skinned from head to toe. Her skin was never located.

More women . . . three . . . eight . . . sixteen . . . until he couldn't bear to continue counting. Each mutilated in a different way after death.

Raymond's penchant for invention—unique among serial killers, most of whom stick to a particular modus operandi— earned him the nickname of "the Artiste." Some authorities speculate that Raymond's versatility was taught to him by his uncle as a method to confuse police and prevent his killings from being linked. Others, including the psychologist who interviewed Raymond after his capture in nineteen ninety-eight, believe that he grew bored and developed a taste for ever-greater depravities in an attempt to satisfy his unquenchable lust for killing.

A man in his sixties sitting behind a desk. Wire-frame glasses, pronounced bald spot in the middle of his white hair, wearing a business suit and projecting a scholarly manner.

"The case of Scott Raymond is a very interesting one, for it begs a central question: are such human predators born or are they made? On the one hand, the fact that two serial killers should be so closely related—uncle and nephew—would seem to indicate they shared a genetic propensity for murder. But on the other hand, there is no record of Raymond committing anything even approximating a crime before he came to live with his uncle. His school records indicate that he had a temper. He'd occasionally snap at his teachers, get into tussles on the playground. In the sixth grade, he even broke a boy's collarbone in a fight. But while these incidents are suggestive, they in no way form a clear pattern, they do not create a picture of a young boy on the road to becoming a notorious serial killer.

"So again, we're forced to return to the age-old question: Was it nature, or was it nurture? Or perhaps a little of both?"

A picture of a small two-story house in a modest suburban neighborhood.

In nineteen eighty-three, Leonard Raymond was found dead at the home he shared with his nephew. Of all Scott Raymond's killings, this one was the most horrific.

A police officer in his fifties. Jowly, uniform too tight, roll of flab hanging over the collar, brown mustache in need of trimming.

"We didn't find a body, per se. What we found were . . . pieces, I guess you could say. None of them larger than a man's thumb, not even the bones. They were placed all over the house. Some were out in plain sight, others we had to . . . search for. We found an eye in a pickle jar in the refrigerator, a toe in the toilet tank, that kind of thing. It was like a madman's idea of hide and seek. We searched for nearly three days, and we're still not sure we found everything. In the end, the county had the house burned down and the ruins bulldozed. It's still a vacant lot. No one wants to build on it, you know? In case any of the pieces are still there, buried beneath the ground."

The announcer's voice again.

Raymond's bloody rampage came to a temporary halt when he was captured by authorities in nineteen eighty-eight, ten years after first coming to live with his uncle.

A stack of legal pads resting on a table. Twenty of them, maybe more.

Like many serial killers, Raymond wrote about his murderous activities in order to relive them later. Police found these notepads, and many more like them, when they searched Raymond's apartment in Grover Beach, California. Though filled with strange, dreamlike fantasies, authorities were able to separate fact from fiction enough to create a reasonably accurate portrait of Raymond's career as the Artiste.

The psychologist again.

His writings were often incomprehensible. Along with details of specific murders—complete with elaborately rendered maps of crime scenes that were of great help to police—he wrote about a delusion he had that there was a separate dimension co-existing with what most of us regard as reality: a dark, nightmarish place. He claimed his uncle had ushered him into this world, and that he could travel through it as easily as you or I might walk down a street. Serial killers often believe they are superior beings with special powers, but Raymond's fantasy was more unique than most. He wrote that this ability to step into another aspect of reality—an aspect the rest of us are for the most part completely unaware of—was his greatest strength as a predator and had helped him elude capture for so long."

Announcer.

This notion of a shadow world is clearly the product of a lunatic mind. And yet, when Scott Raymond escaped from a high-security cell only days before his trial was due to begin—a feat authorities insisted was impossible—some began to wonder: what if it wasn't a delusion? What if Scott Raymond could walk in shadow . . . and what if he walks there still?

Scott hit the STOP button on the VCR remote and stared at the television screen once more.

None of that had happened—and yet, according to the tape, it had. He wanted to believe the video was some sort of elaborate joke, maybe a fake Miranda had concocted as another move in the strange game she was playing. Or maybe it was just another hallucination?

No . . . he no longer believed he'd been hallucinating these past few days. He believed that what he had seen—all of it—was real, in its own fashion. And if that were the case, then this tape was real, too. It was like he'd somehow rented a video from a parallel world, one where he'd grown up to be a serial killer instead of a neurotic true-crime writer.

He remembered the dream he'd had of mutilating the

dead cat in Gammy's back yard. Remembered what she had told him.

There's a battle going on, Scott. A war between what is and what-might-have-been . . . each individual's existence is like a road stretching out before them. Sometimes this road is straight, sometimes it's curvy and twisty, and sometimes it takes unexpected turns. But these roads have . . . well, I suppose you could call them side roads that branch off from the main one. These branches represent all the different paths a person's life might take, if only one or two things were changed.

Sometimes, though, the branching off points are so close together, the circumstance that makes one or the other of them become real so minor, that both exist. And that's what's happened to you, Scott. You've become two different people living two different lives at the same time. But in the end, only one life path, one you can be the real one. And that's what we're fighting for—to see which one of you survives.

He remembered something his uncle had said about Gammy and Miranda.

She and that little cooz you've hooked up with have been trying to destroy my Scotty-boy. And I won't let that happen.

His Scotty-boy. The one he had raised and turned into a killer. Scott's other, shadow self.

"No." The word was barely more than a whisper. Sure, he was attracted to darkness, fascinated by it, but only to the point of writing about it. He'd never felt any actual desire to kill. No matter what, he could never become the Scott Raymond on the videotape.

How often do you get angry? Your fingers curling into fists, hands eager to lash out and strike a blow. How often do you imagine wrapping those hands around the throat of the person who inspired that anger and squeezing the life out of them? How often do you think about doing something even worse?

Those were just thoughts, just feelings. Not actions.

How often did you get mad at Gayle and David? Yell at them? Grab them? Shake them?

Never hit. Never that.

But you wanted to; it was inside you.

Yes.

If there's a spark, then a flame is possible, isn't it?

Nature versus nurture, the psychologist on the tape had said. Scott had to admit he possessed the former—a core of anger burning within him—but it seemed his other self also had experienced the latter, in the form of dear old psychotic Uncle Leonard, a.k.a. the Surgeon.

The idea was insane . . . but then again, no more insane than anything else he'd experienced since Miranda had come into his life. So if it was true—and for the moment he was willing to at least pretend that it was for the sake of argument—the question before him was a simple one: What the hell was he supposed to do now?

He didn't have a clue—but he knew who did.

Miranda.

He was about to get up from the couch and go look for her when someone knocked on his door.

Chapter Twenty-three

Scott went to the door and peered through the Judas hole. He saw a fish-bowl image of two uniformed police officers—one male, one female. While he looked, the man knocked again, causing Scott to jerk his face away from the peephole.

His first thought was that this visit had something to do with the restraining order Gayle had taken out on him. Maybe the officers were acting as agents of the court and had come to serve him papers. He had no idea what the process for instituting a restraining order was, though; everything he knew about the law pertained to crimes like murder and abduction. His second thought was much worse: something had happened to Gayle and David, something terrible. The hideous fate Miranda had forecast for them had already come true.

Fear pierced his heart like a spear of ice. *Please, God . . . let them be okay.* He wasn't sure he believed in the possibility of a benevolent, not to mention sane, deity anymore, but he had to pray to someone or something, and his vague childhood concept of God—a wise, elderly man with a long white beard who was something of a cross between Santa Claus and Merlin the magician—was all he had to fall back on. He unlocked and opened the door.

The man spoke first. "Scott Raymond?"

The male officer was in his mid-thirties with short black hair that was almost but not quite a buzz cut. His face was squarish, eyes intense, lips pursed in what seemed to be permanent disapproval of the world and everything in it. He stood several inches taller than Scott, and while he wasn't exactly Mr. Universe, he was fit enough.

"Yes," Scott answered, feeling like he was somehow confessing to a crime merely by admitting his identity. After seeing that videotape, perhaps he was.

Then it was the woman's turn. "Sorry to bother you, but we need to ask you a few questions." She didn't sound sorry at all. For that matter, she didn't sound much of anything: her voice was almost completely devoid of emotional inflection. Her eyes were narrowed with cold, calculating suspicion, and Scott could imagine machinery working behind those eyes, relays clicking away like mad as she took in and processed information. She was shorter than her partner, the top of her head barely reaching past his shoulders. Her hair was brown and curly and fell to the nape of her neck. Her face was round, nose thin and long but not patrician enough to be called aquiline. Her lips were bloodless, the same pale color as the rest of her face, making it seem as if they were subsiding into the flesh around her mouth and would be gone entirely before long.

It was drizzling out—April showers, and all that—and both officers were dotted with beads of water. The droplets clung to skin, hair, and uniforms, but didn't slide down their faces, didn't soak into their clothing. It was almost as if they were covered with tiny globules of glass instead of water.

The two officers were silent for a moment, and Scott realized they were waiting for him to respond. "I was just about to go out, but I'll be glad to answer whatever questions you have." *That's right: you're a reasonable, cooperative citizen. Busy, but not too busy to help out the good old men and women in blue.*

The man glanced past Scott's shoulder and into his apartment. "You work at home, Mr. Raymond?"

Scott wondered why he'd asked. Then again, it *was* a weekday afternoon and most people were at work. "Yes, I'm a freelance writer." *And please don't ask me what I write.* The last thing he wanted to tell these two was that he made his living by writing about the sort of crimes they were sworn to prevent and, failing that, help punish. In his experience, cops reacted one of two ways to him: They either thought what he did was cool and told him every anecdote garnered over the course of their careers, each less interesting than the one before, or they viewed him as a vulture who exploited the misery of victims for a fast buck.

"That sounds interesting," the woman said. "You make good money?"

"Depends on what you mean by good, but I get by."

The man nodded. "How long have you lived here?"

"In this apartment? A few weeks."

"You know your neighbors well?" the woman asked.

Neighbors? Nausea roiled in his gut, accompanied by a strange fluttery feeling, almost as if the spider Miranda had given him to ingest the other night was still in his stomach, flailing around in a bubbling pool of acid.

He understood then that these two police officers weren't here to talk to him about Gayle and David. They'd come to ask him about Laura Foster.

His pulse was suddenly racing, and he fought to keep his voice calm. "I'm acquainted with a couple, but just well enough to say hello when we pass, maybe exchange a few words about the weather when we run into each other in the laundry room. I don't even know most of their names." *Careful,* he warned himself. *Don't want to lay it on too thick.*

The man, whom Scott was starting to think of as Square-Head, sniffed the air, nostrils flaring wide. He took in a deep lungful of air and held it for a moment. He looked thoughtful, as if some internal mechanism were scanning the air in his lungs, breaking it apart and classifying each molecule. Then he slowly released his breath, looking at Scott and frowning slightly as processed air passed between his lips.

Scott realized he hadn't showered since returning from the river (*you mean fleeing in terror from the river, don't you?*) and he feared the officer could smell the stink of Laura's corpse on him. But that was ridiculous. Even if such an odor did cling to him, no human had a nose sensitive enough to detect it.

The woman—whom he'd mentally dubbed "Machine Eyes"—took her turn. "Do you know a Laura Foster?"

Here it was: The Question. Scott knew he had to play this one just right. He was going to lie, of course; he could hardly come out and say, *Laura Foster? She's the woman who turns into a giant vagina and impregnates men with humanoid maggots, right?* But how big a lie should he tell? Should he deny knowing her, or should he admit to a casual acquaintance? He supposed it all came down to which response would placate the officers, and so far he hadn't been able to read either of them well enough to get a sense of which way to go.

His mind flashed back through hundreds of different criminal cases he'd researched during his career as a writer. How did all the serial killers, mass murderers, spree killers, rapists, abductors, hit men, child pornographers, and terrorists he'd ever written about answer when they were faced with The Question?

But in the end, the thought that guided him most was this: How would Uncle Leonard respond?

"Sure, she's a drama teacher at the high school. Lives a couple buildings over, in 4A. Did she do something wrong?"

Square-Head ignored Scott's question and instead asked another of his own. "When's the last time you saw Ms. Foster?" His nostrils flared again, as if he hoped to determine the accuracy of Scott's reply through smell alone.

Scott pretended to think about it for a few seconds. "Sunday, I guess. I was having a smoke over by the pool when she came by. She'd just got back from the grocery.

We talked for a couple of minutes until I finished my cigarette, then we both went back to our apartments."

"What did you talk about?" Machine Eyes asked.

"I can't really remember in much detail. It was just small talk, you know? I asked her how school was going, she asked me how my writing was going. That sort of thing."

The two officers nodded in unison, reminding Scott of those plastic dogs with the up-and-down bobbing heads that some folks put in the back window of their cars.

"And you haven't seen or spoken to her since?" Square-Head asked.

"No. Why, has something happened to her?" He didn't want to ask that, but he knew it was a logical thing for a concerned if not particularly involved neighbor to ask, so he went ahead.

"She didn't show up at school today," Machine Eyes said. "And she didn't call in sick. When the principal phoned her house, there was no answer. The principal became concerned because, according to him, Ms. Foster is rarely sick, and when she is, she always calls in."

Scott felt his facial muscles working toward a frown, and he concentrated on keeping them relaxed. Machine Eyes was telling him an awful lot, which he found odd. In his experience, police vastly preferred getting information over giving it.

Square-Head picked up his partner's thread. "The boy that was murdered in the park Monday night was one of Ms. Foster's students, making her sudden absence seem more suspicious than it ordinarily might."

He almost asked, *Do you think the murder and her absence are connected?* but he stopped himself in time. Criminals often made the mistake of asking for too many details when being questioned by police—either because they wanted to find out how much the police knew or because they got off on listening to cops talk about a crime they themselves had committed.

So instead, he said, "I hope she's okay."

"So do we," Machine Eyes said, and then both of the officers smiled.

Those smiles—twin mouthfuls of tiny shark teeth—hit Scott like a punch to the throat. He remembered what Miranda had said about Laura back at the river.

Ever wonder why there are so many bad people in the world? People who are just plain rotten through and through? Creatures like her make them.

Square-Head and Machine Eyes were the get of a brood-mother, perhaps even of Laura herself. She didn't—*she's dead; use past tense*, he thought—hadn't appeared to be old enough to be their dam, but Scott doubted appearances meant very much when it came to creatures like these. And now the two of them were standing before him, displaying their teeth and waiting for him to respond.

People—normal people, that is, people who hadn't had their psychic blinders forcibly stripped—would take no notice of those teeth. Oh, they'd see them, but they wouldn't actually *see* them. Scott knew there was only one way to play this: He had to pretend he was still one of the blind. If it hadn't been for everything he'd seen since meeting Miranda, not to mention several decades of trying to keep his rag-doll psyche from coming apart at the seams, he wouldn't have been able to do it. But he'd had more than a little experience at presenting a facade of sanity to the world, and he fell back on that experience now.

He kept his expression neutral, made sure he breathed normally. He smiled himself—sane people met smiles with one of their own, right?—but not too big a smile. After all, they were talking about the possible disappearance of one of his neighbors.

"Is there anything else I can do to help?"

Machine Eyes and Square-Head didn't speak or even glance at one another, but Scott nevertheless had the impression that they were conferring on some deep, hidden level that he was unaware of.

"No, you've been most cooperative," Square-Head said.

"If you think of anything else, please call the station and let us know," Machine Eyes added.

"I will." Scott had questions of his own: *Have you gotten the apartment manager to let you into her apartment yet? Have you searched it? Have you found the bloodstains?*

The officers bid him good day, Scott replied in kind, and he closed the door as they turned and began walking away. He hesitated, then pressed his face to the door and peered through the Judas hole. The two cops didn't head for any other apartments so they could continue questioning residents. Instead, they continued walking through the complex toward the parking lot. They were leaving.

When they were lost to sight, Scott stepped away from the door. All the emotions he had suppressed during the questioning caught up with him, and he began shaking uncontrollably. He went into the living room, sat down on the couch and waited until the tremors passed. It only took a few minutes, but that was more than enough time for him to think. He supposed it was possible that he was the last resident the police—if they really *were* police—had questioned, but even though he now lived in a world where things like broodmothers and dream visits from dead relatives occurred (which meant he'd come to believe that just about *anything* was possible), he doubted it. Something had drawn Square-Head and Machine Eyes to him. Perhaps some instinct their kind possessed, or perhaps something as simple as Square-Head's sense of smell. His scent was probably all over Laura's apartment, or at least her bedroom. But whatever the reason they had come, they evidently hadn't been able to tie him to Laura's murder, at least not strongly enough to act. Yet. But they'd be back, that was certain, and he was determined not to be here when they did.

He got off the couch and headed for the door, more determined than ever to find Miranda—if she was still alive.

Chapter Twenty-four

Scott made his way carefully down the sloping hill that led toward the river's edge. The rain, light though it was, had made the ground muddier than when he had been here earlier with Miranda. He descended sideways, taking a step, then testing his footing to make sure it was solid before taking another, holding on to the small, thin limbs of undergrowth to steady himself as he went.

His wet hair was plastered to his head, and while his windbreaker kept the worst of the water off his chest and arms, his pants were soaked through and his feet squished in his shoes. His hands were covered with red scratch marks from grabbing at the undergrowth, and the back of his left hand had taken a particularly nasty slice from a thorn bush. Blood dripped steadily from the wound, but Scott barely registered it. He was too focused on getting down the hill and finding his way back to the marshy area where he and Miranda had dumped Laura's body.

At first, he'd been afraid to return here. Not so much because of what he might find—Miranda's body lying on the ground, torn and twisted beyond recognition, her killers floating beneath the surface of the muck that concealed them, patiently waiting for the chance to tear into *his* flesh—though Christ knew that was bad enough. He'd been more afraid that when he reached the bridge, he'd discover a police car already parked there: a car that belonged to Square-Head and Machine Eyes who'd backtracked his scent from the apartment complex to the river. But when he reached the bridge, he'd been relieved to discover it empty. He'd considered trying to find another place to park, somewhere he might be able to conceal his car in case the two shark-toothed cops came sniffing around. He'd crossed the bridge and continued driving for a quarter mile in search for a suitable hiding place, but without success. He returned to the bridge and parked in the same place he had yesterday before his aborted suicide attempt. If Machine Eyes and Square-Head found his car, then they did. At least this way he'd have it relatively close by in case he needed to get the hell out of here in a hurry.

As he continued down the hill, he kept a close eye out for his new "children." *David, I have some good news and some bad news: The good news is you have six half siblings; the bad news is they're vampire maggots.* But though he heard (or thought he heard) rustling in the bushes from time to time—rustling that seemed to be keeping pace with him as he descended—he saw nothing. All to the better; he was hardly in the mood for a family reunion just now.

When he reached the point where the trail curved away

from the river, his feet slipped out from under him and he fell onto his left side. He began sliding downward, and he might have continued all the way to the river if he hadn't caught hold of the trunk of a small tree. He lay there for a moment, holding on to the tree and breathing hard, thinking that it might be easier to just let go and slide down to the water, let the current take him and be done with it. But that wouldn't help Gayle and David. Besides, from what he'd seen so far, even death might well not provide an escape from the madness that had engulfed his life. For all he knew, dying might even make things worse.

With that cheery thought in mind, he got to his feet and continued following the curving path Miranda and he had taken to the marshy area, ignoring the new ache in his left hip and the renewed throbbing in his penis. The damn thing was probably bleeding again, too, but he didn't care. All he cared about was finding Miranda and finally having his questions—*all* of them—answered.

After another ten minutes, and two more falls, Scott came across a red-stained sheet lying crumpled on the ground: Laura's makeshift shroud. He was back.

He looked around. No Miranda, no naked zombies.

He wasn't sure it was a good idea to call out—especially if his wormy offspring were around and hungry—but he did anyway, first speaking, then shouting Miranda's name, pausing to listen for a response, yelling once more when he received none. He had no idea how many times he'd called her name, but eventually his voice began to grow hoarse, so he stopped.

She wasn't here.

Not necessarily. She may be here but not able to answer. It's kind of hard to speak when you've been torn into a thousand pieces, you know.

Scott hated the thought, but he knew at its core it was true. If Miranda were dead, he needed to know. He started combing the area, looking for any sign of what might have happened to her. He found several patches of ground that appeared as if they might have been soaked with blood, but he wasn't sure. The ground here, which had already been wet enough to begin with, had been washed almost clean by the rain. He might be looking at nothing more than dark mud.

The last patch of ground he inspected was near the edge of the bog. There was only one place left to look now. He stood and stared out at the muck.

They came from there; they might have taken Miranda back with them.

So what was he supposed to do? Go wading in the Swamp of the Damned? And what would he do if the women attacked him? He had no weapons—not that he imagined a gun or knife would prove effective against whatever they were. And while he didn't know for sure what they wanted, it was clear that they had an intense interest in him. They'd manifested to Scott often during the last four days: sometimes physically, sometimes as merely a chorus of whispers. He felt if he could just figure out what the hell it was they wanted from him, he might have the key to it all.

What was it Miranda had said when they'd attacked? *It's all right, he's not going to go! He's going to stay and help us!*

He remembered the hatred in the women's eyes—hatred for him—remembered how the women had responded, their voices a cacophony of shouts this time: *Stop him, stop him, stop him, STOP HIM, STOP HIM, STOP HIM!*

Miranda had said they wouldn't hurt her, but the way she'd screamed . . .

He had a terrible thought then. What if, like Laura, Miranda had joined the ranks of the naked dead? What if she too would rise forth from the muck and come toward him, hands outstretched, fingers bent into claws, eager to tear the flesh from his bones?

No matter how you looked at it, walking into the bog was a bad idea. If Miranda's body was in there, it would just have to rest in peace, or in pieces, as the case may be. There was no way he was going to—

The surface of the bog began to ripple, as if large sleek shapes were sliding beneath the muck toward him.

Scott realized that while wading into the bog would have been stupid beyond belief, standing at its edge and mentally debating what to do for so long hadn't exactly been an act of genius either.

His first impulse was to run—and a mighty fine impulse it was, too—but instinct told him that he'd be lucky to take three steps before the first hand burst out of the sludge and wrapped its fingers around his ankle.

Instead, he did the only thing he had time for. He said, "I'm going to help you." As soon as the words passed his lips, he was surprised to discover that he meant them.

For a second, the ripples continued toward him and he waited for the women to begin rising from the muck—*Please, don't let Miranda be one of them*, he thought. *Give me that much*—but then the ripples subsided and the surface of the bog became still once more.

He stood there for a few moments, waiting, but nothing more happened. After a bit, he said softly, tentatively, "Miranda?"

A second ticked by, another, and then small shapes pushed upward from the bog. At first they looked like the backs of a dozen tiny turtles, but as the muck slid away, Scott saw that they were mouths. Women's mouths. Lips parted and two words were whispered in chorus.

Not here.

A serpent of ice coiled around Scott's spine and squeezed. He was actually communicating with them. The thought half-thrilled, half-nauseated him.

"Where is she?"

The mouths were silent. Either they didn't know or they weren't telling. Or maybe they simply didn't want to make it too easy on him.

"All right then. I'll go look elsewhere." He backed away from the bog's edge, unwilling to turn his back on the mouths. Just because the women were talking to him directly didn't mean that they were suddenly his friends.

The sheet.

He stopped and turned to look at the bloody sheet, expecting to be confronted with some awful surprise— maybe Laura would be standing wrapped in it, or worse, Miranda. But the sheet lay where he'd first seen it, still empty.

He turned back to the bog, puzzled.

"What about it?"

Give it to us. Before they come.

Scott wasn't sure what they meant. Evidently, being dead didn't improve one's ability to communicate clearly. Then again, perhaps they were communicating *too* clearly, and he just wasn't getting it. He looked back at the sheet once more, and then it came to him. It was evidence. Evidence for Square-Head and Machine Eyes to discover. Along with Laura's blood, the cloth held his and Miranda's scents. The rain might wash the smell of them from the ground—after all, they'd only walked on it with their shoes—but enough of their scent might cling to the sheet for Square-Head's inhuman nose to detect.

He walked over to the sheet, picked it up, and wadded it into a ball. Then he returned to the edge of the bog and threw the sheet as far as he could. The cloth caught the air and came unwrapped as it drifted down to the surface of the bog and lay there, too light to sink. Like fish, the mouths slid through the murk toward the sheet. Delicately, teeth closed on the edges of the cloth, and then the mouths sank, pulling the sheet down with them. Within moments, the surface of the bog was smooth once more, the evidence well and truly concealed.

Scott smiled grimly. *And if those two demon cops go wading in after it, they're in for a hell of a surprise.*

He turned and headed back the way he'd come, more determined than ever to find Miranda. After all, he'd made a promise to these women, and he intended to keep it— and perhaps by helping them, he'd end up helping David and Gayle. And maybe, just maybe, he might even manage to save his own sorry ass in the bargain.

As he drove back toward town, he passed a police car going in the direction of the bridge. His hands stiffened on the steering wheel, and he kept his gaze fixed on the road ahead of him while he tried to look relaxed and unconcerned: an ordinary man out for an ordinary drive on an ordinary day. But as the car flashed by, he couldn't keep himself from glancing at it. He didn't get a good look, only had an impression of two people sitting in the front seat, and if they seemed to both be grinning with small, sharp white teeth . . . well, that might have been only his imagination.

Once he was back in Ash Creek proper, he decided to look for Miranda in the places where he'd encountered her before. He knew there was no reason why she would be at any of them; after all, she could be anywhere. But he didn't have any other ideas and besides, it felt right.

He started with Gayle and David's apartment complex. He didn't know if his wife had gone ahead with her threat to take out a restraining order on him, or if she had, if it were in effect yet. So far he hadn't received any kind of official notice, so that was a good sign. It was late afternoon and David would be out of school by now, so there was a good chance both he and his mother were home. Scott decided he'd check out the parking lot as quickly as he could and hope neither Gayle nor David saw him, and if they did, that his wife didn't call the police.

He parked near the rental office so his car wasn't right outside Gayle's building. As he got out, he saw movement out of the corner of his eye, and he turned to look in the office's window. A young woman, barely out of her teens, lay atop a desk, blazer open to reveal her bare chest, skirt hiked up around her hips to display an equally bare bottom, legs poised in the air as if she were preparing to undergo a gynecological exam sans stirrups. A man somewhere in his thirties stood before the desk. He wore a gray suit with a blue and red tie, and in his hand he held a flabby, quivering whitish-pink mass with thin dangling tentacles that reminded Scott of a jellyfish.

The jellyfish's quivering increased until the gelatinous creature was shaking so hard it became a blur. Even through the window, Scott could hear a soft, musical humming sound that rose and fell gently, like ocean waves.

In response to the humming, the young woman grabbed the backs of her thighs and pulled her legs even farther apart. The business-suited man grinned, stepped forward, and rammed the vibrating jellyfish into her vagina. The woman threw back her head and screamed, the sound a combination of ultimate ecstasy and agony. But her partner didn't stop there; he continued shoving the thing inside her, his hand disappearing into her writhing and bucking body, then his wrist, forearm, elbow . . .

Scott turned away, thankful he hadn't had anything to eat today because if he had, the remains would be all over his shoes right now. His blinders had not only been removed, it seemed they were off for good. Well, so much the better. Miranda would have a harder time concealing herself in the shadow aspect of existence if he could see into it.

He left the two lovers and their deep-sea marital aid behind and walked across the lot to the place where he had parked the night Miranda had awakened him by knocking on his car window. The space was empty at the moment, and he stood in the middle of it, slowly turning all the way around and scanning the buildings and the lot, but he saw no sign of Miranda. He considered shouting for her, but he didn't want to draw any more attention to himself than necessary. Not only because he didn't want Gayle to know he was here, but because he sensed that if he could see the beings that inhabited the dark nooks and crannies of reality, they could see him too. And if they became aware of him, they might decide to do more than just look; they might decide to scuttle forth from their shadows and touch.

He left the apartment complex and drove toward the convenience mart Miranda and he had stopped at during their nocturnal stroll. He pulled into the lot and parked outside the men's restroom. He checked out the gas pumps—which now resembled giant IV stands, their plastic bags swollen with greenish-yellow fluid—and then went inside. Among the stock items on the shelves—snack cakes, cookies, candy bars, oil, transmission fluid, cigarettes, milk, soda, beer—were balls of barbed wire that expanded and contracted as if they were breathing; severed heads that whispered in each other's ears and giggled at whatever secrets they'd been told; chittering insects double the size of a man's hand with jewel-bright carapaces and abdomens swollen with eggs. There were a half dozen customers in the store; some were normal, some . . . were not, but none were Miranda.

Scott walked back outside, got in his car, and drove off.

On the road, mixed in with the cars, trucks, and SUVs, were vehicles of a somewhat more exotic nature. Conglomerations of bone and sinew that lurched along on dozens of fleshless hands and feet; sinuous scaled coils that undulated sideways in rippling S shapes; something that resembled a land yacht whose sail was made out of stitched-together human skin. Scott barely noticed them. He was completely focused on finding Miranda.

He tried Orchard Park next. The rain had finally drizzled to an end, but the wind had picked up, creating a steady breeze that felt more like it belonged to early March than April. As he parked and got out of his car, Scott thought of the old cliché about Ohio: Don't like the weather? Then just wait around a few minutes. As he walked toward the play area, he saw there were no notices that the park was closed, and no yellow crime scene investigation tape barring entrance. Perhaps the police had finished with the scene but people weren't ready to bring their children back yet. Or perhaps the park was closed, and the cops merely hadn't felt like stretching long lengths of tape between tree trunks. Whichever, Scott had the place to himself.

He checked out the play area, not looking too closely at the spot where Jamey had been killed. The cops had probably removed the worst of the blood-spattered cedar chips as evidence, but if they'd left any behind, he didn't want to know about it. He had the impression that the three heads on the *Wizard of Oz* swing set were watching him as he walked past, but they remained solid, unmoving metal, which was just fine by him. The FOR WHEELCHAIR USE ONLY swing set creaked once, but that might have been due to the wind. The spider climber was still, but Scott sensed an alertness to it, as if it were waiting patiently—and hungrily—for him to get closer. He made sure to give the thing a wide berth.

He came to the paved jogging path and followed it deeper into the park, passing frisbee golf tees that were only metal poles and chain-link baskets, not severed heads on pikes. He thought he felt eyes tracking him as he passed, though he didn't actually see any. Maybe the park denizens were choosing not to fully reveal themselves this time.

Or maybe you're just getting used to this sort of thing.

In some ways, that was the most terrifying thought he'd had since the madness had begun. Bad enough to acclimate to the darkness of the distorted world Miranda had ushered him into; worse to find himself beginning to take it for granted, for that implied he'd come to accept it as part of what he defined as "normal." Worst of all, he was beginning to feel at home among the shadows, almost as if he belonged there.

The thought was too disturbing to mull over for long, so he thrust it aside and he made his way to the fountain at the center of the park. The water was running, clear and clean. He dipped his fingers in it, found it cool. He touched the moisture to his lips; it tasted metallic and overly processed, but that was all.

There was no sign of Miranda.

He sat on the fountain's edge for a few moments and debated what to do next. Should he go to the grocery store where she worked? Go home and check his e-mail to see if she'd sent him another message? Neither choice felt right. He turned and looked over his left shoulder, in the direction of the rec center . . . and Poplar Avenue.

If Miranda had been hurt protecting him from the undead chorus, she wouldn't go to his wife's place or the convenience store, to the park or the grocery. There was only one place she'd go, the only place a scared, injured little girl would ever go.

Home.

Chapter Twenty-five

Scott knocked on the door, waited, knocked again. He sensed more than heard movement behind the door, as if someone were standing there, listening, trying to decide what to do. It wasn't five o'clock yet, and though he didn't know what Mr. Tanner did for a living, he figured there was a good chance the man wasn't home from work yet. That meant he only had to deal with Mrs. Tanner.

He knocked again, then said, loud enough for her to hear, "I need to talk with Miranda." If he were wrong, what

he'd just said would be incredibly hurtful to the woman inside. But he wasn't wrong; he almost wished he was.

The door opened a crack but no more. She'd left the
chain lock engaged. It was a flimsy pretense at home security, Scott knew. A strong kick to the door and the chain
would tear free from the wood and the door would swing
open wide, permitting entry to anyone in the whole damn
world. He was suddenly angry at the woman for insulting
him by leaving the chain lock on, and he experienced an
urge to ram his body against the door and expose the chain
for the fragile psychological defense that it was. But he restrained himself.

"Mrs. Tanner, I need to see Miranda. It's important."

He couldn't see her entire face, only a single eye, a shock
of brown hair, a wan cheek, the corner of a mouth defined
by dry, pale lips. The eye narrowed with suspicion, and he
couldn't blame her; he didn't exactly look his best. His hair
was wet and stringy, his clothes damp and muddy, and the
back of his left hand was crusted with blood. He probably
looked to her like some half-crazed derelict begging door
to door.

"If this is some sort of joke—" There was no energy behind the words, no life. They might as well have issued
forth from the speaker of a child's electronic doll. *Please
change my diaper, Mommy. Mommy, I'm hungry; may I have
my bottle?*

"I know Miranda's inside. I know she's hurt. I'm a
friend. I can help her." He spoke slowly, used short sen-
tences so she might understand. From her toneless voice,
he knew she was in shock. It wasn't everyday your missing
and presumed dead daughter came home.

He heard a baby fussing, knew Mrs. Tanner was holding

Miranda's little brother just out of sight. "She isn't . . . She can't come out to play. She isn't feeling well."

He thought of the way Miranda had screamed as he ran from the marsh. *I bet she isn't.* "I won't take long, and it's really important. A matter of life and death." A cliché, sure, but he couldn't think of a more apt phrase. Whatever the ultimate nature of the strangeness swirling around him, it struck to the very core of such basic concepts as *life* and *death*.

"I can't. She . . . She just got home." Plaintive, almost a plea for understanding.

Scott felt a wave of sympathy for Mrs. Tanner. Despite his years writing about crime, its perpetrators and its victims, he couldn't imagine what it must be like to experience the abduction, and probable murder, of your own child. A year and more had passed since Miranda Tanner had vanished without a trace. The emotional toll those months had taken on Miranda's parents was incalculable, beyond understanding except by those who had endured the same nightmare. Suddenly, the last four days Scott had lived through didn't seem quite so awful anymore, not compared with the agony this woman had suffered.

But he had his own child to worry about right now. Miranda had said something horrible would happen to David if Scott didn't intervene. And as much as he didn't want to cause Mrs. Tanner any more grief—Christ knew the woman had experienced enough for several lifetimes—he had no choice.

He grabbed the edge of the door to prevent her from closing it. "I have to talk to her, Mrs. Tanner. My son's life depends on it."

"I . . . I don't . . ." The confusion on her face cleared, replaced by determination. "No. She's sick. Go away before I call the police." She tried to close the door, but he held it open.

"I'm coming in, whether you call the police or not." He pushed the door open until the chain caught. The only thing preventing him from trying to break the chain was the child Mrs. Tanner held. He didn't want to risk knocking her down; she might drop the boy and injure him. He kept pushing, stuck his foot between the door and the jamb like an old-fashioned salesman. Mrs. Tanner shoved back, but she only had one hand to work with and Scott was stronger. She wasn't going to be able to close the door if he didn't want her to.

After several moments of stalemate, during which the toddler began to cry, Scott reconsidered breaking the chain. He didn't want to hurt the child, but he had to save David, and there was a chance Mrs. Tanner would step out of the way before the door slammed open in order to protect her son. He was about to risk it when he heard a voice call out from somewhere inside the house. It was weak, and he could barely make out the words, but he heard them.

"It's okay, Mom. Let him in."

Mrs. Tanner stopped pushing on the door. She turned as if Scott wasn't there and walked into the foyer, as if trying to get closer so her daughter might better hear. "Honey, I can't. You just got back."

This was his chance. Scott stepped back, lifted his leg and kicked the door next to the knob. The chain held, and it took two more kicks before it finally snapped and the door swung inward. He rushed inside before Mrs. Tanner could return to try and stop him, and found himself standing in an empty foyer. Where was she? He listened. The boy was crying from somewhere inside the house, but he wasn't sure where. Most likely she'd gone to wherever Miranda was in order to protect both of her children. He hoped he could reason with the woman once he found her. If not, he would be forced to . . . *What?* he thought. *Subdue her?* He had no idea how to "subdue" anyone. Would he have to hit her? Tie her up? Tape her mouth shut? What if she fought back? What if she still held the boy?

He decided he'd have to do his best to reason with her—though he didn't think much of his chances for success—and hope for the best. He started down the foyer toward a hallway. He passed a gallery of framed pictures: some were of the boy in various stages from infancy to toddlerhood, but most were of Miranda. Not the Miranda he knew, not Lolita, but Miranda Tanner. He stopped and regarded the images for a moment. A chubby-faced newborn, nearly bald, with squinched-up eyes. A grinning toddler with shining blonde hair and healthy, glowing skin. A six-year-old, hair past her shoulders now, smiling in a way that suggested she was trying to look grown-up. Was there a sadness in her eyes, as if she'd somehow known the fate that lay ahead of her, or was it merely his imagination?

He thought of the Miranda he'd kissed, the Miranda who'd jacked him off in the park, whose hand had been sliced open by his temporarily transformed penis as he came. The Miranda who'd laid beside him in bed that night, cuddled up to him, and he felt sick to his stomach. Despite what he suspected to the contrary, he prayed there was no connection between his Lolita and the Miranda whose all-too-brief life had been imperfectly recorded in these few pictures. His Miranda was an adult woman. Young, yes, but not a child.

He heard a sound and tore his gaze away from Miranda's

smiling face in time to see Mrs. Tanner coming toward him, face twisted into a mask of hatred, a butcher knife gripped tight in her hand, raised to strike.

"YOU CAN'T HAVE HER!" she screamed as she ran at him.

Scott blocked her first downward strike with his left forearm, then shoved her into the wall with his free hand, his fingers sinking into the soft flesh of her breast by accident. Air whooshed out of her lungs, and before she could recover, he grabbed her knife hand by the wrist and slammed it against the wall. He felt the bones of her wrist shift beneath his hand, and he felt a grim satisfaction—which he was instantly ashamed of—to know that he had broken something inside her. A mewling sound escaped her throat, less a cry of pain than defeat, and she released her grip on the knife. The blade fell point-first to the foyer floor, barely missing Scott's left foot, then clattered onto its side.

His left hand kept her wrist pinned to the wall, and his right hand reached toward her throat. He watched the extremity move closer to its target, feeling nothing, as if he were merely an observer without control of or responsibility for its actions. When his fingers were inches from her neck, he snapped out of it and pulled his hand back. Jesus, he'd been about to strangle the woman!

She came at you with a knife. She deserves whatever she gets.

Bullshit. Defending one's self didn't mean killing a woman just for the hell of it.

The best defense . . .

Scott ignored the thought and let go of Mrs. Tanner's broken wrist. She slumped to the floor and cradled the hand in her lap as tears rolled down her cheeks. He knelt to retrieve the knife before she thought to make a grab for it, but there was no hurry. He'd taken the fight out of her, at least for now.

"Don't hurt her," she said softly, as if she were speaking to herself. "Don't take her away from me again."

He wanted to promise the woman that he wouldn't harm Miranda, that everything was going to be okay, but he couldn't. He looked at her for a moment longer before walking past her and into the hallway.

He looked both ways. To his left was a kitchen, to the right bedrooms. He went right.

He passed a bathroom first. The door was closed, no light showing through the crack at the bottom. He kept going.

The next door was closed as well, but he heard the boy crying on the other side. He opened it, saw Miranda's little brother standing in his crib, holding onto the railing, face wet with tears and snot. Scott guessed that while he was busy trying to break in the house, Mrs. Tanner had deposited the boy in his crib then ran to the kitchen to get the knife. It might have seemed a foolish delay to some. What if an intruder—especially one who meant harm—managed to get inside before she'd gotten the knife? But he was a parent and understood. You took care of your children first, and sometimes you relied on blind habit to do so. Can't have the boy wandering around during a break-in, can we? So into the crib he goes.

Miranda's little brother wore a red T-shirt and blue-jean overalls. His feet were bare. The room contained a dresser and a set of shelves filled with stuffed animals. The walls were painted sky blue, with fluffy white clouds here and there. Scott wondered if that had been Mrs. Tanner's idea or her husband's. Probably hers, he decided. It seemed more like a feminine touch.

Seeing the boy reminded Scott of when David had been that age. Sometimes he'd wake up in the middle of the night, stand and grip the edge of his crib and call out in singsong fashion, "Mommy? Daddy? 'ere aw oooooo?" over and over. Not crying, not shouting, not screaming. Just asking, as if he were only mildly curious.

The boy cried out, "Mama! Mama!" and Scott wondered what he looked like to the child, standing in the doorway, disheveled, holding a butcher knife in one hand. Probably like a boogeyman straight from hell.

"It's okay, pal. I'm not going to hurt you. I'm just here to talk to your sister."

The boy shrieked and bounced up and down on his small mattress. Scott knew there was nothing he could say to soothe the boy, so he moved on. There were two more doors at the end of the hallway, one on each side. The master bedroom and Miranda's room, he guessed. But which was which? He tried the one on his right, saw a double bed, covers mussed, a desk in a corner with a computer on top, a stack of papers next to it. The curtains were open and there was enough light for him to see that the papers were fliers with six-year-old Miranda's face on them, homemade HAVE YOU SEEN THIS GIRL? signs. Over a year later, and her parents were still printing fliers, still holding on to whatever meager scraps of hope they could scavenge. Scott wondered if he'd be any different in the same situation, knew that he wouldn't. He closed the door and tried the room on the left.

A child's bed with Winnie-the-Pooh sheets. A white dresser with a ballerina music box on top flanked by plastic model horses. Framed posters on light pink walls: a rainbow arching over a multicolored hot-air balloon, a unicorn surrounded by a sparkly blue-white aura running through a dimly lit glen. He'd found Miranda Tanner's room.

Lying in the bed, sheets drawn to her chin, legs curled up so her too-long body would fit, was *his* Miranda, his Lolita, though she was barely recognizable as such. Her face was swollen, nose crooked, lips distended. One bloodshot eye drooped lower than the other, as if her face were made of wax and partially melted. Her scalp was bare in a dozen places, the patches where hair used to be raw and bloody. As Scott looked closer, he saw fine red seams crisscrossed her face, as if the skin had been torn off and then imperfectly replaced. The sheet was dotted with reddish-brown stains where it clung to her body.

"Remember when I said they wouldn't hurt me?" Her voice was a hoarse rasp, the words thick and mushy as they struggled to make their way past swollen lips.

He nodded as a tear fell down his cheek, and her lips twitched in what he guessed was an attempt at a smile.

"I was wrong."

He crossed to the side of the bed, put the knife on the floor, knelt and reached under the covers for her hand. He found it cold, the fingers bent at odd angles, and the skin shifted at his touch, seams splitting open under the gentle pressure of his hand.

Before he could let go, she said, "It's okay. It doesn't hurt."

He felt blood from the open tears spread across his palm, but he held on.

"I'm sorry," he said.

She made a snuffling sound like an animal with distemper. A laugh, he supposed.

"I'm the one who should be saying that. I got you into this mess, and as bad as it is now, it's only going to get worse."

He felt no response to her prediction. He'd expected as much. "Tell me, as simply as you can, what the hell is going on. Who are you and what do you want from me? And what can I do to save David and Gayle?"

"I'm Miranda Tanner, as you probably already guessed. At least, part of me is. And as for what I want, almost a year ago, I was abducted and killed by a man named Scott Raymond. I came back from the dead because he must be stopped, and you're the only one who can do it."

Scott looked at her for a long moment, trying to process what she'd said. At last, he sighed. "Maybe you should give me the slightly less simple version."

Chapter Twenty-six

"It was a beautiful day. Sunny, a nice breeze. I'd just finished my gymnastics class and I was excited. I'd managed to do a forward somersault on the balance beam all by myself, and I couldn't wait to get home and tell my mom. I was looking forward to seeing my baby brother, too. Andrew was only a couple months old, and he cried a lot, especially at night when I wanted to sleep, but I thought he was really neat, like a doll that had come to life. Mom breastfed him, but sometimes she made him a bottle of breast milk, and she'd said that, if I was real good, maybe I could feed him soon. I was hoping she'd let me feed him today, especially after she heard about my somersault.

"I had just turned onto our street when I saw a man walking toward me on the sidewalk. He said something to me . . . I can't remember what, isn't that strange? I do remember being a little worried—I knew strangers could be dangerous—but he didn't say anything else as I walked past him. And then . . ." She scowled. "My memory is hazy after that. The next thing I knew, I was lying on grass looking up at the tops of trees and the blue sky beyond. The man from the sidewalk was there too, and he started . . . doing things to me. Awful things. He was skilled at his work and he took his time. The pain seemed to go on and on forever, but eventually, it grew less and less, and then, as gently as slipping into sleep, I was gone.

"I floated in warm darkness for a time, not thinking, not feeling, just being. After a while, I became aware of other presences in the dark. They drew closer, whispering words of comfort as they came. I felt them gather around me—a dozen of them, more—felt them wrap me in their arms, or at least the spiritual equivalent, and I felt safe and protected and loved.

"They were the others, the ones who had come before me. My killer's previous victims. All had been adult women at the time of their deaths; I was the only child. Along with love, I sensed great sorrow in them, as well as intense hatred for the man who had stolen our lives. Their hatred sparked my own, and soon I was hating our killer just as much as any of them—more, even, for he had taken my life before I'd had a chance to grow up, before I could tell Mom about my somersault, before I got to give Andrew a bottle! And then . . . something happened.

"I'm not sure if I can explain it to you. I don't have the words . . . I don't think there are words yet. It was like their hatred had been growing for some time, but the addition of mine to theirs tipped some sort of cosmic scale. We reached a spiritual critical mass and we . . . fused, I suppose is the best way to put it. Our many spirits became one. Became me: your Miranda."

Before Sunday, not only wouldn't Scott have believed her, he would've thought she was mad. But now . . .

"Why you? There have been other serial killers, other victims . . . Why haven't they come back?"

She gave a weak shrug. "I don't know. Maybe there was something special about Miranda Tanner, some latent power of mind or spirit that she tapped into at the moment of death that made such a fusion possible. Or maybe other victims *have* joined together and returned, and we just don't know about it. Blinders, remember?

"However it happened, it happened, and together, we had power. Power enough to see things . . . do things. We could touch the shadow aspect of existence, where life and death, the past and the future, don't mean the same things they do in what we call the 'normal' world. And from there, we learned how to return to the realm of the living in physical form for brief periods."

She smiled, gave Scott's hand a feeble squeeze.

"Speaking of physical matters, since most of me is made of the spirits of adult women, technically, I don't think I count as jailbait." She tried to laugh, ended up coughing, and Scott suggested he get her a drink of water, but she waved the offer aside.

"In Shadow, my sisters and I could see our killer, watched as he continued his dark work, welcomed the new victims into our fold and felt our power increase with each addition. Our killer was able to walk in Shadow, too. It helped him stalk his victims and catch them by surprise, as well as avoid capture by the police. When we thought we were strong enough, we confronted him in the dark realm and tried to destroy him, but as powerful as we'd become, he still managed to escape us. We knew then that if we were to defeat him, we needed a champion."

She gave Scott an approximation of a smile. "We needed you."

He frowned as he tried to remember. "My grandmother told me something in one of my dreams. She spoke of life as a road with branching-off points. Different possibilities, different alternatives. She said I've become two different people living two different lives at the same time."

Miranda nodded. "There are two Scott Raymonds. Both suffered a terrible tragedy when his family was murdered one summer evening in a cabin by a lake. Both went to live with his closest relative, his Gammy. But then their life paths diverged. One Scott stayed with his Gammy until he reached adulthood. The other—"

"Went to live with Leonard."

"Yes. And under his uncle's dark tutelage, that Scott became the man who killed me, and all the other women who are a part of me."

"The Scott I watched on the video about serial killers."

She nodded. "A little present I brought you to help you understand."

"Is the tape—and the things I saw on it—real?"

"In your other self's existence, yes. Of course, the tape makes no mention of how Leonard learned to walk in Shadow, and how he taught his nephew to do the same."

"So you're saying I'm a serial killer. Or at least, I had the potential to become one, that I *did* become one in another version of my life."

"Yes."

Suddenly something his uncle had said to him made

sense. *I'm not going to let them do that to* my *Scotty.* Leonard hadn't been talking about him; he'd meant the other Scott Raymond, the killer he'd created.

"I'm sorry, Miranda. At this point, I'm willing to believe in ghosts and shadow worlds and all the rest, but I can't bring myself to believe that I could become . . . a monster."

"You've always had a core of anger in you ever since you were born. The horror of your family's murder intensified this core, made it grow stronger and deeper. And when your other self went to live with your uncle, he was able to use that anger, bend it, twist it, multiply it a thousandfold to make that Scott into what he is today."

Scott remembered what the psychologist on the video had said about nature versus nurture. If what Miranda said was true, then his other self had both of those cards stacked against him.

"I still don't see it. I mean, sure, I get mad sometimes, but who doesn't? And yes, I feel like grabbing people, even hitting them. But I don't." He thought back to the last few months when he still lived with Gayle and David. *Most of the time,* he amended with shame.

She squeezed his hand again, more strongly this time. And did her face seem less puffy, the seams in her skin less pronounced? Maybe.

"You've done a wonderful job fighting the darkness inside you, Scott. You had Gammy's help, and the help of all the psychologists you saw in the years following your family's deaths. You went to college, graduated, and then established a career as a crime writer. You found a supportive wife and eventually had a child with her. You had love, guidance, understanding, opportunity . . . all your other self had was Leonard."

"I guess now I'm supposed to say 'There but for the grace of God,' eh?"

She shook her head. "There's no grace about it, Scott. It just how things worked out—and lucky for you they did."

"So you're trying to stop Killer Scott, and Uncle Leonard wants to save him. Where does Gammy fit in?"

"Ever since her death, her spirit has watched over you. When I first made contact with you, I accidentally created a . . . a connection between you and the realm of the dead. A bridge that other spirits could use to reach you."

"Other spirits like Gammy . . . and Leonard."

She nodded. "When your Gammy sensed what I was doing, she used that bridge to contact you, though her primary motivation was to guide and protect you. Unlike myself and Leonard, as a single spirit with no experience in the world of Shadow, she couldn't manifest physically, but only come to you in your dreams."

"But she can't visit my dreams anymore, can she?"

"By killing her on the dreamplane, Leonard cut off her access to you. She's not dead, exactly. That concept doesn't apply to spirits, but you'll never be in contact with her again. Not as long as you live."

"And the other victims? If they're part of you now, why do they manifest separately? And why did they hurt you?"

"We may be one, but that doesn't always mean we're in agreement. Every individual has conflicts within himself or herself. We do, too. But ours tend to be more . . ." she touched her not-quite-so-swollen face. "Dramatic."

"I've had dreams in which I seem to be him. The other Scott, I mean. Dreams where I'm stalking a victim . . . killing her."

"Your life paths are so close that they intertwine and intersect, allowing each of you to glimpse bits and pieces of the existence he might have led and—in the case of your other self, who can travel through Shadow—even physically cross over from one life path to the other."

Scott felt dizzy, as if he might pass out. Now that he was getting the answers he had sought, it seemed his mind was doing its best to shut down and avoid them. He took several deep breaths, and when he felt more or less in control again, he said, "All right. Assuming I believe all of this, what exactly is it that you and . . . your sisters want from me?"

"While you didn't become the killer your other self did, inside you is the same dark fire. We hoped that if we could fan that fire into a blaze, you'd be able to stop him."

"Stop him. You mean kill him, don't you?"

Miranda didn't answer.

"You've been trying to turn me into a murderer like him?"

"No, not like him! We just wanted to . . . unleash the hidden strength inside you. We wanted to fight fire with fire."

"It takes a killer to catch a killer, eh? So that's why you've shown me the delights of the shadow world. You were trying to tutor me the same way Leonard tutored my other self!" He pulled his hand away from hers and stood.

"Please, listen!" Her voice suddenly sounded like that of a little girl on the verge of tears. "We first needed to show you there was more to existence than you thought, otherwise, you'd never believe that I was a ghost and you had a doppelganger who was a serial killer. As for the rest . . ." She trailed off and closed her eyes. "It's true enough in its way. We hoped we could awaken the same savagery in you that your other self used against us. We hoped to make you our weapon of revenge." She opened her eyes again, and her voice was once more that of his Lolita. Strong, far more mature than her apparent years, with an undercurrent of sympathy and, perhaps, even love.

"We want more than revenge, though. If he isn't stopped, your other self will continue to kill unhindered. And with his ability to walk in Shadow, he'll never be brought to justice by ordinary means. Only you can stop him. Only you can prevent the deaths that are to come."

Scott remembered a segment on the serial killer video that discussed how "Scott Raymond" had mysteriously escaped from police custody. He understood now; his other self had merely shadow-walked away.

Another thought struck him then, a terrible thought, most probably the worst he'd ever had, and his breath caught in his throat.

"Deaths that are to come. . . . You're talking about Gayle and David, aren't you? He's going to kill them, isn't he?" When Miranda didn't answer, he grabbed her by the shoulders and shook her, not caring if he hurt her. "Isn't he?" he demanded.

Softly, sadly. "Yes."

He released her and stepped back from the bed. "Jesus, I have to call Gayle, tell her she and David are in trouble. No, she'd never believe me. I have to go over there and warn her in person." He thought about her threat to take out a restraining order. She'd never let him into her building. "Maybe it would be better if I called the police, tell them my family is in danger." He turned, intending to run from Miranda's room in search of a phone, but he stopped before taking a single step.

Standing in the doorway, son on her hip, was Miranda's mother. She smiled with grim satisfaction. "You don't need to call the police. I already have."

There was a pounding at the front door.

Chapter Twenty-seven

"David, do you have any homework you should be doing?"

David sat on the couch in front of the TV set watching a cartoon about robots that could change into dinosaurs. His mom was in the kitchen making supper: spaghetti, broccoli, and garlic toast. Again. He liked spaghetti just fine, especially with lots of parmesan cheese sprinkled on top, but his mom made it a lot. Whenever he complained, she said she didn't have time after working all day and then picking him up at after-school care to fix anything more elaborate. David understood that part. He wasn't asking for anything fancy, just something *different*.

"No, Mom," he lied. He had some math to do, and there was a vocabulary test on Friday that he should study for. But he was *really* into this cartoon, and he just *had* to find out if the good-guy Herbitrons were going to defeat the evil Predatorrs. He kind of hoped they wouldn't. Sure, the Predatorrs were bad guys and all, but they were *way* cooler than the Herbitrons, whom David thought were kind of wimpy, even for good guys. He'd pretend to suddenly "remember" his homework after supper.

He wished his dad were sitting on the couch with him. He'd always watched cartoons with David and he seemed to like them pretty good, though David thought that he was mostly interested in just spending time together, but that was okay. That was what David liked best, too.

Plus, since his dad stayed home to write, he'd always been there when David got home from school. He'd make sure David did his homework right away (which kind of stank, but at least it got done). After that, they'd watch some cartoons before making dinner together. Dad wasn't a gourmet chef or anything—Mom was probably the better cook—but at least he had the imagination to try different things. Sometimes a whole month would go by before he'd repeat a recipe.

The kitchen area wasn't very far from the living space (David didn't think of them as "rooms"; there were no real division between them), and he glanced at his mother. She was stirring the spaghetti and staring into the steam as it rose from the boiling pot. David remembered watching a cartoon where a wizard gazed into a magic pool to see the future, and he wondered what his mom was trying to see. She stared off into space a lot these days, thinking about whatever it was that grown-ups thought about. Dad, probably. That was what David thought about most of the time.

He'd hoped that having breakfast together at McDonald's the other morning might make things better between his parents, but for some reason he couldn't figure out, it had only seemed to make them worse. He knew his mother had talked to a lawyer on the phone a couple times, and David was worried she was finally going to go ahead and divorce Dad. He wanted to ask her about it, but he was too afraid. He didn't know what he'd do if they got divorced. He supposed he'd live through it. He'd known lots of kids back home whose parents had split up, and though he hadn't made many friends at his new school yet, he was sure there were plenty of kids there whose moms and dads were divorced, too. But he couldn't imagine life continuing like this. Hardly ever seeing his dad, hardly ever getting to talk to him on the phone. . . . He blamed his mom. Just because *she* didn't want to see Dad shouldn't mean that David couldn't. But she seemed determined to keep them apart, almost as if she were trying to punish them both. But what she thought she was punishing them for, David couldn't figure out. Sometimes he got so mad at her, he'd like to . . . like to . . .

On the TV screen, a Predatorr called Tyrannosaurus Ax used his sharp-edged face to chop a flying Herbitron named Triceracopter in two. David grinned as the separate halves of the robot dinosaur crashed into the prehistoric jungle and exploded. Man, what he wouldn't give to be a Predatorr! He could make the rules then, and if people didn't like it, he'd change into Tyrannosaurus Ax and chop! chop! He'd be so tough and scary that nobody would mess with him!

He turned toward the kitchen and looked at his mother once more.

Nobody.

He sat on the curb in front of the building opposite Gayle and David's, smoking a cigarette made from cancer cells and rolled in gangrenous flesh. Though his gaze was trained on their window, his awareness was focused elsewhere. He took a long drag on his cigarette, then exhaled greasy, foul-smelling smoke. He watched as the breeze grabbed the small black cloud, bent and twisted it into arcane shapes each more strange and obscene than the last, before the smoke finally grew too diffuse to read.

He had dwelt in Shadow for half his life now, and he

well knew how to read the ebb and flow of its dark tides. It was time.

He stood, took a last pull on his cigarette, then dropped it to the blacktop. He ground it beneath his shoe, knowing that by doing so he not only snuffed out the cigarette's fire but also the life of the person who'd donated the cells and skin. He didn't care in the slightest.

Showtime, he thought. He grinned and started walking across the parking lot.

Gayle dished out spaghetti onto David's plate, then her own. She knew he was probably irritated to be having spaghetti again so soon—she'd fixed it Sunday night—but that was tough. The way she felt these days, he was lucky to get a home-cooked meal at all. She wished she had more money in the bank; that way they could eat out more often, or at least bring home take-out. But not too many social workers got to be millionaires. Worse, her new job didn't pay as well as her old one in Cedar Hill had, and she was still dealing with bills that Scott and she had run up when they'd been together—credit cards mostly, and a few utility bills—so it was going to be spaghetti, macaroni and cheese, and Campbell's soup on the menu for the foreseeable future.

She got the bowl of spaghetti sauce out of the microwave, almost dropping it because it was so hot. She set it down on the counter, waved her hands in the air to cool them, then got a large spoon from the silverware drawer. She ladled sauce onto the spaghetti, drowning David's because he liked a lot, then got a container of parmesan from the refrigerator. She covered David's until the sauce was barely visible, then gave hers a light dusting.

She supposed she should press Scott more to pay his

share of the bills—that's what her lawyer had said, any-way—but she knew she would feel like such a bitch doing so. Besides, she wanted to have as little contact with Scott as possible while she tried to figure out what was best for David and her—especially after breakfast the other day. She felt a pang at the thought of how out of it Scott had been. She'd known he had problems almost since the first day they'd begun dating in college; it wasn't as if he'd ever made a secret of it. But she'd been young at the time, and she'd thought that love and understanding could conquer all. Now in her late thirties, she knew that they weren't enough, not by half.

She took the plates of spaghetti out to the "dining room," really just a carpeted space between the kitchen and the front door, then returned to see to the broccoli. It was done, or close enough, and she drained it in the sink, grabbed a fork, and carried the steaming pot over to the table to put some on their plates. Not the most elegant way to serve, but it was efficient. She went back to the kitchen, put the empty pot back on the burner, made sure to turn the burner off, then got a tub of margarine from the fridge. As she walked past the stove, she checked the timer to see how long the garlic bread had left. Five minutes. Shit, when was she ever going to learn to time a meal? Oh well, they could start on their other food and eat the garlic bread when it was ready.

She walked to the table, opened the margarine, scooped out a couple pats with a knife and dropped them onto the broccoli. The margarine began melting at once, and she felt a wave of guilt for not using low-fat stuff, or better yet, vegetable-oil "fake" butter. It would have been healthier, but David hated the taste, and she couldn't bring herself to deny him such a small pleasure as "real" butter, not these days.

The lawyer had told her that a restraining order against Scott, while possible, was problematic. She had never filed any formal complaints against her husband for abuse, and the incidents she'd described to the lawyer were not "extreme" enough, he'd said. Yes, Scott had a history of mental illness, but not one of violence, and without a paper trail and more convincing evidence that her estranged husband constituted a "clear and obvious danger" to Gayle and David, the lawyer was doubtful that a judge would grant her request for a restraining order. Still, he promised to see what he could do, and in the meantime, he urged her to begin formal divorce proceedings.

She felt guilty for calling Scott yesterday and leaving a message on his machine that the restraining order was a done deal, but she hoped it was a temporary lie, that the judge would come through and grant the order soon. And if the judge didn't, at least her lie would keep Scott away from them for a while.

She left the margarine on the table in case David wanted more, then returned to the kitchen to pour drinks.

"David, food's on the table. Turn off the TV and go sit down." She didn't look to see if he'd heard her. She got a couple glasses and poured milk for David, Diet Sprite for her.

It was funny, but she was more comfortable with the idea of a restraining order than she was with divorce. The latter seemed so final, and even though she knew she'd have to do it eventually, she still loved Scott, and divorcing him would be like cutting him off from the only support he had. He had no other relatives, no friends to speak of. He still had occasional contact with a couple of his coworkers from his newspaper days, and there were his agent and various editors, but he wasn't close to any of them, couldn't really talk to any of them. And he wasn't in therapy right now, though he damn well should be. Without David and her, he'd be for all intents and purposes alone in the world, and she didn't know if she could do that to him.

She took the drinks to the table, saw that David was still watching his damn cartoon. "C'mon, David. Right now."

He hesitated another moment before finally turning off the TV and shuffling over to the table to take his place. He didn't look at her as he began eating, didn't say anything, and she decided that was better than listening to him complain about having spaghetti again, so she left him to his silence as she sat and started eating as well.

They worked on their meals in silence for a bit before the stove timer dinged.

"Garlic bread's ready." She got up and headed for the kitchen. She opened the oven and checked on the bread. Light brown around the edges, just right. She got a couple pot holders from the cupboard, took out the cooking tray, and set it at an angle on top of the stove. She put down the pot holders, turned the oven off, then opened a lower cupboard in search of a serving basket.

There was a knock at the door.

Jesus Christ, this was the second time in a week someone had knocked during dinner. Last time, it was some kid selling candy to raise money for his church youth group. Gayle had no idea who'd let him into the building—she didn't think he lived here, at least, she'd hadn't seen him around before—and she politely, but firmly told him they didn't accept sales calls during dinnertime.

Another knock.

She was having trouble finding the bread basket.

"Should I see who it is, Mom?"

"Ignore them. They'll go away in a minute." Maybe she should just say to hell with the basket and carry the pieces out on a spatula. She'd have to take them one at a time and be careful not to drop them, but it would work well enough. She was tired of taking short-cuts, though. She decided to give her search another minute before giving up and once again choosing practicality over style.

The knocking stopped.

Finally. Maybe now they could eat in peace.

"Hey, Mom! Come see who it is!"

She gritted her teeth in irritation. David knew better than to open the door without permission. Now she was going to have to deal with whoever it was, and by the time she'd given them the brush-off, their meals would be too cool, and she'd have to warm them in the microwave, and all she really wanted to do was sit down, eat, and try not to think or worry about David, or Scott, or bills, or anything else for a few goddamn minutes.

She slammed the cupboard door, straightened, and walked to the front door.

David was grinning from ear to ear. "Look, Mom! It's Dad!"

Scott stood in the doorway, smiling. He was clean-shaven and his hair was cut short. She was surprised; he hadn't worn his hair like that in years. He wore a black suede jacket, gray mock turtleneck, new jeans, and expensive running shoes, the kind that athletes hawked on TV. Scott had never owned a pair of shoes like that in his life, had always told David no when he'd asked for some.

"They're too much money for something that you only walk on," he'd say. The clothes were nicer than he usually wore, too, and she'd never seen that jacket before. She couldn't help thinking that he looked pretty good.

"Hi, Gayle. Would you believe me if I said I was in the neighborhood and decided to drop by?"

His voice was softer, with an edge of mocking humor she found jarring. There was a confidence to it, too, that complemented the way he carried himself. A sureness, as if he thought—no, *knew*—that there wasn't any situation he couldn't handle.

A chill rippled along her spine. Something was wrong here, seriously wrong. She wasn't sure what, but instinct told her it would be a big mistake to let Scott in. She moved past David and took hold of the door. She was afraid to get closer to Scott, but she couldn't let him stand so near David, and she needed to get the door closed and locked—with Scott on the other side—*now*.

"I left you a message about the restraining order," she said. "I don't want to call the police, but I will if I have to. Why don't you just leave without making a scene"—she glanced pointedly at David—"and we can talk about things later on the phone. All right?" She didn't like the anxious, pleading tone to her voice, but she couldn't help it.

"I think it would be more productive if we talked face to face, don't you?" His smile remained firmly in place, but his eyes glittered like frost-covered diamonds. "Or perhaps I should say fist to face."

Before she could react, his hand punched forward and struck her between the eyes. Bright light flashed along her optic nerves and then darkness rushed in to swallow her whole.

*   *   *

David looked at his mother lying on the floor, not believing what he was seeing. Dad had been rough with
them a few times back in the old house, but he'd never hit
either of them before. *Never.*

Dad closed the door and locked it before turning to
David. The same smile was still on his face; it hadn't varied
a fraction since David had first opened the door, almost as
if it were painted on.

"I'd like to say I'm sorry you had to see that, but I'm not,
so I won't."

Suddenly David realized he'd been wrong to blame his
mom for keeping Dad away from them, and he wished he
hadn't gotten up from the table when the knocking had
continued, hadn't jumped up to look through the peephole, hadn't opened the door when he saw it was Dad.

He opened his mouth to shout for help, but Dad
grabbed him by the back of the head with one hand and
covered his mouth with the other.

"Normally I like it when my playmates make noise, but
with so many neighbors around, I think it would be better
if we played quietly tonight. We wouldn't want anyone calling the police and interrupting our fun, now would we?"

A tear ran down David's face, the first of many to come.

Chapter Twenty-eight

Miranda's mother gave Scott a last smug smile before turning and heading down the hallway. She went slowly, almost
as if daring him to come after and stop her.

"It's not her fault," Miranda said. "My coming back like

this"—Scott didn't know if she was referring to her more adult form, her injuries, or both—"was quite a shock to her. I didn't really plan on coming here. It was just instinct, I guess."

Scott heard the front door open, and his muscles tensed in response. His mind was swimming with everything Miranda had told him. It was all far too much to absorb right now, but it wasn't important that he understood it. All that mattered was his other self intended to hurt (*don't be euphemistic: you mean* kill) David and Gayle. He needed to go to them, warn them, protect them from his murderous doppelganger by any means necessary—and he couldn't do that if he were in police custody. Even if he were only questioned and released, he couldn't afford the delay.

He heard voices coming from the front entrance: Mrs. Tanner and two others, male and female. Sudden recognition hit him. Of course, who else would it be but Square-Head and Machine Eyes?

"Come here." Miranda stretched wounded, scarred arms toward him.

Footsteps in the foyer, holsters being unsnapped.

"I don't think we have time for that," he whispered.

"Trust me."

Footsteps in the hall, coming closer.

After everything that had happened between them, Scott knew he'd be a fool to trust Miranda again. But he didn't have any choice. He went to her side and knelt down. She touched her fingers to his cheeks—her skin was corpse-cool, but there was a hint of warmth to it, as if she were beginning to recover—and guided his face to hers. She kissed him with swollen, cracked lips, and he felt her tongue, dry and leathery, dart into his mouth and gently graze his. She breathed into his mouth, and something shivery-cold collected on his tongue, the roof of his mouth, the backs of his teeth.

He started to pull away, but she held him tight with the strength that had surprised him before. *Of course she's strong,* he thought. She had the combined might of all his other self's victims to draw on.

She pressed the index and middle finger of her right hand to his lips. "Don't open your mouth, and hold your breath as long as you can. I've passed along a little bit of Shadow to help hide you. Once you open your mouth, it'll escape and you'll be seen."

Scott almost asked her to explain, thereby opening his mouth and screwing up whatever it was she had done, but just then her mother and the two police officers walked into the room, and there was no more time for questions.

Mrs. Tanner glanced around the room, scowled, then looked at her daughter. "Where is he, Miranda?"

Miranda lowered her hands and folded them over her chest. "I don't know, Mom. He left as soon as you went to the door."

Scott's two favorite cops took in the room at a glance, but as Miranda had promised, neither saw him. Square-Head's nostrils flared as he scented the air, but evidently Miranda's gift masked Scott's scent too, for the cop stopped sniffing, and then he and his partner trained hard gazes on Miranda.

"Where did he go?" Machine Eyes asked.

"I don't know. He didn't say anything; he just left."

Scott had remained in the same bent-over position he'd been in when Miranda kissed him, and now his lower back was starting to protest. He risked straightening, moving slowly so as not to draw any undue attention to himself and strain whatever spell was protecting him, but not a single eye so much as flicked in his direction, not even Miranda's.

Square-Head turned to his partner. "I'll go check out the rest of the house; you get the girl's story."

Machine Eyes nodded stiffly, as if her neck needed oiling, and Square-Head vanished into the hallway. The woman came into the room, and Scott backed away from the bed to give her room. He had no idea if Miranda's gift would continue to mask his presence if someone bumped into him, but he didn't want to find out.

Machine Eyes drew a small notebook and pen from the pocket of her uniform. She flicked the cover of the notebook back and poised the pen over it. "Tell me everything you know about this man, and don't hold anything back. We have reason to believe he might be dangerous."

Scott had never heard anyone actually gasp before, but Mrs. Tanner did then. "I knew it! See, Miranda, haven't I always told you not to trust strangers?"

Miranda closed her eyes. "Yes, Mom."

Good advice, Scott thought. Too bad six-year-old Miranda hadn't heeded it a year ago.

From somewhere within the house, Square-Head called out, "Mrs. Tanner, could you come here a moment?"

Miranda's mother hesitated, obviously not comfortable leaving her newly returned daughter alone with Machine Eyes. Scott didn't blame her; when it came to strangers, Machine Eyes was just about as strange as they came.

"It's all right, ma'am," Machine Eyes said. "I just need to ask her a few questions."

Little Andrew began to squirm in his mother's arms—perhaps he sensed the true nature of the events taking place around him, or perhaps he was just getting tired of being held. That more than anything else seemed to decide her.

"All right. You answer the officer's questions the best you can, Miranda, you hear?" Without waiting for a reply, Mrs. Tanner left with Andrew riding on her hip to see what Square-Head wanted.

Scott wasn't sure what to do now. His lungs were starting to ache, probably more from the knowledge that he shouldn't breathe than from any real need for oxygen yet. Could he breathe through his nose? Miranda hadn't said, and he decided not to chance it. He had another problem, though: the bit of Shadow that Miranda had passed into his mouth was getting colder, making his mouth feel as if it were coated with ice that refused to melt. More, the cold seemed to be growing more solid and shifting around, as though it were alive and moving. He thought of the spider-drug Miranda had given him, and stomach acid bubbled in response. He experienced an almost overwhelming urge to open his mouth and release whatever the hell was in there, but he kept his jaw clamped tight. If he opened his mouth, he'd lose Miranda's gift and Machine Eyes would see him. And if that happened, Scott was confident Machine Eyes wouldn't hesitate to give a few of her bullets a new home in his body.

Once Mrs. Tanner was gone, Machine Eyes put away her notebook and pen, and then bared her shark teeth.

"We know he was in here, slut. My partner may have a better nose, but even I can smell the stink of him on you. Tell me where he is or I'll make you regret it in a thousand ways."

Miranda made a show of sighing. "You brood-get are all the same: posturing and empty threats. I'm already dead. What more can you do to me?"

"Oh, you'd be surprised. But as fun as that would be, there are easier ways to get you to talk. Take your little brother, for instance. It's been a while since my partner and I had a morsel as sweet as him to snack on. Two, maybe three whole days." Machine Eyes grinned, her mouth stretching wider than a human's should. "You tell us what we want to know, and maybe we'll hit a donut shop instead."

Scott couldn't let them hurt Andrew. He took a step forward. He had no clear idea how, or even if, he could prevent the two hell-cops from doing as they pleased, but he had to try.

Miranda shook her head quickly, a gesture he sensed was meant as much for him as for Machine Eyes. He didn't know if Miranda could still detect his presence or if she was merely covering all the bases. Whichever the case, he stayed where he was.

"I can't tell you because I don't know. He *got the hell out of here* as soon as he heard you coming."

That message was unmistakable. He couldn't hold his breath forever. He needed to go now, else he risked squandering Miranda's gift. Still, he hesitated, reluctant to leave Miranda, Andrew, and their mother to the less-than-tender mercies of Square-Head and Machine Eyes.

"He said something about his wife and son. He was worried something was going to happen to them. *Something bad.*"

This second message was also crystal clear, and it decided Scott. He nodded to Miranda in case she could see him then walked quietly toward the door.

"What do you mean, something bad?"

Scott forced himself to ignore Machine Eyes's continued

interrogation and moved into the hallway. Once there, he experienced a powerful urge to run like hell for the front door, but he restrained himself. Not only might such sudden movement shatter Miranda's spell, it would use up the rest of the oxygen stored in his lungs, forcing him to breathe. Though it was one of the hardest things he'd ever done, he made himself walk at a normal pace down the length of the hallway.

He could hear Square-Head talking to Mrs. Tanner in the kitchen.

"The patio door is still locked, and you're certain the front door was also locked when you answered it?"

"Yes. He'd broken the chain, but the lock on the knob still works. After I called you, I went to the door and locked it."

A pause, and Scott imagined Square-Eyes sniffing the air. "Then he has to still be in the house somewhere."

Scott reached the foyer, turned, walked toward the front door. He could see it was unlocked—of course; there was no need to relock it when you had police officers in your house—but he didn't know whether the protection Miranda had granted him would conceal the sound of his opening the door. He couldn't hide in a corner of the foyer and wait for someone else to open it for him so he could slip through. His lungs felt as if they were on fire, and the thing in his mouth (and it *was* a thing, he was sure of that now) was definitely moving, pounding against the roof of his mouth and tongue, as if it were desperate to be free. Scott knew just how it felt.

He went to the front door, grasped the knob, turned it slowly, listening for sounds of alarm from either Square-Head or Machine Eyes. He heard none. He opened the door just wide enough to get through, stepped outside, and closed it once more, being careful not to shut it all the way in case the *snick* of the latch engaging made too much noise.

He almost exhaled then, but he forced himself to continue holding his breath. The longer he could keep himself concealed from the two nightmare cops, the better. He crossed the lawn, heading in the direction of his Subaru, half wishing he'd parked in front of the Tanner's residence so he wouldn't have so far to walk, half grateful that he'd parked several houses down so Square-Head and Machine Eyes wouldn't have automatically taken note of his vehicle. Their car was parked in the Tanner's driveway, and he had the impression that it was somehow watching him as he departed. A few days ago, he would have dismissed such a feeling as another sign of his increasingly fragile mental state. Now he knew it was all too possible. If he could just manage to keep holding his breath until he was behind the wheel of his car . . .

A tickle at the back of his throat, as if tiny hairs were brushing his uvula. He swallowed once, again, but the urge to cough continued to build until, coupled with the desperate need for air, he was unable to resist.

He opened his mouth and let out a barking cough. Something cold leapt forth at the same time, and he watched a black butterfly take to the air on glittering wings of obsidian ice, leaving behind the taste of winter midnights and silent snows to linger on his tongue. From the Tanner's driveway, a siren screamed.

He whirled around, saw the lights on the police car flashing baleful red. Now that Miranda's spell was broken, he was visible. The vehicle had detected him and was alerting its masters.

That's just fan-fucking-tastic, he thought, and ran for his car.

Scott managed to get in his car, hit the ignition, and pull away from the curve just as the two brood-get rushed out of the Tanner's house. In his rearview mirror, he thought he saw the police vehicle's doors spring open of their own accord as the hell-cops approached, but it might've just been his imagination. He tore his gaze from the mirror and concentrated on the road ahead of him.

He reached the end of Poplar and, sending out a prayer to whatever gods watched over insane men being chased by sharp-toothed monsters, he gunned the engine and whipped through the intersection without waiting to see if any cars were coming. A horn blared and he saw a flash of an oncoming mini-van through his windshield, but he avoided it—barely—and was barreling down the road, the impression of a furious face and an upraised middle finger seared into his mind.

His little Subaru had always done well enough by him, but now he wished he drove something with more pick-up. He had the pedal mashed to the floor, but the engine whined and rattled as if it were powered by rubber bands and exhausted gerbils running on exercise wheels. Whatever was beneath the hood of the brood-cops' vehicle—assuming that it *was* a car and not something which merely resembled one—it was bound to have more *oomph* than his tinkertoy excuse for an engine. There was no way he could hope to outrun Square-Head and Machine Eyes, and he knew it.

But luck was with him for a change, or perhaps it was some aftereffect of Miranda's enchantment, for behind him he heard squealing tires then the sound of metal colliding.

He looked in his rearview mirror and saw that the black-and-white had broadsided the mini-van. The vehicles spun through the intersection and came to a rest in a tangle of crumpled metal resting half on the street, half on the opposite sidewalk.

Scott let up on the gas without thinking, and his car slowed. He watched in the mirror as Square-Head and Machine Eyes got out of their vehicle. The former walked around to the rear of their car, wrapped his arms around the trunk—seeming to sink his fingers *into* the metal as he did—and started tugging as he walked backward. Scott couldn't hear, but he could imagine the sound of groaning, protesting metal as the brood-get pulled his vehicle free of the mini-van.

Machine-Eyes walked to the driver's side of the van, and with a single swift, fluid motion tore off the door and flung it into the grass. She grabbed the driver—a fiftyish woman with a blood-smeared forehead from where she'd struck the windshield—by the scruff of her coat, yanked her out, and threw her onto the ground. Machine Eyes bared her teeth and then fell upon the woman. Scott heard a high-pitched scream, but it didn't last long.

The hood of the police vehicle was caved in and the front wheels were turned inward at odd angles. Scott, whose own car was idling now, barely inching along the street, guessed that the radiator was probably cracked and the front axle likely broken. There was no way Square-Head and Machine Eyes would be continuing their pursuit now. He felt terrible about the woman in the mini-van, but at least now he would have a chance to—

In his rearview mirror, he saw the hood of the police car quiver as metal began reforming, tires straightening, hood flattening and smoothing out. The goddamned car was healing itself! Square-Head stood by the rear of the vehicle glaring at Scott. Machine Eyes straightened, wiped blood from her chin and walked over to stand by her partner, and together they watched him as they waited for their car to finish its repairs.

Scott didn't know how long it would take for their vehicle to become roadworthy again, but whether through fate or blind luck, he'd been given a chance, and he wasn't about to squander it. He pressed the gas pedal to the floor once more.

"C'mon, you damn gerbils," he muttered. "Give me everything you got!" This time as he drove away, he didn't look in his rearview mirror. He didn't need to. He knew that sooner rather than later they'd be coming. He just hoped he could reach Gayle and David before the brood-get caught up and did to him what they'd done to the woman in the mini-van.

With that cheery thought as his sole company, Scott headed for his wife and son's apartment.

Chapter Twenty-nine

Scott had a bad feeling long before he pulled into a parking space in front of Gayle and David's building. He'd never been psychic or anything like that—and the concept of "psychic" seemed quaint after everything he'd experienced recently—but the feeling had started soon after he pulled away from the hell-cops and continued to build as he drove across town. It was a cold, gut-churning fear . . . no, more than that, a growing, bleak certainty . . . that it didn't matter how fast he drove because he was too late.

He was so upset that he almost forgot to turn off the engine after he parked. He cut the ignition, got out of the car, closed the door, and pocketed the keys. He ran to the building's entrance, feeling as if he were moving in the slow motion of dreams: head balloon-light, arms and legs lead-heavy. He reached the door, tried the knob, found it locked. He'd forgotten this was a security building.

He reached for the intercom, index finger poised to buzz Gayle and David's apartment, but then he hesitated. Which one was theirs again? For a moment, he thought he was going to have start pressing buttons at random, as he had the last time he'd been here, but then it came to him: 2B. *2B or not 2B*, he thought, and immediately wished he hadn't. He pressed the button.

The intercom squawked as he held the button down, then grew silent as he released it. He waited, the thready whisper of his pulse in his ears ticking off the moments. He was about to try the button again when the intercom buzzed and the door lock *snicked* open. He frowned. The buzzer seemed to have an insolent, mocking tone, but that was ridiculous. It was just a buzzer, right?

He opened the door before the lock could re-engage and stepped into the building.

He took the stairs two at a time, moving through air thick with cooking smells—fried meat, overdone vegetables, rank onion and garlic—and the muted sound of television news, game shows, and syndicated sitcoms. The sounds and smells of people living their lives should've felt normal, but instead they felt oppressive, as if the mingled noises and odors had combined to form a physical barrier between him and apartment 2B. He had to lean forward, gripping the wooden rail for leverage as he pushed upward, as though the stairway was choked with a clear, viscous sludge.

It seemed to take forever to gain the top of the stairs, but then he was there, standing before the door to 2B. He raised his hand to knock, then lowered it. Instinct told him to try the knob. It turned easily in his hand, and he pushed the door open and stepped inside.

Dining table on its side, spaghetti sauce smeared on carpet and walls. TV on the floor, cyclopean eye shattered. Couch upholstery shredded, stuffing scattered around the room like clumps of artificial snow.

No David, no Gayle.

He tried to call out to them, but his throat refused to work. He walked into the apartment, leaving the door open behind him. *Maybe they were gone when he got here, and he tore the place apart in a rage,* Scott told himself, but he knew it was a desperate, foolish hope. If they hadn't been home, how did his other self get in? And why would they leave food on the table? No, they'd been here, the other Scott had found them, and now they were dead.

Stop it! You don't know that!

He heard sounds coming from down the hall where the bedrooms were. Wet sounds.

Oh, yes I do. He started down the hallway, taking one measured step at a time. No need to hurry now. The first two doors were closed, the last one open. He reached the doorway, turned, and his eyes were flooded with crimson.

"I'm considering calling it *Return to the Womb*, but then again, that might be a little too obvious. What do you think?"

The carpet, the walls, the curtains were smeared with

red handprints, and the bed upon which the remains of his wife and child lay was positively drenched in blood. Scott couldn't believe that two human bodies could possibly contain so much fluid. It was like a set from a bad slasher movie where the hack director keeps screaming "More blood!" at the special-effects crew, who reach one more time for plastic jugs of red-colored corn syrup. Gayle and David were naked, and there was no question whether or not they were dead. Gayle lay on her back, staring sightlessly up at the ceiling, mouth covered with duct tape, an assortment of well-used kitchen knives lined up on the mattress beside her. Her lower abdomen had been split by a vertical incision, and David had been positioned to make it seem as if he were . . . were crawling . . .

Scott felt his mind beginning to shut down. Gray nibbled the edges of his vision, and he knew it would only be moments before the darkness of oblivion followed. With any luck, his other self would take advantage of his unconsciousness and kill him. Scott certainly hoped so; there was nothing left to live for now.

Doppelganger Scott's mouth and chin were sticky with drying blood, and his smile revealed red-slick teeth. Both of his hands were coated so thick with crimson, it was almost as if he were wearing blood-colored gloves. Thick globs fell from his fingertips to patter onto the carpet, the drops steady as rain. Otherwise, he was clean, not a single stain on his jacket, shirt, pants, or shoes.

As if he'd read his other self's mind—and who knows, perhaps he had—Doppel-Scott said, "When you've done this sort of work as long as I have, you know how to avoid making a mess." He glanced at the grisly tableau on the bed. "A mess of yourself, I mean."

Scott's knees felt watery, and he didn't know how much

longer they'd hold him up. He stared at the killer he might have been, and was surprised to find that it wasn't at all like looking in a mirror. Yes, there was an undeniable physical similarity, despite the differences in hairstyle and clothing, but the cold emptiness in the other's eyes and the cruel, mocking expression twisting his face were nothing at all like the visage Scott saw when he brushed his teeth, combed his hair, shaved. This wasn't a mirror self; it was a shadow self. It was the bug under the rock, the pus-filled wound that refused to heal, the cancer cell eager to reproduce itself and begin feeding on its host. Maybe it had once been a boy and then a man called Scott Raymond, but decades of indulging every dark desire had purged anything even remotely human from its rotten excuse for a soul.

It was, pure and simply, evil.

And this realization gave Scott the strength to fend off unconsciousness. He wanted to live, if for no other reason than to destroy the thing that stood before him. If this was his darkest self, the worst of all that was or ever could be in him, then it was up to him to stop it. Who else was there?

Doppel-Scott arched an eyebrow, as if he were re-evaluating his other self. "Decided to fight, have you? I'd love it if you'd try, but I only feel it's fair to warn you what you're up against. After all, we are in a sense brothers, aren't we? Closer even than twins, because for the first dozen years of our life, we were the same person.

"When I killed Laura Foster, I made sure to leave enough fingerprints behind—not to mention a few knives that I hid so you and Miranda wouldn't find them—to make the police believe you did it. And just in case Ash Creek's finest are a little slow on the uptake, I decided to make it nice and clear for them this time." He held up a bloody palm. "If their evidence technicians can't get decent prints from this crime scene, then they don't deserve to catch you."

The red handprints that covered the walls seemed to swim in Scott's vision, and he bit down on his lip, teeth piercing soft flesh, warm blood running into his mouth. He welcomed the pain; it helped him focus.

"You mean catch *you*," Scott said. "You're the killer, not me."

Doppel-Scott wiggled his fingers. "We have the same prints, exact down to the tiniest whorl. And when I leave here, I'm going to take your piece-of-shit car—I don't need one myself, not on the dark roads I travel—and dump it somewhere out of town, making sure to leave plenty of forensic evidence in the process." He flicked his fingers and a daub of blood smacked Scott below his left eye. Whose blood was it, Scott wondered. Gayle's? David's? A mixture of both?

Suddenly he was a little boy cowering beneath a kitchen table, a pool of his mother's blood spreading on the floor close by, one edge gliding slowly toward him.

He bit his lip again, and once more the pain brought him back. He made no move to wipe away the blood running down his cheek like a tear. He wouldn't give his other self the satisfaction.

"Why such an elaborate plan? If you and Uncle Leonard want me out of the way so badly, why not just kill me and be done with it?"

"I could, you know. I could do it so swiftly your life would end in less time than it takes your heart to pause between beats, or I could draw your death out as long as I choose, sustaining your agony for days, even weeks."

"So? Why don't you?"

Doppel-Scott shrugged. "I already killed you once, and I

hate to repeat myself. I have something of a reputation as an artist, you know. Besides, killing you wasn't particularly satisfying." He grinned. "I'm finding it much more fun to frame you this time."

"I don't understand. What do you mean, 'this time'?"

His other self laughed. "You don't really think you're the first version of Scott Raymond that Miranda sent to stop me, do you? I killed Number One as soon as I became aware of him. You're Number Two."

"There was . . . another?"

"Yessir. How does it feel to be a second stringer, bro?"

Scott couldn't grasp this latest revelation. There'd been too much, too soon: everything Miranda had told him at her house, finding Gayle and David slaughtered, confronting his darkest self . . . The idea that there had been *three* Scotts instead of two would have to wait until such time—if any—that he could deal with it.

Thinking of Miranda brought another question to the forefront of his mind.

"I saw a documentary about you," Scott said. "All your victims were adult women; the video said nothing about you murdering children. Serial killers rarely deviate from their hunting patterns. So why did you abduct and kill Miranda Tanner?"

"Why the sudden curiosity? Thinking of writing a new book? Maybe you could call it *The Killer Who Was Me*, by Scott Raymond." His other self regarded Scott for a moment. "All right, why not? I suppose I could say that I'd grown bored with killing women and decided to broaden my repertoire, and that's true enough as it goes. But years of walking in Shadow had made me sensitive to other levels of existence, especially the alternate paths my life might have taken. One of those paths was yours, bro. I saw you had a reasonably successful career as a true-crime writer, a wife and a son." He nodded to their dead bodies. "I decided it was high time I had a child, too. So I did." He licked blood from his lips and grinned. "And I had her in every way imaginable."

The full implications of what his other self was saying hit Scott like a hammer in the gut, forcing out a cry of rage and sorrow. He ran toward his distorted reflection, fully intending to tear him apart with his bare hands, but one of Doppel-Scott's own bloody hands shot forth and caught him by the throat, stopping him in mid-charge.

"I'll give you this; there's more fight in you than the last Scott Miranda sent up against me. But there's no way you and that little bitch can beat me, bro. No way in hell."

He tried to respond, but all that came out of his mouth was a soft gurgling noise as his other self squeezed Scott's throat with fingers strong as iron. This time, no matter how hard he tried, Scott couldn't keep the darkness at bay, and as his consciousness ebbed, part of him hoped that this would finally be the end of it, that he would die and gain release from the nightmare his life had become. But the rest of him knew he wouldn't be so lucky. Then, for a time, he knew nothing at all.

The first thing he became aware of was the sensation of wet carpet pressing against the side of his face. He opened his eyes, saw the edge of a comforter, the empty space beneath a bed. No dust bunnies yet; Gayle hadn't lived here long enough for any to collect.

Gayle.

He tried to sit up, but the attempt made his head pound; it felt as if his skull was contracting, threatening to squeeze his brain out his ears. All he could do was lie on the carpet and breathe while he waited for the pain to subside to a manageable level. After several moments, the pain didn't get any better, but he thought he could deal with it. He tried sitting up again and was successful this time.

He wiped the cheek that rested on the carpet and his hand came away crimson. He'd been lying in blood. He examined his clothes and saw that along with the mud stains from the river, his jacket, shirt, jeans, and tennis shoes were smeared with blood. Before taking his leave, his other self had paused to rub some "forensic evidence" on Scott. He struggled to stand, losing his balance at one point and having to grab the comforter to steady himself. It began to slide off the bed, and he fell backward onto his ass as the comforter, the kitchen knives, and the bodies of his wife and son tumbled onto the floor in a heap of cloth, metal, meat, and blood.

"I'm sorry," he whispered, though there was no one else alive in the room to hear him. He got to his knees and started toward Gayle and David—he refused to think of them as *the bodies*—intending to pick them up and put them back on the bed, to restore some measure of dignity to them in death. But just as he was about to reach out and touch one of David's blood-slick bare feet, he hesitated. He wasn't worried about leaving any more evidence behind for the police. He didn't care what happened to him anymore. Scott had no idea how long he'd been unconscious or how much of a head start Doppel-Scott had, but the longer he remained here, the farther away his other self got. There was nothing he could do for his wife and son now. But there was plenty he could do to the man who'd killed them—*if* he could catch up to him.

"I'm sorry," he said again. "For everything." Hardly an adequate eulogy, but it was all he had time for. He tried to stand on his own this time and managed to get to his feet without falling. He took one last look at the room—the remains of his wife and child on the floor, the bloodstains on the carpet, the red handprints on the walls—and he let the hurt and the pain and the anger boil up inside him.

Miranda had wanted to awaken the killer in him so that he might be able to destroy the man who murdered her.

"Congratulations, Miranda," he said, tasting his own blood in his mouth and finding it sweet. "Mission accomplished."

As he walked down the stairs, he saw a young woman standing outside the entrance to the building pushing intercom buttons frantically, trying to get someone to let her in. He was not surprised to see it was Miranda.

So absorbed was she in pushing buttons that at first she didn't notice him open the door and step outside. Then she looked up and smiled in relief, but her smile quickly died when she saw the blood on his clothes.

"Are they . . . did he . . . ?"

Scott nodded.

Miranda was dressed in her usual black outfit, and while her skin was still bruised in places, she'd healed quite a bit since he'd left her. The seams in her flesh now had the appearance of weeks-old scars and most of her hair had grown back.

"I thought I felt their passing, but I'd hoped . . . oh, Scott!" She came to him and hugged him, pressing her body against his bloody clothes without a second thought and sobbed.

He felt an urge to wrap his fingers around her neck and

see if he couldn't make her permanently dead this time. If she hadn't tried to make him into a weapon to use against his other self, David and Gayle would still be alive right now, and he wouldn't be . . . what he'd become. But the way she cried, as if she'd lost two members of her own family, restrained him and he hugged her back.

When she pulled away, he looked into her eyes, and he saw something new there. Something familiar.

"They're a part of you now, aren't they? Just like all his other victims."

"Yes."

He pressed his fingers against her breastbone, trying to connect to the amalgam of spirits that resided within the vessel called Miranda. Then he leaned forward to kiss her, and in doing so, kissed more than her shell. After a moment, he drew back and gave her a smile that came more easily than he imagined it would.

"Let's go get the bastard." He reached out and took her hand.

She returned the smile and nodded. Holding onto his hand, she led him into the parking lot and toward a Honda Civic. It was parked at an odd angle, and the right fender was dented.

"Aren't you going to . . ."

"What?"

"You know, open some sort of doorway so we can catch up to him faster."

She gave him a look.

"Well, after all this 'walking in shadow' talk, I just thought—"

"It took a great deal of my energy to—literally—pull myself back together. Ordinarily I wouldn't waste power

on healing. That's why I had the cut on my hand for so
long, the one I got in the park?"

It was the hand he was holding, and he realized it was
now smooth and undamaged.

"But I didn't have a choice this time, not if I was going to
be any help to you. So even with the addition of your wife
and son's spirits, I don't have enough power to help us
travel. I do, however, have this." She brought them to a halt
before the Civic.

Realization hit him. "You borrowed your mom's car?"

She frowned. "It's not like I have one of my own." She
suddenly looked sheepish. "Sorry it took me so long to get
here. I, uh, never learned how to drive. I *was* only six when
I died, you know. I tried drawing on the memories of the
other women inside me, but . . ."

Scott looked at the crumpled fender and was surprised
to find himself having to fight to keep from laughing.
"Don't worry about it; I'll drive."

She smiled in relief. "I was hoping you'd say that."

Chapter Thirty

Concentrating on the mundane tasks of driving—hands at
ten and two o'clock, gaze moving from sideview mirror to
windshield to rearview and back again, foot pressed lightly
on the gas pedal (*Imagine there's an egg beneath it*, his driver's
ed instructor once told him)—helped take his mind off the
image of Gayle and David's desecrated bodies lying on the
floor where he'd left them. He was able to retreat into

the comfort of the rituals: keep one car length's distance between your vehicle and the one ahead for every ten miles you were traveling; signal well in advance of each turn; take your foot off the gas to slow down before you brake; and when you do, don't tromp on the pedal, pump it gently.

He needed the mental refuge driving provided, not only to shield him from the memory of seeing his wife and child's corpses but from the sights and sounds of the distorted streets Miranda and he traveled. Perhaps it was because she was with him, or perhaps it was due to whatever shift his psyche had undergone after meeting his other self, but Ash Creek no longer resembled a medium-sized Ohio town. The sky was the grayish white of a drowned, water-bloated body, and the trees had become curving, jagged lengths of bleached bone thrusting upward from cracked, barren soil. The road on which they drove was covered with a hard, pebbly surface resembling rhino or elephant hide instead of asphalt, and it rose and fell gently as they passed over, as if it were breathing. Buildings no longer adhered to established principles of architecture, or even the laws of physics for that matter. Some resembled gigantic conch shells, others double-helixes made of crystal and algae. There were structures formed from quivering pink flesh covered with thousands of screaming mouths, and lattices of glistening insect wings that slowly beat the air to no apparent purpose.

Scott glanced at Miranda, and she shook her head.

"I'm not doing it; I don't have the strength. I think maybe you are."

A creature made of a dozen interlocked spinal columns skittered onto the road, and Scott had to swerve to avoid hitting it. He didn't know if the thing would be injured if they struck it—hell, he didn't even know if it were even alive in any meaningful sense of the word—but he didn't want to risk damaging the car. Without it, they wouldn't be able to catch up to his doppelganger. Worse yet, they might be stranded in this nightmarish version of Ash Creek forever.

"I think you forged a connection with your other self when you met," Miranda continued. "He's taking a shortcut through Shadow, and in a sense, he's pulling us along after him."

Up to this point, he'd only had hints and glimpses of the true darkness that existed alongside what most people thought of as reality. Now he was experiencing the totality of what Miranda, Uncle Leonard, and his alternate self referred to simply as *Shadow*. He could've done without it, thank you very much, but if driving these dark roads would help him catch the other Scott Raymond, then drive them he would, and be glad of it.

Miranda pointed. "Look! Isn't that your car?"

Scott saw the flashing lights of a black-and-white that had pulled over to the side of the road. Parked in front of it was a Subaru that, if it wasn't his, sure looked a hell of a lot like it.

He smiled. This was too damn good to be true.

He slowed as they drew near, and they saw two police officers struggling with a man in a vacant lot where shards of glass grew from the ground instead of vegetation. It seemed Square-Head and Machine Eyes had finally cornered their quarry.

Scott remembered what his other self had said about their possessing identical fingerprints. *Guess what, asshole? Looks like we share the same scent, too.*

The two hell-cops weren't having an easy time of it, though. Doppel-Scott was armed with a black metal blade that looked large enough to be a short sword—his personal weapon, Scott guessed. The cloth over Machine Eyes's right shoulder was torn and bloody, and her arm flopped uselessly at her side as she fought. Doppel-Scott had managed to cut away a good-sized chunk of her partner's skull, making him Oblong-Head now, Scott supposed. Despite his hideous injury, the brood-get continued fighting, teeth bared, fingers transformed into hooked talons. Both of the cops' weapons remained holstered at their sides. Maybe firearms didn't work in the realm of Shadow, Scott thought. Or maybe his other self didn't give them time to draw their guns. Or maybe the hell-cops simply thought it more fun to fight claw to blade. If the latter, they were paying for it now.

Not that his alternate self had gone unscathed. His forehead, cheeks, neck, and hands were covered with bloody slash wounds. It was a wonder he could see from all the gore pouring into his eyes, or maintain a grip on his dark blade with blood-slick fingers. But then again, he was a superpredator, quite possibly one of the most dangerous killers who'd ever lived. He was holding his own against his inhuman attackers, and given time, he might even prevail over them. Might.

Scott experienced conflicting emotions as he brought the Civic even with his Subaru. On the one hand, he felt cheated out of his revenge—Doppel-Scott had killed *his* wife and child, and *he* should've been the one to take him down—but on the other, he was relieved to find Square-Head and Machine Eyes doing his dirty work for him. Seeing his other self fight like a sort of martial demon made him realize that no matter what changes Miranda wrought in him, he'd never stand a chance against his dark doppelganger.

"What should we do?" he asked her.

She answered without hesitation. "Keep driving. With any luck, they'll cut each other to ribbons."

"I was hoping you'd say that." Scott started to press down on the gas pedal but then, on impulse, touched the switch to roll down the driver's side window, thrust his arm out, and flipped his other self the bird. Then he hit the gas and the Civic lurched forward as they accelerated away. After a couple moments, he pulled his hand back inside and rolled the window up once more. Doppel-Scott had probably been too busy fighting for his life to catch his farewell gesture, but damn if he didn't feel better for making it.

They drove through the Dali-esque landscape in silence for a bit after that. Scott hoped that the world would return to normal if he waited long enough, but it showed no sign of doing so.

Eventually, he said, "That's it, isn't it? I mean, I suppose there's a chance my other self will survive, but there's an equally good chance he won't. All we have to do is give them some time to finish fighting, then circle back to see who won. If we're lucky, the brood-get will have finished off the other Scott—and not only will he be dead, hopefully the hell-cops will be satisfied that they've avenged the death of their broodmother and lose interest in me. The career of Scott Raymond, serial killer, will be over, you and your sisters will have had your revenge, and maybe Gayle and David will be able to rest easier knowing their murderer is dead."

He glanced at Miranda, but she didn't respond. She was staring out the windshield, lost in thought.

"Not exactly the happiest of endings, I'll grant you, but—"

"It wasn't supposed to happen this way." Tears slid down Miranda's scarred cheeks, and she sounded more like a little girl than ever, and a lost little girl at that.

"I don't understand," Scott said. "I know he might survive, but he might *not*. And if he does, he'll be hurt . . . weakened, and we'll stand a greater chance of—"

"That's not the point!" she sobbed. She turned to him and wiped her eyes with the heels of her hands, first one, then the other, the way a child would. "I didn't just want to kill *him* . . . I wanted to save *me*!"

"I'd say you lost me, but I've been lost since this whole mess started. What are you talking about, Miranda?"

"I'm talking about a way to save the life of the six-year-old girl I once was. All we have to do is—"

"Uh-uh. No more. I'm sorry, but I've experienced more death and madness the last few days than most people do in their entire lives, and while I'm not confident I'm going to come through this with my sanity intact, it's beginning to look like I might at least keep from getting killed, and I'm shocked to discover that still matters to me. So whatever else you're scheming, you can forget—"

"We can save Gayle and David, too, Scott. Not only can we restore them to life, we can change events so the past few days never happened for them. The other Scott Raymond will have never gone after them, never done the things he did to them."

Scott didn't respond right away. He continued driving through the twisted landscape of the Shadow Realm, only now he barely noticed the oddities they passed. He was too busy thinking.

You can't trust her. She's proven that time and again.

She helped me escape from the hell-cops, and then she followed me to Gayle and David's.

Remember what your double said. You're not the first Scott Raymond she's used in her plot for revenge—and the other one was killed.

Maybe.

Let the brood-get deal with your other self! You're no fighter: You're just a failed husband and father who's a half-step away from being institutionalized for life! If you're smart, you'll cut your goddamned losses and get the hell out of Dodge right now!

If there's even a *chance* I can save Gayle and David . . .

No, no, no, no, no, no, no!

He turned to Miranda. "What do we have to do?"

Chapter Thirty-one

Orchard Park looked much the same in the Shadow Realm as it did in what Scott had come to think of as the "real world," though that term held little meaning for him anymore. The sky was still the color of dead flesh and the trees broken lengths of bleached bone as in the rest of Shadow, but the play area appeared normal enough, if one ignored the way the FOR WHEELCHAIR USE ONLY swing swayed listlessly in the still, stale air, the occasional sideways glances from the *Wizard of Oz* heads crowning the swing set, and the quivering anticipation of the spider climber as it waited patiently for potential prey to make the mistake of coming too close.

Miranda sat on the swing beneath the Tin Woodsman's head, hands holding the chains, legs stretched out in front of her, twisting gently from side to side. Scott sat cross-legged on the cedar-chip covered ground in front of her, idly picking up chips, fingering one for a moment before tossing it aside and reaching for another.

Though Scott had seen no hint of a sun in the corpse-colored sky, the shadows in the park were growing long, and he knew night wasn't far off. If what he'd experienced during the day in this place was any indication, he wasn't looking forward to what might come out to play under cover of darkness.

"My other self said you'd tried to stop him before, that you'd recruited another version of me to go up against him. He said he killed that Scott easily."

Miranda looked surprised, but she said, "It's true. I first made contact with a Scott Raymond on a different life path from either you or the man who killed me. He had been raised by your grandmother and gone to college, but while he'd dated Gayle a few times, they didn't stay together."

"I was still pretty messed up in those days . . . drank too much, did too many drugs . . . Gayle almost left me, but I managed to get my shit together enough that she stayed. I guess this third Scott didn't." He tried to imagine the man's life—*his* life—if he hadn't married Gayle, if there hadn't been any David, but he couldn't.

Miranda nodded. "He went to work for a small weekly paper in northern Ohio, eventually moving up to the crime beat. He tried writing freelance articles, but with only modest success. He'd completed one book and was still trying to get it published when he was fired from his job—

unlike you, he was still struggling with alcohol and drugs. He managed to land another job with the paper here in Ash Creek."

"Managed?"

Miranda smiled. "With a little supernatural assist. I made contact with him, introduced him to Shadow, as I did with you. He . . . took to it more easily, though. Almost seemed to enjoy it."

Scott wasn't surprised. Without the influence of Gayle and David in his life, that Scott Raymond had likely lived on the edge of darkness for so many years that the transition to Shadow wasn't that great a leap for him.

"I made the mistake of telling him the whole story too early, and he chose to go after his other self alone, before he was fully prepared."

"He didn't stand a chance, did he?"

"No," she said softly.

They fell silent then, Miranda twisting slowly on her swing, Scott playing with cedar chips.

After some time, he asked, "Why didn't you tell me?"

"I don't know. There was so much weird stuff that I *had* to tell you, I guess I didn't want to overwhelm you any more than necessary. And . . . I'd gotten to know that other Scott a little before he died. Despite his faults, he was a good man with a strong inner core of decency—the exact opposite of the man who killed me. In the short time we were together, I . . ."

Scott looked up from the cedar chips and met Miranda's gaze. "What?"

Her reply was so soft, he wasn't sure he heard her right. "I came to love him." Before he could ask her to repeat herself, she hurried on, more loudly this time. "I almost gave up then rather than risk the life of another version of you. But my sisters felt . . . otherwise. They aren't self-aware, not in the same way I am. They are emotion incarnate— agony, sorrow, fury—and they exist solely for revenge. They won't let anything get in the way of seeing their killer brought to justice." She touched her fingers to one scarred cheek. "Not even me. So we searched through dozens of life paths, looking for the one Scott Raymond who possessed the most suitable balance between light and shadow. A good enough man to want to stop his other self, but one with enough darkness in him to actually do it."

"And you chose me."

"Yes." A smile. "You're our champion, our knight in shining armor."

"More like tarnished armor." He smiled back at her and found himself wondering if, out of all the possible directions his life might have taken, if there was one road he traveled with a human woman named Miranda. "So now here we are."

"Yes."

He stood up and brushed clinging cedar chips from the seat of his jeans. "Now what? Do I challenge Killer Scott to a duel? Butcher knives at a dozen paces?"

A breeze blew through the play area then, gentle but cold, like the air wafting forth from an open freezer. Carried on the wind was the nearly inaudible sound of whispering.

Miranda got off the swing and walked over to him. "Not yet. If you go up against him now, you won't fare any better than the first Scott who tried. You need to prepare yourself."

He didn't like the sound of that. "And I do this by . . . ?"

"Facing the darkness inside you and mastering it. Only by doing this can you find the strength to defeat your shadow self."

The whispering grew stronger, clearer, and he thought he could make it out now, a single word, repeated over and over.

Yes, yes, yes, yes, yes, yes, yes, yessssss . . .

"I don't suppose you can be a little more specific?"

She took his hands and gripped them tight. "I would if I could." Tears welled in her eyes. "The truth is, I don't really know what you'll experience; I just know you have to do it."

"And if I *do* do it, whatever *it* is, there's still no guarantee I'll beat my other self, is there?"

"No. But you'll have a chance, I do know that much."

A chance. And from the sound of it, not a big one. Still, Scott knew he had no right to expect otherwise. What more did life ever offer anyone except an uncertain chance at an unguessable outcome? Real world, Shadow Realm . . . in the end, there was no appreciable difference. The rules were still the same and just as simple. You pay your money and you take your chance; the only real choice you have is whether or not to spin the wheel in the first place.

Scott brushed away a tear from Miranda's face. He thought of the six-year-old girl whose face he'd first seen on missing-child posters . . . thought of Gayle and all they'd shared over the years . . . there'd been fights, yes, harsh words and hurt feelings, but there'd been far more loving touches, late-night talks, and shared laughter . . . he thought of David, remembered first hearing the soft *whoosh-whoosh-whoosh* of his heartbeat as the obstetrician pressed an ultrasound device to Gayle's swollen belly, remembered the sight of him emerging into the world, slick with blood and somehow all the more beautiful for it, remembered first words, first steps, first teeth, and hundreds, no, thousands of other such moments that had not only taught Scott what the word *love* truly meant but redefined and broadened the word beyond anything he could've possibly imagined before becoming a father.

In the end, there was really no choice. For Miranda, for Gayle, and above all for David, it was time to spin the wheel.

"How do we do it?"

Miranda leaned forward and kissed him gently. When she pulled back, she whispered, "Thank you," and her words were echoed and re-echoed upon the air.

She released his hands. "First we need a spider. Not a dried one this time, but a live one."

He turned to look at the spider climber.

"In the bushes behind it," she said.

"Are you sure?"

"Yes. 'One pill makes you larger, and one pill makes you small.' "

"Yeah, but Alice didn't have to get past a giant mommy spider in order to get to Wonderland." He started walking toward the climber, trying—and failing miserably—not to think about how it had sprung upon one of the brood-get that had attacked them the night they'd spied on Laura and her children.

As he drew closer, he sensed the climber's attention focusing on him, though there were no outward signs of this. It remained, in appearance at least, a child's plaything made of metal and paint. But Scott could feel the air around the climber vibrating as it quivered in anticipation of his approach. How was he supposed to get past the thing? He had no weapons, and as soon as he was close enough, he knew the climber would shimmer and transform into the monstrosity that had pulled a brood-get youth into the bushes to feed.

When he was within a yard of the creature, the ground in front of him bulged, and a hand thrust through the cedar chips. A woman's hand. He stopped and watched as a naked form of Laura Foster pulled itself free of the earth.

Her skin was blue-white, and her abdominal cavity yawned open, her internal organs hanging out, loops of intestine touching the ground. She smiled at him, reached down, gathered a coil of intestine and threw it over her shoulder as if were a feather boa.

"Get the bastard for us," she hissed, then grinned, showing teeth as sharp as any of her children's. "And don't say I never did anything for you." Then she turned and walked toward the climber.

When she was within a foot of it, the air around the thing wavered and the fanged, furred arachnid pounced on her. She didn't cry out as the spider pulled her off her feet, didn't struggle as it injected venom into her body cavity and then began dragging her toward the bushes. She merely gave Scott a jaunty wave and a wink, and then both she and the spider were gone.

He hesitated for a moment, then walked to the bushes, and gently pushed the branches apart so he could see.

Behind the green, the mother spider continued pumping Laura with venom, softening her flesh for the thousands of smaller spiders that swarmed over her body, climbed onto her exposed organs and scurried into her abdominal cavity to explore the secret wet recesses inside.

Clamping his jaw tight against nausea, Scott carefully reached for the closest baby spider—he only needed one—and snagged it by a single furry leg. He pulled his hand back before the mother spider noticed, and returned to Miranda, making sure to kept the wriggling baby at arm's length so it couldn't bite him.

"Now what?"

"Down the hatch."

He looked at the spider struggling in his grasp and thought of its siblings, thousands of them, busily devouring Laura's corpse behind the bushes.

"You've got to be kidding."

"They're far more potent alive," Miranda said. "It won't work if we kill it."

Scott sighed, closed his eyes, and slowly brought the spider toward his open mouth. He popped it in, but before he could bite down, the thing scurried down his throat, as if eager to find out what delights this new body had to offer.

Scott coughed, wheezed, gagged, and thought he was going to puke his guts out, but since he hadn't had anything to eat in so long—and since the spider seemed reluctant to be expelled—all he did was dry heave for a few moments, bringing up only a few mouthfuls of bile he spat on the ground. Finally, his digestive system gave up and settled down, and the urge to vomit passed.

"Now what do I do?"

Miranda took his hand and pulled him down to a sitting position. They sat cross-legged, facing each other, Miranda continuing to hold onto his hand and stroking the back of it with her thumb.

"Now we wait for the spider to relax and begin dreaming. It shouldn't take long. And Scott?"

"Hmmm?" A pleasant warmth was beginning to suffuse his body, and he found it hard to focus on Miranda's words.

"Good luck."

He tried to say *thanks*, but the word wouldn't come out, and then he was someplace else.

Chapter Thirty-two

There is the smell of old wood and musty curtains. Above him is the underside of a table; below, a wooden floor, knots and whorls plainly visible in the boards. He's wearing shorts, socks, a brand-new pair of tennis shoes, but his legs are thin, hairless, and smaller than they should be. He's wearing a T-shirt with a cartoon image of a fish standing on the edge of a lake with an angler's hat on its scaled head and holding a fishing pole. On the other end of the line, jumping out of the water, is a man in a brown shirt and pants, and although the detail isn't clear, presumably the hook is buried in his cheek. The fish is winking and the caption below the picture reads I'M HOOKED ON LAKE HOPEWELL. He thought the shirt was funny when his mom bought it for him at the lodge gift shop. He doesn't think it's so amusing right now.

He touches his chest and finds it scrawny, can feel the ribs close under the skin. Touches his head, finds his hair short and fuzzy, almost a buzz cut, and a strange thought drifts through his mind.

I am nine years old, and I am hiding beneath the table in the kitchen of our cabin at Lake Hopewell because my uncle is killing my family.

And then he becomes aware of the screams, realizes he's been hearing them all along, but hasn't allowed them to sink in. He knows what he's supposed to do now: make his hands into fists and jam them against his ears in the vain hope he won't be able to hear the screams then. And he starts to—after all, he has a part to play and his role was choreographed a long time ago—but he hesitates. Something is different this time, but he's not sure what.

The scuffle of feet nearby, a final sharp shriek and then a woman falls to the floor, her face turned toward him, eyes wide and staring. It's his mother.

Blood runs from a dozen different wounds and collects beneath her. The pool widens, and its leading edge begins to spread toward him. He's supposed to be concerned about the new shoes his mother got him before their vacation, supposed to worry about what she'll think if he gets them all bloody, but he doesn't give a damn about his shoes. That's his *mother* lying there, sundress shredded, one breast visible, a last small indignity, one that hardly seems to matter given the enormity of what's happened to her. She's gone, and she's never coming back.

More scuffling feet. Two men are fighting—one in shorts, the other in khaki slacks. He recognizes the hairy legs of the man in shorts. They belong to his father. He's supposed to sit here and watch his father die too, wait for him to fall, one arm flopping across his mother's body in a final awkward embrace, almost as if their corpses were posed like a pair of window-display mannequins in a department store in hell.

But he doesn't sit. He crawls out from beneath the table,

avoiding the widening pool of his mother's blood, and stands. His father has hold of his uncle's wrists, a blood-slick hunting knife held tight in the latter's right hand. They take one step forward, two steps back as they fight, looking almost as if they're dancing. His uncle's eyes are wild, his mouth stretched wide in a lunatic's grin. His light brown short-sleeved shirt, pants, and black shoes are dotted with blood, almost as if he's a painter who's been a little sloppy as he worked.

He's struck by how much his father and uncle resemble each other. They're brothers, of course, Leonard the older of the two by several years, but it's more than just a physical similarity. There's a feverish gleam in his father's eyes, a cruel twist to his mouth as he struggles against his sibling, and he realizes that his father and uncle share something besides the same set of parents: the same dark fire burns inside them both. It blazes far more strongly in Uncle Leonard, though, and it's obvious to him that his father doesn't stand a chance. He has to do something.

He's only nine years old and he's terrified beyond words, but he's also three decades older and mad as hell. He rushes toward them, grabs hold of his uncle's knife arm. At nine, his body doesn't have much muscle or weight, but he hopes to slow Leonard down enough to give his father an advantage. He imagines his father wrestling the knife from Leonard, killing him, and then rushing to the phone to call an ambulance. He knows it's too late for his mother, and likely so for his sister and brother, as well as his paternal grandparents whose bodies all lie elsewhere in the cabin. But at least the call would be made, and if there's even a spark of life left in any of them . . .

Uncle Leonard looks at him. "You might as well not bother, Scotty. Nothing you do here will change what hap-

pened on that fine summer evening at Lake Hopewell." His
uncle shifts to the side, slams him against the kitchen wall.
The air whooshes out of his lungs and he loses his grip on
Leonard's arm. He falls to the floor, sits, gulps air as he
desperately tries to breathe.

"Leave him alone, you sonofabitch!" his father shouts,
and Leonard laughs as he renews his efforts to get the knife
away from him.

"You're just a fragment of your son's memory, brother.
Little more than a walking, talking paper doll." With a sudden burst of strength, Leonard flings his brother back,
breaking his hold on his wrists. His brother staggers back,
his right shoe steps in his own wife's blood, and his foot
slides. His legs fly out from under him like one of the
Three Stooges taking a spectacular pratfall, and he falls
hard, landing next to his dead wife. There's a snapping
sound as he hits, and Scott knows something has broken
inside. The fierce light in his father's eyes dims until
they're just the eyes of a scared, hurt man who knows that
he's lost.

Leonard takes his time walking over to his fallen
brother. "There's no real need to kill him, you know," he
says, speaking to his nephew who's still struggling to pull
air into his lungs. "Only you and I are real here. But if I
don't, he'll just keep interfering, like a mechanical toy
whose battery refuses to run down. So . . ." He kneels, and
with a single swift stroke slices his brother's throat open.
Blood gushes forth, running down either side of his neck,
spreading across the floor, some of it mingling with that of
his wife. He's lying in a different position this time, and his
arm isn't across her, but he's next to her, and that's close
enough.

Leonard wipes the blade clean on his brother's chest,

then stands and walks over to Scott. "Do you remember what I said to you next, when this really happened?"

Scott manages to draw in enough air to answer in a croaking voice. "You said it was my turn."

Leonard is younger, thinner, and has more hair, but his mouth is still the same cruel slash, his eyes still those of a hungry predator. "That's right, but I didn't kill you. Instead, I turned and walked away. Do you remember why?"

"No." It's a lie. He hasn't remembered for thirty years, has worked goddamned hard *not* to remember, but here, now, in this place fashioned from the very substance of memory, he can't help but recall.

"You were huddled beneath the kitchen table, fists jammed against your ears, your ass soaking in your mother's blood. When you wouldn't come out, I pushed the table aside and reached for you, and then—"

He doesn't want to say it, but he'd rather the words come out of his mouth than his uncle's. "I dipped my finger in Mom's blood and touched it to my lips." A wave of self-loathing and revulsion crashes through him, and he wants to cry, wants to bawl his fucking eyes out, but he fights the tears. He knows he can't afford them now.

"And you didn't know why, did you?"

He shakes his head.

"It was instinct, Scotty-boy. The killer buried in you found a way to communicate to the killer in me. Found a way to say, 'Look, I'm just like you.'"

"No." But denial was useless in this place of memory. He knew Leonard was right.

"And that's why I spared you. Your father had the dark fire in him." He turned and gave his brother's leg a contemptuous kick. "When we were kids, we used to have all sorts of fun with animals. We started with frogs and turtles, eventually working our way up to cats and dogs. But somewhere along the line, he lost the taste for blood, and he turned away from his true nature. I thought it was temporary, that he was merely frightened by the greatness that lay within him and that one day he'd return to it. When we were adults—years after I'd graduated to using humans as my playmates and the papers began calling me 'The Surgeon'—I made the mistake of telling your father about my burgeoning career. Not directly, of course. I sounded him out by pretending they were only fantasies that I hadn't acted on yet. I hoped . . . well, that doesn't matter. He told me that I was sick and should get psychological help as soon as possible, and that if I didn't seek it on my own, he'd make sure I got it, one way or the other."

Leonard smiles. "He should've known it was a mistake to threaten me. Three weeks later, your family went to Lake Hopewell for a week's vacation. Halfway through the week, I made a surprise visit. I came to kill your father so he wouldn't give me away, and while I was here I killed everyone else—my niece, my other nephew, my sister-in-law and my own dear, sweet parents—just for the fun of it."

Scott is feeling better now, but he doesn't try to stand, senses it would be a mistake to so much as move. "Why?" He's not sure what he means by the question, just knows he has to ask it.

Leonard has no problem understanding. "Here's the hell of it, Scotty-boy. *There is no reason.* My parents were good, loving people who did everything right, or at least as close as anyone could. My childhood was a place of warmth, safety, and happiness. I guess, like Popeye, I simply yam what I yam. And you have the dark fire in you, too—or at least *my* Scott does. Who knows? Perhaps it smolders in your David as well."

That brings him to his feet. "Never. Not my son."

Leonard grins. "Nature versus nurture, Scotty-boy. You may be able to exert some influence on the latter, but not the former. I am what I am, you are what you are, and your son . . . well, only time will time, eh?"

Scott starts toward his uncle. He has no idea what he's going to do when he reaches him, but he figures kicking in that goddamned smiling mouth of his is a fine place to start. But Leonard, with a movement as lithe and graceful as any jungle cat, moves his arm and now the bloody hunting knife is pointing at Scott, only inches from his scrawny nine-year-old chest.

"You know why you're here, don't you? I'm your *bete noir*, your black beast. The idea is that if you can face and defeat me, you'll discover the inner strength to confront my Scott and stop him. Absurd, isn't it?"

There's something in his uncle's tone that tells Scott *he* doesn't think it's absurd. In fact, he sounds as if he's a little scared and trying hard to cover it up. "I don't know," Scott says. "I'm not hiding under the table anymore. I'm standing right here in front of you, face to face."

Leonard sounds thoughtful now. "Perhaps you *do* have a thread of steel running through you. But a thread isn't enough. I suppose that little cooz of yours has told you that she's been trying to 'awaken the darkness in you' or somesuch nonsense."

Scott sees no point in lying to his uncle. In this place of the mind, he's not sure deception is even possible. "Yes."

"That's a pretty way of saying she's trying to turn you into a killer. Do you know what the real reason behind your first visit to the park was? Miranda wanted you to be discovered by the brood-get and attacked. She hoped that if you were placed in a life and death situation, the killer in you would emerge. But it didn't because the dark fire is too weak in you, just as it was in your father. Oh, you fought, but you didn't *kill*, not purposefully, with your own hands."

Scott realizes something. "That's why you stepped in and killed Jamey. You weren't trying to save me; you were afraid that eventually I'd be forced to kill him and be one step closer to destroying your Scott. You're worried that Miranda was right."

Leonard doesn't answer.

"You killed Gammy's spirit on the dreamplane, or at least severed my connection with her by seeming to kill her. I'm not sure I understand the difference, but it doesn't matter. If her spirit can die in a dream, that means yours can die here, doesn't it? In this place, I *can* kill you, and you know it."

Still no answer.

"And if I kill you, I'll gain the power to kill my other self."

Finally an answer. "The power to make the attempt, at any rate. But such power demands a high price, one that you might not want to pay. The realm of Shadow is like Nietzsche's abyss: one cannot walk its dark paths without being changed by them. To defeat my Scott, you'll have to become as he is. And once he's gone, who's to say you won't be just like him? Perhaps even worse? You'll succeed in removing one killer from the world only to replace him yourself."

Scott knows there is no trickery in his uncle's words. What he says is true. "It's a chance I'm willing to take."

Leonard cocks his head to one side, as if truly seeing Scott—*this* Scott—for the first time. "You might be able to do it. Do you know the moment when your life path and that of my Scott's broke away from each other? When your dear Gammy had a heart attack not long after you moved in with her. You found her lying on the kitchen floor and called 911 just in time. If you'd called any later, she would've died. Well, my Scott *did* call later. As he was riding his bike home, he saw a crow perched on a farmer's fence post."

Scott remembered that crow. Biggest and blackest one he'd ever seen, as if a piece of night itself had been given feathery form.

"You were tempted to stop and throw a rock at the bird, but you remembered how your Gammy was always telling you to be good, and you kept on riding. My Scott decided to ignore his Gammy's advice, and he stopped. He had a good arm, too, clipped the crow's head on the first try. The bird fell to the ground, and my Scott ran to get it before it could recover and fly away. He had a pocketknife, and he put it to good use. Altogether, he spent a half hour playing with the bird, and by the time he finished, wiped his hands in the grass and rode home, Gammy was dead. And so, with no other living relatives who would take him in, he came to stay with me. And under my tutelage, the spark of his dark fire was fanned into a burning ebon flame."

"Maybe I could've become like your Scott once, but our paths branched off long ago, and I'm a much different person than he is. Whatever happens here, however I change as a result, I won't become a killer like him."

"Perhaps, but it's a moot point. My Scott easily killed the first double that came after him. He found the experience disappointing and decided he'd rather play with you a bit this time, and I went along. But playtime's over. My Scott may not be the child of my blood, but he's my son in darkness, and I won't let you harm him." Leonard turns the hunting knife slowly this way and that, and light glints off the blade, mirroring the light gleaming in his eyes. "And don't think you're safe because we're meeting on a mental landscape. If you die here, you die, period."

Scott realizes that, whether by accident or subconscious design, he's chosen a dangerous battlefield upon which to face Leonard. His uncle is young and strong here, and while Scott possesses the mind of his adult self, his body is that of a nine-year-old. Leonard is an experienced, ruthless killer, and Scott doesn't have a single weapon.

His stomach roils then, and he feels a tickling sensation in his esophagus. Maybe, he realizes, he *does* have a weapon.

Leonard raises the hunting knife, its metal still wet with the blood of Scott's mother and father. "It's been fun, Scotty-boy, but you know what they say: all good things come to an end."

Scott opens his mouth as if to speak last words, and his uncle hesitates. It's all the time Scott needs. His abdominal muscles buck and an uprush of acid sears his throat. In a spray of vomit, the baby spider he swallowed in the park—he doesn't question how it can also be here in the realm of memory, it just *is*—shoots out of his mouth. It flies through the air, its trajectory a perfect, beautiful thing to behold, and lands on Leonard's mouth. Immediately, its legs work to pry open the lips of its new host, eager to scuttle inside and see what new dreams this one has to offer.

Leonard flails at the spider, stumbles backward as he tries to dislodge the bile-coated arachnid from his mouth. Scott hopes that he'll lose his grip on the knife and drop it, but he doesn't. Scott rushes forward, grabs his uncle's wrist and tries to shake the knife loose, but Leonard holds fast to the blade, almost as if it's another appendage of his body. He finally manages to knock the spider onto the floor, and before it can skitter away, he stomps on it with one of his blood-spattered shoes. There's a short, muffled cry, almost like a human infant's, and then silence.

Scott knows he only has a split second before his uncle's attention turns his way, and he does the only thing he can think of: he sinks his teeth into Leonard's wrist. The serial killer once known to authorities as the Surgeon emits a high-pitched shriek like a little old lady, and Scott finds it surprising that a creature used to doling out pain to others should react so strongly to his own. Blood rushes into Scott's mouth, the coppery tang familiar enough, but there's also a strange taste that he can't identify, as if his blood is seasoned with exotic spices—or perhaps tainted by years of dwelling in Shadow.

Leonard's fingers spring open and the knife falls to the kitchen floor. Scott feels a surge of triumph as he pulls his teeth out of his uncle's flesh and makes a grab for the blade. But before he can reach it, Leonard lashes out with the back of his fist and Scott is knocked backward into the wall. Again, the breath is forced from his lungs, and he can do nothing but slump to the floor and gasp for air.

Leonard examines his bleeding wrist, then looks at Scott and grins. "Nice try, boy. But your old Uncle Leonard isn't that easy to kill." He holds his wrist out for Scott to see, and as he watches, the blood flows backward into the wound, which then seals itself neatly until the flesh is smooth, pink, and unmarked.

"The problem with the real world is that it's too stubbornly solid. The realm of Shadow, as well as mental landscapes like this one, are more malleable. *If* you know what you're doing." The knife on the floor sprouts a hundred metallic centipede legs and quick as a flash, climbs onto Leonard's shoe, up his trouser leg, across belly and chest, over shoulder, down along his right arm and into his waiting hand. When it's once again safely in his grip, the legs melt back into the blade's metal. "This entire place is a potential weapon, but you don't have the experience to use it against me. Now let's see, where were we? Oh, yes. Not to repeat myself, but . . . *it's your turn*, Scott."

Leonard steps forward, mouth stretched into a grin, eyes bright with the fire of madness. Scott knows there's nothing he can do now but die.

He sees movement out of the corner of his eye, and his gaze is drawn to the pool of blood that surrounds his mother and father. As he watches, wet red slides across the floor, separating, coagulating, forming shapes. No, not merely shapes. *Letters*. Letters that spell out a simple message.

IN YOUR POCKET.

Scott has no idea what this means, but he trusts his parents. He reaches into the pocket of his shorts, and his fingers close around an object that he could swear wasn't there a moment before. But it's there now, and that's all that matters. He pulls it out, looks at it, sees that it's his half of the wishbone, the one that he and Gammy broke in his last dream of her. The one she'd told him to hold on to. Now he knows why.

As Leonard draws near, Scott makes a wish and lunges toward him. Leonard's knife arm is fast, but this time Scott is faster, and he buries the broken end of the wishbone in his uncle's chest, right above his heart.

Leonard screams and the universe shatters into a million pieces.

Chapter Thirty-three

When the universe reassembled itself, Scott found himself standing in a darkened room. The curtains were drawn, but a thin sliver of light between them told him it was daylight out. The air was thick with the smells of shit and piss, mixed with the rank odor of slow-rotting flesh. He touched his chest and found it broad and solid once again; he was no longer nine years old.

As his vision adjusted to the dimness of the room—a bedroom, he realized—he saw that it was sparsely furnished: single bed, nightstand, dresser. The floor beneath his feet was made of old wood and creaked whenever he shifted his weight. It felt as if the whole house were fragile, that one good stomp could bring the whole thing crashing down like a child's game of jackstraws.

As seconds ticked by, and his eyes continued to acclimate to the darkness, he became aware of the faint sound of breathing—thready and labored—coming from the bed, and he realized that he wasn't alone in the room.

"Who's there?" he asked, the words sounding loud as

gunshots in the silence of the room, though he spoke normally.

"Who else?" The voice was barely more than a hoarse whisper, but it was recognizable as Uncle Leonard's.

Scott stepped toward the nightstand, and fumbled for the switch on the bedside lamp. Sour yellow illumination splashed the room, and the scarecrow lying on the bed closed its eyes and turned its skull face away from the light. Its movements were slow, like a lizard that had basked too long in the sun.

Scott walked to Leonard's bedside, unconcerned that he was placing himself within striking distance of the infamous serial killer once known as the Surgeon. He knew there was nothing Leonard could do to hurt him now. His uncle's skin was dry as parchment, and liver spots dotted his nearly bald head. The few wisps of hair that clung to his pate were white and looked as if they might fall out any moment. His eyes had receded into his skull, as though they were retreating from a world that they had seen far too much of. The sheet that covered him was stained with phlegm, blood, urine, and feces, like a shroud composed of bodily fluids.

Leonard turned to face Scott, opening his eyes, but keeping them squinted against the light. "I suppose congratulations are in order. I honestly didn't think you could defeat me. I guess there's more of my Scott in you than I thought." He paused after each sentence as if to build up strength for the next. When he was finished, he coughed several times. Not a deep, violent spasm as Scott expected, but an almost breathless *kaff-kaff*, as though his lungs weren't strong enough to do any more.

"You'll forgive me if I don't take that as a compliment," Scott said.

Leonard laughed, the sound barely distinguishable from his coughing. "He'll still kill you in the end; you know that, don't you?"

Scott ignored the gibe. "Where are we?"

"Another memory. Mine this time. Do you know how I died?"

Scott remembered from the serial killer documentary. "Your Scott hacked you to pieces and hid the bits around your house. The authorities never did find all of you."

Leonard chuckled, the sound dry and rough as rattling bones. "That's right. But what no one besides Scott and myself knew was that I was already dying from cancer. I asked Scott to kill me. Not to release me from the pain." He grinned, displaying soft gray teeth and bleeding gums. "I rather liked that part, actually. But I wanted a more dignified death, one suitable for the Surgeon. Scott made it last: he used every dark trick I taught him and more than a few that he invented on his own. It was delicious. And then to scatter my parts around the house . . . what a delightful joke to play on the police and the coroner, don't you think?"

"I'm afraid I don't have much of a sense of humor right now."

"Pity. It's true that they never found all of me, but that wasn't entirely due to Scott's skill at concealment. One of my parts was missing—my heart. Can you guess what happened to it?"

A chill gripped him and he had to suppress a shudder. "I'd rather not."

"Scott ate it, of course. As a final tribute to me, a way of keeping my glorious darkness alive in him. I thought I was strong in the ways of Shadow, and I'd taught Scott all I knew of it, but when he devoured my heart, his ability to walk the dark roads increased tenfold. He had added my power to his, becoming stronger than I'd ever been."

"I don't think I like where this is going."

Leonard grinned and pulled the sheet down to his waist with trembling claws that had once been hands. His naked flesh was covered with running sores, and on the left side of his chest, precisely where Scott had struck him with the wishbone Gammy had given him, was an open wound.

Leonard reached toward the gash, stuck his claw fingers inside and pulled the ragged edges apart. The ribs beneath had rotted away, due perhaps to the magic of Gammy's weapon, leaving nothing to protect the pitch-black organ that served as Leonard's heart. Instead of beating, the foul thing quivered and lurched, an old, broken-down engine about to shudder itself apart.

"*Bon appetite.*" Leonard smiled, his eyes blazing a challenge at Scott.

Scott looked at the rotten lump of black meat, his nose wrinkling in disgust at an odor of corruption that had nothing to do with physical decomposition. There was no-way-in-hell he was going to eat that thing.

But he knew it was the only way if he wanted to save Gayle and David.

With far less hesitation than he expected, Scott reached into his uncle's wound, clasped his fingers around the tremulous heart, and pulled. It came loose with little resistance, like a piece of cotton candy being separated from the main mass of spun sugar. The removal of Leonard's heart didn't seem to pain him any, nor for that matter did it cause his death. He continued to watch, eyes bright, as Scott lifted the still-beating black muscle to his mouth, and then the Surgeon laughed, the sound seeming to echo throughout all the corridors of eternity, as his nephew took the first bite and began to chew.

Scott opened his eyes. He saw Miranda sitting cross-legged on the ground in front of him, her scarred face radiating concern.

"Are you . . . did you . . ." It was clear she had no idea exactly what to ask him. It didn't matter. Whatever her question, his answer would be the same.

"Yes." His voice was flat, emotionless, and it seemed to catch Miranda off guard. She stared at him for a moment, peering into his eyes as if trying to divine what sort of change had taken place in him. He knew she would see nothing, though. There was, quite literally, nothing inside him.

He stood. "I'm ready. What do we do now?"

She hesitated, almost as if she were waiting for him to help her to her feet, but when he didn't extend a hand, she stood on her own. "I . . . *we* have the power to send you back to the time of our birth, when our spirits coalesced into a single self-aware entity. Once there, you can confront your other self and stop him from killing Miranda Tanner." She smiled. "We're sending you back to save my life, Scott."

Before, her words would've struck him as ludicrous, but now that Leonard's black heart beat inside him, they seemed perfectly reasonable, the task she proposed as simple as catching a cross-town bus.

"And Gayle and David?"

"If you stop your other self in the past"—and by *stop* it was clear she meant *kill*—"then you will undo everything he did in the past year, including the murders of your wife and son."

He considered this for a moment. "Why not send me

back to when he first went to live with Leonard? That way I can kill them both and save even more lives. For that matter, why not send me back to the moment before Leonard slaughtered my family? Then I could not only end the Surgeon's career before it ever gets started, I could save my family's lives and prevent my doppelganger from ever coming into existence." Such a change would destroy him, too, he realized . . . erase most of his past and create a brand-new Scott Raymond, one who'd never suffered the trauma of seeing his family murdered before his eyes. And that Scott's life path would be so different, he might well never meet Gayle in college, never father David. In a way, he'd be killing them all over again. Even worse, because they'd never have existed in the first place. Still, their sacrifice seemed worth it to save the dozens, perhaps even hundreds of lives Leonard and the other Scott had taken—together or separately—over the decades.

"If I could, I would," Miranda said. "But I can only send you back to the moment I was born, no further. Spiritually, I still exist in that time, and in a very real way, I've never truly left it."

Scott didn't understand what she was talking about, but he didn't care. It sounded as if he'd still be saving some lives, especially Gayle's and David's. More to the point, he'd get a chance to kill his double, and that was really what mattered most to him now. He was almost looking forward to it.

"How do we do it?"

Miranda took his hands then and squeezed them. He let her, though he didn't squeeze back.

"You know that old saying, 'Be careful what you wish for because you just might get it'?" she asked.

He nodded. "Why?"

She smiled sadly, stood on her tiptoes, and kissed him lightly on the lips. Then she pulled away and released his hands. "Just something I was thinking."

She stepped back. Her mouth began to move, but he couldn't hear anything. He tried to read her lips, but though it was clear she was forming words, they were none he recognized. Perhaps, he thought, she was speaking some language known only to the dead.

The whispering that had become so familiar to him over the past few days grew louder, until it became a chorus of voices chanting in Miranda's strange language. Some voices were stronger, some weaker, but all were feminine, full of sorrow and anger, but now there was another emotion in the mix as well: hope.

They rose from the ground slowly, cedar chips sticking to their bloody flesh. Two . . . eight . . . a dozen . . . so many he couldn't count. They filled the play area, standing shoulder to shoulder, mouths open and chanting with increasing energy and speed. Miranda took her place in the front row, joining her sisters who, in a real sense, were her, for Miranda was all of them, and they were her.

And we are all together, koo-koo-kachoo, Scott thought, but without any humor.

Miranda was crying as she chanted, tears running down her face, and he wondered why, until he realized the implications of what he was about to attempt. If he saved Miranda Tanner in the past, then this Miranda, the amalgamation of a hundred or more murdered spirits, would be forever one soul short of critical mass, and she would never come to be.

This, then, was good-bye.

He knew he should feel something—and maybe he did, somewhere inside—but all he could think about was getting his hands on that other Scott and testing his newfound dark strength against a man who, more than ever now, was close enough to be his twin.

Miranda's gaze moved upward, and he turned to see what she was looking at. The middle head on the *Wizard of Oz* swing set, the Tin Woodsman, was larger than its companions now, and continuing to increase in size. Double, triple, quadruple the mass of the Scarecrow or the Lion. The support bar of the swing set began to bend under the increased weight, and the Tin Woodsman sagged slowly toward the ground. Metal groaned, resisted, but finally had no choice but to give in. With a *thump!* the Tin Woodsman's chin hit cedar chips. The head was now almost the size of a grown man, and its mouth stretched open wide, tin grating on tin, and Scott could imagine the metal man mumbling, *Oil can! Oil can!* Inside the mouth, darkness swirled and roiled like an endless ebon ocean.

He didn't need Miranda to tell him this was his rabbit hole. He looked back at her, tears still running down her cheeks, and she spoke two words that he couldn't hear above the chanting of her sisters, but he was able to read her lips this time.

Good luck.

He nodded. He turned, stepped into the Tin Woodsman's mouth, and let the darkness take him where it would.

Chapter Thirty-four

The creak of swing chains; the soft *swoosh* of jean-clad bottoms sliding across shiny metal; the muted pounding of athletic shoes on cedar chips; youthful voices shouting, laughing, calling out to friends.

Scott stood before the *Wizard of Oz* swing set, the Tin Woodsman restored to his normal size and position alongside his compatriots. This play area was a far different place from the one he'd just left. A dozen children of various ages ranging from barely walking to almost ready for junior high ran, climbed, swung, jumped, dodged, hid, and chased around him. Most were white, but there were a few black, Hispanic, and Asian children in the mix. Parents—mothers, mostly—stood on the fringes of the play area, chatting with each other or talking on cell phones. One woman sat on a bench near the spider climber breastfeeding a baby, a receiving blanket providing modesty. Even from where he stood, Scott could smell the sweet-sour tang of breast milk, and he wondered if the scent excited the mama spider. Probably. Lucky for the human mother that there were too many people around for the climber reveal its true nature and attack.

Sights, sounds, and smells were far sharper than he recalled their ever being before. A side effect of stepping through the portal Miranda had opened? Or perhaps a change wrought in him by ingesting Leonard's heart? If the latter, then he understood his other self a fraction better. That Scott had devoured Leonard's heart also. If his senses were this sharp, then the act of murder—the sounds of pleas, screams, hitching sobs, and last sighing breaths; the smells of sweat, blood, urine, and feces; the feel of flayed skin, exposed organs, and blood-slick bone—would result in a high more intense than that of any drug . . . of a dozen drugs combined. How could anyone resist—

He noticed adults turning to look at him, like animals that had just caught wind of something dangerous in their environment. They took notice of the dried mud and blood covering his clothes, his unkempt hair and beard, and whatever it was that they saw in his eyes, and they turned away, searching for their children to make certain they were safe. A couple parents walked into the play area, took their children's hands, and ushered them away, moving slowly, casually, so as not to attract the attention of the stranger who had appeared seemingly from nowhere.

Not from nowhere, Scott thought. *From eleven months in the future.*

The air was warm and welcoming, the sky a piercing clear blue; the trees were covered with green leaves, and the grass outside of the play area was thick and lush. It was May 12: the day of Miranda Tanner's abduction and murder by the serial killer sometimes known as the Artiste, but whose real name was Scott Raymond.

I'm Scott Raymond, and after today, I'll be the only one.

The Tanner's street was just beyond the other side of the park. He started running in that direction, children scattering out of his way, parents yelling for him to watch where he was going, unable to keep from sounding relieved that he was leaving. He had to hurry; there wasn't much time.

. . . I can only send you back to the moment I was born, no further, Miranda had said. His Lolita had come into existence with the death of the girl called Miranda Tanner.

But perhaps there was a build-up to the event itself, a spiritual equivalent of human labor. If so, then there would be a grace period—however short—between the time his doppelganger abducted Miranda Tanner and the moment she died. If so, then he had a window of opportunity in which to save her. If not, if she were already dead . . . then at least he would have the chance to avenge her and hopefully save the lives of Gayle and David in the process.

And so he ran, heart burning in his chest like a fiery black furnace.

Miranda hummed "Old King Glory" as she walked. It was her favorite song of all the ones she'd learned in music class in first grade, and she always hummed it when she was happy. Today in gymnastics class she had tried a forward somersault on the balance beam—with the teacher's help—and she'd done it! She couldn't wait to get home and tell Mom. She was so excited, she was tempted to run all the way from the rec center to her house on Poplar Street, but she didn't. Despite her happy mood, she was tired. Her baby brother Andrew had been up crying half the night. Mom thought he was getting an ear infection, and Miranda was sorry about that, but whenever Andrew didn't sleep, no one else in the house did either. Still, she liked her little brother well enough. Mom said she might even let Miranda give him a bottle soon. Maybe after Miranda told her about the somersault, she'd let her do it today.

It was a warm, pleasant afternoon. So warm that Miranda had left her school clothes in her backpack and walked out of the rec center wearing her purple leotard and white leggings. She wished she'd brought a different pair of shoes to wear: her white tennies didn't go with her outfit. Her black shoes with the silver buckles would've been much better. She liked wearing her leotard. She imagined she was a superhero—the Amazing Gymnastics Girl!—patrolling the streets of the city, on the lookout for crime. When she encountered a supervillain, she'd use her incredible tumbling and stretching powers to bring him to justice.

Still humming "Old King Glory," she turned onto Poplar Street.

"That's a pretty song."

She blinked. There was a man standing on the sidewalk in front of her, which was really weird because she could've sworn he hadn't been there a second ago. Maybe she was more tired than she thought.

She almost said *thank you*, but her mother and her teachers had all told her it wasn't a good idea to talk to strangers, no matter how nice they seemed, and so she looked down at the sidewalk so she wouldn't have to meet the man's gaze—there was something about his eyes that made her *need* to look away—and detoured into a neighbor's yard to go around him.

She was past him and moving down the sidewalk again, walking faster now and no longer humming when she felt a cold hand fall on her shoulder.

"There's no need to be in such a hurry, little one." He'd knelt down and now his voice came from beside her ear; she could feel his breath on her skin like a kiss of winter. His hand tightened on her shoulder until it started to hurt. "It's so much better if you take your time. *So* much better."

*   *   *

By the time he reached Poplar, Scott's lungs felt as if they were shriveling up inside him. The dark power he'd stolen from Leonard might have surged through his body, but that didn't make up for decades of little to no exercise. His legs ached, his heart pounded, and he gulped for air like a fish in serious danger of asphyxiation. But all discomfort was forgotten the moment he saw his other self with Miranda.

He was kneeling on the sidewalk behind her, clasping her shoulder with one hand so she couldn't get away and whispering in her ear. Scott was too far away to make out what his double was saying, but whatever it was, it made Miranda cry.

Scott's own heart had been armored in cold steel since he'd eaten Leonard's, but the sight of sweet little Miranda in her purple tights, with her shining blonde hair and blue eyes—why had he expected them to be an unearthly amber, like his Miranda's?—standing terrified on the sidewalk not more than a few dozen yards from her house caused an echo of sorrow to sound deep within him. Adrenaline surged through his body and renewed strength flowed into his limbs. He picked up speed, legs tired no longer, and he called out to his other self.

"Leave her alone, goddamn you!"

His doppelganger started, as did Miranda, and Scott experienced a sudden wave of vertigo, as if the world had tipped over onto its side for a moment before slowly righting itself. He nearly tripped and fell, but he managed to stay on his feet and keep moving toward his other self. It seemed that Doppel-Scott and Miranda had felt the unsettling sensation too, for they both were swaying as if trying to regain their balance. For a brief moment, Scott hoped that his double would lose his grip on Miranda, allowing her to escape, but despite whatever dizziness he might be feeling, the serial killer known as the Artiste managed to hold on to her.

Scott thought he knew what had happened. Simply by being here and yelling at his other self, he had begun to change things. What they had just experienced was the awkward judder of the universe jumping from one track onto another. Now it was up to Scott to see how profound a change he could make.

The doppelganger stood and turned to meet the man running toward him, turning Miranda around with him. He looked much the same as when Scott had first confronted him in Gayle's apartment, though that moment was almost a year in the future for him. Black suede jacket, black pants, black shoes. The shirt was white this time, and his hair was a little longer, but he was still clean-shaven. *When you've got a look that works for you, why mess with it?* Scott thought.

Doppel-Scott flashed a hail-fellow, well-met smile, though his eyes narrowed as his funhouse mirror self approached. "Would I risk seeming obvious if I said there's something familiar about you?"

Fuck the banter. Scott didn't reply as he ran straight for his double, intending to tear the bastard's throat out with his teeth if he had to. Doppel-Scott grinned and waited until his other self was close, then fast as a striking cobra, his fist lashed out and caught Scott just below the Adam's apple. Scott gagged, wheezed, and fell onto the grass. He curled into a fetal position as he tried to pull breath into a throat that seemed to have suddenly swollen shut.

"I don't know who or what you are, and to tell the truth,

I don't really care. I should T-P the neighborhood with your intestines for interfering with my fun, but then I might lose hold of my little sweet-meat here, and she's far too tasty to risk that."

Scott wondered why his double didn't recognize him, and then he remembered. At this point on his counterpart's life path, the two of them hadn't met yet.

Miranda whimpered softly, and as Scott lay on the grass struggling for breath, he thought, *You can still breathe! Suck in some air and scream your goddamn lungs out!* But Miranda made no other sound. Perhaps she was too frightened, or perhaps his other self had performed some Shadow Realm hoodoo to silence her voice. Whichever the case, it was clear Miranda would not be calling for help.

"I know it's rude to take my leave before we've been formally introduced, but Sweet-Meat and I would like a little privacy so we can get to know one another better. So if you'll excuse us . . ." The doppelganger yawned his mouth open wide and leaned his head back. With his free hand, he reached up and inserted his fingers into his mouth, grasped hold of something, and then pulled it forth. Like some kind of demonic sword-swallower in reverse—*a sword-regurgitator,* Scott thought—he slowly drew an ebon blade from within his gullet.

Scott remembered seeing his other self fighting the brood-get police with a black sword. Now he knew where his double kept the weapon sheathed.

Doppel-Scott raised the sword and brought it down in a vertical slash. The air sizzled, there was a scream more felt than heard, and a gash appeared in the very fabric of reality. It was an open wound in the side of the universe, through which nothing but darkness was visible. No, now that Scott looked again, he could see that there were things

moving around in there . . . distorted shapes even darker
than the blackness that surrounded them.

His other self lowered the swordpoint until it was level
with Scott's face. "You're lucky I'm in a hurry. Interfere
again, and I'll do things to you that will make you beg for
the relief of eternal damnation." He turned Miranda toward the portal, said, "In you go, love," and shoved her
through. She screamed now, but the sound was distant and
faint, as if it came from a long way off. Then, without a
backward glance, Doppel-Scott stepped into the darkness
and was gone.

Scott remembered the reports of Miranda's disappearance that he'd researched for his book. She'd disappeared
in broad daylight without anyone witnessing her abduction, and now he knew why. His double had opened a portal into Shadow and taken her through it. Doppel-Scott
didn't need a car, not on the roads he traveled. And even if
anyone had looked directly at the ragged gash in the air,
they wouldn't have actually seen it, not as long as they had
their blinders on.

Scott struggled to get to his feet. He didn't know how
much longer the portal would remain open, and if he had
any hope of following them, he needed to—

The portal began to shrink.

"Fuck." It was more of a croak than a word, but at least
he'd managed to draw enough breath to give it voice. He
staggered to his feet and threw himself toward the gateway
his other self had created. He crashed to the sidewalk, a
bright spear of pain shooting through his right elbow as it
struck concrete. He was too late; the portal was gone.

He lay there a moment, cheek pressing against cold sidewalk, knowing that he had failed. Failed Miranda, failed
Gayle, failed David. Scott didn't know exactly how gate-

ways to Shadow worked, but he knew there was no way to guess where the one his double had created led to. It could've conceivably opened onto any point in the Shadow Realm, and from there, another could be opened that led back to any place on Earth, if his other self so desired. They could be anywhere in the worlds of Light or Darkness, anywhere at all. It was over. He had lost.

A whisper of thought tickled at his consciousness, struggling to be born. His doppelganger might be far more experienced in the ways of Shadow, but Scott had one advantage over him. He knew the future, or at least some of it. He sat up and cast his mind back over the last few strange days of his life path, searching his memory for some bit of information, a hint, something he'd seen or read, perhaps a phrase someone had spoken, *anything* that might give him an indication as to where his other self had taken Miranda.

And then he had it. After his double had murdered Laura Foster, Miranda had helped Scott dispose of her body by taking it to the marsh along the river. The location had been her suggestion, and at the time Scott had been so upset he hadn't thought to ask why she'd chosen that particular place. It had simply seemed a logical place to get rid of a corpse. But maybe Miranda had chosen it for a different reason. Maybe she'd been trying to show him something. Something important.

He remembered the shapes of women rising from the bog, their bodies covered with slime and muck. There had been one form among them smaller than the others, small enough to have been that of a child.

He knew where his doppelganger was taking his little "sweet-meat," and he knew what he intended to do with her body once he was finished playing with her. The only question was, could he get there in time?

A VW bug pulled onto Poplar, and slowed as it passed Scott, the driver frowning as she looked at him. Evidently mud-encrusted men sitting in the middle of the sidewalk weren't a common sight in this neighborhood. The woman pulled into a driveway two houses down from where Scott sat. She got out of the car and looked at him again, trying to look as if she *wasn't* looking, and then she popped the trunk and began unloading white plastic bags filled with groceries.

Scott had left his car at Orchard Park, eleven months in the future. If he had any hope of getting to the marsh before Miranda was killed, he needed a ride. And it looked like he'd found one.

He stood and began walking toward the woman.

Chapter Thirty-five

The ground was dry and Scott had an easier time negotiating the narrow path that led down to the marsh than when he'd last been here. He remembered reading somewhere in his research that this area of Ohio had suffered a drought for several weeks prior to Miranda's abduction. *Was* suffering a drought, he corrected, because then was now, wasn't it? It was all too damn confusing, and he decided not to worry about time anymore—what came first, what came next. . . . he was here, now, and he had a job to do. That was all that mattered.

He half ran, half skidded down the slope, dirt crumbling under his shoes, a dust cloud rising in his wake. The day was warm enough, but this close to the river, the air was humid and heavy. Sweat ran down his face, trickled from his underarms, rolled down his chest and back, making his shirt cling to his body like a second, wet skin. He would've stopped to remove his windbreaker if he could've afforded the delay. But he doubted his other self would be so obliging as to postpone his fun while Scott made himself more comfortable, and so he kept moving and did his best to ignore the heat and humidity.

The path leveled off, and Scott turned to the left and kept going. Everything looked so different now. The trees were filled with leaves, and the undergrowth was far thicker than the last time he'd come this way. Plus, he'd been too busy carrying Laura's body—not to mention too upset by her death—to pay more than passing attention to his surroundings. (Laura Foster was alive in this time, perhaps even still at the high school, finishing up the day's work before getting ready to go out for the evening and create another litter of her sharp-toothed children.) Ordinarily he might have hesitated, unsure that he was going in the right direction, but he continued making his way toward the marsh with confidence, almost as if he had a lodestone lodged between his eyes drawing him toward the killing ground his doppelganger had chosen. Perhaps eating Leonard's heart had forged a stronger link between the two of them, allowing him to sense the presence of his other self. Or perhaps it was merely the knowledge that every second brought Miranda Tanner closer to her death. The time for hesitation had long since passed.

He smelled the bog before he saw it: stagnant water, decaying vegetable matter, the rich earthy odor of mud . . .

and did he smell traces of human sweat, some of it sharp with terror? Maybe.

He found them by the edge of the marsh, a cloud of insects hovering around them like living, seething fog. Miranda lay naked and spread-eagled on the ground, her wrists and ankles held tight by thick, scaled coils, as if his other self had used serpents as shackles—and perhaps he had—their heads and tails buried deep in the soil, tips held fast in their mouths like tiny ouroboroses. Miranda was whimpering softly, but as near as Scott could tell, there wasn't a mark on her. She'd urinated, from fear, no doubt; he could smell her pee soaking into the ground between her legs. Thankfully, he smelled no blood, but that didn't mean his doppelganger hadn't been busy. Leonard's black heart whispered in his ear that there were all sorts of nasty things one could do without breaking the skin or raising a bruise—many that could be done with the spoken word alone. It had taken Scott almost twenty minutes to drive to the river from Poplar Street and then make his way to the bog, and he knew his other self had made every one of those minutes count.

Miranda's tights were folded neatly and rested next to her shoes and backpack several yards off from where she lay. His double's jacket was folded next to them, but he hadn't removed any of his other clothes yet.

Give him time, the black heart whispered. *He's just getting started.*

The voice wasn't all that different from the one that ordinarily spoke to him from time to time, and Scott wondered if he were truly hearing an echo of Leonard, or if these were merely his own thoughts and had been all along. The notion was far from comforting.

Doppel-Scott knelt next to Miranda, slowly trailing the

fingertips of his right hand across her sleek belly as he made his way toward her smooth, hairless pubis. Though he seemed to merely be touching her, Miranda took in hissing breaths of air, as if he were causing her pain, and maybe he was. Scott knew there were many dark tricks to be learned from Shadow, and taking shortcuts was the merest of them.

"Stop it." He spoke without emotion or inflection.

His other self didn't respond at first, but he removed his hand from Miranda's belly, and the girl sighed in relief. Then he stood and turned, each motion deliberate and economical. No rush, no wasted motion.

He smiled. "Whoever you are, you're persistent, I'll grant you that."

Scott began walking toward his funhouse mirror reflection, going slowly, in no hurry. "I can't let you do this."

If his other self was concerned by Scott's approach, he gave no sign. "What makes you think you can do anything about it?" He sniffed the air. "You have no weapons on you."

Scott hadn't thought to arm himself. He hadn't had the time. But he knew conventional weaponry—though his double often employed it in the creation of his dark art— would be useless against him. He felt the cold beating of Leonard's ebon heart within his chest.

"There are weapons, and then there are weapons," Scott said. When he was just out of arm's reach of his doppel-ganger, he stopped.

This earned him a mocking smile from his other self. "How cryptic." Killer Scott scented the air again, then frowned this time. "There's a trace of corruption about you that I haven't smelled for some time."

"It's a legacy from our dear departed uncle."

"Our?" He examined Scott more closely, and Scott had

the impression his double was employing senses beyond mere sight. "You're the other me, aren't you? The Scott Raymond who never went to live with Leonard, who never found the courage to become his true self."

"Maybe *you're* the one who never found the courage."

"Maybe," but his light tone indicated he thought otherwise. "I've managed to catch glimpses of your life from time to time, in dreams, primarily. Seems boring as hell. Makes me glad that old bitch Gammy died when she did—otherwise, I might be you."

"Instead of what? A predator who kills without real need? A butchering robot programmed by Uncle Leonard?"

"Oh, I have needs, Scott. Dark, lovely needs that you couldn't begin to imagine, and I take great delight in fulfilling them. And Leonard didn't program me; he awakened me to the true nature of existence."

"Which is?"

"That the worlds of Light and Darkness are merely overlays for a vast, unending Nothingness. There is no reason, no sanity, no love, no hope. Nothing but action and reaction, stimulus and response, appetite and satiation."

After all he had experienced since meeting his Lolita, Scott felt the tug of his counterpart's words. *It's true, you know,* the voice whispered. *You can feel it deep within the core of your being. Everything is . . . nothing.*

But then he thought of Gayle and David, of Miranda's tears and her last farewell kiss, and the emotional numbness that had encased him like invisible armor vanished, in the end no more substantial than a thin layer of ice melting beneath the light of a summer sun.

"You're wrong. There's *us* . . . people, I mean. We're real, and we matter."

His other self laughed. "What makes you think we're any less of an illusion than the rest of existence?"

"If I believed that, I'd be you: a bottom feeder who makes nothing, builds nothing, accomplishes nothing but death. Where's the trick in that? Everything dies eventually. At best, you're merely an accelerant for a natural process; at worst, you're a little boy who still gets off on mutilating dead animals. You act like you're some terrifying force of nature, when in reality you're just an asshole who likes to cut people up."

Doppel-Scott held his smile, but it was obviously a strain. He nodded back over his shoulder at Miranda. "We could share her, you know. Two brothers glorying in the wonders of pain and blood. And when we're done, I can show you every fell secret Leonard taught me and all I've learned since on my own. We will stride through Shadow as two dark princes, and none shall stand in our way."

Scott considered his other self for a moment. "You're jealous of me, aren't you? You've seen bits and pieces of my life, and fucked-up though it's been, it's a damn sight better than anything you've managed to create. You'd give anything to be me, but you can't. It's the one hunger you can never satisfy."

His counterpart's smile shattered and his face twisted into a cold mask of hatred. "I don't know how you got here, or why you want to prevent me from having my fun with the little sweet-meat over there, and I don't give a damn. I'm going to break your arms and legs, and then make you watch as I inflict such agony on the girl that her screams will shred your soul. And when I'm finished with her, I'm going to start on you. The longest I've ever been able to keep a victim alive was thirteen days." He grinned. "I'm going to try to set a new record with you."

Before Scott could react, his double's arm shot out and backhanded him across the face. White bursts of light exploded in his vision like fireworks as he flew backward and hit the ground. He blinked away tears of pain as he struggled to get to his feet, but Doppel-Scott stepped forward and kicked him in the gut. He rolled over onto his side, cradling his abdomen and feeling as if he were about to vomit forth his internal organs.

Scott looked up at his other self, his vision clearing enough to see the man lean his head back and reach toward his mouth.

He's going to draw his black sword, Scott thought. There was no way he could hope to stand against such a weapon, and he knew it. He was going to die without even managing to take a single swing at his doppelganger. He looked over at Miranda. The girl's head was lifted up so she could watch what was happening. Was there hope, however desperate, shining in her eyes? He couldn't tell from where he lay.

Looks like you chose the wrong champion, Miranda. I wish you better luck with the next Scott you recruit.

His double began to pull the ebon blade from his mouth. Scott stared at the sword's color—or rather, absence of color—a thought pounding at his consciousness, demanding attention.

The sword was black . . . just like Uncle Leonard's heart. His doppelganger had eaten Leonard's *physical* heart, absorbing the power of all the evil their uncle had accumulated in life. But Scott had eaten Leonard's *spiritual* heart, absorbing the dark energy their uncle's ghost had built up after death. And that meant—

He rolled onto his knees and gave in to the urge to throw up. It felt as if claws raked his esophagus as he coughed and hacked, and then a mass of darkness was expelled from his mouth. It lay in a tarlike puddle on the ground before him, and he reached out and gingerly touched the black mass. The puddle shifted, lengthened, grew hard and sharp. He now held the hilt of a sword in his hand.

He sensed the strike coming toward him, and he rolled onto his back just in time to bring his own blade up to meet it. The sword was light—it *was* made of Shadow, after all—and he was able to move it into position easily. Doppel-Scott's blade crashed into his, not with a metallic *clang!* as he'd expected, but with the howl of a frustrated animal denied its prey.

His counterpart let out a cry that echoed that of his sword, and he lifted the blade for another strike. Scott scuttled backward and the blade bit into the earth where he'd been. He jumped to his feet, adrenaline singing through his veins, and he stepped forward and swung at his other self's head.

Doppel-Scott ducked beneath the swing with ease, and Scott lost his balance and stumbled forward several steps, but he managed to keep from falling. He turned quickly and saw that his double was bringing his sword around for another strike. Scott reversed the momentum of his swing and brought his blade back around to meet the other's blow. This time both swords screamed their fury at being balked.

Doppel-Scott pressed forward, putting his weight behind his blade, and Scott did the same, and they stood like that, sword to sword, each pushing against the other in a temporary stalemate.

"You can't defeat me," the double said through clenched teeth. "You're nothing!"

"Funny, I was thinking the same thing."

With a roar of rage, Doppel-Scott shoved forward, breaking the impasse and sending Scott stumbling backward. He caught a glimpse of the trees surrounding them, saw they had become structures of intestines coiled around twisted, broken lengths of bone, their limbs covered with large, black-shelled beetles instead of leaves. As they'd fought, the two of them had slipped into Shadow.

The doppelganger came charging forward, and Scott waited until the last moment before stepping out of the way. His other self continued on several steps before managing to stop.

Scott glanced in Miranda's direction and saw she had crossed over into Shadow with them—or perhaps they had brought Shadow to her?—still bound wrist and ankle by scaled shackles, only now the ground beneath her, beneath the three of them, was brownish-red, bumpy, cracked and oozing in places, as if they stood upon a plane of scabrous flesh.

Something dark shimmered in the corner of his vision, and he turned to see the air where they had been fighting was crisscrossed with ebon slash marks, and Scott thought of the way his other self had sliced open the air to create a portal into Shadow. It seemed their swings were doing something similar. What would happen if either of them bumped into one of those gashes? Whatever the result, he doubted it would be pleasant. He'd have to be careful.

Doppel-Scott had turned around and was coming toward him again. But he stepped slowly this time, moving the tip of his blade back and forth in a horizontal figure eight as he approached. It appeared his initial fury had given way to sly calculation. Insects buzzed around him as he came, small as gnats, but with tiny grinning skulls for heads.

Scott backed up, careful to keep one eye on the shimmering rips in space so he didn't walk into one. He thought he detected a sound emanating from one off to his right—a soft, high-pitched mewling, like that of a lost kitten, but with an almost human quality. It sounded familiar, but he couldn't quite—

His counterpart rushed forward suddenly, swinging his sword in a wide backhanded slash. Scott jumped backward, sucking in his stomach to keep from having his gut split open. A corner of his mind noted that the mewling sound had become louder, but he didn't have time to worry about it. His double was bringing his sword back around for another strike, and Scott realized the first swing had been a feint designed to force him off balance. He brought his weapon up to defend himself, but while he managed to get it in place, his wrist was in an awkward position, and when Doppel-Scott's blade struck his, he lost his grip on the hilt, and the ebon sword tumbled through the air, coming to rest point-first in the scabby ground with a *chuk!* and a spray of pus-like fluid. The ground shuddered beneath their feet as if reacting to the injury, but quickly grew still.

Scott steeled himself for the feel of black metal piercing his flesh, but the expected blow never came. Grinning, his double lowered his weapon and walked over to where Scott's sword stuck out of the red, cracked ground. With his left hand, his other self drew the blade free with an oozy sucking sound, and for an instant, Scott thought his doppelganger was going to return the weapon to him, as fighting men of honor always did in old-time movies. But instead, he placed the tip of the blade between his teeth, bit down, and lifted his head back. He opened his mouth and the sword slid down his throat and vanished.

Scott felt a wrenching in his chest, and his heightened senses abandoned him. It seemed as if his eyes had filmed over and his ears and nose were packed with cotton. His limbs felt thick and stupid, clumsy elephantine things that he could barely operate. But he hadn't been disabled, merely returned to normal. The power granted him by Leonard's heart was gone, stolen by his dark counterpart.

Doppel-Scott smiled, the air around him seeming to crackle with energy. "I'm twice the man you used to be, my friend. You can't possibly defeat me now. Nothing can." He started forward, his sword held easily at his side. As he walked, ebon fire erupted along the blade's length, spread across the hilt, covered his hand, then rushed up his arm. There was no heat, no smell of burning cloth or sizzling flesh. It was a cold flame, but Scott feared no less deadly, at least for him.

He experienced an urge to run, but he knew it wouldn't do any good. His other self would be on him like a ravening hound before he got three feet. It was over.

He heard the mewling again, louder, closer, and he sensed a presence on the other side of one of the gashes in space. No, *presences*, and then he realized where—and when—he'd heard that sound before. It seemed the wounds in the air weren't only portals in space; they were portals in time as well, at least here in Shadow, where the laws of cause and effect had their own way of doing things.

He waited for his counterpart to draw near the rent in space from which the mewling came, and then he shouted, "Here! I'm here! Come to Daddy!"

The first one leapt through the dimensional rift, sank clawed fingers and toes into Doppel-Scott's hair and fastened its tiny shark teeth on his neck. He howled as the brood-child of Scott and Laura Foster began chewing furiously on his flesh, blood jetting forth from a suddenly severed carotid.

The others came through then, one after the other, grabbing onto Doppel-Scott's face, shoulders, chest, and back; clawing, biting, and chewing, swallowing bits of flesh and washing it down with gulps of hot blood. They'd changed a great deal since Scott had last seen them. No longer maggoty things, they resembled white-fleshed, hairless infants, each about nine inches tall, their arms and legs all lean muscle and bone, hands and feet sprouting black claws, eyes wide and black, teeth deadly as hell.

Scott almost felt a father's pride watching his children go about their work. Almost.

The dark fire that flickered along his doppelganger's arm extinguished as if blown out by a strong wind. He shrieked in pain, grabbing at the brood-children, swatting and smacking them with his free hand, twisting his body back and forth as he attempted to dislodge them, but the six little bastards held fast, scurrying away from his blows before they could land, sinking teeth into fingers once they were out of the way, digging into the next patch of flesh when they were withdrawn.

Scott thought that would be it, that his monstrous offspring would strip their "uncle" to the bone like a school of piranha that had evolved to hunt on dry land, but of course it wasn't that simple. Though he was bleeding from a dozen serious wounds, Doppel-Scott stopped fighting and stood completely still. It was as if he had managed to ignore the pain, shut it off entirely, and Scott realized he probably had. From the glimpses he'd had of his counter-

part's life, he knew that Uncle Leonard's lessons often involved more than a little agony for his student. His other
self had made friends with pain a long time ago.

Doppel-Scott angled his sword toward his body, and the
blade split down the middle into six sections that whipped
the air like tentacles, lashing out and wrapping around
each of the brood-children's tiny necks, and plucking
them off the doppelganger's body one by one. The tentacles held the nightmarish infants in the air for a moment as
they howled and thrashed, and then the coils around their
necks tightened, and their heads popped off like the tops
of dandelions. The headless bodies slipped through the
tentacles' loops and fell lifeless to the ground where their
heads already rested, eyes sightless and staring.

The brood-children were monstrous, misbegotten things,
and better off dead, but even so, Scott felt a twinge of sadness at their demise.

The tentacles weren't finished with their work yet. They
lashed out again, this time dabbing at their master's
wounds, leaving behind a bit of darkness wherever they
touched, sealing his injuries with their own substance. It
took only seconds, and when they were finished, Doppel-
Scott's face, neck, shoulders, chest, back, arms, and hands
were virtually covered in black. What remained of the tentacles rejoined, and now the sword was little longer than a
carving knife, but still sharp, still quite capable of killing,
Scott was certain.

"I must admit I didn't expect that," his other self said,
his black-patched lips distorting his words, making them
barely intelligible. He glared at Scott out of his only visible
eye. "Bravo. But I've walked in Shadow for too many years
to be stopped by mere injuries to my flesh. I've learned to

manipulate the very substance of this realm, work it like putty, and that includes my own body. In a very short time, I'll be whole and healthy again, and ready to resume my dark dance with the little sweet-meat. A shame you won't be here to see it."

He gestured, and Scott felt himself sinking, as if the ground beneath his feet had suddenly turned into thin, watery mud. He sank up to his ankles before the ground grew solid again, holding him fast. He tried pulling free, but it was no use. He realized that his counterpart had only been toying with him up to this point, that he could have used his mastery over Shadow to entrap him whenever he wished. But now playtime was over. His doppelganger started forward, ebon knife clutched in white-knuckled fingers, ready, Scott knew, to bury it up to the hilt in his chest. There would be no more fucking around, just one swift, final blow that Scott couldn't hope to avoid.

The death's-head insects circled his head now, chittering soft derisive laughter in his ears.

But something his other self had said sparked an echo of memory in him: Uncle Leonard, back at the cabin—or rather within his *memory* of the cabin—just before Scott stabbed him with Gammy's wishbone.

The problem with the real world is that it's too stubbornly solid. The realm of Shadow, as well as mental landscapes like this one, are more malleable—if you know what you're doing. This entire place is a potential weapon, but you don't have the experience to use it against me.

He thought of that night in the park with Miranda, watching Laura copulate with her children . . . thought of how his penis had transformed within Miranda's hand . . . and he understood that not only was the Shadow Realm a potential weapon—he was too.

His doppelganger kept coming. Ten feet. Seven. Four. One.

He grinned, drew his knife back to strike. "See you later, alligator."

Scott smiled grimly. "After a while, crocodile." He thrust his hand—which had become a gleaming silver blade—into his other self's gut.

Doppel-Scott gasped, and his visible eye widened in surprise as he experienced a pain he could not ignore. Scott gritted his teeth as blood splashed from his counterpart's belly onto his, and with his other hand he gripped his double's shoulder to steady him and slowly began sawing his way upward.

The doppelganger stiffened, dropped his own knife, and then slumped forward. Scott released his other self's shoulder and shoved him forward. He slid off Scott's blade, which had become five fingers again, all slick with dark blood, and he fell to the ground.

The death's-head insects scattered and the scabrous earth loosened its grip on Scott's feet. He pulled himself free and then stood over his dark reflection, watching blood bubble over the man's lips. The shadow patches that covered the wounds inflicted by the brood-children vanished, and he began bleeding anew from a dozen different places. Blood pooled beneath him on the ground, just as it once had beneath his—beneath *their*—parents in a cabin by a lake many years ago. No matter what fell magics his counterpart had learned in the realm of Shadow, Scott knew he couldn't stave off death much longer.

"Con . . . congratulations." A liquid cough, a spray of blood. "Now you can have her all to yourself."

At first Scott didn't know what his double was talking about, but then he realized that even as death approached, the sonofabitch thought that Scott was like him, eager to "play" with Miranda. He might have caught glimpses of Scott's life from time to time, but it was clear his other self had never truly understood what he saw.

"I suppose you'll finish me off now, so you two can be alone." Another cough, the blood much thicker and darker this time.

Scott thought for several moments. "Death didn't stop Uncle Leonard. His spirit was still able to manifest on the dream plane, and even in the physical world sometimes. If you truly are his protégé, then you know how to do that too."

The doppelganger said nothing, but his eyes were focused intently on his other self.

"I can't let you die, not if I'm really going to stop you."

His double gave a wet snuffling sound that Scott took for laughter. "And just how do you plan to keep me alive?"

"How else does one keep a dangerous animal? In a cage. And there's only one cage I can think of that will hold you."

Doppel-Scott's eyes widened and he shook his head feebly. "No . . . you wouldn't . . ."

Scott smiled. "Wouldn't I?" Gammy's spirit had told him this moment would come, a moment when he would have to make an awful choice—and he'd made it. He knelt by his double's side and opened his mouth wide, wider, and yet wider still, like a constrictor dislocating its jaw as it prepared to feed. When he was finished, he was alone. At least physically.

Scott stood, brushed a bloody hand across his chest, looked down at the mark it left on his shirt. "You be good in there, you hear?"

A distant echo of a furious, confined scream was his only answer.

He looked up and saw grass, trees, blue sky . . . the world had slipped out of Shadow. He looked for Miranda, saw her sitting naked a dozen yards away, knees hugged to her chest. Evidently her bonds had vanished when everything returned to normal. He walked over to her, smiling.

"It's okay, sweetheart. Everything's going to be all right now."

She was shivering as if it were the dead of winter instead of the middle of May. He bent down and reached out to touch her with blood-stained fingers. She looked at his hand and shrieked, and he quickly withdrew it.

She stared at him with wild, terrified eyes. "Don't hurt me, please, God, don't hurt me, don't hurt me, don't hurt me, please . . ." She buried her face against her legs and sobbed.

He longed to touch her, to hold and comfort this little girl who would never become his Miranda, but he knew it would be better for her if he didn't, and maybe better for him, too. He decided it was enough that she was alive. It had to be.

"I'll go get your clothes," he said, and went to do so, realizing as he did that he was now wearing a black suede jacket.

Chapter Thirty-six

Scott sat on his bed, hands resting on his lap, and stared at the featureless wall of his cell. His court-appointed psychiatrist had taken him off his latest antipsychotic medicine several days ago, and he was enjoying having a clear head for a change. It let him think better, and thinking was pretty much all he could do these days. Although his behavior had been so good since he'd been taken into custody—he was completely cooperative with the guards and the medical staff—that his doctor intended to recommend that he be let out of his cell for an hour a day so he could get some exercise: under close supervision, of course. Scott hoped that hour might include a visit to the prison library. He looked forward to reading again, and maybe even being allowed to write.

His cell was located in the psych wing of a maximum security prison, and though he had written about such facilities in some of his true-crime books, he'd never actually been inside a cell before his capture. It was just as bleak as he'd always imagined: hardly larger than a good-sized walk-in closet, with a single bed, sink, and a toilet. The door was metal, with a small window that provided a lovely view of the cell door opposite his, and a sliding panel through which his meals were delivered. He wore an orange coverall and black shoes that both fastened with velcro; prisoners as dangerous as he weren't allowed access to such potentially deadly weapons as zippers or shoe-strings. At least the walls of his cell weren't padded; he'd managed to avoid that indignity.

His trial, the first of several, was due to get under way soon, and although it would at least get him out of the cell for a time, he wasn't looking forward to it. The media had been frothing over his story ever since his capture—TRUE-CRIME WRITER REVEALED AS INFAMOUS KILLER—and he knew the trial would be a mad circus.

Actually, I'm rather looking forward to it.

Scott ignored the voice. He'd found that responding just made it worse.

After defeating his other self, he'd returned Miranda Tanner to her home. Her mother, worried at her daughter's delay in returning from gymnastics class, had called the police, and a cruiser was sitting in the driveway when Scott and Miranda pulled up. In retrospect, he should have dropped her off and gotten the hell out of there, but he'd been so relieved to have saved her life that he walked her to the door and rang the bell. After listening to Miranda's nearly incoherent story—and taking note of the blood all over Scott's clothes—the police (a pair of normal, *human* officers) took him in for questioning. At that point, he still hoped that everything would turn out okay. But when they took his prints at the Ash Creek police station and ran them through various databases, they were revealed as a match for a wanted criminal—a serial killer referred to by the media as the Artiste.

Everything had been so confusing in those early days, but eventually Scott worked it out. Somehow, by absorbing his doppelganger he had merged their two life paths. He was still Scott Raymond, author of true-crime books, husband to Gayle and father to David. But he was now, as far as this reality was concerned, also a vicious serial killer responsible for the deaths of who knew how many women.

You know, I lost count along the way myself. Let's see . . . one, two, three . . .

By saving Miranda Tanner's life, he had succeeded in changing events so that Gayle and David were never murdered. In this reality, they were alive and safe, though he hadn't spoken to either since the first few days after his capture, and he doubted he ever would again. Gayle had filed for divorce, or so a visiting lawyer had informed him, and he didn't plan to contest. He could only imagine what they were going through, believing that all the time he had been living with them as husband and father, he also had a secret life as a murdering monster. He worried about David, especially. What would it be like growing up thinking your father was a killer? What might such a trauma do to a young boy?

We know all about childhood trauma and what it can do, don't we, bro?

Scott remembered what Leonard's spirit had said about David, that perhaps he too carried the seed of darkness within him. Might that seed now begin to sprout and grow? Scott desperately hoped that it wouldn't, that Gayle would be able to help their son cope so that he might reach adulthood as well-adjusted as possible, given the circumstances. But there was no way to know for certain; he would just have to wait for the years to tell their story.

During all the interviews with psychiatrists and psychologists—and there'd been a lot—it seemed everyone with an M.D. or Ph.D. after their name wanted a piece of his psyche in order to advance his or her own career. He'd never told the full story of what had happened. He knew if he had, they'd mark him down as hopelessly insane, and his body would be pumped full of high-powered tranquilizers for the rest of his life. He had no hope of ever being released from prison, he knew that, but he really didn't want to be. Considering what he kept jailed inside him, it was probably safer for the world that he remained right where he was. But at least he could be free in his own mind—if not alone.

Tell me something, bro. Was it worth it?

Scott mulled this over for several minutes. He'd done what he'd thought right at the time. What else could anyone do?

"Yes," he said softly.

You're an idiot. The voice broke into laughter.

In the corner of his cell, between the foot of the bed and the sink, shadows gathered and deepened. The hairs on the back of his neck stood up, and he peered into the blackness, almost as if he were searching for something within it. A scent drifted into the air, a combination of bubblegum and after-sex musk, and he rose to his feet, heart pounding.

She stepped out of the shadows as if parting an ebon curtain. Amber eyes, blonde hair, dressed all in black, just as he had first seen her on that Sunday afternoon so many months ago. His Lolita had returned to him.

Looking good. The thought was accompanied by flashes of slit throats, flayed skin, and glistening, exposed organs. Scott pushed them out of his mind and walked over to Miranda. Up close, he saw that her skin was smooth and unmarked. The last of her scars had healed.

"This isn't possible," he said. "You're not dead. I mean, Miranda isn't. I mean—"

She pressed fingers to his lips, her flesh cold as always,

but he didn't care. "Shhhh. I know what you mean. It's okay."

She withdrew her fingers and stepped back then. He felt an urge to embrace her, but there was something about her facial expression and her body language—a wariness and uncertainty—that kept his arms at his sides.

"How?"

"When you fused with your other self, your separate life paths became as one. Each life path couldn't remain completely intact—you couldn't have been raised by both Gammy *and* Uncle Leonard, for example—so elements from each were cobbled together into a new whole. But there were . . . leftovers, I guess you could say. Like extra pieces of a puzzle that don't fit anywhere else." She smiled. "I'm one of those pieces: the ghost of a girl who never died."

He grinned. "That's wonderful!" But quick as it came, his grin fell away. "No, it isn't. It means we didn't succeed. We didn't save you."

She shrugged. "We saved *a* Miranda Tanner. I've peeked in on her a few times. She's almost eight now, and although she still has nightmares about the day she was abducted, she's alive. Her mother and father have their daughter back, and Andrew will grow up knowing his big sister. I'd call that a success, wouldn't you?"

"A success for them, but what about you?"

She ignored his question. "And don't forget Gayle and David. Their lives may be more troubled now since you've been imprisoned, but at least they *are* alive. That's the main thing, right?"

Maybe they'd be better off dead, a voice whispered, and he couldn't tell if it was his or his doppelganger's. Maybe both. But no, Miranda was right. Gayle and David's lives weren't easy right now, and they might never be again, but at least those lives had been restored.

"And then there are the women your other self killed in the year after Miranda Tanner's death," she added. "Their deaths were undone as well."

"Including Laura Foster?"

Miranda made a face. "Unfortunately. She's alive and well and probably out there somewhere breeding as we speak."

He smiled sadly. "Not exactly a happy ending, is it?"

She returned his smile. "That all depends on your definition of *happy*, I suppose."

An awkward silence fell between them then. There was a question Scott wanted to ask . . . no, needed to, but he wasn't certain that he wanted to hear the answer. In the end, he asked it anyway.

"Why did it take you so long to visit me?"

Miranda paused a moment before answering. "I spent almost all my energy to send you back in time, holding only a small portion of power in reserve in case you didn't succeed. After you left, I waited for oblivion to claim me, wondering if I would wink out of existence, or if it would happen more gradually, like a slow unraveling. But neither occurred, and after a time, it became clear that oblivion had stood me up. I was afraid you'd lost the battle with your double, but I was too weak to find out. I couldn't do anything but rest and regain my strength.

"I stayed in the park for a month: a weak, pathetic creature existing half in and half out of Shadow, sleeping in bushes, on tables in picnic shelters, hiding wherever I could. And even when I was finally strong enough to fully enter Shadow once again, it still took me a while to understand what had happened. The living may think the dead are all-knowing, but it still takes us a while to observe and learn."

"Be careful. The Guild of Spooks and Specters might not be happy that you're giving their secrets away."

His joke elicited only a weak smile. "But the main reason I didn't come before this was that I didn't know if I really *wanted* to see you again. The man who killed me—*all* of me . . ."

"Lives inside me now."

She nodded. "I didn't know if I'd be able to put that aside. Whenever we were together, I knew *he'd* be there. Watching, thinking . . ."

You know it, sister! And oh what thoughts I'd think! Spraying blood, tearing flesh, echoing screams . . .

Scott closed his eyes and again pushed the images away. When his mind was clear once more—was *his* once more—he opened his eyes. "I can see where that would be a problem for you." For both of us, he added mentally.

You mean the three of us, don't you?

Shut up.

"I guess what I really needed was time to think, and you know what I decided?"

He shook his head.

She walked up to him and touched his cheek. He gently took her wrist and turned her hand to examine the palm, saw that a faint scar cut across the breadth of it. It was the scar from the wound she'd received that night in the park, the only time they had even a semblance of sex.

"I don't know why that one wouldn't heal all the way. I guess . . . I wanted to keep it as a reminder."

He looked into the depths of her strange, amber eyes and wondered what secrets lay within. "You were about to tell me what you decided." He let go of her wrist and took her hand.

"I realized that if anyone could understand what's happened to you, it's me. I'm the combination of dozens of different women, an amalgam of personalities, histories, desires, and fears . . . thousands of pieces that don't always mesh as well as I'd like."

He thought of the afternoon by the marsh, when she and her other selves had argued, to put it mildly.

Tore her to fucking pieces is more like it. Wish to hell I'd been there to see it.

"I guess what I'm really trying to say is—"

"Nobody's perfect?"

She grinned. "Something like that. But in the end, it came down to one thing. I realized that even the dead can love."

A faint chorus of feminine whispers tickled his ears. *Can love, can love, can . . .*

Miranda and Scott kissed then, and his other self was silent for a change. When they parted, still holding hands, he asked, "Now what?"

Miranda nodded to the corner of the room, where shadows roiled and seethed like ebon tides.

Scott hesitated. "It might be better if I stayed. In here, there aren't any distractions and I can concentrate on keeping my other self caged. But out there . . ." He gestured toward the writhing shadows. "Who knows what might happen?"

"Not me," Miranda said. "But I can tell you this: You're stronger than you think, Scott Raymond, and I believe in you." She smiled. "After all, you saved both my life *and* my death. If you can do that, I think you can manage to keep the spirit of one measly serial killer bottled up."

"And if I can't?"

Miranda looked at him for a long moment. "There are no guarantees, Scott, no matter what road you travel. But I can promise you this: I'll help you all I can." A pause. "We'll help each other."

Don't do it! You know you can't trust the little bitch, not after how she used you to get to me!

Fuck off, Scott thought. Aloud, he said, "Let's go."

Hand in hand, they entered the darkness together.

IN
SILENT
GRAVES
GARY A. BRAUNBECK

Robert Londrigan seems to have it all. He is a newscaster with a rising career. He has a beautiful wife, Denise, and a new baby on the way. But in just a few short hours Robert's world is turned upside down. Now his family is gone—but the torment only gets worse when his daughter's body is stolen from the morgue by a strange, disfigured man. . . .

Robert is about to begin a journey into a world of nightmare, an unimaginable world of mystery, horror and revelation. He will learn—from both the living and the dead—secrets about this world and things beyond this world. Though his journey will be grotesque, terrifying and heartbreaking, he will not be allowed to stop. But can he survive with his mind intact? Can he survive at all?

THE WIND CALLER
P. D. CACEK

Listen to the leaves rustling. Hear the wind building. These could be the first signs that Gideon Berlander has found you. They could be the last sounds you hear. Gideon hasn't been the same since that terrifying night in the cave, the night he changed forever—the night he became a Wind Caller. But the power to call upon and control the unimaginable force of the wind in all its fury has warped him, twisted his mind, and unleashed a virtually unstoppable monster. Those who oppose Gideon are destroyed . . . horribly. No one can escape the wind. And no one—not even Gideon—knows what nightmarish secrets wait in its swirling grasp.

THE WYRM
STEPHEN LAWS

Something hideous is about to happen to the small town of Shillingham. Why does a madman shoot at the workers tearing down the old gallows at the crossroads? Why are the children drawn to play in its shadow, as if by a silent command? What is the eerie, thickening fog that surrounds the village, cutting off the inhabitants from the outside world?

Beneath the ground, something stirs. As the workers continue working and the bulldozers roll on, a dark and unimaginable evil, imprisoned beneath the gallows for centuries, slowly awakes. It is alive. It is powerful and cunning. And it wants revenge.
